· EXIT DYING ·

"Stand at the foot of the tub."

Jerry complied.

"Now grab my ankles."

Reaching into the warm water, he took hold of Charlotte's ankles.

"Now pull."

Jerry pulled her ankles gently. She slid forward.

"No good," she said. "You're being too gentle. Let's try it again—this time for real. Jerk my ankles, hard. And then push them up into the air so that my head is forced under water. As if you were forcing me to do a backward somersault."

His hands tightened around her ankles. Charlotte felt her legs being yanked forward. Then she felt her hamstrings stretching as Jerry pushed her legs over her head. The warm, fizzy water rushed into her nose, her mouth. A hand was holding her head under. Try as she might, she was unable to get her head above the surface. Then she felt nothing.

She had blacked out.

MURDER
AT THE
SPA

STEFANIE MATTESON

CHARTER/DIAMOND BOOKS, NEW YORK

MURDER AT THE SPA

A Charter/Diamond Book / published by arrangement with
the author

PRINTING HISTORY
Charter/Diamond edition / November 1990

ISBN: 1-55773-411-9

Charter/Diamond Books are published by The Berkley Publishing
Group, 200 Madison Avenue, New York, New York 10016.
The name "CHARTER/DIAMOND" and its logo are trademarks
belonging to Charter Communications, Inc.

PRINTED IN THE UNITED STATES OF AMERICA

10 9 8 7 6 5 4 3 2 1

To my mother

MURDER
AT THE
SPA

· I ·

CHARLOTTE GRAHAM SAT on the terrace of her brownstone on East Forty-ninth, sipping tea and savoring an unaccustomed feeling of leisure. She was an elegant woman in her early sixties, dressed in a starkly tailored suit of navy blue linen. She always wore white, gray, black, or navy blue—these were the colors that best complemented her alabaster complexion; her glossy black hair, which, though now dyed, still had only a few streaks of gray; and the striking features that were as familiar to three generations of movie-goers as those of their closest relatives. She pondered the day that lay ahead of her: a long window-shopping walk down Madison Avenue perhaps, or a walk along the river with its view of the somber flatlands of Queens.

It was ten o'clock on a cool, clear Saturday morning in June. A sweet chirrup caught her ear. A wren had laid claim to a birdhouse that hung from the branch of an old crab apple. She followed his movements as he fluttered his wings with pride and popped in and out of the birdhouse—"See what a beautiful nest I've made," he bragged to the female. After disappearing for a few minutes, he reappeared with a twig to add to the nest's foundation. If the female accepted his proposal, she would feather it herself with feathers from God-only-knew-where. It always amazed her how nature managed to adapt to the hostile environment of the city. The eastern cottonwood that grew on top of one of the towers of the Queensboro Bridge; the Atlantic Ridley turtles that, having ridden the Gulf Stream up from Mexico, paddled happily about in Jamaica Bay under the flight paths to and from Kennedy; the peregrine falcons that nested on the girders of the Throgs Neck, oblivious of traffic to the Hamptons below. All seemed to her small miracles of Darwinian adaptation. And now her wrens. But then there was the example of the pigeon: adaptation carried to its loathsome extreme. Several had built nests in her gutters. She would have to call an exterminator to get rid of them; their excrement could destroy the masonry of a building faster than acid rain. She also noticed that the chimney needed pointing up, the shutters needed painting. Now that she finally had some time, she would have to take care of some of these things.

She had just made three movies back to back. Two were expected to be big hits. There was talk of another Oscar. (She already had four on her living room mantel.) She was, thank God, hot, the way she had been early in her career. She was also bone-tired—she no longer possessed the stamina of her youth. But she wasn't complaining; she was happy to be working. She had finally emerged from that stagnant stage in her career in which she was too old to play middle-aged women and too young to play old women. Grieving widows, monstrous matriarchs, and dotty maiden aunts—all were now grist for her mill. And since most of the actresses she'd started out with back in the forties were now sick, dead, or retired, she was back in demand. For a long time, Hollywood had ignored her. She had mentally labeled that period her "black years"—a ten-year stretch of little but television offers and precious few of those. But she had survived, thanks to Broadway, which had welcomed her with open arms. And now Hollywood had summoned her back. She loved Broadway; there was nothing like the rapport between player and audience—the big black giant as it was called in the business. But in many ways she preferred the movies. For one thing, they weren't as physically taxing, which was an important consideration at her age. In the theater, even something as simple as talking on the phone was affected; you were always saving your voice for the next performance. For another, there were no nerve-wracking opening nights. And if you flubbed a scene, you had the luxury of doing it over. But mostly it was the size of the audience: not just a few hundred show-goers at a pop, but millions—

millions!—of people, all over the world. She was a famous person who liked fame.

Overhead, the sunlight trickled through the leaves. She would have to have the trees trimmed too; it was getting too shady. There was shade enough from the neighboring buildings without a dense canopy of leaves blocking the sunlight as well. She looked up; the leaves rustled in the breeze off the river. When she sat out here, it was hard to believe she was in New York. Not that she didn't want to be in New York. It was unfortunate she didn't get to spend more time here. She loved it. Her home here was her oasis, her refuge from Hollywood, where she had spent most of the last forty years. She liked fame, yes. But she also liked a break from it once in a while, and from the glitz that went along with it. Here she could put on an old pair of walking shoes and a pair of sunglasses and walk for miles without being recognized.

Her thoughts were interrupted by a voice from above. She looked over at the rear of the house. It was Julie, her Chinese housekeeper, who lived with her husband Jim on the fifth floor. They had been with her for years; they were like family. A cinemaphile friend had long ago nicknamed them Jules and Jim. Julie was leaning over the wrought-iron balcony that opened off of the third-floor library. Charlotte noticed that the grillwork needed painting too. The place was going to wrack and ruin.

"Miss Langenberg's on the telephone," she said. "Don't get up. I'll bring the phone out to you." She waved the telephone and giggled.

It was a new portable telephone. Charlotte had bought it a couple of months ago, but the gloss hadn't worn off. Julie still got a thrill out of taking it out to the terrace. Being able to talk on the phone out-of-doors gave Julie almost as much of a kick as being able to barbecue on the grill indoors. Despite her origins, Julie had a distinctly American taste for novelty. Charlotte wondered why Paulina was calling. It wasn't like her to call herself. Usually, her secretary called for her. Unlike Julie, who was gadget-happy (in addition to the indoor grill, the kitchen was equipped with everything from a built-in electric wok to a faucet that emitted boiling water), Paulina had a primitive distrust of modern conveniences. The telephone was her special bugaboo. She held it at arm's length and yelled into the mouthpiece, as uncertain about the outcome as Alexander Graham Bell must have been when he spoke the first words over the telephone: "Mr. Watson. Come here. I need you." Charlotte suspected that Paulina was also wary of being bugged. In the competitive atmosphere of the beauty industry, corporate spying was not uncommon.

Paulina was the giantess of the beauty industry, one of the most famous, one of the richest, and one of the most fascinating women of her day. To say she was Charlotte's friend would be a misstatement. It would be as difficult to harness Paulina in the yoke of friendship as it would be to harness a force of nature. But they had much in common: they were institutions of a sort, monuments of American culture. It was Paulina, along with her two competitors, who had founded the beauty industry when the century was still young. But Paulina deserved the credit because she had been the first. And she would be the last. Her competitors, to whom she referred as "That Woman" and "The Eye Shadow Man" (never allowing their names to be spoken in her presence), had both died eight years ago, coincidentally within only days of each other. Paulina had made wearing makeup respectable; before her, only actresses and loose women dared to wear it in public. The story was a legend: she had begun with the twelve jars of her mother's homemade face cream that she'd packed in her trunk when she set out from her native Budapest as a young woman to visit relatives in Canada. (The date of this event was shrouded in mystery because of Paulina's wish to keep her age, which was somewhere around eighty, a secret.) Her Canadian friends and relatives, whose skin had suffered from the harsh Canadian climate, envied her milky complexion. To her admirers, she passed out samples of her mother's cream. Before long, she was sending home for more. The demand eventually became so great that she started selling her Crème Hungaria Skin Food in her own "salon." (Paulina was also the first to recognize the cachet of French in selling cosmetics.) It was only a matter of time before she had opened salons in New York, London, and Paris. She would turn a dozen jars of her mother's cream into the country's most profitable cosmetics company: a company with forty thousand employees in over a hundred countries and annual sales approaching two billion.

That was Paulina.

Julie emerged from the house with the phone and handed it to Charlotte. The voice that assailed her over the airwaves was deep and throaty, with a thick eastern European accent. "Is that you?" it bellowed. To avoid injury to her hearing, she moved the receiver a few inches away from her ear.

As Charlotte listened, Paulina went on in a garbled way about the murder at the Morosco case. Several years before, Charlotte's co-star in a Broadway show called *The Trouble with Murder* had been shot dead on stage. It was actually Charlotte who had pulled the trigger; a real bullet had been planted in a stage prop. The case had been a sensation: the press had dubbed it "Murder at the Morosco," after the Morosco Theatre. Charlotte was the one who had gathered the evidence that eventually put the murderer away. As a result of the book describing her role, which became a best-seller, she had developed something of a reputation as an amateur detective. It was for this reason that Paulina was calling her, she gathered. But Paulina's message was hardly any more sophisticated than Bell's. What it boiled down to was, "Miss Graham. Come here. I need you." Someone was trying to sabotage her spa business, she said. She wanted Charlotte to find out who and why.

Charlotte tried to ferret out more information, but Paulina, as usual over the telephone, was cryptic. She demanded that Charlotte come to the spa immediately. The details could wait. Ever imperious, she alluded to the fact that she wasn't used to being disobeyed.

Charlotte hesitated at first if for no other reason than she wasn't used to being bossed around; a rude demand was apt to make her dig in her heels. But she quickly realized that it was a good idea. Paulina had been urging her to visit the spa ever since it had opened five years ago. ("Having the stars—it's good publicity," she always said.) Charlotte had turned her down, but now she was tempted. She needed a rest—a real rest, not one in which she had to play general contractor, which was what she'd be in for if she hung around home. She had never stayed at a spa before. She didn't usually approve of

indulging herself. She had a streak of the kind of Yankee
asceticism that embraces cold showers and Spam, a streak that
had been nurtured by her revulsion for the excesses of
Hollywood. But this time, she felt as if she deserved to be
pampered like a star. Because she *was* a star once again.

And so she agreed.

Although she had never been there, she knew quite a bit
about Paulina's precious spa. For years, it had been Paulina's
dream to open a spa—not a spa like That Woman's famous spa
in Maine, which was little more than a fat farm for overweight
celebrities, but a spa like the continental spas to which she
retired every year for the cure, returning recharged with her
legendary energy. For Paulina, as for other Europeans, the
annual spa visit was a vital necessity to health. The European
spa had never fallen out of favor like its American counterpart;
it had remained in the medical mainstream, promoted by
European balneologists who studied the therapeutic virtues of
the mineral waters. The idea of a spa had also appealed to
Paulina because of its link with her roots: like most Hungarians, she had spent hours in the tub rooms at Saint Gellert or
Széchenyi; no other city in the world was as richly endowed
with mineral springs as her native Budapest. But she had also
been shrewd enough to recognize that a European-style spa
would never go over in the United States. Even the most
luxurious of them had a depressingly clinical air, vaguely
reminiscent of an old-age home or a mental institution. Her
dream had been to create a new hybrid, a spa that rejuvenated
its guests like a traditional European mineral spa, that pampered them like a luxurious American beauty farm, and that
prodded them into shape with diet and exercise like the spartan
camps of the natural hygienists.

A decision by the New York state legislature to lease a
run-down upstate spa to a private investor provided her
opportunity. The time was ripe: interest in health and physical
fitness was at an all-time high, and only someone like Paulina
had the money, vision, and power to realize such an undertak-
ing. Two years and twenty-one million dollars later, it was
finished—the Paulina Langenberg Spa at High Rock Springs.
From the moment it opened its elegant bronze doors, it was a
fabulous success, the jewel in the crown of the Queen of

Beauty that Paulina had hoped it would be. But it wasn't just a showplace; like all of Paulina's enterprises, it was a money-maker as well. The rich and famous paid four thousand dollars a week and more to be soaked, whirlpooled, massaged, manicured, pedicured, and coiffed. To say nothing of being starved on a diet of twelve hundred calories a day—a diet that was a feast for the eye, but for the eye alone. And the clientele wasn't mostly women as it was at other spas. Paulina had recognized early on that in order to make real money, she had to attract men. To do so, she had spent a small fortune to groom the overgrown fairways and lumpy greens of the existing golf course to smooth green perfection. Lured by the golf course, the husbands flocked to the spa for its famous cardiac rejuvenation program. And if golf held no appeal, there was indoor tennis and outdoor tennis, an indoor pool and an outdoor pool, skeet shooting, bridle paths, cross-country skiing—you name it. The ratio of staff to guests was a sybaritic three to one. In short, the spa offered everything the most demanding spa-goer could ever want.

Charlotte was looking forward to it.

She left the next day. Paulina's secretary had booked her for the Ten-Day Rejuvenating Plan, which started on Monday. She set out in her rented car late that morning, happy to be getting out of the city. Although it had been cool, a heat wave had been forecast, and there was nothing worse than New York in the heat. It took only a little more than three hours to follow the Hudson a hundred and twenty miles north to the plateau at the foot of the Adirondacks where the town of High Rock Springs was situated. From the exit on the Adirondack Northway, she turned onto a local highway, and from there onto the approach road leading to the spa, a narrow road lined by a double row of majestic pines that wound its way through a two-thousand-acre state park to the spa. At the end of a curve, the Avenue of Pines, as it was called, opened up onto a vista of hotel and spa complex laid out in symmetrical splendor against a background of pine groves and misty blue mountains. Charlotte turned left onto Golf Course Road and headed toward the hotel: an imposing building of red brick whose neoclassical facade was dominated by a glass outdoor elevator (a Langenberg addition

that allowed the guests to view the distant Adirondacks) and by
a columned entrance portico in front of which stood a fountain
in the form of a phoenix, symbolizing the rejuvenative powers
of the mineral waters. To either side of the portico were
screened verandas where busboys in red jackets were setting up
for dinner.

After dropping off her car keys at the rental desk, she
checked in and took the glass elevator to her room. Her room
was at the rear of the hotel on the sixth floor, which was the top
floor (except for the seventh, which was occupied by Paulina's
penthouse). It faced south, overlooking a lovely lake called
Geyser Lake, which, the bellman explained, took its name
from the geyser that spouted from its island center under the
pressure of carbonic acid gas from an expiring underground
volcano. Charlotte counted; every three minutes, the geyser
magically erupted, shooting a plume of white water ten feet
into the air. The bellman proudly informed her that it was one
of seven geysers at High Rock Springs—the only spouting
springs east of the Mississippi. Her room was luxurious: large
and high and filled with the sweet fragrance of fresh lilies. It
was decorated in typical Paulina Langenberg style. If one were
to give it a name, one might call it riotously eclectic: a
chrome-based glass coffee table stood next to a marble-topped
Empire dresser; an abstract expressionist reproduction hung
above a Greek caryatid lamp. The effect was dramatic,
original, sumptuous; it made Charlotte feel spoiled. Which was
the whole idea. After settling in, she called Paulina to
announce her arrival. Then she took a few minutes to study the
program for the Ten-Day Rejuvenating Plan (herbal wraps and
mud packs and Swedish massages—it sounded delicious) and
to read the literature on the spa. After that, she headed out. Her
destination was High Rock Spring, the famous spring from
which the spa took its name.

The spring stood at the center of a long lawn called the
esplanade, which was spread out in front of the hotel like a
carpet of green baize. The esplanade was crisscrossed by
gravel paths, but they were deserted; there were no people to
mar the geometry of the neatly spaced rows of pollarded plane
trees. It was the time of late afternoon naps or of before-dinner

"cocktails" (which here consisted only of fruit punch lightly laced with white wine). In the hazy afternoon sunlight, the atmosphere was one of peaceful tranquillity. The muffled clink of silverware drifted across the esplanade like the sound of wind chimes. Even the grass had taken on a golden glow over which the shadow of the pavilion that housed the spring fell like the reflection on a lake. The only note of color was a bold Chinese red, a color known as Langenberg red for its association with Paulina's theatrical style in the same way that a delicate shade of floral pink was associated with the more ladylike style of That Woman. The geraniums that hung in baskets from the wrought-iron lampposts were Langenberg red. As were the park benches that lined the walkways and the roses that were planted in beds in the center of the lawn. Both Paulina and That Woman had varieties of hybrid tea roses named after them, but there were no pink roses here. For that matter, there were no pink flowers at all. Paulina would never have stood for it.

At the pavilion, Charlotte took a seat facing the cone of the spring—the "rock" of High Rock. The cone, which had been built up over the millennia from minerals deposited by the mineral water—stood about six feet high and about twelve feet wide. From a well in its center the water gushed, pulsing with the pressure that would thrust it skyward. Like the spring at the center of the lake, it was a geyser. On its surges, it shot a column of water twelve feet into the air. At its ebb, it bubbled fitfully, occasionally regurgitating a belch of water that would overflow the lip of the well with a gurgle of satisfaction. For eons, it had been thus: the salty, mineral-rich waters of a primeval underground sea had been forced to the surface of the earth by a charge of carbonic acid gas. In the last century, she had read, inquisitive scientists had raised the cone with a giant crane to find out what lay below. They had found only layer upon layer of muck and mineral, and, at the bottom, seventeen feet below the apex, the charred remains of a three-thousand-year-old campfire. The mysterious aboriginal people who had built their campfires here were lured by the abundance of game, which was attracted by the water's salty taste. Later came the Indians of the Iroquois Confederacy, who called it the

Medicine Spring of the Great Spirit. On the lintel of the
pavilion were engraved the words of a Mohawk Indian song:

> *Far in the forest's deep recess,*
> *Dark, hidden, and alone,*
> *Mid marshy fens and tangled wood,*
> *There rose a rocky cone.*

According to what she had learned of the spa's history, the
first white man to visit the spring was Sir John Williams,
the Superintendent of Indian Affairs for the British crown. The
early explorers had heard tales of the healing powers of
the waters that spouted from a rock in the forest, but until
Williams, the Indians had kept its location a secret. Williams,
who was much beloved by the Indians, first visited the spring
in 1767. He was carried there on a litter by Iroquois braves for
treatment of a wound. He recovered, and word spread of the
spring's powers. Before long, a settler named Elisha Burnett
had opened a tavern where visitors could quench their thirst
with stronger stuff than that which issued from the spring. And
so the spa at High Rock, as it came to be called, grew. The
Elisha Burnett Tavern was enlarged again and again. By the
Civil War, it had become the High Rock Inn, and by the turn
of the century, the High Rock Hotel, a faux French extrava-
ganza modeled after the palace at Versailles. At the time it was
built, the High Rock Hotel was the largest in the world, with
a thousand rooms, a mile of piazzas, and a dining room a city
block long. New springs were discovered. The Union and Sans
Souci springs became almost as famous as High Rock Spring.
The Washington Bathhouse was built, where Victorians
suffering from dyspepsia, arthritis, and the general debility
known as "nerve fag" or "Manhattan madness" took the cure
in the effervescent mineral waters. And when the spa outgrew
the Washington Bathhouse, the Lincoln Bathhouse was
built—the world's most modern and luxurious. The spa had
become the playground of the nouveau riche.

And then, in 1900, it burned. Only the cone survived, the
mineral waters spilling down its sides saving it from the
conflagration. The spa lay idle for a while, but by the twenties,

it had become the dream of Dr. Rudolph Flexner, a German balneologist, to build a new spa that would rival the great European spas like Baden-Baden and Montecatini. Dr. Flexner didn't live to see his dream come true, but his son, Samuel, did. Samuel, a friend of the governor of New York, Franklin D. Roosevelt, interested Roosevelt in the scheme. It wasn't difficult; Roosevelt was a proponent of mineral baths, having taken the waters at Warm Springs, Georgia, for his polio. Roosevelt's interest in the spa continued once he was elected president. It was built in 1935 with New Deal funds: two and a half acres of red-brick neo-Georgian buildings. Nothing was spared in terms of quality: the finest craftsmen were imported to lay the floors of multicolored Italian marble, to raise the Doric columns of pale pink Indiana limestone, to forge the ornate wall sconces of heavy wrought iron. The result was dignified, patrician, elegant.

The new spa enjoyed enormous popularity, until the war. The war ushered in a new era in medicine. The generation that had put its faith in the healing powers of mineral waters was replaced by a generation that believed in antibiotics and inoculations. The number of spa-goers dwindled. The buildings fell into disrepair. Rain poured through holes in the slate roofs. The paint peeled; the masonry crumbled; the marble floors became coated with a layer of slime. Mineral deposits clogged the pipes. So precipitous was the spa's fall from grace that by the fifties the elegant Hall of Springs was being used as a storage depot for Civil Defense equipment. What to do about the spa became a public issue. After long debate, the legislature decided to lease the spa and the bottling plant, which still bottled High Rock, Union, and Sans Souci waters, to private investors.

It was then that Paulina stepped in.

And so Charlotte sat in the High Rock Pavilion, a replica of the rustic Victorian pavilion that had burned in the great fire, sipping a glass of the famous mineral water. She knew that sipping wasn't what you were supposed to do. Sipping didn't allow the bubbles to perform their miracles on the digestion; you were supposed to toss it back like a belt of whiskey. She also knew that the water was best taken on an empty stomach, preferably before breakfast. But she wanted to sip, to taste the hint of iron, to feel the fizz of bubbles in her nose. She slowly drank the rest of her glass. It had a not-unpleasant saltiness, like something you'd gargle with for a sore throat. A rustic sign mounted on a column proclaimed: "High Rock Spring: A naturally carbonated saline alkaline mineral water. Contains more minerals than any other water in the world." Another sign asked visitors not to chip souvenirs off the famous mineral cone.

Rising from her seat, Charlotte tossed her plastic glass into a trash basket and headed across the esplanade to dinner.

· 2 ·

CHARLOTTE BEGAN HER Rejuvenating Plan with breakfast on the veranda. It consisted of half a grapefruit, a low-fat bran muffin, and a cup of peppermint tea. The grapefruit and muffin weren't so bad—she seldom ate much for breakfast anyway— but the peppermint tea was a sorry substitute for her morning coffee. The night before, she had taken dinner in her room and gone straight to bed. Breakfast was to have been her first chance to look over the other guests. She had wanted to see if there were others of her advanced years. But the dining room was deserted. Although it was only eight, most of the guests were already out on the esplanade. In front of the High Rock Pavilion, a group of sweat-suited figures of indeterminate age and sex was doing aerobics under the direction of an energetic blonde in a pink leotard. A recorder blared a fast-paced disco tape, to which the sweat suits pulsed, bounced, and dipped. Another group jogged in strict military formation around the esplanade behind a young man with bulging biceps. Strict military formation, that is, except for the three fatties who lagged behind, alternately lurching forward in determination and falling back in distress. Charlotte didn't smile; she would be happy not to be the only one bringing up the rear.

After breakfast, Charlotte headed toward the lobby, where she was to meet her personal exercise advisor, Frannie La-Beau. Frannie was a thin blonde with metal-rimmed granny glasses. As Charlotte's personal exercise advisor, she explained, she would be responsible for overseeing Charlotte's spa stay. She would review Charlotte's program daily, making adjustments and suggestions. Charlotte thought this sounded

vaguely despotic. She wondered if a black mark would be
entered against her name if she didn't do the required number
of push-ups. In fact, her impression turned out not to be far off
the mark. The first event on her schedule was a two-part
Fitness Appraisal. The first part, Frannie explained, would be
a physical evaluation, the results of which would be fed into a
computer along with information from Charlotte's pre-
admission physical. The second part would be a computer
interview, the subject of which would be her health habits.
From this data, the computer would calculate her biological
age (as opposed to her real, or chronological, age). "Hope-
fully," said Frannie, "your biological age will be younger than
your chronological age."

Frannie explained most of this as they walked across the
esplanade. Or rather, Charlotte walked. She had a long leggy
stride, as forthright as a man's. Frannie kind of lurched, her
body convulsing with the effort of moving a leg that was
withered to a thin spindle. It was the kind of disability that had
been common before the polio vaccine, but Frannie was too
young to have had polio. Charlotte wondered: a birth defect,
muscular dystrophy? On the foot of the withered leg, she wore
an orthopedic shoe whose sole was built up to compensate for
the shortened leg. But even with the shoe, she walked with a
limp, swinging the leg forward stiffly in a kind of choppy
rhythm, like an exaggerated dance. They were headed toward
the spa quadrangle, which was entered via a set of low steps
flanked by wisteria-covered pergolas. The steps, which Frannie managed with a surprising degree of sprightliness, brought
them face-to-face with the Hall of Springs, an imposing brick
building with a hipped slate roof. To either side stood the two
other buildings of the spa: the Roosevelt Bath Pavilion and the
Flexner Health Pavilion. The symmetry of the design was
completed by a reflecting pool in the center of which stood a
graceful bronze sculpture of an Indian maiden filling a gourd at
High Rock Spring, and by the open-air colonnades linking the
three buildings, giving the quadrangle the contemplative feel
of a medieval cloister.

From the steps, they set out across the quadrangle toward the
Health Pavilion, startling the peacocks that strutted proudly at
the edge of the pool. Entering under an entrance portico whose

pediment was adorned with a bas relief of Hygeia, the Greek goddess of health, they found themselves in a lobby, which, with its two-story rotunda, its massive Doric columns, and its glossy black-and-white-tiled marble floor, reminded Charlotte of the lobby of the Bowery Savings Bank on East Forty-second. In the center stood a fountain from which High Rock water flowed continuously. A pair of elliptical staircases led to the second floor. At the stairs, which were steeper than those at the spa entrance, the rhythm of Frannie's stride was broken. After pausing to grip the brass banister, she proceeded to slowly and tortuously make her way to the top. Reaching the top, they proceeded down a corridor to the Diagnostic Room, a mirror-lined chamber the size of a classroom, in which twelve stations were laid out, each marked by a large red number on the wall. At each station, a different fitness parameter was measured—height; weight; blood pressure; chest, hip, thigh, and arm measurements; and so on.

For the next hour, Frannie put Charlotte through her paces, prodding and measuring with the brisk, impersonal efficiency of a sergeant at a Marine induction center. After the basic measurements came the cardiovascular stress assessment: after being wired with electrodes, Charlotte was asked to pedal hell for leather on something called an ergometric lifecycle. Next came the skin fold analysis, in which the unsightly folds of flesh on the undersides of her upper arms—her bat wings, Frannie called them (somewhat indelicately, Charlotte thought)—were gripped between the menacing pincers of a set of jawed calipers. Then came the pulmonary analysis, in which she had to blow into a balloonlike contraption called a spirometer. And so it went—grip strength, stress profile, flexibility, posture analysis, musculoskeletal assessment. As she made her way from station to station, Charlotte was assailed by words that conjured up a frightening image of degeneration: dowager's hump, which, thank God, she didn't have; bunions, which she did. Sagging breasts, liver spots, chicken neck—what grim specters of the grave Frannie didn't invoke, Charlotte readily imagined for herself. She found it all mildly disturbing. The state of her flesh wasn't a subject to which she ordinarily gave much thought. She preferred to

banish it from her consciousness in the same way that she
disguised her bat wings by wearing long-sleeved dresses.

While Frannie fed the results of the physical evaluation into
a computer, Charlotte was directed to a cubicle where she
spent the next half hour being questioned by its nosy mate. The
green characters that appeared so impersonally on the screen
demanded answers to intimate questions about her sex life
(none) and her bowel movements (regular), as well as to less
intimate ones about her smoking, dietary, and drinking habits.
Next came a series of stuffy questions about her fitness goals.
What would she like to accomplish most? What did she
consider her area of greatest weakness? Where would she like
to be in five years? The answer to that question was easy:
alive and kicking, which she was coming to view as an
accomplishment in itself.

She now sat in the office of the spa administrator, Anne-
Marie Andersen, awaiting her "personal consultation," in
which she would be presented with the computer's verdict. The
walls of the office were hung with photographs of mountain
peaks. They were pyramid-shaped and ridged, domed and
saw-toothed, sheathed in ice and strewn with rocks. Seeing
them, Charlotte remembered that Anne-Marie was a mountaineer. In fact, she had been the leader of the first all-female team
to climb some Himalayan peak or other. Several of the photos
were of the blonde who had been leading the aerobics class,
whom Charlotte concluded must be Anne-Marie. In one, she
was standing atop a snow-covered peak, an ice ax raised in
triumph to the sky. In another, she was sitting with a fellow
mountaineer on a narrow ledge, their sleeping bags wrapped
around their dangling legs. Others showed her camping on
alpine glaciers or crossing raging torrents on flimsy rope
bridges. If the photographs were meant to be intimidating, they
were. Charlotte wondered what the intrepid mountaineer
would have to say in judgment of an over-the-hill movie star
with a weakness for manhattans and marzipan.

Anne-Marie was familiar to Charlotte by reputation. Charlotte had often heard Paulina speak of her. She was a Swede
whom Paulina had discovered at the famous Bircher-Benner
Clinic in Switzerland, where she was working as an exercise

instructor. Paulina had hired her away to supervise the exercise programs at the two-hundred-odd Langenberg salons around the world. Since joining the Langenberg organization, she had gone on to become a celebrity in her own right. She was the author of several books extolling the virtues of exercise and good nutrition, which, breezy in tone and replete with common sense advice, had been very popular. Another book recounted her adventures as leader of the all-female mountaineering team. In addition, she had played a large part in the creation of the spa. It was Anne-Marie who had drawn up the guidelines, chosen the treatments, hired staff, and purchased equipment. In beauty industry circles, she was widely regarded as Paulina's confidante. Although it could never be said of Paulina that her decisions were subject to any judgment other than her own, to the extent that she required a sounding board, it was Anne-Marie who served that function.

But any image Charlotte might have had of Anne-Marie as a less-than-feminine body cultist were dispelled by her appearance. She was muscular—compact would be a better description—but far from masculine. In fact, she was the kind of radiant, tawny-skinned blonde who had earned Scandinavian women their reputation for beauty. Although she looked thirty—an impression fostered by her round, rosy cheeks and her short, boyish haircut—Charlotte suspected she was at least fifteen years older.

Taking a seat, Anne-Marie introduced herself and told Charlotte how happy Paulina was that Charlotte was finally visiting the spa.

Charlotte made the appropriate replies, all the while eyeing the green-and-white-striped computer printout that would tell her whether her name was entered in the debit or the credit column of the giant ledger in which second helpings and late-night parties were recorded by a merciless celestial hand.

Anne-Marie chatted on about the spa: that it wasn't a fat farm or a clinic, but a holistic center that dealt with the entire individual—physical, mental, and spiritual—and that its goal was to provide guests with the tools to overcome bad health habits. "We're what's called a permissive spa. We don't demand that our guests attend classes. We don't post monitors in the dining room. These are futile exercises: what good do they do if our guests go back to stuffing themselves with chocolate chip cookies the minute they get home?"

She paused for a reply. But Charlotte had no answer to the chocolate chip cookie question. Why not go back to stuffing yourself with chocolate chip cookies the minute you got home? She knew a lot of chocolate chip cookie eaters and candy bar eaters and potato chip eaters (to whose ranks she belonged) who had led long, happy, and productive lives.

Anne-Marie continued. She spoke in earnest tones: "We believe the way to conquer bad habits is to restore the broken link between the inner self and the body. Most of us exist only from the neck up." She held her hand out palm down beneath her chin. "We feel alien in our bodies. It's our aim to help our guests restore the connection. But not by setting rules—if we try to fight our bad habits, we only create conflict, which leads to anxiety and depression—but by purifying and conditioning the body through exercise and nutrition. Through exercise and nutrition, we can create the kind of spiritual atmosphere in which our bad habits will give *us* up." Leaning back, she smiled brilliantly. She was one of those blondes who are all teeth and hair.

"That sounds like quite a trick," said Charlotte. She also thought it sounded vaguely heretical, as if doing push-ups and drinking carrot juice were somehow the key to spiritual salvation.

"I think you'll find that it works. We'll see in nine days, won't we?" She smiled again, and then passed the computer printout across the desk. "I expect you're anxious to find out how you did."

"Yes," replied Charlotte. She had the odd feeling that the printout would divine her fate, like tea leaves in an empty cup or the pattern of cracks on a heated bone. She donned her eyeglasses; they were reading glasses with tortoise-shell frames that gave her a professorial air.

"At the bottom," said Anne-Marie, pointing with a long, tanned finger.

Charlotte scanned the rows of figures. "Forty-nine?"

"Yes. Are you surprised?"

No, Charlotte thought.

It was true that she was as adept as anyone at lying to

herself: the five or six cigarettes that were really half a pack, the one or two glasses of wine that were really three or four. But when it came right down to it, she knew what the score was, and that it was a pretty good one. She had her gauges: her mirror, her scale, her joints—the watchdogs that reproved her for her excesses and congratulated her on her restraint. What did surprise her was how smug she felt, as if the computer really was prescient. She wanted to believe in the infallibility of the bookkeeper in the sky who said she was entitled to an extra thirteen years for good behavior. But she also knew he wasn't as punctilious as the Anne-Maries of the world would have her believe. It was her experience that he was as prone to foolishness and whimsy as anyone else. His ledger was apt to be full of errors and omissions: debits in the column of the health food devotee, credits in the column of the chocolate chip cookie binger. She put people who believed they could forestall death by drinking carrot juice in the same category as people who believed that everything will go right for them if they go to church every Sunday. They were both in for a rude awakening.

She handed the printout back. "Not really," she replied.

"The guests who are older than their biological ages rarely are. It's the ones who are younger who are shocked." She turned her attention back to the printout. "You have at least one area where there's room for improvement. Can you guess what it is?"

"The cocktails," replied Charlotte.

Anne-Marie nodded. She urged Charlotte to switch to white wine spritzers and to limit herself to one or two.

In fact, Charlotte thought her biological age would probably be higher were it not for her nightly manhattan. She was a firm believer in the psycho-therapeutic virtues of alcohol, and said as much. For soothing the spirit, Lord Byron had said, apply rum and true religion.

But Anne-Marie, invoking the specter of shriveled gray cells to add to those of bat wings and liver spots, wasn't convinced. She returned her attention to the printout, a disapproving frown slipping across her viking brow. "I see another area. What about the cigarettes?"

Charlotte damned the computer. She could hardly argue that

cigarettes were therapeutic, but she had managed for most of her adult life to keep her habit to ten or less a day, an achievement that she, at any rate, considered an outstanding example of self-control.

"You realize, don't you, that there's no threshold for lung cancer?" Anne-Marie leaned forward, her arms folded on the desk. "In other words, there's no point below which you are not subjecting yourself to a risk." She raised a forefinger. "Even one cigarette is a risk."

In her mind's eye, Charlotte saw the celestial hand making an entry in the debit column of the giant ledger in the sky. Meekly, she pledged to refrain, or at least to cut back.

Anne-Marie set the printout aside.

Charlotte leaned back in relief.

"You'll be in C-group—for those whose biological ages are forty-five and above. All our guests take the same classes, but the workouts are tailored to individual fitness levels. Here's your exercise prescription." She handed Charlotte a booklet with an engraving of the Indian maiden on the cover. Inside there was a page for each day of Charlotte's stay. The pages were marked off in half-hour intervals: six A.M., wake-up; six-thirty A.M., mineral water prescription; seven A.M., Awake and Aware; seven-thirty A.M., breakfast; eight A.M., Terrain Cure; and so on.

"Six o'clock?" said Charlotte.

"We like you to get up early to take the waters. The spa physician, Dr. Sperry, will be giving you your mineral water prescription and your bath prescription this afternoon. We generally reserve the afternoons for treatments at the Bath Pavilion or at L'Institut de Beauté."

"I'm glad to hear that," Charlotte said. She had been looking forward to her spa stay in terms of a long, luxurious soak in the tub, but it was beginning to sound more like boot camp—without the food.

"Don't worry. It's not as strenuous as it looks," said Anne-Marie with a smile that was intended to be reassuring. "I'm sure you'll enjoy it." With that, she rose, signaling the end of the interview. "Frannie will take you down to the locker room now; your first class is in twenty minutes."

Charlotte thanked her and shook her hand. She had the grip of a heavyweight champion.

Frannie was waiting for her outside Anne-Marie's office. She smiled her crooked smile. Next to the robust Anne-Marie, she looked like a case study in bad health. Her posture was poor, her complexion pasty, her hair thin and lank. Even her eyes, which were magnified by her glasses, were dull and pale. She reminded Charlotte of the baby mice—blind, pink, and helpless—that she had once found nesting in an old orange crate as a child.

"How did you do?" she asked as they headed toward the stairs.

"Group C," confessed Charlotte. She felt as if she was admitting to being relegated to the slow track in ninth grade.

"I mean, your biological age," said Frannie. She descended the stairs with much less difficulty than she had climbed them.

"Forty-nine."

"I guessed forty-eight."

"How did you know?"

"By your appearance. Generally speaking, if people look younger than they are, their biological age is younger than their real age."

"So much for the wisdom of the computer."

Frannie smiled. They had reached the foot of the stairs. Frannie headed across the lobby to a door on the far wall.

"This is the treatment area," she said as she entered. She reeled off a list of treatments, which ranged from biofeedback to herbal wraps to tanning beds. "A typical treatment cubicle," she added, opening a door on a small room with a cot. "It also happens to be the one where I work."

"What do you do?" asked Charlotte.

"Shiatsu," she replied. She briefly explained the Japanese system of finger massage. "You asked how I estimate biological age. One way is by appearance. Another is by touch. If I've done a massage on a person, I can usually estimate their biological age pretty accurately."

"Why's that?" asked Charlotte.

"Oh, it's not hard. Skin quality, muscle tone . . ." she replied. "If someone's poisoning their body, it will show up in a massage. The body is supposed to be the temple of the spirit, but some people treat it like a hotel room." With that, she opened a door leading to the weight area.

A hotel room? Charlotte pondered the metaphor for a while and decided that it didn't hold up. It wouldn't be right to treat your body like a flophouse, but as a temporary abode in which you were privileged to reside—a first-class hotel, so to speak? That hardly struck her as so reprehensible.

"Sometimes I can even tell about past lives from a massage," Frannie added as they entered a room filled with gleaming chrome exercise machines.

"Past lives?"

"Sure. The body is imprinted with every incarnational event the soul has ever experienced—not only from the present lifetime, but from every lifetime. Every cell is a storehouse of the energy of experience. Have you ever had the feeling that you've been somewhere before?"

"Yes," replied Charlotte, wondering what she was opening herself up to.

"That's because you *have* been there before, in another life. Ordinarily, you don't remember because it would interfere with your functioning. You're prohibited from remembering by a veil of forgetfulness. But once in a while, the veil lifts. That's when you have the feeling of déjà vu."

Here we go again, thought Charlotte. Mozart, who was composing at four because he'd been a musician in a past life. Patton, who was strategically familiar with the battlefields of Europe because he'd been over them before as a Roman commander. She raised a skeptical eyebrow.

Frannie paused next to a machine into which a young woman was strapped on her back, ready for takeoff. Her ankles were tucked under padded cylinders, which she raised by extending her legs.

"This is our compound leg machine; it exercises the quadriceps muscles. We have twenty-three machines," she said. "Each machine exercises a different muscle or muscle group. I'll be showing you how to use the machines later in the week. But first we have to get you conditioned. What were we talking about?"

"The veil of forgetfulness."

"Oh, yes. The veil lifting. It happened to me with my husband. The first time we met—it was in a metaphysical bookstore in the Village—I had this feeling of closeness, as if I'd known him before. I wasn't into reincarnation then, but he was. He felt it too; he knew right away what it was."

As she spoke, a young man entered the room. He had black hair, a black beard, and a black belt that identified him as a martial arts instructor.

Frannie's face lit up. "I was just talking about you."

"Oh?" He grinned. "Anything nice?" He spoke with a soft southern accent that Charlotte pegged as North Carolina or Tennessee.

"I was just telling Miss Graham how we met. Miss Graham, this is my husband, Dana LaBeau."

He extended his hand. "Pleased to meet you."

"It wasn't until Dana regressed me that I realized we were soul mates," Frannie continued. "Not twin souls. Twin souls are quite common—people who've had a relationship of some sort in another life. Soul mates are very rare; our souls vibrate at the same electromagnetic frequency."

"They were created together at the time of the Big Bang," added Dana.

"How romantic," said Charlotte with a twinge of sarcasm that went unnoticed. She studied Dana more closely: he was good-looking enough, with strong white teeth, a pleasant smile, and deep green eyes with long, silky lashes, but Charlotte thought him disappointingly unprepossessing for someone whose soul dated back to the Big Bang.

"I mean, it all makes sense if you think about it," said Frannie.

Charlotte withheld comment.

"If you're interested in finding out more about your past lives, you can take our course," said Dana. "It's called Other Lives/Other Selves. It's on Wednesday nights. It's a prerequisite for Past Life Regression. If you want to sign on, just tell Frannie." He extended his hand with a warm smile. "It was a pleasure meeting you. I hope we'll be seeing you again on Wednesday."

"Maybe," said Charlotte, returning his handshake.

"Dana teaches karate in the morning and works as a bath

attendant in the afternoon," Frannie explained after he left.
"He was a samurai warrior in a previous life; that's why he's
so interested in the martial arts. We often remember our past
lives through our interests and predilections."

"Does that mean that I was an actress in a previous life?"

"I wouldn't be surprised. If you take our course, you'll find
out. It often helps you advance spiritually if you're familiar
with your past lives. It's easier to work off your karmic debts
when you have a clear idea of what they are. You know—
coming to terms with your cosmic responsibilities."

"I think I'd prefer not to know."

Frannie shrugged. "Some people just prefer to live in a state
of cosmic ignorance," she said with a good-natured smile.

The tour ended at the women's lounge, where Frannie issued
Charlotte a white terry-cloth kimono, a pair of red rubber
thongs, and a white sweat suit with racing stripes of Langenberg red. Then she directed Charlotte to her locker, wished her
good luck, and bade her good-bye.

Charlotte wasn't sure which was worse: Anne-Marie's
overbearing enthusiasm or Frannie's metaphysical malarkey.

She found herself sharing a corner of the locker room with
a woman who was struggling to stuff a large leather tote bag
into a narrow floor-to-ceiling locker. She was of the type who
used to be called voluptuous, but was now just called fat.

"For four grand a week, you'd think they'd give you a
bigger locker," she complained as she slammed the door.

She was a short woman with frizzy brown hair cut in a
twenties-style bob and a piquant mouth that turned up at the
corners. But underneath its expression of wry amusement, her
face was careworn: the forehead was deeply creased and the
skin hung in yellowish folds under distant gray eyes.

"Are you a new inmate?" She enunciated her words carefully, as if she wasn't sure they'd come out right if she didn't.

"I guess you could say that." Charlotte did have the feeling
that she was being treated like a mental defective confined to
some sort of institution—the childlike days plotted out for her
in half-hour segments, no decisions to make, not even what to
wear.

"It's a nice place," the woman said. Taking a seat on a

bench, she removed a pack of cigarettes from her pocket. She pulled out one for herself and then offered the pack to Charlotte. "Want a smoke?"

"Do they allow it?"

The woman lifted her shoulders in a shrug.

Charlotte smiled and sat down next to her, taking her up on her offer. She liked her immediately.

"I see you're in the backward group too," the woman said as she offered Charlotte a light. Charlotte noticed that her hand shook.

"You're in C-group." She nodded at Charlotte's sweat suit. "We're color-coded—dark gray, light gray, and white. White is for the backward group, those of us whose biological age is forty-five and over." She gestured at the booklet in Charlotte's hand. "Do you have Swing and Sway now?"

Charlotte checked her booklet. "Yes."

"Good. So do I. There are only four from the backward group in that class and two are men. It'll be nice to have some more female company."

"How is it?" asked Charlotte.

"Swing and Sway isn't bad. It's Backs and Bellies and Absolutely Abdominals that are the killers. In case you haven't noticed, they're big on alliteration here," she added with a little smile. "The real killer is Awake and Aware—that's the one at seven."

"At that hour, I'm more like semiconscious and stupefied."

The woman laughed. "I know what you mean. What age did you clock in at?"

"Forty-nine."

"Hey!" Drawing away, the woman gazed at Charlotte in wide-eyed admiration.

It was true that Charlotte didn't look her age. Outside of her hair style and a few crow's-feet, she still looked much as she had in her twenties. The years had dealt lightly with the fine structure of her face. As for her body, she had gained a few pounds, but she still had a good figure and she carried herself with the lightness and grace of a woman half her age.

"Congratulations. I clocked in at forty-eight, but that's not much of an achievement. I'm really only thirty-eight. My name's Adele Singer, by the way," she added, extending her hand.

"Charlotte Graham."

"I know. I recognized you right away. I always imagined you would be tall. But so often movie stars turn out to be a lot shorter than you think—you know what I mean?" She continued: "I'm a fan. But don't worry. I'm not going to hound you for an autograph."

"Thanks," replied Charlotte. She hoped the same would be true of the other guests. She was counting on the guests at a posh spa like this one to be considerate enough not to harass their celebrity fellows.

As Charlotte changed, Adele filled her in on the other C's. The two men were Art, a middle-aged chemist who had been ordered to the spa by his cardiologist, and Nicky, an obese young man who worked as a counter boy at his father's Greek deli in Astoria, and who had been eating more than he sold. He had sold the Buick he'd saved three years to buy to pay for his stay. The third C was Corinne, a model who'd come to the spa to promote a new line of Langenberg products, the chief ingredient of which was mineral water. Corinne had technically been assigned to A-group—she'd clocked in with a biological age in the teens—but she'd voluntarily relegated herself to the ignominy of C-dom. Her attitude was that she'd come to the spa to do a promotion, not to torture herself, which Adele thought a sensible attitude indeed.

As she entered the exercise room a few minutes later in her white sweat suit, Charlotte felt like a spa virgin about to be sacrificed on the altar of physical fitness. Her usual idea of athletic wear was a sturdy pair of walking shoes and her usual idea of exercise a brisk walk up the sunny side of Fifth Avenue. The front of the room had been claimed by the dark gray sweat-suited A's, who awaited the commencement of class with grim seriousness of purpose. Adele wisely staked out their turf at the back next to Art and Corinne, whose face Charlotte recognized from magazine ads. She was a vague-but-whole-some-looking beauty who wore sweatbands around her forehead and wrists to match her low-cut plum leotard, which was definitely not spa-issue.

While they waited, Charlotte chatted with Art, the chemist.

By now, she had recognized "What's your biological age?" to be the conversational equivalent of "How do you like the weather?"—the icebreaker that established a bond of shared experience. For Art, the report wasn't good. His biological age was seventy-three, a disastrous sixteen years older than his real age. Forty pounds overweight and with a cholesterol level in the stratosphere, he was a prime candidate for a coronary. His doctor had sentenced him to the fourteen-day cardiac rehabilitation program as restitution for a nightly shakerful of martinis, a four-pack-a-day cigarette habit, and little exercise outside of an occasional expedition onto the golf course.

Charlotte liked him enormously. He had a wonderful face: long and narrow, with prominent temples from which his thin blond hair had long ago receded; eyebrows suspended like circumflexes over small, deep-set blue eyes; and a long nose leading down to a narrow mouth filled with small, even teeth. It was a Gothic face, a knight's face. He looked, with his furrowed brow and pugnacious jaw, like a St. George who had wearied of slaying dragons.

The class commenced with the arrival of the teacher, a limber young woman named Claire who led them through body circles, waist twists, and scissor kicks to the gentle strains of easy listening music. A stylish and energetic leader, she regularly interrupted her routine to cheer on her students with exhortations of the "Come on, you can do it" variety or to demonstrate variations they could do at home or in the car.

Art graciously took it upon himself to be Charlotte's guardian, showing her how to position her uncooperative limbs and reassuring her in moments of distress that she needn't complete every count.

But if Art saw no need to complete every count, a lean-and-hungry-looking man in a dark gray sweat suit did. When Art stopped at six counts, he went on to twelve. When Art dropped out of the routine, red-faced and gasping, the man in the dark gray sweat suit went on to finish effortlessly. If Art was the class dunce, the man in dark gray was its star.

"See that guy there?" whispered Art between exercises.

"How could I miss him?"

"His real age is fifty-one—he's only six years younger than

me. But his biological age is only twenty-three. Fifty years'
difference." He shook his head. "Fifty years!"

Charlotte studied the man in amazement. Narrow-waisted
and sharp-featured, he wore a New York Marathon T-shirt.
What miracles of rejuvenation had he performed on his body
that the computer should assign him an age fifty years younger
than a man only six years his senior?

"One of those guys you want to kill," said Art. "Mr.
Physically Fit. Our Role Model, I call him."

"Keep those heads up," admonished Claire. Moving around
the room, she adjusted here and advised there. She had a
bright, cheerful manner and a wide, pale face with a high
forehead and a light dusting of freckles. It wasn't a pretty face,
but it was intelligent and forthright.

"What does our role model do for a living?" asked Charlotte
as she and Art struggled to swing their legs into the air. She
noticed that the Role Model accomplished this feat without a
grunt or groan, thanks no doubt to rock-hard stomach muscles.

"An investment banker. Specializes in hostile takeovers,"
said Art. He named a prominent New York firm.

Charlotte nodded. She knew the type: up at dawn for a
ten-mile jog around the reservoir, lunchtime racquet ball at the
athletic club, meals of yogurt and fruit juice and vitamins taken
on the run. Physical fitness in the name of the Almighty
Dollar. New York was full of them.

After a final series of neck twists, Claire announced the
conclusion of class. "That's it, ladies and gentlemen," she
said. The announcement was met with a burst of applause, in
gratitude partly for the style and vigor of Claire's leadership
and partly for the welcome fact that class was over.

Charlotte exited behind Art and the Role Model: one pasty,
flaccid, and jowly; the other tan, trim, and sharp-featured.
They could be, she decided, the contrasting symbols of the Era
of Physical Fitness.

· 3 ·

AFTER CLASS, CHARLOTTE and Adele headed over to the Hall of Springs for lunch. The Hall of Springs was the most imposing of the spa buildings, modeled as it was after the *trink* halls of the European spas. To Charlotte, its main room, the Pump Room, looked like the nave of a cathedral or perhaps the set of a thirties champagne musical. It was a vast room, a hundred and fifty feet long and three stories high. Huge crystal chandeliers hung from the barrel-vaulted ceiling, which was supported by files of massive Doric columns through which shafts of sunlight poured down through clerestory windows. Encircling the room was a band engraved in roman-style lettering with a quotation from Ecclesiastes: "The Lord hath created medicines out of the earth, and he that is wise will not abhor them." Above the band was a running frieze depicting episodes from the spa's history: the Indian maiden at the spring, the arrival of John Williams on a litter, Elisha Burnett's log cabin surrounded by Indian tepees. The highly polished marble floor was laid out in a geometric pattern. Set at intervals along its length were three circular altars where the mineral waters flowed from brass spigots labeled High Rock, Union, and Sans Souci into fonts of dark green marble. Behind the altars, acolytes in crisp white jackets served up the water to modern-day supplicants, the sophisticated counterparts of the pilgrims to Lourdes. The water was served like the Russians serve tea, in glasses with metal holders. For some, it was heated to the prescribed temperature at heaters behind the counters.

But despite the architecture, the atmosphere was far from

reverential. Guests sat at marble tables amid the potted palms talking, drinking, or eating lunch to the accompaniment of a Strauss waltz played by the string quartet that concertized three times a day on the terrace outside.

Charlotte and Adele threaded their way among the tables to an empty one in a corner and sat down. A young woman wearing a starched white shirt and a small red bow tie brought them their menus and took their mineral water order. Charlotte played it safe and ordered High Rock water; she had yet to get her mineral water prescription. Adele ordered Union water, heated.

"Actually, I'd prefer a martini," she said once the waitress had gone, "but I've got to purge my system of the toxins I've been pouring into it. Quote, unquote. Excuse me if I bolt halfway through lunch. Union water is guaranteed to produce swift results."

Charlotte laughed, the curious husky laugh for which she was famous.

Adele studied her menu. "I hope you're not fruits and nuts."

Charlotte smiled. "No. Cuisine Minceur."

"Good. The fruits and nuts people are bad enough. But the juice people are even worse."

She was referring to the spa menu plans. La Cuisine Minceur was the low-calorie continental plan. There was also a low-calorie vegetarian plan—what Adele called fruits and nuts—and a juice plan for the real zealots. La Cuisine Gourmande was for those who didn't need or didn't want to diet.

"Not much to choose from," said Charlotte, scanning the offerings. There were only three La Cuisine Minceur entrées. Each was marked with a calorie count. A maximum of twelve hundred calories a day for women and fifteen hundred calories a day for men was recommended.

"I agree. There's not much of a selection, but I can assure you that it's all delicious," said Adele. "What this chef can do with twelve hundred calories is incredible. Michel Bergeron—he's very famous for cuisine minceur. I recommend the grilled veal chop—it's out of this world."

"That sounds fine to me," said Charlotte.

The waitress brought their water and took their order. In

addition to the veal chop (two hundred and twenty calories), they ordered crayfish in court bouillon (fifty calories), and a field salad with chives (seventy-five calories). By dessert, they would have used up their entire lunch allotment.

"How do you like it so far?" asked Adele suddenly. She spoke proprietarily, as if she wanted Charlotte to enjoy her stay as much as she was.

"So far, so good. But I haven't been here that long."

"Who's your advisor?"

"Frannie LaBeau."

"Mine's Claire. She's an absolute doll. But I hear Frannie's very good too. I know one thing—she's the best masseuse here. I've tried them all, but Frannie is tops. She may be a little cuckoo, but she gives a hell of a massage. Did she give you the reincarnation bit?"

"The body as the temple of the spirit?"

Rolling her eyes heavenward, Adele twirled a forefinger at her temple. "I wanted her to tell me what I was in my last life, but she said I'd have to take the course. All she would say was that I'm living on borrowed time." She hoisted her glass. "I'm poisoning my physical envelope."

"Your physical envelope?" said Charlotte. She raised her glass to Adele's in a toast. "Here's to poisoning your physical envelope." She sipped her drink, feeling the bubbles fizz in her nose. Like Adele, she would rather have been poisoning her physical envelope with a glass of wine.

Over a lunch that was artfully presented to look like more than it was, the garrulous Adele gave Charlotte a series of brief reviews of the treatments. She praised the Salt Glo, in which you were rubbed down with coarse salt from the Dead Sea; and panned the Herbal Wrap, in which you were wrapped, mummylike, in warm sheets soaked with herbs: "It's supposed to be a quasi-mystical experience, but I felt like I was being buried alive." From zone therapy and biofeedback, she went on to the latest gossip on the spa physician, Dr. Sperry, who, she said, used to be spa director. Paulina had reportedly demoted him because of problems caused by his skirt-chasing habits. "Irate husbands and the like," was how she put it. "He told me I had a Reubenesque figure," she added with a giggle. The new spa director was Paulina's son, Elliot. It was Elliot, who was something of a health food nut, who had introduced the fruits and nuts and juice plans. "But if it weren't for Anne-Marie, Dr. Sperry would have been fired outright," said Adele.

"What did Anne-Marie have to do with it?" interjected Charlotte between bites of her tiny veal chop, which was indeed delicious.

Adele explained that Dr. Sperry was Anne-Marie's ex-husband. But they remained on good terms. It was Anne-Marie who had talked Paulina into keeping Dr. Sperry on, if only as spa physician.

Anne-Marie struck Charlotte as being too smart to have married someone like Dr. Sperry. She said as much to Adele.

Adele shrugged. "Who knows? Sometimes even intelligent women make mistakes. I'm sure we can all think of some examples."

Charlotte smiled. It was known to all the world that she had been married four times. "Touché," she said.

"You're not the only member of the club."

By the time the raspberry tart (seventy-two calories) arrived, Adele had moved on to her own life story, which wasn't very pretty. In short, she was a pill junkie. For more than a dozen years, she'd been "riding the pill roller coaster." She had started with amphetamines, prescribed to help her lose weight, and gone on to barbiturates, prescribed to help her sleep. And then to other drugs: Valium, Dalmane, Quaalude, Librium, Seconal, Percodan, Darvon—the names rolled off her tongue like a list of old, beloved friends. She spoke slowly and determinedly. Occasionally she'd lift a hand to her throat, as if her memories interfered with her ability to breathe. "I didn't consider myself an addict," she explained. "My pills were all prescribed by doctors. Every time I went to the doctor, I was given another prescription. In all that time," she said, her voice rising, "no one ever said to me, 'Adele, don't you think you ought to cut back?' "

Charlotte listened. She was a good listener. Unlike many actors, she had the ability to be intimate with people; it was an ability that few actors keep, which few ever had. Her role was that of the sympathetic stranger. It was always easier to confess your problems to someone you didn't know than to someone who might be around to remind you of what you wanted to forget. She knew the importance of letting Adele unburden herself. By telling her story, she was putting it behind her, making it history. Besides, Charlotte didn't need to ask questions. In her business, it was a familiar story: the need to be on, to perform, day after day, whether sick or well, up or down, demanded incredible stamina. It was hard to resist the pill that gave you the oomph to get through another performance, and then, when you were too keyed up to sleep, another pill or the bottle to bring you down again. For people like Adele, who were doing their best to pull themselves out of a nose dive, Charlotte had nothing but respect. She had known all too many over the years who had failed.

Gradually, Adele's life had unraveled. Her husband left her, taking the children with him. Her eldest son died tragically in a plane crash. She began drinking, swallowing her pills with booze. She ended up in a cheap hotel on the Lower East Side where she was free to spend her days taking pills and her nights in neighborhood bars. The end came one cold January night when she was found frozen to the sidewalk next to a leaky fire hydrant. She was taken to Bellevue and treated for hypothermia.

The waitress reappeared to clear the dessert dishes.

"In AA terms," Adele said after the waitress had left, "I had reached rock bottom. For some, rock bottom is something as minor as making a fool of yourself in public. For others it's a drunken driving conviction or passing out under the dining-room table. But until you've hit it, you're not going to change. For me, it was being picked up off the sidewalk like a Bowery bum." Her voice shook. She paused to compose herself and then went on. "AA got me off the booze. I haven't had a drink in four months. But," she added with a wry little smile, "I'm still on the pills."

Reaching into her leather tote bag, she pulled out a compartmentalized plastic box of the type used for storing thumb tacks and safety pins. "My security box," she said. Each compartment was filled with pills of different shapes and colors. "These are for me," she said, picking out three or four red capsules. She reached into her bag again. "And this is for us," she said, the corners of her mouth lifting into a smile.

"Contraband." She pulled out a bar of Swiss chocolate—the dark, bittersweet kind that was Charlotte's favorite—and broke off two squares for Charlotte and two for herself.

"Does Anne-Marie know about this?" teased Charlotte.

"No, and she doesn't know about these either," she said, swallowing the pills with a swig of mineral water. She continued: "I've been cutting back. But I'm not ready to go cold turkey yet."

She had, she said, in "moments of sanity" flushed her pills down the toilet, but she'd always ended up going back to a Dr. Feelgood or buying more pills on the street. But this time she was determined to lick her "pilling." She'd resolved that when she got home, she would flush her pills down the toilet for good. "I'm poor, I'm sick, but I've never felt better in my life," she said. She was counting on her spa visit—the generous gift of an old friend—to give her the strength of mind to carry through. Her voice carried a note of determination, as if by announcing her intention, she was making a pledge to herself to carry it out.

Charlotte wished her strength, and luck.

Charlotte sat in Dr. Sperry's waiting room, reading a magazine. After lunch, she had walked over to the Health Pavilion with Adele, who was now in Dr. Sperry's office. Unlike the A's and B's, who required no checkups after the initial one, Adele and the other C's were required to see the spa physician daily for a checkup and blood-pressure reading.

The door to Dr. Sperry's office opened and Adele emerged, rather unsteadily. For a moment, it looked as if she would bark a shin on the corner of the glass and chrome coffee table, but she managed to successfully maneuver herself around it. Noticing Charlotte, she paused, waved a glassy-eyed good-bye, and floated out into the hall.

Standing in the doorway, Dr. Sperry looked out after her, his forehead creased in a worried frown. Once she had gone, his attention shifted to Charlotte. "You can come in now, Miss Graham," he said.

In contrast to Anne-Marie's spartan quarters, Dr. Sperry's office was Park Avenue plush. A stereo played a Mozart sonata and signed lithographs by well-known artists hung on the walls. The windows overlooked the reflecting pool. Charlotte wondered how he had ended up with a woman whose idea of ideal accommodations was a pup tent at a Himalayan base camp.

Dr. Sperry closed the door behind her. For a moment he stood and stared, his knuckle raised to his mouth in contemplation.

She could see how the ladies would find him attractive. He was tall, with silver-gray hair and sideburns, heavy black eyebrows, and a long, thin face tanned to a medium bronze, probably by the tanning bed downstairs. It was heavily lined—craggy, some would have called it. He wore a knee-length white lab coat over a navy blue turtleneck. A stethoscope hung from his neck.

"It's remarkable," he said.

"What's remarkable?"

"How beautiful you are." He smiled. "I'm sorry. I didn't mean to make you uncomfortable."

"You haven't," replied Charlotte matter-of-factly.

"That's right. I suppose you're accustomed to compliments," he said. He pulled out a swivel chair upholstered in dove-gray leather. Gray was the color theme, with a charcoal-gray carpet and vertical blinds: stylish, soothing, masculine. "Won't you take a seat?"

At one side of the room was an examination couch. From what Adele had said, it got quite a workout. Next to it stood a blood-pressure unit.

"Thank you," said Charlotte. To her surprise, he offered her a cigarette. A sign in a chrome frame on the desk said, "No smoking, people breathing."

"I see that you smoke," he said, nodding at the folder that lay on the teak surface of his desk.

"Yes," she replied. "About six a day."

"Good. The important thing is moderation." He removed a gold lighter from his pocket and lit her cigarette. She noticed that his fingers were stained yellow-brown from nicotine. "I smoke too," he said, removing a cigarette from the pack and lighting it. "Are you shocked?"

"No."

He smiled. "I drink too. I know I shouldn't. But I can

moderate myself. Moderation—that's the important thing. I
don't believe in this simon pure business." Like Anne-Marie?
thought Charlotte. "I also don't smoke in front of the guests,
usually. I like to set a good example."

Charlotte nodded.

He had a British accent and a voice that oozed solicitude. He
also had a way of wrinkling his nose when he smiled that she
supposed many women found boyishly appealing. But she was
immune to the blandishments of boyish charm, having once
been married to one of Hollywood's most charming leading
men.

For a few minutes, he reviewed her chart.

"I don't see any special health problems. Except for a little
arthritis in your knee. How are you feeling?"

"Okay."

"Are you on a salt-restricted diet?"

Charlotte shook her head.

"Any kidney stones, ulcers?"

She shook her head again.

"Then I'm going to prescribe the usual: two eight-ounce
glasses of High Rock water one hour before breakfast. Down
the hatch; no sipping. It's not wine, it's mineral water. Also,
one eight-ounce glass before lunch, one before dinner, and one
before bed. Do you have your prescription booklet?"

Charlotte withdrew it from her pocket and handed it to him.
"What will the water do for me?" she asked.

"It's a mild laxative; it contains sodium sulfate and magnesium bicarbonate. Not that you have any problems of that
nature. If you did, I'd prescribe Union water." He smiled. "It
produces what the local people call action-within-fifteen-
minutes."

So that's what Adele had been talking about. "I hope the
Union Spring isn't far from the hotel," said Charlotte.

He laughed. "No. It's not. Actually, fifteen minutes is
overstating it a bit; it usually takes about an hour."

Charlotte was reminded of the old saying about knowing a
man by his drink; it took on a special significance at a mineral
spa.

Dr. Sperry went on to explain that the waters of the spa fell
into three categories: the saline waters, such as Union water,

were highly cathartic. They were generally taken before meals and warmed. The saline-alkaline waters, such as High Rock, were mildly cathartic, and were prescribed as a tonic for the kidneys, bowels, and digestion. They were also taken before meals, but at room temperature. The third type, the alkaline-saline, of which Sans Souci was the best example, were digestive aids. They were generally taken after meals by people with digestive disturbances or liver disease.

"Then I presume I'm taking High Rock water as a tonic," said Charlotte as Dr. Sperry recorded the prescription in her booklet.

"Exactly," he replied. "But many guests also find that it helps their arthritis. To say nothing of diabetes, gout, rheumatism, neuritis."

"Oh? Why is that?"

"Frankly, we don't know. Mineral water is like acupuncture: we know it works, but we don't know how. A lot of studies have demonstrated that the waters help certain conditions, but identifying the chemical that's responsible is like finding a needle in a haystack. High Rock water, for instance, contains more than nineteen thousand different chemicals."

"I see," said Charlotte.

"The baths are different. There we know that most of the benefit comes from simple relaxation. As far as the baths go, we'll start you out with a daily bath and massage, what we call our 'ninety-minute unwinder,'" he said, making another notation in the booklet. He studied her chart again. "Frannie indicates here that your shoulders are tense. Is that true?"

"Yes." She accumulated tension in her shoulders the way others did in their faces or their guts, but she wouldn't have thought it obvious. She gave Frannie credit for her perspicacity and wondered if she was walking around with hunched shoulders. "I'm surprised Frannie noticed it."

"Are you?" He smiled, wrinkling his nose. "I'm also going to prescribe a hot pack for your knee and fango for your shoulders." He made another notation in the booklet. "Fango is mud therapy: mud has excellent heat-retention properties." He leaned back. "You shouldn't be. We can tell a lot about a client's physical and mental condition from her appearance."

"So I see," replied Charlotte.

"For instance," he continued, "I can tell that you're a happy, well-adjusted person." He wrinkled his nose again.

Charlotte raised a dark, winged eyebrow in the skeptical expression that was one of her screen trademarks, along with her clipped Yankee accent and her starkly tailored suits.

"You are open, vibrant, alive," he continued, staring at her appreciatively. "I can tell just by looking at you that you are beautiful in your soul as well as in your person."

She returned his stare. She wanted to tell him to cut the crap.

"Unfortunately, I can't say the same for a lot of our guests," he went on. "Many of them are very unhappy. They're often going through widowhood, or divorce. Their faces are masks of anxiety and depression; their skin has sagged; their lips are compressed. We can't do anything about their personal situations of course, but we can help them feel better about themselves."

If outward appearance were the key to character, Charlotte thought, Dr. Sperry's narrow, thin-lipped mouth and long, pointed teeth put him in the wolf family. The kind that prey on lonely, middle-aged women.

He paused to offer her another cigarette, which she turned down, and then lit one himself from the tip of the one he was smoking.

"Some of our guests are in very bad shape indeed. Like that woman who was just in here. Her biological age is about the same as yours, but she's actually twenty-four years younger. She doesn't need a spa, she needs a detox program. We get a lot of guests like her. We ask our guests to refrain from using drugs or alcohol, but we can hardly search their luggage, can we?"

His voice had taken on an intimate tone, as if they belonged to an elite of which Adele was not a member. Charlotte's mild dislike was progressing to outright hostility. What he said about Adele was no doubt true, but it was unprofessional to be talking with her about it.

"Dr. Sperry, I'm not interested in discussing the medical histories of the other guests," she said firmly.

She could imagine him telling the next patient: "Oh, yes, Charlotte Graham. Well preserved, I'd say, for a woman of sixty-two. Wouldn't expect it with the life she's led. Four husbands would take its toll on anyone. To say nothing of those notorious love affairs."

"Oh, quite right," he said, startled at her rebuke. "Well, do you have any questions?"

"What is the pack for my arthritis?" she asked, studying the booklet he had returned to her.

He described the hot pack, and then, their interview at an end, she rose to leave. He walked her to the door, his arm draped familiarly around her shoulders. She wanted to shake it off, like a surly adolescent.

As they reached the door, she felt him gently squeeze the muscle at the back of her neck. "We'll take care of those shoulders for you," he said.

After leaving Dr. Sperry's office, Charlotte crossed the quadrangle to the Bath Pavilion, which was a mirror-image of the Health Pavilion except for the relief on the pediment, which here depicted Asclepius, the Greek god of healing. An inscription read: "A gentle craftsman who drove pain away/ Soother of cruel pangs, a joy to men,/Bringing them golden health."

At the reception desk, she was directed to the women's wing, where she was greeted by the director of the women's baths, a middle-aged woman named Mrs. Murray who wore a white nurse's uniform and the firm expression of someone who was used to dealing with difficult guests. A starched white nurse's cap floated on the stiff waves of her charcoal-gray hair like a paper boat on a stormy sea. Mrs. Murray introduced her to Hilda, who would be her bath attendant. Hilda was a stocky woman with a round face encircled by the platinum curls of an ill-fitting wig. Her face had a hint of the Tartar about it, with prominent cheekbones and fierce yellow eyes above which eyebrows had been penciled on in a perennial expression of surprise. She bobbed her head and smiled broadly, revealing a wide gap between her protuberant front teeth. Then she shuffled off down the corridor in her corduroy slippers, leaving Charlotte to follow behind.

Charlotte found the bath cubicle to which she had been assigned to be surprisingly utilitarian by comparison with the

rest of the spa. It was large, with a high ceiling, glossy
white-tiled walls, and a black-and-white-tiled floor. It was
simply furnished with a white wicker table and chair and a
white-painted metal cot covered by a starched white sheet. The
walls above the tile, which looked as if they once had been
painted a depressing hospital green, were now papered with a
gay floral print. On the table stood a pot of red geraniums. One
corner was occupied by the treatment tub, which was both
wider and deeper than an ordinary tub. Charlotte noted with
pleasure a heated towel rack of the type that was the one
redeeming feature of British bathrooms.

She felt right at home. Except for the matter of bath
etiquette. Was she supposed to disrobe in front of Hilda? She
was about to ask when Hilda led her into an adjoining
bathroom and handed her a white terry-cloth robe and what
appeared to be a towel, but was actually a turban. Emerging a
few minutes later, she took a seat while Hilda drew the bath,
using fishtail faucets for the mineral water that bubbled up
from a well at the bottom of the tub and ordinary faucets for the
tap water that was used to adjust the temperature.

"It smells rusty," observed Charlotte.

"*Ja,*" replied Hilda. "The iron in the water. It's what clogs
the pipes." She spoke with an accent that Charlotte could
identify only as eastern European.

"How long does the bath last?" Charlotte asked.

"Fifteen minutes. Then I check you. If you want, you stay
in another ten minutes. If the water is too cold, I add more hot.
Then I wrap you in warm sheets and you rest—thirty minutes.
I turn the lights out. After the rest, you have a massage." She
looked back at Charlotte and smiled. "Okay?"

"Okay." It sounded wonderful. "Where are you from?"
she asked.

"Budapest." Hilda explained that she was a refugee of the
1956 revolution, one of many to whom Paulina had given
jobs. For twenty years, she had worked as a maid at the
Chicago salon. But when the spa opened, she had moved east.
She came from a long line of bath attendants. In Hungary,
she explained, spa jobs were passed along from mother to
daughter.

Raising herself onto one knee, she gestured for Charlotte to step into the tub. Above her hemline, Charlotte could see the bulge of flesh that overflowed the thickly rolled top of her cotton lisle stocking.

Charlotte removed her robe and gingerly dipped a foot in the water. Hilda supported her, gripping her tightly by her upper arm.

"Your arms are strong."

"*Ja,*" said Hilda. She flexed her biceps like a body builder. "Very strong. In Budapest, the spas are used for physical therapy—cripples, amputees. The attendants have to be strong to lift them in and out of the tub. Is too hot, the water?" She checked the bathometer that bobbed on the water's surface. It read ninety-four point five. She explained that the temperature of a mineral water bath is lower than that of an ordinary bath because the water feels hotter. "The bubbles are insulation," she said. "If you want, I can adjust."

"No, thank you," said Charlotte, gently lowering herself into the water. She liked her bath water hot. "It's fine."

The tub was recessed a foot or more below the level of the floor. Sinking into it, she found herself up to her chin in the warm, effervescent water.

Hilda had disappeared into the bathroom. She returned momentarily with a white plastic pillow, which she placed under Charlotte's head, and a linen hand towel, which she floated on the water under Charlotte's nose.

"What's the towel for?"

"The gas," replied Hilda. "The carbon dioxide; it can make you woozy." She revolved her head in a circle, her eyes rolled upward. Then she leaned over to dip her hand in the water. "The temperature, is okay?"

Charlotte nodded.

"Would you like a glass of mineral water? Is good to drink the mineral water in the bath—you don't get dehydrated."

Charlotte replied that she would, and Hilda shuffled off to fetch a glass of High Rock water from the fountain in the lobby.

The bath was incredibly soothing. The waters of High Rock spa were unique, she had read. Not only were they among the most highly mineralized in the world, they were also the most effervescent. The waters emerged from the earth supersatu-

rated with carbon dioxide gas. During a bath, the carbon
dioxide penetrated the skin, dilating the capillaries and reliev-
ing pressure on the heart. The result was supposed to be a deep
feeling of relaxation.

Hilda returned with the glass of water and handed it to
Charlotte. "I come back in fifteen minutes," she said, and left.

Charlotte leaned back, glass in hand. Her body was totally
sheathed in tiny iridescent bubbles; they made her skin tingle.
She felt like the swizzle stick in a giant champagne cocktail.
Every time she moved, clouds of bubbles floated to the
surface. The water was unexpectedly buoyant. Her hands and
feet floated as if they were made of rubber. Noticing a toe hole
at the end of the tub, she tucked her toes under it to keep them
from rising. Then she set down her glass and surrendered
herself to the waters. For a while, she thought about the spa,
then about her work, and finally about nothing at all. Sounds
too faded from her consciousness. At first, she heard the sound
of splashing in the next cubicle. Then the dull thud of a door
closing and the light tread of footsteps. After that, only the
gentle murmur of bubbles breaking on the water's surface and
the soft sough of her breath.

She dozed off, soothed by the massage of a million tiny
bubbles.

It was the sensation of cold that awakened her. Fifteen
minutes had surely elapsed, but Hilda hadn't returned. She
waited awhile, and then decided to get out of the tub. She was
drying herself when she heard a door slam. The slam was
followed by the sound of someone running down the hall. And
then more footsteps, a general commotion. From the next
cubicle came the anxious murmur of voices. She heard
someone in the hall ask: "What happened?" And then other
voices: "Is she all right?" and "Has someone called a doctor?"
She quickly threw on her robe and opened the door. A small
cluster of white-uniformed staff members and white-robed
guests stood solemnly outside the cubicle adjoining hers. At
the front was Hilda, her yellow Tartar eyes gleaming with the
thrill of calamity. A worried-looking Mrs. Murray stood with
her arms outstretched in front of the door like a school crossing
guard.

As they stood there, a young man in a white lab coat

appeared at the far end of the hall. Charlotte recognized him as Frannie's husband, Dana. Behind him came two other men in white lab coats. They were carrying an olive-green metal case of the type used for storing oxygen equipment. All three were walking rapidly, almost running. As they reached the end of the corridor, their pace slowed and the onlookers parted silently to let them through. Then they disappeared into the cubicle with Mrs. Murray.

Spotting Corinne's pale profile, Charlotte edged her way through the crowd to her side. "Do you know what's going on?" she asked.

"It's Adele," she replied. "They think she's drowned."

· 4 ·

CHARLOTTE FOUND OUT what the Terrain Cure was the next morning. It was a series of walks at increasing gradients. The idea was to start with the most gradual grade and move up to the steeper grades as your spa stay progressed. The Terrain Cure route began on the esplanade and headed down a wooded path to the Vale of Springs, a gorge that followed the fissure in the earth's crust through which the mineral waters escaped to the surface. At the base of the gorge, the route joined a winding stream and followed it for some distance before turning back up the hill toward the esplanade. It was on the ascent that the Terrain Cure routes varied. The most difficult route ascended via a steep ravine nicknamed Heartbreak Hill after the famous hill in the Boston Marathon. All three groups began with the easiest route, the difference being the pace at which they took it—the A's at a run, the B's at a jog, and the C's at a brisk walk. At regular intervals, participants paused to take their pulses at benches that were provided in scenic spots for this purpose. The aim was to reach, but not exceed, a target heart rate. When a certain fitness level was achieved, participants moved up to the next grade, an accomplishment that earned them a merit pin for the lapels of their sweat suits.

The idea of the Terrain Cure was explained by a muscular young man named Jerry D'Angelo, who then jogged his charges slowly around the esplanade in close-order drill formation (it was this that Charlotte had witnessed the day before) before sending them off down the hill. Charlotte had risen at six in order to drink two glasses of High Rock water at six-thirty, take Awake and Aware at seven, and eat breakfast at seven-thirty. By the time Terrain Cure rolled around at eight, she felt as if she'd already put in a day's work. As did Art, her comrade in white. They brought up the rear of the two-by-two formation. By now they were fast friends, having shared a table at dinner the night before, glum meal that it was. They had both been shaken by Adele's death. Dr. Sperry, who had arrived on the scene shortly after Charlotte, had unofficially attributed the cause of death to drowning subsequent to a drug overdose. He had tried unsuccessfully to revive her. As had the ambulance crew that arrived not long afterward. Her body had been taken away, and that was that. Where had the body been taken to? Would there be a funeral? Who would make the arrangements—the friend who had paid for her spa stay? Charlotte knew next to nothing about Adele—not even where she was from. Her death was strange in that respect; it was as if she had just been spirited away in the night.

With Adele gone, the only other C left (she didn't count Corinne, who hadn't shown up yet anyway) was Nicky, who'd already fallen so far behind the group that he might as well be considered a dropout. As the group headed down the path toward the Vale of Springs, they had left Nicky circling the esplanade for the first time. "At least," said Art, "we're not D.F.L." It was, he explained, with apologies for the language, a sailing term for dead fucking last. Charlotte smiled; without Nicky, they would have been D.F.L. for sure. They were walking briskly along a broad flagstone-paved path bordering Geyser Stream, a winding, boulder-strewn ribbon of green that gurgled under bridges and through pine glades to its terminus at Geyser Lake. Ahead was the spring from which the stream took its name: the Island Spouter, a geyser that spouted twenty feet into the air from the center of an island formed of the same mineral as the rock at High Rock Spring. Drawing near a bench overlooking the geyser, they stopped to take their pulses. Or rather, Charlotte stopped to take her pulse, Art sat with his head hanging between his knees, gasping.

Charlotte hadn't realized he was in such bad shape. His appearance was alarming. "Are you all right?" she asked.

He removed his baseball cap, revealing a bald spot like a monk's tonsure. "I will be in a minute. Jesus," he said, his voice tense with frustration. "I can't even take a damned walk." After a minute, he went on: "Every time a pain hits my chest, I think it's the big one. But do you think I've done a damned thing about it? Nope. I've just been sitting around on my fat ass."

"You're here," said Charlotte. "That's doing something about it." Charlotte herself was, as Anne-Marie had put it, communicating with her body. If communication with her body had been only intermittent before, it was now all too continual. Her legs ached and her lungs felt as if they were on fire.

Art looked up. "Did that crippled masseuse give you the 'your body is a temple, but you treat it like a hotel room' bit?"

Charlotte nodded.

"Well, I've been thinking about it. I've decided she's right. I've been treating my body like a hotel room, or rather a motel room: the kind that rents for fifteen bucks a night, the kind that's out on a highway in the Southwest somewhere, with holes punched in the doors and cracks in the mirror."

Charlotte laughed. "I know the kind you mean. A blinking neon sign out front and motorcycles riding by all night long."

Art looked up at her with his navy blue eyes. "You've got it. Scheduled for demolition. New highway project coming through."

"Maybe it's time to move up to better quarters. Why don't you try the Ritz? You deserve it."

He shook his head. "The Ritz. Why not the Ritz?"

For a few minutes they sat in silence, catching their breaths. Every three minutes the geyser erupted, shooting a white plume of mineral water into the deep blue sky.

After a while, Art spoke: "The preliminary coroner's report is in on Adele. It's official—drowning as the result of an accidental overdose. Barbiturates—apparently the concentration in her blood was sky-high."

Charlotte nodded. She wasn't surprised. She remembered how Adele had looked when she left Dr. Sperry's office.

"Apparently she was carrying a drugstore around with her."

"Her security box."

"What?"

"She carried around this plastic box filled with pills. She

called it her security box." She looked over at him. "How did you find out?"

"Jerry told me before class. He used to be a homicide detective—in New York. I guess he has connections with the local police. He talked with the coroner's office last night." He shook his head. "Poor gal."

"It seems so unfair," said Charlotte. "She was just getting her life pulled together." She felt a tug at the back of her throat. "She told me that she'd licked the booze and was about to start working on the pills."

"She was moving up to better accommodations," said Art. He looked up and smiled, blinking away the tears that had risen in his deep blue eyes. "I hardly knew her," he added, as if mystified at his reaction.

"Want a hanky?" She offered him a tissue from her pocket.

"Thanks."

They were both blowing their noses when a small pack of A's reached the foot of the path. It was their second time around. The Role Model was in the lead. He ran with the springy stride of the trained athlete.

Ignoring Art and Charlotte, the group ran past, depositing Jerry in its wake. "We were wondering what happened to you two," he said. He was jogging in place. "Come on," he gestured. "Up and at 'em."

He had a wide grin, which the dimples in his round cheeks and the slight gap between his front teeth couldn't help but make appealing.

Art groaned. "Okay, coach," he said, rising reluctantly to his feet.

Charlotte and Art completed the rest of the course at a gentle pace. By the time they got back up to the esplanade, it was already a quarter past nine. Charlotte headed directly back to her room, where she showered and changed for her ten o'clock appointment with Paulina. At five of, she was riding the glass elevator up to the penthouse that doubled as Paulina's office when she was in residence at the spa. Back when she was starting out, Paulina had always lived "over the shop." She prided herself on the fact that she still did, at least part of the time. Her apartments in London, Paris, and Rome were all located above Langenberg salons, in buildings that she owned.

Upon leaving the elevator, Charlotte was accosted by a taciturn guard who allowed her to pass into the foyer, where she was greeted by Paulina's secretary, a young man named Jack whom Charlotte had met before. Jack was the latest in a long line of handsome young protégés. He had been with Paulina for four years, an achievement that was extraordinary in light of the fact that the usual term of service was only a few months. In fact, he had more than once been banished to publicity—the gulag for out-of-favor Langenberg employees—but he always managed to work himself back into Paulina's good graces. Tall and elegant, he wore beautiful clothes that were always a bit threadbare—Paulina was not known for her generous salaries.

The apartment was small. In fact, it was the smallest of Paulina's residences, but it was also one of her favorites on account of the magnificent view of the Adirondacks, which today glowed like amethysts against the deep blue sky. The decoration was opulent: rose-colored silk wallpaper, an exuberantly patterned carpet in a water lily design, leopard print upholstery. The wall space that wasn't taken up by windows was hung with art. At first glance, Charlotte recognized works of Picasso, Matisse, and Braque, as well as a stunning Bonnard pastoral and a Renoir portrait. There was also sculpture—a streamlined Brancusi bird, an abstract Lipchitz figure, and, in a bronze and glass room divider, a collection of African masks.

"Come in, come in," said Paulina. She sat next to Anne-Marie on a Victorian couch upholstered in chartreuse velvet. She sat like a peasant on a milking stool, with her legs apart and her feet planted squarely on the floor. In her hand was a paring knife with which she was stabbing a slice of sausage. She was a tiny woman, less than five feet tall, but she had enormous presence. Her grand features—the strong jaw; the broad, high cheekbones; the small, slightly slanted eyes; the noble nose with its flaring nostrils—were set off by glossy blue-black hair that was pulled tightly back from her commanding forehead into a chignon at the nape of her neck. The result was stern, severe, majestic. She wore a loose caftan patterned in reds, oranges, and greens in which she looked like a gypsy fortune teller.

"Good morning. I see you've met my confidential secretary."

"We've met before," said Charlotte. She smiled at Jack.

Like all Paulina's male employees, he was handsome, with eyes so blue and eyelashes so curly that they might have been a china doll's. Although he must have been in his mid-thirties, he had a boyish face that was marred only by the faint scars of a once-bad complexion and a tendency toward puffiness. But it was his manner that was the key to his success with Paulina. He was pleasant, polite, and efficient, but more importantly, he could be at the same time both independent and ingratiating, dashing and deferential. He wouldn't let Paulina bully him, but nor was he insensitive to her demands. He was the perfect companion-escort-secretary for a forceful and difficult old lady.

Jack escorted Charlotte to one of the chairs facing Paulina, a rococo Louis XV upholstered in a leopard print. As always, Charlotte found herself conscious of Paulina's odor: a not-unpleasant old lady smell overlaid by the spicy fragrance of one of her own perfumes. In this case, the concert of smells also included the garlicky low note sounded by the sausage.

"Eat, eat," she bellowed. Like many elderly people who are slightly hard of hearing, she spoke too loudly. She offered the tip of the knife to Charlotte with a small neat hand embellished with a cabochon ruby that together with its showy gold setting was the size of a golf ball.

"Thank you."

"Crackers?" she asked, offering Charlotte a box of soda crackers from the coffee table, one of several that were scattered around the room.

Charlotte accepted gratefully. She was hungry after her meager breakfast and the Terrain Cure workout.

"Anne-Marie?" said Paulina, offering her the sausage.

"No thank you."

"I know, calories." With a forefinger, she pressed the tail of a cloisonné turtle on the coffee table, producing a loud ring.

Jack, who had disappeared into the adjoining office, reappeared.

"Jack, get Anne-Marie some crudités. Carrots, celery—you know."

Jack accepted Paulina's bullying with grace. She was like a willful spoiled child, but you couldn't help being seduced by her youthful vitality. It was this quality of gameness that Charlotte admired in Paulina. At eighty, she was still curious, still looking for new challenges.

Anne-Marie turned down the offer, explaining that she had to leave.

"Get them anyway," commanded Paulina. "Sonny's coming. Then I want you to take Miss . . ."—she hitched a thumb at Charlotte—"around." She addressed Charlotte: "Will you excuse us while we talk shop for a few minutes?" Without waiting for a reply, she turned to Jack. "Show her the art."

While Charlotte awaited Jack's return, Paulina and Anne-Marie talked about the new Body Spa line, designed to appeal to a younger, more active woman than the other Langenberg lines. It appeared that Anne-Marie was responsible, if not for the original idea, then for its development and marketing.

Jack reappeared shortly with the crudités. He then proceeded to give Charlotte a brief tour of Paulina's collection, about which he was gracious and knowledgeable. Charlotte had often visited Paulina's New York apartment, where most of her collection was displayed. In fact, it was through Charlotte's fourth husband, who was also an art collector, that she had become friendly with Paulina, although they had known each other for years. Charlotte's husband collected on a modest scale, but Paulina was one of the great collectors of her generation—patron would be a better description, for she had been buying from artists like Braque and Léger before anyone had ever heard of Cubism. Likewise, she had been among the first to collect African art. Both turned out to be, like everything she put her hand on, good investments.

The tour ended back in the living room.

"How did you like it?" asked Paulina.

"Very impressive. I would have thought all your masterpieces were in New York, but it looks as if you have a few here as well."

Paulina grinned. "Some of them aren't so great, but I keep them because they remind me of the good old days, the days when you could still buy good art for cheap. Tell me, which one did you like the best?"

"The Matisse in Jack's room," replied Charlotte, referring to a stunning odalisque. It was a testimony to the scope of Paulina's collection that a masterpiece worthy of a great museum was hanging in her secretary's bedroom.

"It's his favorite too. I bought it from Matisse in Nice. You wouldn't believe what I paid for it. What do you think of that one?" She pointed to a large abstract hanging next to a Picasso drawing.

It was a pleasant enough painting, but it appeared to be the work of a talented amateur. "Very nice. Who's the artist?"

Paulina looked smug. "A discovery of mine. In fact, you might call him my creation." Her eyes twinkled. "You'll meet him later. I knew you'd appreciate it. Most people can't tell a good painting from a bad."

Charlotte took the compliment with a grain of salt.

"We were talking about the poor woman who died. Did you meet her?"

"Only briefly."

"Anne-Marie was just telling me that she was a drug addict. Drug overdose—it's better. We can't be blamed. After all, we can't be babysitting our clients every last minute of the day."

Anne-Marie had risen to leave.

"Before you go, I want to ask you something," said Paulina. "Tell me"—she took Anne-Marie's hand in hers—"are you interested in the Seltzer Boy?"

It was one of Paulina's many idiosyncrasies that she couldn't remember names. It wasn't just her age; it had always been true. But she had nicknames for everyone. Charlotte guessed that the Seltzer Boy was the president of High Rock Waters, with whom Anne-Marie's name had been linked in the gossip columns.

"The Seltzer Boy." Anne-Marie smiled. "I like that. I'll have to tell him. He'll like it too. Yes, I am interested."

"Aha," said Paulina. She pounded her chest with her fist, rattling the gold beads that cascaded down her bosom. "I knew it. I know what's going on." She raised a red-lacquered fingernail to her cheekbone. "Nothing escapes these old eyes." She smiled benevolently. "I'm very happy for you, my dear."

"Thank you. I don't know if anything will come of it—" She kissed Paulina good-bye on the cheek.

"It will, don't worry. Paulina knows. I'll see you tomorrow," she said as Anne-Marie headed toward the door.

Once Anne-Marie had left, she turned her attention back to Charlotte: "Tomorrow is our five-year anniversary," she explained. "We're having a lawn fete. A publicity stunt—you know. We're going to launch our new line—the Body Spa line. Would you like to be our guest?"

"I'd be delighted."

"Good. I'll have Jack send you an official invitation." She returned to the subject of Anne-Marie: "She deserves a good man." She held a cracker between her thumb and forefinger, her little finger cocked. "After that creep she used to be married to."

Charlotte thought it an apt description of Dr. Sperry.

"My Mistake, I call him. I should fire him. I should have fired him a long time ago. I've only kept him on as a favor to her." A look of love crept into her sharp old eyes. "She's like a daughter to me. My daughter—I should be so lucky. Then I wouldn't have any problems. Such problems!" She waved the cracker in the air, bracelets jangling. "All my life, I've worked to build the business." She popped the cracker into her mouth. "And now my health is giving out." She pulled up her hem to display a knee swollen to the size of a cantelope. "My heart, my circulation . . . I'm not going to live forever."

"I wouldn't take any bets on it," said Charlotte.

Paulina looked over at her with a twinkle in her eye. "I don't do badly for an old bag, do I?" Leaning over, she picked up a black leather notebook from the coffee table. Pasted to the cover was a typed label reading: "The Last Will and Testament of Paulina L. Langenberg." "But what am I going to do? Leave it all to my Sonny?" She tossed the notebook back on the table. "He'd ruin me in five minutes. *Après moi, le déluge.*" She pressed the turtle buzzer again. "Bring us some mineral water," she yelled. "And don't forget my vitamins."

Her attention had switched to her guest's appearance. "You look very chic," she said admiringly. "You always wear neutral colors—very chic." Sticking her neck out like a chicken, she peered into Charlotte's face. "What do you use on your skin?" she asked.

"Paulina Langenberg," Charlotte replied. "Crème Hungaria."

Paulina grinned like a Cheshire cat. "I knew it. I can tell. Such good skin. See, it works. After all these years, it's still my biggest seller. People wouldn't keep using it if it didn't work." Sticking her neck out again, she scrutinized Charlotte's face suspiciously. "And for lipstick?"

Charlotte confessed to using a product manufactured by That Woman.

"How *can* you?" Paulina moaned. Leaning over, she reached into a drawer and pulled out a lipstick in a distinctive mint green tube. "From our new line. You'll like it." She removed the cap and twisted the end to display the color. "It's a good color for you." She thrust it into Charlotte's hand.

"Thank you," said Charlotte, depositing it in her pocketbook. Every time she visited Paulina she went home with a new lipstick.

"The Body Spa line has over a hundred new products." She pulled a mint green jar out of the drawer. "Every one contains mineral water." She pointed to the silver label, which read: "Contains mineral water from the famous High Rock Spa." "Mineral water is very high in magnesium. That's why Hungarians have such beautiful skin—the waters of Budapest are very high in magnesium. Look!" She ran her fingers down an olive cheek that was remarkably free of wrinkles.

"Amazing," said Charlotte, who was accustomed to being called upon to admire Paulina's complexion. "I've never known a woman of your age with such a youthful complexion. But I didn't know it was the mineral waters of Budapest that were responsible," she teased. "I thought it was Crème Hungaria."

"That too," said Paulina, smiling. "I'm a good advertisement, no?"

The doorbell rang, and Jack went to answer it.

The man who entered was conservatively dressed in a navy blue pin-striped suit and was carrying a leather attaché case. He wore horn-rimmed eyeglasses in a fashionable shade of blond tortoise shell. "Good morning, Aunt Paulina," he said. Coming over to the couch, he kissed Paulina on the cheek.

"Leon!" said Paulina, returning his kiss.

Charlotte noticed a family resemblance. He had Paulina's olive complexion, prominent nose, and high forehead. But his face lacked the drama of Paulina's, an impression that may have been fostered by a weak jaw, beneath which was blooming the beginning of a double chin.

Jack emerged from the kitchen with the mineral water and vitamins.

"Put it there," said Paulina, gesturing toward the coffee table. Jack set the tray down and retreated into the office.

"Leon, I want you to meet someone very important . . . A movie star—one of the greatest. My nephew, Leon Wolfe."

"Charlotte Graham," proffered Charlotte, coming to Paulina's rescue.

They exchanged greetings. Charlotte put his age at about fifty; his curly black hair had long ago receded from his prominent temples and he had a definite paunch. She noticed as he sat down that he wore bright purple socks—the only flamboyant note in his otherwise conservative attire.

"Do you want something to eat, Leon?" Paulina asked, her hand reaching out for the turtle buzzer.

Leon placed his hand over hers. "If I do, I'll get it myself. You're going to run Jack ragged. Besides, that thing drives me crazy."

"Okay, okay," said Paulina.

"Are you involved in the Langenberg business?" asked Charlotte.

"Yes," he replied.

"Leon takes care of the money," interjected Paulina. She downed her vitamins with a swig of mineral water. "I'd be lost without him."

"That's what she says, but she won't make me an officer of the company," said Leon. He spoke in teasing tones, but his words were barbed.

"I give him a job, I give him stock—now he wants to be an officer of the company. He wants everything yesterday," Paulina complained. She turned to him. "You have to learn patience. You'll get what you want—in time. You are my rock; I can rely on you. You're not like that airhead of a son of mine." She nodded at a photograph of a bearded man at the helm of a sailboat. "How many times have we bailed him out,

Leon?" Shielding her eyes against the answer, she asked, "Where is it going to end?" She addressed Charlotte: "You wouldn't believe what we're paying his ex-wives. And not one of them loved him." Her expression turned sympathetic. "Poor Sonny—all they were after was his money. *My* money," she added, pointing at her bosom. "His low-life friends are even worse. When they're not sponging off him, they're getting him into trouble. Like that drug business last year." She stabbed another slice of sausage. "How much did that end up costing us, Leon?"

"About fifty thousand as I recall."

"Fifty thousand. Do you believe it? Fifty thousand to get him off. The year before that, it was the drunk driving charge." She proceeded to recite a litany of scandals, business failures, and "cockeyed schemes" that her son had been involved in. "Now I give him a nice job—a much better job than managing the San Francisco salon—and he turns my spa into a hippie commune." She turned to Leon. "How much are we paying that hippie in the kitchen?"

He opened the attaché case and removed a notebook, which he passed over to Paulina. Charlotte noticed that his nails were neatly lacquered with clear nail polish. He also smelled strongly of Langenberg for Men, Paulina's successful line of men's cologne.

Paulina donned a pair of heavy black eyeglasses. "Just as I thought," she said. "My wastrel son is ruining me. I hire the finest cuisine minceur chef on the continent. Now he wants to go back to Lyons. Why? Because my son is paying some California hippie almost as much to make tacos."

Her diatribe was interrupted by a knock. *"Entrez,"* she said imperially.

The man in the photograph entered. By contrast with Leon, who had the fleshy appearance of the man who spends most of his time behind a desk, he was lean and fit. He was slight, with a pleasant, slightly sunburned face and a red beard going to gray. He was dressed in jeans and a cotton madras shirt.

The small group stared at him.

"I see you've been talking about me," he said.

Paulina smiled sweetly. "We were just talking about what a good job you're doing, my darling." Her voice was like honey.

"Yeah, Ma," he replied. He sat down in one of the leopard print chairs.

"This is Miss . . . My son, Elliot Langenberg."

"Charlotte Graham," said Charlotte. "Nice to meet you."

Elliot nodded.

"My son is artistic," Paulina announced. She pointed to the painting about which she had just asked Charlotte's opinion. "That's one of his." She beamed with maternal pride. "Miss . . . thought it was very good."

"Thank you," said Elliot politely, giving her a look as if to say, "We both know this is a farce." Which was no surprise, considering that all of Paulina's guests were probably coerced into praising his work.

"Sonny," said Paulina, "come here." She patted the place beside her. "Look at this," she said, pointing to a notation. "I'm paying some California hippie seven hundred a week to make tacos—only three hundred less than I pay one of France's finest chefs. This is how you're running my spa—by letting some hippie steal me blind? If it weren't for Leon, I'd be ruined."

Elliot, who had stood up to look at the notebook, shot Leon a look of overt hatred over his shoulder.

Charlotte was puzzled at his manner. He seemed at once both defiant and fearful, like a newly freed prisoner who is kept from standing up to his jailer out of sheer force of habit. He also seemed profoundly bored. He had clearly been over this ground before.

"Ma, haven't you heard of California cuisine?"

"No, I haven't heard of California cuisine," she replied sardonically.

"Well, that's what he's cooking—a low-calorie version. People are tired of the same old continental stuff. Veal marsala, shrimp scampi, beef bourguignonne. They want something different."

"Are you telling me I don't know my customers? After sixty years in the business? I'll tell *you* something—my customers don't want health food. At least the ones with money don't. And we don't want the ones without."

Elliot looked pained. "Ma, you're eighty years old. You're not in touch with what's happening anymore. You'll never attract a younger clientele if you keep offering the same old boring food." He paused. "Pretty small potatoes. Haven't you got something better to bitch about today?"

Paulina, thrown momentarily off balance, had no reply.

Elliot turned. "Then I'm going," he said, taking a handful of carrot sticks. He headed toward the door.

"Eighty is right," Paulina bellowed after him. "And I've never eaten a sprout in my life." She pronounced is *shprout*. The door slammed.

"Sprouts," she snorted. "I'll tell you how to live long. Hard work—that's how. Work you love." She turned to Leon. "Out," she commanded. "I want to talk to . . ."—she hitched a thumb at Charlotte—"in private."

Leon docilely packed up his attaché case and left.

After he had gone, Paulina continued: "I suppose I could leave the business to Leon." She addressed Jack, who had shown Leon to the door: "I've thought of it, haven't I, Jack?"

"Many times," he replied.

"When I'm mad at Sonny, I always threaten to change my will. But I never do. What else can I do? Sonny's my flesh and blood." A sentimental smile stole across her stony mouth. "Besides, Leon's smart, but he's boring. For the beauty business, you need imagination. Good with money he isn't, my Sonny. But at least he's got some imagination."

"I don't think you have to worry," said Charlotte. "It looks to me as if you've still got a lot of time to go, eighty or not."

Paulina smiled. "Look." She gripped the ridge of an ear, shaking the ornate gold hoop that hung from an earlobe stretched like a Buddha's from decades of wearing heavy earrings. "I have big ears, like an elephant. That means I'll live forever." She paused to think, and then continued: "If Sonny had children, it would be different—someone to carry on. Feh!" She shook her head. "Married two times, and no children. Or even if Leon had children. But he's forty-eight and he's still a bachelor." She continued on a cheerier note: "But maybe I shouldn't give up hope. I hear Sonny has a new girlfriend. What's her name, the health nut with the freckles?"

"Claire Kelly," replied Jack.

"The one who teaches the exercise classes?" asked Charlotte.

"Yes," replied Paulina. "Do you like her?"

"She's a very good teacher."

"Feh! Thick ankles. No chic. But she'll probably be cheaper than the last one—the fashion model. That one cost an arm and a leg. This one with the freckles, she's young. Maybe she'll have a baby." She waved an arm. "But forget that—let's get down to business."

"I was beginning to wonder when we'd get around to that."

Paulina smiled. "I think you can help me." Reaching over, she gently stroked Charlotte's arm. "Jack, get the clipping."

Jack fetched a newspaper clipping from a massive Louis XVI desk at the front of the room and handed it to Charlotte. It was from *The New York Times* and was dated Friday, June 8. The headline was, "High Rock Water Held Unsafe." It read:

HIGH ROCK SPRINGS, N.Y.—The New York State Department of Health has reported that the waters of four springs at the Paulina Langenberg Spa at High Rock Springs contain levels of radium that exceed federal safety limits.

In a report issued yesterday, the department of health warned consumers to limit consumption of water from the contaminated springs to one glass per week or less. Radium is known to cause cancer and other illnesses. The report recommended that signs be posted at the contaminated springs.

The report said the waters from the four springs contain up to 400 picocuries of radium per liter—about four times the recommended level. The springs are the Lincoln No. 3, the Lincoln No. 5, and the Lincoln No. 6, and the Old Red. The Lincoln waters are used for baths at the High Rock Spa.

The level of radium in water that is bottled and sold by High Rock Waters, Inc., however, was found to be below levels set by the United States Public Health Service for ordinary drinking water.

Gary A. Brant, chairman and chief executive officer of High Rock Waters, Inc., said the water is routinely tested and found "safe" for consumption. High Rock water is the country's leading mineral water. Sales of High Rock water are expected to reach about $250 million this year, Mr. Brant said.

The report drew no conclusions concerning the effect on people who bathe in the radium-contaminated waters, but workers at the spa, which is leased from the state by Paulina Langenberg, Inc., a beauty products company, expressed concern that the report may frighten away spa customers.

The report may also have a negative effect on sales of a new line of Paulina Langenberg cosmetics, in which water from the Old Red Spring is a major ingredient. The new line, Body Spa, is scheduled to go on sale next week at cosmetics counters in department stores around the country.

Charlotte read no further. "Is this true?" she asked.

"It's baloney," replied Paulina.

"Then how did it get in the newspaper?"

"That's what I want you to find out. It's true, but it doesn't mean anything. Yes, the waters have a little radium, but they've always had a little radium. This is nothing new. There's a report issued every six months that says the same thing. The signs have been up for five years."

"Then what difference does it make?"

"It makes a difference because it's affecting business. It doesn't matter that it's baloney—people worry about it anyway. It's affected business already. Our stock dropped seven points after this article came out. I'm not worried about the stock—it will recover; it already is . . ."

"I would hope so," interjected Charlotte. "I'm a stockholder." In fact, she was a very satisfied stockholder. Her Langenberg stock, which she had bought at Paulina's urging years ago, had steadily appreciated—with the exception of a recession here and there—and had paid substantial dividends.

"You're a stockholder!" Paulina gazed at her as if she were a long-lost cousin. "A stockholder, and you don't use our products. Tsk tsk." She went on: "I'm not worried about the stock. But I am worried about who did this. Maybe they'll do something else. Someone is trying to sabotage my business."

"Or High Rock Waters's business."

"Or High Rock Waters's business. Actually it's worse for him. People worry more about what they drink. I want you to find out who."

"Do you have any ideas?"

Paulina shrugged. "I don't know. But you have connections. You can find out who planted this article, can't you?"

"I'll do my best," said Charlotte.

· 5 ·

CHARLOTTE HAD MANAGED to miss her morning exercises the day before because of her meeting with Paulina, but today there was no getting out of them. As if Awake and Aware and Terrain Cure weren't enough, she had dutifully suffered through Backs and Bellies and Absolutely Abdominals. But at Swing and Sway she had drawn the line. She had had enough. Besides, she had to be back at her room by noon to await a return call from Tom Plummer. Tom was the reporter who had written the book about the murder at the Morosco case. They had been good friends ever since. If anyone could find out who had planted the radium story, it was he. She had called him shortly after speaking with Paulina. She had been skeptical of Paulina's implication that a story could be planted in a reputable newspaper like the *Times*. But Tom had disabused her of this naive notion: the techniques were just more sophisticated. It wasn't merely a matter of sending out a press release or standing a reporter to lunch. It was cultivating connections, applying pressure in the right places.

Back at her room, Charlotte collapsed onto her bed. In a short while, she would have to start getting ready for the fete. It was a perfect day for it: cool and clear, with a light breeze that ruffled the waters of Geyser Lake. Standing up, she walked over to the balcony. Directly below was the red-and-white-striped canopy of the tent that had been set up the day before. From here, it looked like a giant trampoline; she had an odd impulse to jump. Waiters and busboys scurried in and out of the hotel, making last-minute preparations. Turning back to her room, she removed a bottle of High Rock water

from the hospitality bar (not for the spa hotel the usual stock of
liquor and soft drinks) and turned on the television. The big
story on the local news was the radium controversy. The mayor
was blustering about "the nut" who had leaked the radium
story to the press. "Whoever did this is an enemy of our city,"
he said. A voice over some old footage of the downtown
explained that before Paulina Lagenberg took over the spa,
High Rock Springs had been just another decaying upstate
community. If the radium rumor were to have an adverse effect
on spa business, it could mean a major economic setback for
the community. Charlotte was reminded of the lines from
Byron: "While stands the Coliseum, Rome shall stand; When
falls the Coliseum, Rome shall fall."

Next came an interview with a man named Regie Cobb who
had been the spa's chief of maintenance before retiring to a
part-time job as driver of the jitney bus that ferried guests to
and from town. Cobb was interviewed at the Lincoln No. 3
spring, which spouted from a fountain under a bus-stop-like
kiosk. A dapper old fellow, he wore a straw boater and a
striped shirt with a sleeve garter. The newscaster explained that
Cobb had been stopping at the Lincoln No. 3 on his way to
work every day for the last thirty-two years. The camera
zoomed in on a sign that read: "This is a highly mineralized
water that contains radium. Its continuing or excessive use may
be harmful to your health." From there, it panned to Regie
taking a deep draught. "I've been drinkin' this water every day
for the last thirty-two years, and I've never been sick a day in
my life," he said. His grandmother, he added, had also drunk
the waters and had lived to be ninety-six. "Of course," he went
on, "if she hadn't drunk the waters, she mighta lived to be a
hundred and ten." With that, he bared his teeth in a broad smile
as if he'd been standing in front of the cameras all his life.
Charlotte wondered how many camera-shy locals the crew had
interviewed before coming up with that snippet of footage.

But the main radium story wasn't Regie Cobb. It was a
mysterious "fleet-footed Mineral Man" who had been popping
up around the city passing out literature extolling the virtues of
the waters. The screen showed a man in a commedia dell'arte
costume doing a pantomime in front of city hall.

The phone rang, and Charlotte switched off the news. It was

Tom; he had talked with the reporter who wrote the story. The reporter had been assigned the story by his editor, who had gotten a tip from a friend. The friend just happened to work for one of the big public relations firms.

Charlotte asked if the firm had been representing the state.

Tom didn't know, but he would try to find out and get back to her.

Charlotte hung up and began getting ready for the fete. Tom's information wasn't much help. The important thing was to find out who the client was. If the client was the state, it would dash Paulina's sabotage theory. But if the client were someone else, Paulina could just be right.

From below, she could hear the murmur of conversation. The early arrivals had begun to cluster at the bar that had been set up on the terrace. A pianist at a white baby grand played Cole Porter. A few minutes later, she was ready. She wore a tailored white linen dress with a white shawl collar. Her glossy black hair—once worn in a famous pageboy—was now pulled back into a chignon. Like Paulina, she chose a chignon for the sake of convenience and like Paulina, her hair was colored, but not as blue-black as Paulina's. But where Paulina's hair style was dramatic and sculptural, Charlotte's was looser and more natural. With her soft, delicate features and her pale skin, the effect was both gracious and elegant.

She took the glass elevator down to the lobby. In the distance, the mountains stood out crisp and clear against the deep blue sky. Emerging at the rear of the hotel, she headed directly for the bar. It was odd how being denied alcohol made her want it all the more. At home, she often went a week or more without a drink; now she was craving one after only three days. Manhattan in hand (she hoped she wouldn't bump into Anne-Marie), she stood back to survey the scene. At least a hundred people had already arrived, all looking very stylish: the men in navy blue blazers and white trousers, the women in flowery dresses and wide-brimmed hats. The press, which was present in full force, wore red carnations and name tags. In the center of the terrace stood a department store cosmetics counter, looking as out of place as a yacht stranded on a Kansas prairie. On it was displayed "the product": bottles, boxes, and countertop display stands of the Body Spa line, all richly packaged in mint-green and silver. The counter was flanked by store easels displaying poster-sized replicas of the national ad: a close-up of the flawless face of Corinne, the Body Spa girl. Nearby, Paulina was posing with the lean and leggy Corinne herself, next to whom she looked like a potato dumpling. Paulina made an unlikely Queen of Beauty, but it was part of her genius that she put her dumpiness to work for her. "If she can make herself look glamorous, then I can too," went the rationale of the millions of dumplingesque, middle-aged ladies who were the backbone of her business.

It seemed to Charlotte that the concept behind Body Spa line was equally inspired. If she hadn't already owned Langenberg stock, she would have bought some, despite the radium rumor. The Body Spa line was aimed at a different market, one whose appetite for beauty products had yet to be fully exploited. While the regular line appealed to the wealthy, idle, older woman, the market for the Body Spa line was a fresh, active, younger woman. For the Body Spa woman, beauty was less an embellishment than a part of fitness and health. To promote the idea of its being modern and scientific, the product was being sold by beauty "consultants" whose mint-green lab coats gave them an aura of scientific authority. Another gimmick was the "computers" (basically just question and answer boards) that the consultants used to assess skin type.

A group of expertly made-up consultants was circulating among the crowd, inviting guests to try the computer. Charlotte was about to take one of them up on it when she caught sight of Paulina charging in her direction, her red straw bowler bouncing up and down like the bobber on a fishing line. Jack followed like a lady in waiting to the queen. She was wearing an embroidered chemise-style tea gown with a matching shawl in Langenberg red, in which she looked like the Red Queen on a rampage. In her wake marched a retinue of red-carnationed press people. Emerging from the throng, Paulina stopped dead, raised an arm, and pointed at Charlotte. "There she is," she said. Charlotte had the feeling she was about to add, "Off with her head."

The press had espied their quarry. They were massed behind Paulina like the Red Queen's retainers, only instead of clubs they carried cameras and notebooks. Why, they're only a pack of cards, thought Charlotte, I needn't be afraid of them. As she reached Charlotte, Paulina grabbed her drink and set it on a nearby table. Then she pulled a jar of Body Spa cream out of a bag Jack was carrying and stuck it into Charlotte's hand. "Okay, shoot," she ordered, striking a smiling pose. As the shutters clicked, Charlotte felt her face redden in anger. Dispensing free ink was a profitable sideline for many celebrities. Designer gowns, hotel suites, fine antiques—all were available on the cheap to those who were willing to have a picture taken here, drop a name there. But Paulina wasn't playing by the rules. She hadn't reduced Charlotte's rate. All she had offered was a free lunch, which Charlotte would have turned down had she known what she would be asked to do in return. She was ordinarily indulgent of her fans—she would gladly sign autographs by the hour—but she resented having her face used to promote products.

The shutters stopped clicking and Paulina retrieved the jar from Charlotte's hand. "For *Society* magazine," she offered by way of explanation. "Very important—over a million circulation. Good publicity—for you and for me." But before Charlotte could object, she had marched back into the crowd in search of some other celebrity to have her picture taken with.

Charlotte gazed after her, still seething with resentment.

"Taking advantage, was she?"

The voice was Jerry D'Angelo's. She realized she must have had a sour expression on her face. Sour enough to spoil the picture, she hoped. "Oh, well," she said. "It was my own fault. I should have known Paulina had an ulterior motive in inviting me."

"The boss lady never misses a chance to rustle up some free publicity. Can I get you a drink?"

"If you won't snitch on me to Anne-Marie." The glass that Paulina had taken from her had disappeared.

He smiled. "What will you have?"

"A manhattan—on the rocks, thanks."

She watched as he made his way through the crowd at the bar. His broad back was squeezed into an ill-fitting suit that puckered at the seams. He looked more at home in a T-shirt and sweatpants.

He returned a moment later carrying her drink, which he

handed to her, and a beer for himself. "Shall we sit down?" He nodded toward the tables, which were shaded by green and white umbrellas suggesting High Rock water and lime as "the perfect thirst quencher."

"I've been meaning to talk with you," he said as they took their seats on the red bentwood chairs. "I think we have a friend in common."

"Who's that?"

"Tim Connelly."

Charlotte smiled. It was a different smile from the one she wore in public. Her private face had never been frozen, as had those of so many of her colleagues, into an expression that was too dazzling, too intentional. For friends, her smile was still as warm as a fire on a chilly night.

"Really!" she said delightedly. "How is he?" Tim Connelly was the detective with whom she'd worked on the Morosco case. Over the course of the investigation, her respect for his professionalism and her appreciation of his sense of humor had blossomed into a deep friendship.

For a few minutes, they reminisced about Tim and the other members of Manhattan Homicide with whom she had worked. Tim, it turned out, had been Jerry's mentor. That is, before Jerry quit police work.

"Why did you leave? Or shouldn't I ask. Maybe it's none of my business."

He held up the forefinger of his right hand. Half an inch was missing from the tip. "I got out on a disability pension—three quarters. It's what's known in the business as winning the lottery. Some cops make it happen: they slam their hand in the car door or slice the tip off their trigger finger. I had it done for me by a wacko with a gun."

"You don't sound too happy about it."

He shrugged. "I wasn't, at first. I'm adjusting. In a lot of ways, it's better. A cop's life isn't the life for a man with a family. That's why a lot of cops end up in divorce court. The money's better here too. With my disability, we can live pretty well. Before, I was trying to support a wife and four kids on twenty-six grand a year. In New York. It was tough."

"How did you end up here?"

"After I got out, I worked in a health club for a while.

Somebody told me about this job. It's a trade-off, like anything else. I'm not the guy in the white hat anymore, but I'm outside a lot, I'm making good money, and I don't have to go home to the wife and kids day after day and pretend that I didn't see a guy with his head split open lying in the gutter."

A waiter came by with a tray of hors d'oeuvres.

"They didn't serve grub like this at the station house either," he added, helping himself to a cracker piled with caviar. "Actually, it wasn't Tim that I wanted to talk with you about; it was Adele."

"Adele Singer?" said Charlotte, puzzled.

"Yeah." He spoke with a thick Brooklyn accent. He was leaning forward in thought, his beer glass cupped between his knees. His brow was furrowed. "I don't think she died of a drug overdose."

"What do you think it was? Suicide?"

"I don't know. That's the problem. It sounds good, drug overdose. Most bathtub deaths *are* overdoses, or suicides. Except that I saw the body, and it didn't look right; it wasn't in the position you'd expect."

Charlotte remembered that Jerry had been one of the men who'd carried in the oxygen resuscitator. "What position was it in?"

"Her feet were hanging out over the end of the tub." He pulled over a chair and draped his legs over the back. "Like this," he said.

"But didn't they find drugs in her blood?"

"Yeah. But that doesn't mean anything. She was an addict. She could have swallowed enough to kill a horse and not even have felt it. I thought you might be able to help me figure it out. Why would her feet be hanging out like that? Some arcane female ritual that I'm not aware of?"

Smiling, Charlotte raised a skeptical eyebrow in an expression that had withered many of the screen's leading men.

Jerry grinned. He had delightful dimples.

"Could she have been shaving her legs?" Charlotte offered. She leaned back in thought, stretching her long legs out in front of her. Her hand was draped languidly over the arm of the chair, her glass dangling from her fingers. She still possessed

the distinctive liquid grace—at once both feline and ethereal—
that was part of her sexy, radiant screen presence.

"No razor."

"Maybe her legs were too long to fit in the tub."

"She was short. And even if she wasn't, she could have bent
her legs. I've seen a lot of tall men get in and out of these tubs,
but I've yet to see one who's stuck his legs out over the end like
that."

Jerry was right—it was odd, unnatural. But she was damned
if she could figure out why. She tried to think back to that
moment. She remembered the footsteps. But that didn't tell her
much except that they weren't Hilda's. She would have
recognized Hilda's shuffle. "Did you tell the police?"

"Yeah, but they weren't interested. They've got everything
neatly wrapped up. They don't want some smart ass from the
Big Apple telling them they shouldn't be so eager to close the
file."

Under the tent, the guests were taking their seats. Jack
disengaged himself from a group of red carnations at the other
end of the terrace and headed toward them, dispatched no
doubt by Paulina. He looked like a southern planter in his
fashionably rumpled white linen suit.

"Here comes the boss lady's lapdog," said Jerry.

"I gathered he's at her back and call."

"She's all but got him on a leash," he said disdainfully.

Jack arrived at their table. "Are you ready to dine, madam?"
he asked with mock formality, offering her his arm.

"Yes, thank you," said Charlotte. After saying good-bye to
Jerry, she headed toward the tent with Jack. The tent poles
were festively decorated with garlands of flowers and mint-
green banners bearing the Indian maiden logo. Bouquets of
green balloons floated above the tables. At each place, there
was a gift certificate for twenty dollars and a miniature
mint-green shopping bag filled with samples of the product.
Wine them and dine them and give them presents—Paulina
knew how to spend her money where it would do the most
good.

Jack escorted Charlotte to Paulina's table. In addition to
Paulina and Jack, those at the table included Leon, Anne-
Marie, Gary, and one of the ubiquitous red carnations, a

heavily made-up reporter from *Society* magazine named Miss
Small with inch-long orange fingernails and a straw hat to
match. The topic of conversation was the radium scare. In
response to Miss Small's question about the effect of the
radium scare on business, Gary replied that sales of High Rock
water had started to slip. Wisely choosing to ignore the
question, Paulina unsuccessfully tried to steer the conversation
to the Body Spa line. But Gary persisted. He said he wasn't
concerned. "It's going to be tough sledding for a while, but
we'll come out of it smelling like a rose," he said with the
businessman's knack for mixing metaphors.

Miss Small conscientiously recorded every word in a reporter's notebook, her charm bracelet jingling. It would make a
nice item: "President undismayed by dip in sales. 'High Rock
water will recover,' he says." But the romance between Gary
and Anne-Marie would have made much better copy. Charlotte
could see now why Paulina thought him a good match for
Anne-Marie. Like her, he glowed with vitality. He wasn't
handsome: he was losing his hair and he had an underbite. But
he was magnetic, with heavy black eyebrows; small, intense
brown eyes; and a pointed chin with a deep cleft. He was short
in stature—no taller than Anne-Marie—but he had the presence of a much larger man. He struck Charlotte as smart,
shrewd, and unabashedly ambitious.

Charlotte had often come across his picture in the gossip
magazines in the doctor's office, jogging or skiing across the
pages. A former West Point cadet, he had gone on to become
a Madison Avenue ad man, and was widely considered a
marketing genius on account of his uncanny knack for spotting
trends. Yogurt, blue jeans, running shoes—all had been largely
Gary Brant creations. When the state put the High Rock
bottling plant up for lease, he smelled a new market and
decided to strike out on his own. He repackaged the water in
sleek leaf-green bottles, marketed it as a chic alternative to soft
drinks, and advertised like crazy. In just five years, he had
turned a dusty upstate New York label into one of the country's
most popular beverages. In doing so, he had virtually created
the mineral water market, just as Paulina had created the
cosmetics market more than fifty years before.

Indeed, it was clear from Paulina's indulgent expression that she considered Gary a man in her own mold. It was another of Paulina's idiosyncracies that she had no interest in people who had inherited money. Titles, blue blood, family fortunes—these impressed her not at all. But when it came to people who had *earned* fortunes, she wanted to know what they ate for breakfast. Charlotte suspected that Paulina was quite impressed by the Seltzer Boy, although she never would have admitted it. He had, after all, amassed a small fortune, and he had done it very quickly.

"Sales will bounce back," he was telling Miss Small. "The consumer is a lot smarter than most of us give him—or her—credit for, and a lot more loyal. As long as the product is okay, the consumer won't desert the ship. He'll recognize that the product's image has been unfairly tarnished. The important thing is to get the message out."

The conversation was interrupted by the arrival of the first course, oysters served on the half shell by a squadron of efficient waiters in black bow ties. With the oysters came goblets of champagne.

Miss Small was still listening intently. Gary had her wrapped around his little finger. His dark, sharp face combined with his muscular physique gave him a Panish quality, slightly playful, slightly lascivious, that Charlotte imagined many women would find very appealing.

"Then there's nothing wrong with the water?" she asked, still on first base with her notebook.

"Nothing," replied Gary. He went on to talk about the safety tests to which the water was subjected and about the fact that the contaminated waters were not among those bottled by High Rock. Miss Small took it all down, oblivious to the fact that she was being led around by the nose.

Charlotte was impressed; he had turned a potentially embarrassing situation into one that was to his company's benefit.

After the oysters came the entrée: lobster with truffle sauce and filet mignon. With it came an assortment of fine wines, both red and white. And, of course, High Rock mineral water. It was quite a spread.

"What about the stock?" asked Miss Small in a fleeting moment of skepticism before digging in to her lobster.

"Oh, that's dropped too," Gary replied blithely. "But it will come back."

"Eat," Paulina urged her.

Miss Small nodded and settled down to her meal. In fact, the stock had dropped precipitously. After talking with Paulina, Charlotte had checked. By comparison with the drop in High Rock Waters stock, the drop in Paulina Langenberg stock was nothing. But what society reporter was going to bother to check the stock listings, particularly with a bellyful of lobster?

During the main course, Paulina finally succeeded in steering the conversation away from radium. The new subject was jewelry, specifically the rubies that bedecked Paulina's throat, wrists, and earlobes. A ruby brooch was even pinned to her hat. While Miss Small oohed and aahed, Charlotte took stock of her surroundings. The neighboring table was occupied by Jerry and his wife, a dark, plump, pretty woman; Elliot and Claire, who looked like a throwback to the sixties in her Mother Hubbard skirt; and Dr. Sperry and Corinne. The table grouping was completed by another red carnation. Across the room, Charlotte noticed Frannie and her husband sitting at a table with some other spa employees. With her hair done and her face made up, Frannie actually looked pretty, proof of Paulina's dictum that there are no ugly women, only lazy ones.

By the time Charlotte returned her attention to the conversation, it had moved on to the yellow stone on Paulina's finger. "You like it?" Paulina asked. Removing it from her finger, she thrust it into the hand of the astonished reporter. "It's yours," she said. "For luck." It dawned on Charlotte that Paulina must have worn the jewel—probably an inexpensive quartz—for the purpose of making just such a show of generosity. When it came to manipulating the press, Gary had nothing on Paulina.

The waiters returned to clear the dishes and to serve dessert and coffee. As dessert—an ice cream bombe—was served, the ceremonies began. The first speaker was an official who talked about what Paulina's stewardship of the spa had meant to the state. Before Paulina Langenberg, he said, the state had been subsidizing the baths to the tune of ten dollars each. Five years later, the royalties paid by Paulina Langenberg were enriching state coffers by hundreds of thousands each year. The story was similar for the bottling plant. After a few platitudes about a profitable future, the official went on to introduce Gary, who was the featured speaker.

Gary excused himself and made his way up to the mint-green-skirted podium. He had the broad shoulders, straight back, and narrow hips of the natural athlete. He also had a very good tailor. He mounted the podium with an energetic jump. After starting off with the obligatory joke, he moved on to the substance of his speech:

"In the summer of the year 1767, Sir John Williams, who had just returned from a visit to High Rock Springs, wrote a friend: 'I have just returned from a visit to a most amazing spring, which miraculously effected my cure.' These words launched the spa that would become famous throughout the world as High Rock Spa. The story of the development of High Rock Spa is a story of the American entrepreneurial spirit, the spirit of hard work and dedication and the ability to respond to the needs of the marketplace, the spirit that built this country and made it great."

Paulina sat with one hand cupped around the back of her ear. "What did he say?" she asked Anne-Marie in a loud voice.

Anne-Marie repeated the gist of his words.

Paulina nodded, smiling.

"High Rock's first great entrepreneur was Elisha Burnett. It was Elisha Burnett who had the vision and fortitude to clear High Rock's famous spring, to build its first inn, to lay out its streets and roads. In his footsteps followed other entrepreneurs, men who carved a city out of the wilderness. One of these was Dr. William Allen, who was to become High Rock's second great entrepreneur." He went on to talk about Dr. Allen, who, on a visit to High Rock in 1820, was so impressed by the number of visitors who had come to take the waters that he purchased the spring and set up a bottling plant. A new industry was born.

"Today, we are celebrating the anniversary of the third stage in High Rock's history, a stage in which the trends established by Elisha Burnett and by Dr. Allen—the spa and the bottled waters—have come together, producing a rebirth of High Rock Spa. Five years ago, High Rock Spa was taken over by Paulina Langenberg and High Rock Waters. The result has been nothing short of miraculous: together, these companies have given the spa a new lease on life; together, these companies have put High Rock Springs back on the map."

The speech was interrupted by applause. Miss Small gave a jingling ovation, orange fingernails flashing. As she clapped, Paulina bounced up and down in her seat like a child. Charlotte felt a jab in the ribs. "Smart, eh?" said Paulina. She leaned toward Anne-Marie. "This time, you've got a good one. 'A' number one." Addressing Charlotte, she added: "He's not a creep like the last one." She shot a sidelong look of distaste at the adjoining table, where Dr. Sperry was nuzzling Corinne with unseemly familiarity.

Gary cleared his throat. "It is therefore fitting," he continued, "that today we are commemorating the commencement of another stage in the history of the spa, a stage that will marry the two trends in High Rock's history—the spa and the mineral waters—a stage in which Paulina Langenberg and High Rock Waters will look toward the future, together."

"How nice," Paulina whispered, "he's going to plug the spa line."

Gary glanced over at their table. "What I'm about to say may come as a surprise—even as a shock—to some of you, but I can assure you that there is no cause for concern. The future that we will share together will be even brighter than our separate futures might have been."

A shock? Charlotte didn't understand.

"Oh, God," muttered Leon, who was sitting to Charlotte's right. He removed a handkerchief from his breast pocket and used it to wipe his brow, which had begun to perspire profusely despite the cool breeze.

Paulina had stopped bouncing. With a puzzled expression, she cupped a hand around her ear.

Gary continued: "I am proud to announce that as of today High Rock Waters, Inc., is the majority shareholder in Paulina Langenberg. High Rock Waters has acquired a twenty-five percent share of Paulina Langenberg. Our goal is a thirty-four percent share. High Rock Waters's tender offer will be announced in the financial pages of tomorrow's newspaper."

For a moment, Paulina's jaw hung slack. Then she glanced around the room like a beleaguered general seeking the support of his troops. There was a buzz of conversation as it dawned on the guests what was happening.

"In the future," Gary continued, "High Rock Waters and Paulina Langenberg will be working together. The merger is a natural for both companies." Gary went on to talk about mutual interests, marketing compatibility, and increased growth and profits.

But no one was listening.

It was a takeover, plain and simple. Charlotte watched Paulina in fascination as the realization took hold that the empire over which she reigned had been attacked. Corporate raider—the term was perfect. For the first time in her life, Paulina would have to answer to someone else.

Paulina looked stunned.

How had it come about? Charlotte wondered. High Rock Waters—however profitable—was still only small fry by comparison with Paulina Langenberg. How had David felled Goliath? Then Gary let the other shoe drop.

"I want to stress that High Rock Waters is acquiring stock in Paulina Langenberg with only the friendliest of intentions. We have every expectation of working to make our two corporate cultures fit together. Toward that end, I have another announcement. As of today, I am resigning my position as president of High Rock Waters. I will, however, stay on as chairman of the board. The new president will be Elliot Langenberg, who, as you know, is director of the spa and executive vice president of Paulina Langenberg, Inc."

Gary went on, but everyone's eyes were on Elliot, who managed to look both triumphant and sick at the same time. In fact, he looked as if he were about to crack his cookies—or rather his filet mignon—on the spot.

It was then that Charlotte realized what had happened: Elliot had sold his stock in Paulina Langenberg to Gary. As Paulina's son, Elliot undoubtedly owned a lot. Gary had probably thrown in the presidency of High Rock Waters to grease the deal. By adding Elliot's block of stock to shares purchased on the open market, Gary could easily accumulate enough to meet his goal.

In fact, a David gaining control of a Goliath probably wasn't so unusual in the business world nowadays; it seemed as if there was nothing too big to take over or to try to take over. All it took was good credit and a lot of nerve. Gary apparently had plenty of both.

Leon was bending consolingly over his aunt. "I'm sorry. The letter of intent came this morning. I wanted to tell you myself. To break it gently."

"Do you think I'm senile?" she snapped.

Leon went on: "Thirty-four percent is slightly more than a third. According to our bylaws, High Rock Waters's ownership of thirty-four percent will give them negative control. Which means that all major decisions will require their approval. To put it another way: he's got us hamstrung."

"I know what negative control means," hissed Paulina.

Leon shot Elliot a dirty look, which Elliot returned. The exchange made Charlotte realize why Elliot had done what he had. He was afraid Paulina would someday carry out her threat to leave the company to Leon. With negative control, he could block any effort to install Leon at the head of Paulina Langenberg. In fact, he could defeat any proposal he cared to contest.

Gary was still talking—about what an honor it would be to work with Paulina. But the flattery was going over her head. She was over being stunned; her face was a study in fury. Her nostrils were flared, her lips compressed. She stood up, giving Anne-Marie a look that would scorch the desert. Grabbing Charlotte's arm, she said, "Come on. Let's get away from this scum."

Anne-Marie looked up importunately, as if she were being rejected by her own mother. Either she was a good actress, or she had had no idea that a tender offer was in the works.

With the dignity of a dethroned monarch, Paulina, resplendent in her red gown and her red jewels, tossed her shawl over one shoulder and marched over to the table where Elliot sat with Claire and the others.

She stood squarely in front of him, her hands on her hips. "Traitor," she said. "Rotten, rotten, traitor."

And then she spat on him.

· 6 ·

"BETRAYED ME. YOU betrayed me," shouted Paulina. "My own son. How could you? The company that I've worked my entire life to build. Sold out from under me. I don't believe it. I don't believe it."

In her hand, Paulina held a letter, which she passed to Charlotte in evidence of her son's treachery. It was from High Rock Waters, describing the terms of the tender offer and the plans for the future of the company.

After being hustled out of the fete on Paulina's arm, Charlotte had been dragged back to Paulina's apartment. She now sat at the side of Paulina's bed, the unofficial witness to the family melodrama.

Elliot stood at the foot of the bed, his face as white as if it were smeared with a layer of Langenberg cold cream.

For the last ten minutes, Paulina had been delivering a tongue-lashing that was mesmerizing in its drama. Always extravagant in her use of gesture, she had embellished her performance by alternately raising her fist to the heavens and beating her breast. Now she was signaling an unofficial time-out by burying her face in the pile of silk pillows at the head of her huge Chinese bed. She was huddled on her knees, her hands gripping her elbows. Her chignon was coming apart. Strands of blue-black hair hung down her back. She rocked back and forth, keening like an Indian squaw for her dead brave.

Charlotte took advantage of the break in the melodrama to survey the room. The rosewood platform bed was covered by a canopy and enclosed on three sides and part of a fourth by a

latticework railing. On the purple wall above the bed hung a
spectacular Picasso, a mother and child. One wall was lined
with windows over which were drawn rose-colored brocade
draperies. The overall impression was a combination of French
bordello and opium den—one that had just been ransacked:
newspapers were heaped next to the bed, clothes overflowed
the dresser drawers, food lay uneaten on plates on the bedside
table.

Entering with a brandy snifter on a tray, Jack gently shook
Paulina's shoulder. "Here, drink this," he said softly. "It will
make you feel better."

Paulina raised her head. Her cheeks were streaked with
mascara, the corners of her mouth smudged with lipstick.
Picking up the snifter, she downed its contents in a gulp.
Revived by the brandy, she wiped her nose on a corner of the
pink satin sheet and pitched into her son with renewed vigor.

"Ingrate. Ingrate," she shouted. She had risen to her knees.
"That such a monster could come from my own loins." She
raised her fist to the ceiling. "I rue the day that I ever gave
birth to you. All that I've done for you, and you sell me down
the river—me, you own mother."

Elliot's face reddened. Stepping forward, he gripped the
latticework railing at the foot of the bed. "I've betrayed you.
That's rich. How many times have you betrayed me? Huh? I'm
asking you, Ma. How many times have you threatened to leave
everything to Leon? I'll tell you. One too many."

At first uncomfortable, Charlotte was now settling in, like
the audience after the curtain has gone up. Her head moved
back and forth as if she were following the ball at a tennis
match.

"That's right," Paulina replied. "Too many times I've
threatened. This time, it's no threat. This time, it's for real.
You'll see." Her eyes narrowed. "You won't get one red cent
out of me." Reaching over, she pressed the tail of another
turtle buzzer on the bedside table.

Jack appeared at the door. "Anne-Marie is here to see you,"
he announced.

"Another traitor. I won't see her. I'd like to fire her, but I
can't spare her. But I'm going to sack her ex. I'm not going to

keep him around any longer just as a favor to her. Make sure he gets his walking papers this week."

Jack pulled a small leather notebook out of his breast pocket and made a notation. It appeared that in addition to being Paulina's lapdog, he was also her hatchet man. Then he turned to leave.

"Then come back," said Paulina. "I want you to get out my will." She looked pointedly at Elliot. "I'm going to disinherit my son."

Elliot had been standing by silently as if waiting for his mother to recant. "So you're finally going to carry through," he said, realizing that she wasn't going to change her mind.

"Did you think I wouldn't?"

Elliot didn't answer. "Well, you're mistaken if you think I'm upset. I'm sick and tired of your fucking black notebook; I'd like nothing better than to see it dragged out for the last time."

"That's right. The last time." Paulina stared at him.

He turned away, his hands thrust deeply into his pockets. "Go ahead, leave all your money to Leon. But I'm the one who'll have the last laugh. Leon will never run Paulina Langenberg. I've made sure of that."

"Traitor. After all I've done for you."

"All you've done for me?" said Elliot, spinning around. "Ha. That's very funny." He threw back his head. "Ha, ha, ha, ha. Do you know what you've done for me? Made my life miserable, that's what. You never cared about me. All you ever cared about is money. Money, money, money."

Paulina let loose a wail and buried her head in the pillows.

Charlotte was sure Elliot's accusations were quite true. He must have had a lonely childhood—the only child born late in life to a world-famous businesswoman, his father having died while he was still a boy, shuttled off for safekeeping to posh boarding schools. But Charlotte couldn't blame Paulina. It was simply too hard to do both—to be a career woman and a mother too. If Charlotte had had children, they probably would be leveling the same accusations. Anyway, Paulina hadn't done that badly. Elliot struck her as a decent person, which was saying a lot these days.

"Oh," said Elliot sarcastically, "the inconsolable mother

act. Well, let Leon console you this time. He's being well paid for it."

Paulina's wailing stopped. She looked up, surprised that her bid for sympathy hadn't worked. Score one for Elliot.

"See? It was just an act, like everything you do. You are a despicable old woman, always manipulating people with your money. Well, Ma, I'm not going to be your puppet anymore. I don't need your fucking money. I have all the money I need. I have a job where I'm respected . . ."

"Not for long," Paulina sneered. "You won't be respected for long. The Seltzer Boy will find out what a no-good bum you are. You're just like your father: a rotten, lazy, no-good wastrel. I slave to build the company, and you sell it out from under me. You're a parasite, just like he was."

Elliot's face flushed to his bald temples.

Elliot's father had been a handsome womanizer who had gambled away thousands of Paulina's dollars before she finally divorced him. Her second husband, who had died some years ago, had been an impoverished European aristocrat a dozen years her junior whom she married for the glamour of his title. Not that she was impressed by it, but she thought others would be. Much to everyone's surprise, the second marriage had worked out very well. His relaxed personality was an effective counterpoint to Paulina's volatile one. But it was her first husband who had been the love of her life.

"But you respected him, didn't you?" Elliot replied. "Because he took money from you. You only respect people who are clever; people who can match wits with you. Well, maybe you'll respect me now."

Paulina gave him a scathing look. "Where's my will?" she bellowed, pressing the buzzer again in irritation.

Jack reappeared at the door.

Reaching into her bosom, Paulina withdrew a key and handed it to him. From a glass vitrine in the corner he extracted the black notebook that Paulina had shown Charlotte on her earlier visit and set it on the bedside table, a Louis XV bombé commode topped by a cupid lamp.

"My glasses too," ordered Paulina.

Kicking off her shoes, she got under the covers, pulled the sheets up around her waist, and arranged the pillows behind her back. With exaggerated care, she carefully reknotted her chignon and reapplied her makeup. Then she leaned back, balanced her glasses on the tip of her nose, and lifted the notebook onto her lap. "A pen, please," she said. "*Not* a pencil," she added, making the point that she had no intention of erasing anything.

Once Jack had brought the pen, she slowly opened the cover of the notebook. From where she was sitting, Charlotte could see that it was alphabetically arranged. Paulina turned to E for Elliot. Solemnly leafing through the pages, she made a great ceremony of crossing out this and writing in that. It was, Charlotte conceded, a hypnotic performance.

Elliot looked on mutely.

"Everything to Leon," she said finally, closing the notebook with an air of finality. Then she addressed Jack: "Jack, call the estate lawyer. The One with the Blond Wife. Tell him to get up here on the double."

Elliot, who had taken a seat on one of the bedside chairs, looked miserable. He was actually wringing his hands. "Ma . . ." he implored.

Paulina ignored him.

Rebuffed, he sat immobile, as if turned to stone. Finally he rose and headed toward the door. Pausing at the door, he turned. "You spit on me," he said, his teeth clenched in anger. He pointed at the spot of dried spittle on the lapel of his blazer. "You spit on your own son."

"So what," said Paulina implacably. "You deserved it."

"I'm going back to the city."

"Good. By the way, you're fired. Anne-Marie can run things until we find someone else. Jack, clear out his room. Then have Leon's stuff moved up here. And give him that," she said, pointing to his photograph. "The one in the living room too. I don't want to look at his traitorous face."

Jack picked up the photograph and gently handed it to Elliot, who opened the door and quietly left.

Paulina watched him leave, stone-faced. During this interval, Charlotte tried to leave herself, but Paulina wouldn't let her. Once Elliot had gone, Paulina ordered Jack to summon Leon, who had been waiting in the living room until the scene with Elliot was over.

"Sit," said Paulina as Leon entered. She patted the edge of the bed. The notebook lay open on her lap. "Leon is my good boy," she said, taking his hand. She gazed at him benevolently through eyes moist with tears of self-pity. "The son of my beloved sister. Leon would never betray me."

"No, Aunt Paulina."

Her tone changed: "He just doesn't tell me when my company is being sold out from under me."

"I'm sorry," said Leon, looking contrite. "I was going to tell you. I didn't know he would announce it at the fete."

Paulina's expression turned benign again. "The estate lawyer will be here tomorrow. You'll be my sole heir. Sonny has fixed it that you can't be head of Paulina Langenberg. But don't worry." She waved her arm. "I'll make you a rich man. Everything will go to you." Turning around, she pointed to the painting above the bed. "Including the art."

Leon looked up at the painting disinterestedly. It was clear he could care less about art. Charlotte detected a sour expression cross Paulina's face as she registered his lack of interest.

"I'm honored, Aunt Paulina," said Leon. He looked like the cat who's just swallowed the canary.

"Now, Leon," said Paulina. "What can we do?"

"About what?"

"The Seltzer Boy, dummy!"

Leon shrugged. "He's got us. We might have been able to do something if he'd just been going after the outsider stock, but with Elliot's block, he's already got twenty-five percent. All he needs to gain negative control is another nine percent, and he'll probably have that locked up by tomorrow."

"Can't we sue?"

"On what grounds?"

"Antitrust."

Leon looked pained. "Aunt Paulina, he bottles mineral water; we make lipstick."

"I don't know," said Paulina. "The lawyers should be able to think of something. Jack, look in my book. I have the name of a firm, specialists in defending corporations against hostile takeovers. The best in the business. They'll find a way to put an end to this."

"You could tender your shares," offered Leon. "Retire a rich woman."

"Ai," wailed Paulina. She picked up a magazine from the table and whacked Leon over the head with it. "For this kind of advice, I pay you all that money? Tender my shares." She snorted. "Leon, I am not interested in retiring. 'A rich woman,' he says. I *am* a rich woman."

"It was just an idea."

"Never mind. I should have known better than to ask you. Now get out. I want"—she pronounced it "vant," like Garbo—"to be alone." Clutching the black notebook to her breast, she slipped down under the satin sheets, a small lump of pink in the middle of the huge bed.

Led by Jack, the three of them tiptoed out. From the bed came a low whimper, muffled by the pillows.

"Is there anything I can do?" asked Charlotte.

"Thank you," replied Jack. "But I can take care of her."

Charlotte said good-bye and left.

It was the next afternoon, Charlotte's fifth day at the spa. She sat at a table shaded by a High Rock umbrella on the sunny terrace in front of the Hall of Springs. She was sipping a glass of High Rock water. Her table stood next to a balustrade topped by urns of red geraniums. Beyond the balustrade lay the lawn, where a white peacock strutted back and forth looking for handouts from the guests, presumably those on the cuisine gourmande program. Charlotte had nothing to spare; her cuisine minceur lunch had consisted of only an artichoke and a tiny lobster salad. Beyond the lawn, the green surface of the reflecting pool rippled in the cool, pine-scented breeze. A string quartet played "The Blue Danube." It was all very pleasant. She felt as if she could have been at Baden-Baden or Montecatini. But High Rock was different from a European spa, she had decided; it had a feeling of vigor that was missing from its European counterparts. In Europe, the lack of activity was the chief attraction of a spa stay. The aim of the monotony of the routine was to alter the perception of time, slowing its flow. But the idea of savoring monotony was alien to the American psyche. The American wanted to control time, not surrender to it. Not for the American the endless hours on a sunny terrace wrapped in a tartan lap robe, but a morning coffee break sandwiched between exercise machines at nine and Absolutely Abdominals at ten-thirty.

Despite all the activity, Charlotte was enjoying her stay. Between Adele's death on her second day and the fete and its aftermath two days later, it had gotten off to an unnerving start. But she had finally settled into the routine, with Art as her guide and companion. She was now recuperating from a morning on the machines, to which she had graduated after a training session with Frannie, who had assured her that by purifying the temple of her spirit, she was hastening her progress on the journey to spiritual enlightenment. She enjoyed the feeling of using her muscles, but the pointlessness of the routine put her off. She couldn't get over the feeling that something should be accomplished by such an output of energy: a garden weeded, a floor scrubbed, a walk to the store. It was, she supposed, a sign of her age: in spite of her success, she was still a child of the Depression, when physical effort was too valuable a commodity in the struggle to survive to be squandered on exercising for the sake of physical fitness. She suspected the current passion for physical fitness was also a reflection of the times. In a world that was prosperous and secure, people tended to invent their own hardships, create their own challenges. Why else would they mortify their flesh by running themselves ragged on treadmills going nowhere and repeating the same movements over and over again on exercise machines?

She was reminded of the Role Model, who had looked on with haughty disdain as Charlotte and Art had piled their plates with low-calorie delectables at the buffet last night, ignoring the sample plates that showed how much food was within the limits of the prescribed calorie regimens. Taking only an apple and a glass of orange juice, the Role Model explained that he was on the fruit fast. He even turned down a dish of low-fat yogurt, dismissing it as "mucus forming." The question Charlotte asked was, to what end were he and others like him pursuing their goal of physical perfection? To what end were they piling up those credits in the giant ledger in the sky? She doubted that it was to become a better person, or to better serve humanity. She even doubted that health had much to do with it.

She suspected, with her generation's disapproval of the culture of narcissism, that it was out of selfish motives: to feel powerful, to be admired, to get ahead. God knows, the hardships experienced by her generation hadn't all been imposed by the Depression and the war. Charlotte for one was quite adept at inventing her own hardships. But she liked to think that the hardships invented by her generation tested the mettle on a loftier plane than that of the mere physical.

For all her cynicism as to the motives of her fellow spa-goers, however, she had to admit that she felt better: fit, relaxed—even thin, or thinner. She had no illusions, though, that her transformation would last. A visit to the spa was like taking Fido for a bath and clip: whatever Anne-Marie might say about our-bad-habits-giving-us-up to the contrary, she knew that it would take only a few weeks back in her natural habitat before she would revert to her former physical condition, which stood somewhere on the map of physical fitness between unregenerate slothdom and a base camp in the Himalayas.

The concert ended with a rousing number from *My Fair Lady*. The silence that ensued was punctuated by a booming voice: "Hello Humanoids," it said. It was the fleet-footed Mineral Man from the television news. He had popped up like a jack-in-the-box at the center of the terrace. A tall, gangly, young man, he was wearing a court jester's costume consisting of a black and gold diamond-paned tunic, a gold cape, and rust-colored tights. His face was covered by gold makeup, and his head by a floppy gold cap trimmed with bells. On his feet he wore boots with upturned toes, also trimmed with bells. As he moved, he jingled.

After launching his act with a less-than-perfect cartwheel, he performed a few magic tricks. As magician's assistant, he had drafted Nicky, who, like most obese people, appeared embarrassed at having to stand up in front of an audience. After a few minutes, however, he got into the spirit of the act, supplying the Mineral Man with props from his red knapsack, and acquiescing with good humor to having gold coins produced from behind his ear and lengths of rope pulled out of his pockets. After these feats of prestidigitation, accomplished only with the aid of a few abracadabras and hocus-pocuses, the Mineral Man launched into his spiel:

"Ladies and Gentlemen," he said, taking off his cap and bowing to the audience. "I am the Mineral Man. I conjure water from the center of the earth to make Humanoids feel wonderful!" With that, he pulled a bottle of High Rock water out of his cap. The crowd applauded politely. "The water I conjure from the center of the earth is effervescent, full of bubbles." Setting the bottle aside, he took some white balls out of the knapsack and proceeded to juggle them, tossing them into the air in imitation of a geyser.

As an acrobat, he wasn't much, but as a juggler, he was very good. From juggling the balls in the usual manner, he went on to bouncing them off of his head and his feet, and throwing them under first one leg and then the other. His act was a well-honed combination of acrobatics, mime, juggling, and sleight-of-hand, interspersed with jokes and overlaid with a line of patter about the virtues of the mineral waters. Charlotte was impressed by his professionalism, but baffled as to his motives.

As she watched, a shadow fell over her table. Turning, she found herself looking up at Jerry, who had just ascended the steps at the rear of her table. He was wearing a sleeveless T-shirt, which revealed what she had come to learn was called "deltoid definition."

"May I join you?" he asked.

"By all means."

He pulled out a chair and sat down. Catching the waitress's eye, he asked her to bring another glass of High Rock water.

"This is the first time I've seen this guy. He's pretty good."

"Yes," agreed Charlotte. "Do you know why he's doing this?"

"Haven't a clue."

The Mineral Man was now back to juggling. From cups and saucers, which he had solicited from the guests, he had gone on to knives and forks, and then to napkins, which he miraculously made to appear in knotted lengths from the pockets of members of the audience. But his most remarkable feat was achieved using unopened bottles of High Rock water, which he juggled as if they were juggling pins while the audience sat spellbound, expecting one to smash on the flagstone pavement at any moment.

The act had attracted a crowd from among the guests who'd been lunching in the Pump Room or strolling under the colonnades or sunning themselves by the pool. They stood around the perimeter of the terrace in sweat suits or bathing suits, many with glasses of mineral water in hand. Turning around to survey the crowd, Charlotte noticed Anne-Marie standing behind her. Pulling out the extra chair, she invited her to join them.

Anne-Marie nodded hello to Jerry and sat down.

After a few more tricks, the Mineral Man wrapped up his act with a flip that just barely succeeded. He then withdrew a handful of mimeographed leaflets from his knapsack, which he passed out with Nicky's assistance. The leaflet, which was entitled, "Analysis of the Waters of High Rock Spa," gave a spring-by-spring analysis of the waters. The amounts of radium were highlighted, the point presumably being that the maximum allowable limit was exceeded at only a few springs, and at those only by a slight margin.

After distributing the leaflets, he picked up his knapsack and headed back into the Pump Room to the hearty applause of the audience.

"The kid's pretty good," said Jerry, clapping enthusiastically.

"I guess the point he's making is that the radium scare is a fraud," said Anne-Marie, looking over the handout.

"That's what Paulina thinks," said Charlotte. "She thinks it's an attempt to sabotage her business."

"You mean, she thinks that someone set out to deliberately plant this rumor?" asked Anne-Marie.

Charlotte nodded.

"But who?"

Charlotte shrugged. But the thought had occurred to her that it could have been Gary. The mayor had called the person who planted the rumor "an enemy of our city." Charlotte was reminded of Ibsen's play, *An Enemy of the People*. It was a play she knew well, having appeared on Broadway as the doctor's wife in a revival in the years before her Hollywood comeback. Or rather, the most recent of her comebacks. For as a critic had once noted, her career had been recycled more times than a reusable soda bottle. It was also a play that had been haunting her brain, a play whose plot bore some resemblance to the situation at High Rock. In it, a spa town's livelihood is threatened by a rumor that the waters are contaminated by sewerage. The doctor is accused by the townspeople of planting the rumor in order to depress the price of stock in the baths. According to the townspeople's scenario, the doctor is planning to buy up the stock at the depressed price and then announce that the danger is less critical than he had originally imagined. With the public's fears allayed, the price of the stock would climb and the doctor would make a hefty profit.

Charlotte wondered if the same could be true at High Rock. Perhaps Gary had planted the article in order to buy up Langenberg stock at a depressed price. Hadn't the stock dropped seven points as a result of the article? In any case, it seemed an unlikely coincidence that the article had appeared just before the announcement of High Rock Waters's tender offer.

Anne-Marie, perhaps sensing the tack of Charlotte's thoughts, or perhaps having similar thoughts herself, looked uncomfortable. "How is Paulina?" she asked, changing the subject.

"Unhappy," replied Charlotte. "She thinks Elliot betrayed her."

"She probably thinks I did too," said Anne-Marie, as if reading Charlotte's mind. "She won't let me see her. If you see her, could you please tell her that I didn't know anything about the takeover?"

"Of course," said Charlotte.

"Your boyfriend sure has a flair for the dramatic," said Jerry. "To say nothing of a lot of guts. Why'd he do it? Why take a chance when he's sitting pretty on the mineral water business?"

Anne-Marie shrugged. "You said it—he likes drama, he likes risk. Now that High Rock Waters is a success, it's time to move on. New peaks to conquer, so to speak." She smiled.

Charlotte sensed that she was proud of Gary for making such

a bold move. She also sensed that she was very much in love with him.

"Elliot just happened to come along at the right moment," she went on. "Gary says it happens all the time in family businesses. There's a falling out, and the injured party goes looking for a buyer."

The waitress brought Jerry his drink.

"It was also a matter of eat or be eaten," continued Anne-Marie. "High Rock Waters has big cash reserves. As you can imagine," she explained with a little grin, "there's not much expense involved in bottling water."

"I'll say," said Jerry, hoisting his glass. "Take free water, put it in a bottle, and charge more for it than for beer. What a racket."

"What you mean is," said Charlotte, "that its cash reserves made High Rock Waters an attractive takeover target for some other company."

"Exactly," replied Anne-Marie. "If High Rock Waters hadn't spent its assets on Langenberg stock, it might have been taken over by someone else."

"Of course, he stands to lose a pile too," said Jerry. "I mean, if it doesn't work out. I imagine the boss lady's going to put up quite a fight."

"It should be interesting," said Anne-Marie.

Actually, thought Charlotte, Gary had little to lose. If the takeover scheme worked, he would have a valuable stake in a company that was much larger than his own; if it didn't, he could sell his Langenberg stock—probably at a profit—and move on to something else.

"I have to give Elliot credit for standing up to her," said Jerry. "It took a lot of courage. She's a great lady, but she sure can be a pain in the ass. It must be hell being her son." He added: "But I wouldn't be surprised if she respected him all the more because of it."

"That's just what he said," said Charlotte. "He told her, 'You only respect people who take money from you,' or something to that effect. It got pretty heated: she's threatening to disinherit him. She says she's going to leave everything to Leon."

"She's said that before," said Anne-Marie. "Every time they

have an argument. She calls the lawyers; they make a few minor changes: she'll leave this Picasso to Leon instead of Elliot, or that piece of real estate to her niece instead of Elliot. But that's the extent of it."

"This time she sounds as if she's really going to carry through," said Charlotte. "She's fired him too." She wondered briefly if she should be talking about Paulina's affairs and then dismissed her qualms: there was little if anything that Paulina chose to keep private.

"I wonder who she's going to get to replace him," said Anne-Marie.

"You, for the time being."

Anne-Marie made a face. "As if I don't have enough to do already. Which reminds me, I have to get going," she said, rising from her seat.

After she had gone, Charlotte and Jerry sat in silence for a few minutes, watching Anne-Marie as she strode down across the lawn with the grace and confidence of a professional athlete.

"What do you think about this merger, Jerry?" asked Charlotte after a while. "Do you think it will work?"

"I don't know. Brant admires her. And she feels the same about him, or used to anyway. She liked to think of him as her protégé. I wouldn't be surprised if it did work—after the dust settles, that is. She doesn't have any respect for Elliot's business ability, and Leon . . ."

"What about Leon?"

"He's good on the money end of it, but he's"—he cast her a look out of the corner of his eye—"he's what the British used to euphemistically refer to as 'a confirmed bachelor.' "

"A homosexual?"

"That's probably putting it too strongly. I think he has those tendencies, but I don't think he has the strength of character to act on them. Not that his sexual orientation would interfere with his business ability—but I do think it affects Paulina's opinion of him."

"She knows?"

"There's not much she doesn't know."

Charlotte gazed out over the lawn. She suspected that many self-made men and women found themselves in Paulina's

predicament. *"Après moi, le déluge,"* she had said. After
spending a lifetime building a company, they end up with no
one to leave it to. The relatives are either disinterested or—in
the eyes of the company's founder anyway—unacceptable.
Others in Paulina's position might have sought out a merger
candidate; instead, Gary had sought out Paulina. He might just
be the answer to her problems.

A white-uniformed man had emerged from the Bath Pavilion
and was heading across the lawn. Charlotte recognized him as
Frannie's husband, Dana. He was walking rapidly, as if he had
pressing business. A few minutes later, he had reached the
terrace. He bolted up the stairs and headed directly for their
table. In an urgent tone, he asked to speak privately with Jerry.

Rising from his seat, Jerry stepped a few feet away, where
he conferred with Dana for a moment. Then he returned to the
table, grim-faced. "Come on," he said, waving his arm,
"we've got another one."

As they headed across the quadrangle, Dana explained that
the victim had been found unconscious by another bath
attendant. The attendant, with Dana's help, had tried to revive
him, with no success.

"Have you called the ambulance?" asked Jerry.

"Yes," answered Dana in his soft Carolina accent. "We've
called Dr. Sperry too. We've got Walter on the oxygen
resuscitator." He looked over at Jerry. "But I don't think it's
going to do much good."

Dana led them down the long, white-tiled corridor of the
men's wing. Alert to the signs of something amiss, the male
bathers stood in clusters in the corridor, just as the women had
three days before. With their white towels draped around their
middles, they looked like disciples of Gandhi. Among them,
looking as brown and wiry as Gandhi himself, was the Role
Model.

Dana stopped at the end of the hall and indicated a room on
his left.

Charlotte was hesitant about entering—she wasn't sure her
presence was wanted—but Jerry urged her in. "I want your
help," he said.

The victim was Art. He was lying on his back in the hot,
harsh glare of a shaft of early afternoon sunlight that streamed

through the opaque window, bouncing brilliantly off the gleaming white tile walls. Beneath him, a towel had been spread out over the black-and-white-tiled floor, which was wet in places from the water that had dripped off his body when he was lifted out of the tub. A bath attendant was stooped over the body. He was operating an oxygen resuscitator. With one hand, he pressed the face mask over Art's nose and mouth; with the other, he pushed down on the squeeze bag that was attached to an oxygen cylinder in the metal case on the floor. Lying on the towel next to Art's ashen face were his dentures, removed to clear an airway. His head was fully extended, and his jaw jutted toward the ceiling. The oxygen valve that forced air into the mask was making an eerie whooshing sound.

Charlotte's first reaction was embarrassment at seeing Art naked. His shrunken genitals were dwarfed by the rolls of flesh—now a grayish white—that cascaded down his belly. Then a wave of nausea hit her. She was sure he was dead: his deep blue eyes—the eyes of a kindly knight—stared glassily at the ceiling. She thought of what he had said about the motel: fifteen bucks a night, holes punched in the doors, *scheduled for demolition*.

Jerry knelt down to examine the body. He looked first at the pupils. Then he felt for the pulse in the wrist. As he picked up the wrist, Charlotte noticed with the eye for detail that is heightened in moments of tragedy that Art's arms—tanned to a freckly red below the line of his shirt sleeve—were covered by a fine fuzz of reddish blond hair.

Dropping the lifeless wrist, Jerry felt for the pulse in the carotid artery. "How long have you been at it?" he asked the attendant.

The young man checked his watch. "About ten minutes."

Walking over to the cot, Jerry picked up a starched white sheet, unfolded it, and draped it over Art's body. Only his toes protruded; the nails were already beginning to turn blue.

"Cyanosed," said Jerry, following Charlotte's gaze. "Is there a stethoscope?" he asked.

"In the case," answered the young man.

Dana fetched the stethoscope from the resuscitator case and handed it to Jerry. Pulling down the sheet, Jerry pressed the diaphragm to Art's chest. After listening for a moment, he said, "I think he's a goner, but you might as well keep at it until the ambulance gets here."

Charlotte could hear a siren wailing in the distance.

"How did you find him?" Jerry asked the attendant, a thin, pimply-faced young man with a scared expression.

"In the tub." He nodded toward the tub, where the plastic pillow and the towel were still floating on the surface of the fizzing water. "I was only gone about fifteen minutes."

Dr. Sperry entered and, deferring to Jerry, took a place near the door.

"Nobody's blaming you," said Jerry impatiently. "Just tell me how you found him. Not where, but how."

"How?" asked the young man dumbly.

"Describe the position he was in."

"Well, he was lying on his back."

"Yeah . . ."

"And . . . and his feet were hanging out over the end of the tub." He looked up at Jerry, unsure whether he'd gotten the answer right.

"Very good, Walter." He looked over at Charlotte.

"Just like Adele," she said.

· 7 ·

THE JITNEY BUS pulled away from the curb and turned left onto Golf Course Road, the road that led to the Avenue of the Pines and from there to the highway. The bus—a free service for spa guests—made the trip to town twice an hour. No sooner was it in motion than Charlotte started nodding off. She had slept fitfully the night before. Periods of wakefulness haunted by images of Art's dead body had alternated with periods of sleep haunted by dreams of loss. In her dreams, the loss of Art mingled with that of other loved ones. They were always lost, never dead—her lost husband, her lost mother, her lost dog.

She sat in front next to Regie Cobb. As on the news, he was wearing a Panama hat and a pin-striped shirt. Behind her, two fat women were discussing food binges. "It's Oreos for me," the one was saying. "If I buy a package, that's it. It's gone in nothing flat." Her companion nodded her chin, or rather her succession of chins. Charlotte hadn't noticed the women before. They must have been new inmates, to use Adele's expression. The seat opposite them was occupied by the Role Model, who wore an expression of extreme distaste. He sat as far away from them as possible, as if they were carriers of contagion. The other seats were occupied by the pimply faced bath attendant who had discovered Art's body and by Frannie's husband, Dana, who had nodded pleasantly to her.

Charlotte suspected the three men had been summoned to town for the same reason she had, the investigation into Art's death. Jerry had called the police soon after finding Art's body, and they had responded within minutes. A squad of technicians had immediately set to work taking photographs and making sketches of the scene of the crime—if that's what it was. The scene had been sealed off, and those who were in the building had been held in the men's lobby. One by one they had been called into a room to give their names and addresses. After being admonished not to discuss the case, they had been released with the stipulation that they might be called back for additional questioning. That morning, Charlotte had received a message from a Detective Crowley asking her to report to the police station at ten.

It had been easy and convenient for the police to write Adele's death off to a drug overdose, but it wouldn't be as easy a second time. A heart attack, maybe; but even a heart attack wouldn't explain the position of Art's feet. To her, the similarity of the deaths was too striking to ignore. But if the deaths had been unnatural, how had the victims been killed? To drown a healthy adult by forcing the head underwater would have required considerable strength, yet there was no evidence of struggle—no cries or screams, no wild splashing, no marks of violence—on Art's body, and, she presumed, none on Adele's. Besides, Charlotte suspected that it would soon be impossible for the police to dismiss Art's death as lightly as they had Adele's. The local paper had carried a small item that morning about the "body in the bath" case. It wouldn't be long before the story would be getting bigger play in bigger papers. But conceding that Art's death was unnatural was only the beginning. The hard part would be finding out who had murdered him. The award for the best opportunity went to the Bath Pavilion staff. Likewise the award for the most likely to have noticed anything unusual. Which was probably why the bath attendants were being called in. But the murderer could have been anyone at the spa. For that matter, the murderer need not be connected with the spa at all. The question was why. Why would someone at the spa, which was the most likely, commit murder, much less that of a total stranger?

The loud, gravelly voice of the woman behind her broke into her thoughts. "Not me. Chocolate, I can ignore. But salt. Get me near a can of salted peanuts and I go crazy. Or potato chips. Or pretzels."

The Role Model moved closer to the window.

The bus passed the spa quadrangle and turned onto the

Avenue of Pines. "Over there is the golf course," said Regie.
Ever the performer, he had taken it upon himself to conduct a
guided tour. "High Rock Golf Course is the only therapeutic
golf course in the world: no grade is steeper than five degrees.
As you may know, High Rock Spa gained its fame as a spa for
heart patients. In those days, exercise was thought to be bad for
the heart. Now it's just the opposite." He lifted a hand from the
wheel to point. "If you look over there, you'll see a bunch of
little buildings that look like outhouses. Those are the pump
houses." He turned around to look at the two women, his eyes
twinkling. "I'll bet you lovely ladies think the Lincoln water—
that's the water that's used for the baths—comes from a single
spring. Am I right?"

The two women nodded obligingly.

"That's what most people think. But actually it comes from
a grid of eight springs under the golf course. From there, it's
pumped to the power plant behind the Hall of Springs, where
it's heated. From there, it's pumped to the baths. High Rock
Spa uses one point nine million liters of mineral water a day,
enough to supply the drinking water for a small town."

At the end of the Avenue of Pines, the bus turned left onto
the highway. After a mile or so, the highway strip development
gave way to the flamboyant Victorian "cottages" of the town
proper. One of Victorian High Rock Springs's charms, Regie
said, was its uninhibited celebration of wealth. "The motto of
High Rock Springs," he said, "might have been 'too much is
never enough.' " But Regie had lost the attention of the two
women, who were back on food. From cookies and peanuts,
they had graduated to rum raisin ice cream and beluga caviar.
Charlotte wondered why they were torturing themselves—all
they could expect for lunch was poached fillet of Dover sole
and a couple of spears of broccoli (like the other guests,
Charlotte had taken to studying the menu postings with the
scrutiny she ordinarily accorded the morning newspaper).
Unless they were going into town for the purpose of cheating—
a transgression that probably occurred with more frequency
than the spa management would care to admit, and one that
would demonstrate a shocking degree of moral laxity in two
new arrivals.

Tuning out the beluga caviar, Charlotte shifted her attention

back to Regie. Only a few years earlier, he was saying, many
of the cottages had been destined for the wrecking ball, but the
revitalization of the spa had led to the restoration of many of
the town's fine old buildings. As they passed two particularly
magnificent cottages, Regie explained that they had once
belonged to the actress, Lillian Leonard, and her companion,
"Diamond Jim" Morrissey. Known as "Beauty and the Beast,"
they had been the leaders of spa society. The cottages were said
to be connected by an underground passage.

"Imagine that," said Gravel Gertie, craning her neck for a
better view of Lillian's house, which was a Victorian wedding
cake affair.

Charlotte, too, turned to look. If she could have chosen one
person to have been in a former life, it would have been Lillian
Leonard. For four decades, Lillian had dominated the American stage. Like Charlotte, she had played the virgin and the
whore, the socialite and the social activist, but she had played
them in real life as well. She had blond hair and a creamy
complexion that appealed to the protective instincts of men,
and a reputation that appealed to their baser ones. She was
known for her extravagant displays of wealth—she had once
pedaled around High Rock Springs on a diamond-encrusted
bicycle—but she had also been a leader of the suffrage
movement. Most appealing to Charlotte at this juncture was
her legendary appetite: the Gay Nineties credo that too much
was never enough also applied to female flesh; Lillian had
weighed in at a hefty one hundred and eighty pounds, and the
men had loved her for it. How times had changed.

Gravel Gertie had moved on to cashew nuts.

Regie continued: On their right was the High Rock Casino,
which had once been the country's most famous gambling hall.
It was here, said Regie, that Diamond Jim had proffered his
oft-quoted advice: "Never play another man's game." Alas,
said Regie, the gambling interests had been vanquished in the
early fifties. In an ironic transformation of vice into virtue, the
former gaming rooms now housed the offices of the High Rock
police.

Pulling over to a bus shelter at the far side of the park in
which the casino was situated, Regie announced the first stop.
"If you ladies are going shopping, you might want to get off at

the next stop, in the center of town. Return trips on the hour and the half hour."

"Where do we get off for Mrs. Canfield's?" asked the sweets lover, confirming Charlotte's suspicions. Mrs. Canfield's Sweete Shoppe was High Rock's most famous confectionary, a French patisserie whose delectables were the stuff of the dreams of the starved patrons of the spa.

"I don't know if I should answer that question," said Regie, turning around with a smile. "Ordinarily, regulations prohibit me from discharging passengers at Mrs. Canfield's, but I guess I can make an exception for two such lovely ladies." He tipped the brim of his jaunty hat.

The two women giggled.

Charlotte thanked Regie and got off. The three men also got off and headed in the direction of the casino. The Role Model took the lead, walking quickly and with an unusual stride, his heels rising with each step as if walking itself were a constraint. He was a textbook case of the Type A personality. Charlotte lingered behind, enjoying the lovely park. In a few minutes, she had reached the casino, a red-brick building in the flat-roofed Italianate style. Entering, she found herself in a dimly lit hallway. After taking her name, a dispatcher invited her to take a seat. The decor was heavily Victorian, with dark woodwork, parquet floors, and a huge chandelier. Above the door, plaster cherubs clasped their chubby arms around an overflowing cornucopia—a metaphor, she presumed, for the riches awaiting fortune's favored at the gaming tables.

After a few minutes, the Role Model emerged. It was then Charlotte's turn: a young officer escorted her into what had been the public gaming room. It was an enormous room with a vaulted ceiling perforated by octagonal stained-glass windows depicting the twelve signs of the zodiac. A long mahogany bar ran the length of one side. Tall windows hung with velvet drapes ran the length of the other. Between the windows hung enormous pier mirrors, which had once reflected the action at the faro boxes and roulette wheels, but which now reflected only an ugly warren of office cubicles.

Threading his way through the maze, the young officer led Charlotte to an office at the back, where she was introduced to Detective Crowley.

The interview itself was a letdown. Detective Crowley, a handsome man in his late thirties with a waxen pallor and prematurely graying hair, seemed mainly intent on establishing the chronology of events. He asked a few routine questions about when she had arrived on the scene, who had been present, and what had happened. She presumed that Jerry had already told him about Art's feet, but she reiterated the point anyway. It didn't seem to make much of an impression. In fact, Detective Crowley looked tired and somewhat overwhelmed. The cause of Art's death, he reported, was drowning subsequent to cardiac arrest. But because of Adele's death, they were giving his death more scrutiny than they otherwise might. In response to Charlotte's inquiry, he replied that Art's body had been released to his wife in Maryland. Funeral services would be held there on Monday. He gave her Art's wife's address and that of the funeral home. She intended to write a note and send flowers.

After being dismissed by Detective Crowley, Charlotte was escorted into another room, where her fingerprints were taken. "Elimination prints," the young police officer called them. They would be used to distinguish her prints and those of others present at the scene from those of any unknowns. After the fingerprinting, she was escorted back out to the hallway. She checked her watch; her visit had lasted only fifteen minutes. She would be able to make the next bus. Resisting the impulse to follow her fellow C's down the road to perdition at Mrs. Canfield's, she returned to the bus stop to await the return of the bus and poached fillet of sole.

"Ow!" Charlotte's head reared up in protest against the pain that shot through the bunion of her right foot.

"Points on the foot correspond to parts of the body," said Frannie. She was digging her thumbs into Charlotte's bunion with the determined pressure of someone trying to push a thumb tack into a slab of solid mahogany. "The point near the bunion is usually associated with shoulder problems."

Charlotte lay facedown on a massage table in the shiatsu treatment room, where she had reported after her daily parboiling in the bath. She had the feeling that the shiatsu, which had a reputation for being painful, was about to undo all that the bath had accomplished in the way of relaxation.

"I like to start with the feet. The feet give me an idea of where the problem areas are." She kneaded the spot on Charlotte's foot with her thumbs. "You have a lot of crystals," she said. "Feel them?"

To her surprise, Charlotte could feel the grainy lumps rolling around in the skin under Frannie's thumbs. "What kind of crystals?" she asked.

"Uric acid, calcium. They're an indication of problem areas."

Frannie moved up to Charlotte's neck. Shiatsu, she explained, releases energy that is trapped at points along the body's meridians, or energy pathways. The energy is released by applying pressure to specific energy points, the same points used in Chinese acupuncture.

"That hurts," warned Charlotte as Frannie dug her fingers into a particularly sensitive spot in the middle of her shoulder blade.

"I knew I'd find trouble in your shoulders," Frannie announced. "Feel that," she said triumphantly.

Reaching back over her shoulder, Charlotte could just feel the spot. Under the skin was a knot of muscle the size of a plum.

"Right on your gall bladder meridian."

"It's very painful."

"The pain is evidence of trapped energy. By the way," she said, bending over to look Charlotte directly in the eye, "there would be less pain if you didn't eat so much junk food." Her dull blue eyes gazed at Charlotte reprovingly through her granny glasses.

"What junk food?" protested Charlotte.

Frannie gave Charlotte a look she might have given a dissembling four-year-old. "Liquor?" she asked.

"Well, yes."

"Salt?" She continued to knead the knot. "I can tell. You're so puffy. I bet you live on potato chips. Your body is a temple of the spirit . . ."

"I know," interjected Charlotte. "But I treat it like a hotel room."

Frannie smiled her lopsided smile and tucked a lock behind an ear that protruded from between strands of lank hair. She had ears that were cupped forward like a monkey's. Charlotte found them quite charming. "It's not all that bad," Frannie said. "But it could be better."

"I thought I was doing very well. I don't eat sweets, I don't eat much red meat. What about the people who binge on chocolate chip cookies?"

"You're different. You should know better. You're more evolved. You're an old soul—very pure, very spiritual. That's why your system is so sensitive. You were probably a high priestess in your last life, or a desert hermit who subsisted on nothing but grains and dates."

Looking up, Charlotte raised an eyebrow in the you've-got-to-be-kidding-me look that was one of her screen trademarks. "How do you know?"

"That you're an evolved entity?"

Charlotte nodded.

"Karma," she answered matter-of-factly. "Beauty is a positive karmic consequence, as is success, as is wealth. Your beauty and your success are your rewards for your spiritual progress in past lives."

Funny, Charlotte thought her good looks a gift of nature and her success a reward for a lifetime of hard work. But good genes and hard work apparently didn't count for much among believers in the transmigration of souls. "Then ugliness and poverty are punishments for the sins of past lives?"

Frannie nodded. "Sort of. Educational opportunity would be a better term. You see, we plan our lifetimes before we incarnate in order to work out particular problems. An ugly person might have been obsessed with physical perfection in an earlier life. In that case, being ugly is their karmic consequence."

"What if you're not successful in working out your conflicts? What if you don't *like* being ugly?"

"You won't progress. If an entity fails to improve itself, it will keep on coming back to the school of life. I was a Roman matron in an earlier life. I'm crippled because I laughed at the cripples in the arena. Now I'm paying my karmic debt by helping others. If I didn't, I might come back again as a cripple. Dana was a Roman soldier . . ."

"You were in Rome together?" interjected Charlotte.

"We're soul mates. We've spent all of our past lives together."

"I thought he was a samurai warrior."

"That was in another life. Most of his karmic debt comes from his life in ancient Rome. He was a persecutor of the early Christians—one of the soldiers who fed the Christian martyrs to the lions. Now he's working off his karmic debt by helping others learn about their past lives."

It looked as if Frannie's husband had a pretty heavy debt load. "How do you know all this? It hurts there, by the way." Charlotte sucked in her breath as Frannie dug her thumbs into a point at the back of her skull. She was amazed that the hands of a woman could be so strong.

"Gall bladder twenty," said Frannie, kneading the spot. "It's what I call a yipe point." She replied to Charlotte's question: "The *akashic* records."

"The a-what records?"

"*Akasha*. It's a Sanskrit word for the fundamental substance of the universe. It's like a giant photographic plate; it registers impressions of everything that transpires in the universe. We can learn about our past lives and our future lives through readings of the *akashic* records."

"Readings?" It sounded like the giant ledger in the sky.

"If you're trained, you can learn to pick up the vibrations of the *akasha*. You can find out what it says about your past, or someone else's past. It's not hard. It's just a matter of learning to communicate on the right universal wavelength—kind of like tuning in a radio receiver."

Charlotte had as little use for the determinism of Eastern religions as she had for that of Freud. She was a diehard believer in individual will. Deathbed visions of the godhead, past life regressions, clairvoyance—all these she wrote off to the imagination. She said as much to Frannie.

But Frannie had an answer for the imagination question as well. "But what *is* the imagination? The imagination is simply past-life recall. The *reason* you're able to call a particular image to mind is that you've experienced it before. It's already there, imprinted in your cells."

There was no arguing with that. That was what was so annoying about Frannie's brand of metaphysics—there was an answer for everything.

"How do you learn to read the *akashic* records?" asked Charlotte. She was curious about the exact nature of this process. Did you travel in your astral body to some distant etheric library and look up your records in a cosmic card catalog? Or were they dictated to you over cosmic radio, or what?

"We start with guided meditations. To get our students accustomed to altered states of consciousness. Then we progress to trance work and OOB—that's 'out of the body'—experiences."

"I see," Charlotte said. But she really didn't.

"Some people can tune right in; they use their bodies as a kind of receiver for the *akasha*. Others use an entity from the other side to help them tune in. But you have to be careful with entities. Just because someone's lived and died doesn't mean they're more enlightened than you are. If you open yourself up, you don't know what might come jumping in. But in any case it's not difficult." She was digging her fingers into the back of Charlotte's leg. "We all retain memories of our past lives—it's just a matter of finding a way to connect with that knowledge. For instance, I can tell a lot about a person's past lives from a massage, from the aura. Some people can see it. I can feel it. If I hold my hands above the skin, like this"—she demonstrated, holding her hands over Charlotte's back as if she was warming them over a campfire—"I can feel it. That's how I know you were a spiritual entity in your last incarnation—that, and your positive karma. Your aura is very cool—a blue-green maybe, very energetic and clear."

"It sounds pretty."

Frannie smiled. "Dana and I also teach a course called You and Your Aura. The aura is a reflection of karmic energies. When a person understands his or her karma, the energies of the body flow freely and the aura is healthy and harmonious. When karma is unresolved, the energies are polluted by the karmic impurity and the body becomes sick. The more karmically free a person is, the more healthy he or she is."

"Does that mean that you can diagnose disease from the aura?"

"Absolutely."

Charlotte was intrigued. "What does the aura of someone who's sick look like?" she asked.

"Dull. Cloudy," replied Frannie, who was again working on Charlotte's feet. "Often the energy patterns are fragmented. The auras of some of the people I work on are really a mess. Some start out bad—that's their karma going down. But others create their own disharmony. Which they'll have to pay for in the long run." She ran her hands down the back of Charlotte's legs. "Smoothing the meridians," she explained. "Okay, you can turn over now."

Charlotte turned over onto her back.

"Like that woman who died." She was working the meridian on the inside of Charlotte's arm. "You have to really work at it to be in such bad shape. I mean, you have really got to *concentrate* on neglect. She might as well have moved on to the next incarnation because she wasn't making any progress in this one. Although it's hard to imagine what condition she'll come back in. Pretty bad, I'd imagine. She has a lot of karmic debt to work off."

"Tender," warned Charlotte. Frannie had moved down to her legs. The point she was now pressing was just above her knees.

"Liver-kidney-spleen meridian," said Frannie. "Those toxins again. Don't think you're alone. Most of the people I work on have tender gall bladder and liver-kidney-spleen meridians. It's the American diet—all that fat stresses the organs. Do you eat a lot of fried foods?"

"Only potato chips."

Frannie nodded knowingly and returned to her description of Adele: "Her body was poisoned. I don't like working on heavy people. I mean heavy emotionally. They're like energy sponges. I had to lie down after I worked on her—that's how much energy she sucked out of me. And then people like her think they can undo years of abuse with a few shots. Instant youth. If you ask me, that's what killed her—those shots she was getting."

Charlotte raised her head. "What shots?"

"Cells," replied Frannie, moving around to work on Charlotte's head. "From the embryos of sheep. Dr. Sperry gives them; they're supposed to make you young. They're illegal, but that doesn't stop him. Nobody's supposed to know about it, but I know because I see the marks. If Mrs. Langenberg found out, she'd fire him in a minute." She moved down to Charlotte's throat and jaw. "You have a lot of energy in your throat center," she said. "All creative people do; it's the locus of the creative energies."

But Charlotte's thoughts were on cell therapy: she knew several people who had undergone the expensive treatments, which were supposed to renew the sex life and restore youth. They might have been ineffective, but as far as she knew, they weren't dangerous. "How would the shots have killed her?"

"Allergic reaction. Any time a foreign protein is injected into the body, there's a risk of an adverse reaction. If you're sensitive, you can die from it. Look at penicillin. A shot of penicillin can be life-threatening for the person who's allergic to it. The same goes for a bee sting . . ."

Frannie had a point. It was also true that Adele had had an appointment with Dr. Sperry shortly before she died. But that still didn't explain why her feet had been found hanging out over the end of the tub.

Frannie had grasped Charlotte's wrists and was raising and lowering her arms, which, she explained, had something to do with the heart meridian. Then she announced that the massage was over.

Charlotte wasn't prepared for the way she felt. She had been having Swedish massages every day after her bath, in which her body was pounded, kneaded, and stroked into letting go, but she had never had a massage that left her feeling as if every last drop of stress and anxiety had been wrung out of her body. "I feel like a fillet of sole," she said, thinking of her lunch. But that wasn't entirely true. She felt enervated, but at the same time curiously peaceful and mentally, if not physically, buoyant.

Frannie smiled. She stood over the table with her arms

folded. "Tonight you'll want to take a long soak in the tub. I worked your shoulders pretty hard; they're going to be sore."

Charlotte nodded.

"Are you going to come back?" asked Frannie.

"Definitely," she said.

After her massage, Charlotte headed back to the hotel. Each step was an effort, as if she were walking through heavy sand. She wanted to visit Paulina before dinner. Jack had reported that she wasn't doing well. Charlotte was worried about her: she was strong, but she was also eighty years old, at least. After stopping at the flower stand in the lobby to buy a bouquet of flowers—she chose freesias—she took the elevator up to the seventh floor.

Jack answered the door. He wore a tie and a jacket, again of white—a fashionable silk twill. He looked totally unruffled.

Charlotte handed him the bouquet. "How is she?" she asked.

He shook his head. "See for yourself," he replied. "I'll just get a vase for these." Returning a moment later, he led her down the hall to the bedroom, where he opened the door on a scene that had changed little in two days. As before, the room lay in semidarkness. Paulina was curled up in the center of the bed, facing the wall. Her blue-black hair was spread out in a fan against the pillow. There was something eerie about seeing her so still. Charlotte studied her face: although the flesh sagged, her skin was smooth and shiny and free of lines. In repose, it looked almost childlike.

"I'll put these here so she can smell them," said Jack, setting the vase on the bedside table next to an untouched lunch tray and an unopened bottle of High Rock water. "Mrs. Langenberg, Miss Graham is here to see you," he announced formally. His soft voice carried an imploring note.

The only response was a twitch of the little finger on the rubied hand that still clutched her will to her breast.

Crossing over to the bed, Jack leaned over and whispered in Paulina's ear. "Paulina?" he said. But she didn't respond. He rejoined Charlotte at the door. "I was hoping she might respond to you. But I guess not."

"At least she got undressed," said Charlotte.

She was wearing a simple cotton duster. The red chemise she had worn to the fete was draped over a chair and a discarded girdle lay on the floor. The magnificent ruby necklace was heaped in an ashtray.

"No. I undressed her," said Jack. He breathed a deep sigh. "Has she eaten anything?"

Jack nodded at the untouched tray. "Nothing. I don't think she's had anything to drink either. I haven't even seen her get up to go to the bathroom."

Charlotte's attention was drawn to the adjoining bathroom, which was linked to the bedroom by a closet overflowing with clothes. On a table beside the door stood a magnificent bouquet of roses—Paulina Langenberg roses.

"They're from Elliot," he said, following her gaze. "He might as well have saved his money. She doesn't even know he sent them."

Above the table hung a framed photograph of a young woman in an ostrich-plumed hat. Charlotte recognized the distinctive profile as that of Paulina. She could easily see why the Canadian women had been so impressed by her. To them, she must have seemed as exotic as a bird of paradise.

"She was very beautiful then." He gazed lovingly at his employer. "For that matter, she's very beautiful still." Gesturing for Charlotte to precede him, he quietly left the room, closing the door gently behind him.

"What are you going to do?" whispered Charlotte.

"I don't think there's much I can do," he said resignedly. "I think this is just one of her nervous crises, as she calls them." He smiled. "If it is, she'll get over it. She was like this after her husband died—she didn't move a muscle for three days. After that, she got up and took the cure."

"The cure?"

"A series of baths. That's the pattern anyway."

"Have you called a doctor?"

Jack nodded. "Her doctor in New York. He's the only one she trusts."

"Not Dr. Sperry?"

"No," he said, giving her a pointed look. "She thinks he's a quack. Her doctor is taking the train up tonight."

They had reached the living room.

"Why does she think Dr. Sperry's a quack?" asked Charlotte, her mind still toying with what Frannie had told her.

"First, would you like an iced tea?"

"Yes, thank you."

Opening the sliding glass doors, Jack escorted her out to the terrace, and then retreated into the kitchen to make the iced tea.

Charlotte walked over to the railing. The view was stunning. She could look out in a direct line over the red awning, the phoenix fountain, and the gravel path that bisected the esplanade to the flag flying over the High Rock Pavilion, which lifted itself now and again with the breath of the rising wind. From the peak of the pavilion, the line continued straight as an arrow to the steps leading up to the spa quadrangle, and beyond the steps to the reflecting pool and the Hall of Springs, which stood against a backdrop of dark pines and smoky mountains. A leitmotiv of geometric shapes, echoed by the shadows created by the afternoon sun and accented by a procession of symmetrical arches and columns. Seldom had she known architecture to create such a feeling of restfulness and order, such a unity of form and function. Its formalism and regularity stood in stark contrast to the chaotic world that lay outside its borders. Or rather, she thought with irony, the chaotic world that had once lain outside its borders.

After a few minutes, Jack returned with a tray, which he set down on a patio table shaded by a red canvas awning and surrounded by flowering shrubs and plants in terra-cotta pots. Charlotte could easily see why this terrace had made the High Rock penthouse one of Paulina's favorite residences. Jack handed her an iced tea and took a seat. "Why does Paulina consider Sperry a quack. Well, for one thing, he's not a doctor: he claims to have a British medical degree, but all he's actually got is a mail-order degree from some homeopathic institute in India that's long since gone under. For another . . ." He paused. "Have you ever heard of cell therapy?"

"Yes. Injections of sheep cells, or something—it's supposed to make you young. I'm hoping you're going to tell me it works," she said lightly.

Jack gave her a skeptical look.

Charlotte smiled. In her day, she'd seen a host of rejuvenating crazes come and go: orgone boxes, chlorophyll tablets, grape cures, royal jelly—she was equally skeptical of them all. When it came to rejuvenation, she was in Paulina's camp: what kept you young was hard work, work you love.

"Injections of cells from the embryos of pregnant sheep, to be precise. It's a big thing with celebrities. I daresay you know someone who's had the treatments." He rattled off a list of names of famous writers, artists, politicians, members of royalty, and heads of state.

"I've heard of the treatments, yes," said Charlotte.

"They're given at a posh clinic in Switzerland. It's on Lake Geneva. Anyway, the patients stay a week at a cost of something like six thousand dollars." He paused. "Except that they no longer have to fly to Switzerland . . ."

Charlotte completed his sentence: ". . . because Dr. Sperry's giving the treatments here."

Jack nodded. "One difference. In Switzerland, they use fresh cells; he uses dried. He claims they're only slightly less effective. They're smuggled in through the Bahamas. They're sent to a patient of his in the Bahamas who sends them to a patient of his in New York who sends them to High Rock."

"So it's not legal," said Charlotte, knowing it wasn't.

"No-o-o. It's strictly a word-of-mouth operation. He got started in the U.K., where the laws are less stringent. When he came here, he started treating the Americans he'd been treating in London. What started as a favor turned into a full-fledged business. He calls his treatments Body Servicing."

"I hear he had quite a reputation for that," said Charlotte dryly.

Jack threw back his head and laughed. "Yes, he does."

"Does Paulina know?"

"Of course. As you know, having been recently drafted into her intelligence service, she has her spies everywhere. That's one of the reasons she brought in Elliot to replace him as spa director. She was planning to ease him out gradually. Now of course his departure will be more precipitant."

First Frannie, now Jack. Charlotte decided to see what else she could find out about Dr. Sperry's illegal operation.

There was a lapse in the conversation as they drank their iced tea. The sun had vanished. In the distance, the sky had turned a menacing gray, and dark clouds were massing over the mountains.

"Speaking of Paulina's firing people. All the other secretaries I've known were fired within a few months, sometimes only a few weeks. I'm curious as to how you've managed to stick it out for four years."

"I haven't," Jack replied. "I've been sent to publicity at least three times and banished to Siberia—that's what we call the Houston office—twice. But she always takes me back, just like she does her son."

"Is she going to take him back this time?"

"I don't know. She's threatened to disinherit him before, but she's never done it. But she's never asked me to call the estate lawyer before either. I had to cancel that. She's obviously in no condition to see him."

"Do you think she might forget the whole thing?"

"Maybe, maybe not. I just know that I better damned well have scheduled another appointment because if she still has it in for Elliot when she comes around, there'll be hell to pay if I haven't."

"It must be a demanding job," sympathized Charlotte.

"To be more precise, it's a bitch. I'm on call twenty-four hours a day—usually. Over the past couple of days, I've had a little vacation. Or rather, it would be a vacation if I wasn't worrying about her."

"Why have you stayed?" she asked. But it was clear he thought a lot of his boss. If she could be imperious and domineering, she could also be merry and warm. And one could hardly expect a woman who had single-handedly built one of the world's largest companies to be refined and demure.

"I don't know," Jack replied. He displayed the sole of a hand-sewn loafer, which was dotted with circles made up of concentric rings, like the rings of a tree. "If I have to have these shoes resoled one more time, there won't be anything left of them."

"So it's not the pay." The image of Jack as an oppressed laborer wasn't very convincing anyway. He struck her as savvy enough to take every advantage of his position, holes in his shoes notwithstanding.

"No. It's the glamour I guess. I've grown accustomed to it:

the travel, the luxurious surroundings, the celebrities . . ." He gestured at her. "It's pretty hard to give up, even if I'm nothing but a glorified lackey."

Charlotte thought of the Matisse in his bedroom. Hard to give up, for someone with his refined tastes. She looked at him sympathetically. "I hope you're going to have a queen to be a glorified lackey to."

"That makes two of us," he said, a look of concern crossing his handsome face.

A stiff wind had sprung up, turning it inhospitably cool. The flag, which had been flying desultorily over the pavilion, now stood straight out from its staff. It looked as if they were in for a sudden change of weather.

Thanking Jack for the tea, Charlotte said good-bye and left.

· 8 ·

CHARLOTTE HELD OUT her cup under the stream of water that spouted from the horn of a Triton at Ainsworth's Favorite Spring. Sipping it, she found it tasted faintly briny, like Alka-Seltzer. Her brochure said it was recommended for stomach upset, as well as for hangovers.

Ainsworth's Favorite was the fourth spring on her walking tour of the springs of High Rock Spa.

She had slept hard the night before and had awakened feeling dopey and lethargic. But Frannie had led her to expect that; it would be the second day before she would feel the invigorating effects of the shiatsu massage. Her mood was matched by the weather. The clouds that had been hanging over the mountains had moved in, cloaking the spa in a dank, dismal shroud of gray. She had managed to struggle through Terrain Cure, the lone member of C-group. But instead of taking exercise class, she had returned to the Vale of Springs for the walking tour. She felt as if she needed a walk to regain her balance, to put her thoughts back in order. She preferred to take her exercise in the form of walking anyway, its virtue being that you could both exercise and think at the same time. Instead of occupying your mind with the agony of aching ankles or searing lungs, you could throw it an old problem to chew on. More often than not, it would favor you with a solution. *Solvitur ambulando*, the medieval philosophers had called it: a problem that is solved by walking.

As she had expected, the recent deaths had retreated from their disquieting position at the forefront of her mind, which was now occupied by the simple task of locating the springs.

In fact, her low spirits had given way to the sanguine expectancy of a child at a treasure hunt. The route of "A Walking Tour of the Springs of High Rock Spa," as her brochure was called, followed the banks of Geyser Stream, on either side of which were located many of the springs. At intervals, the route crossed the stream over rustic footbridges from which one could look out over the rushing waters. From Ainsworth's Favorite, she turned to the Elixir Spring, which issued from a twin fountain less than a yard away. Again, she filled her cup from the horn of the Triton. But the water of the Elixir Spring, which the brochure described as "a fine table water of high mineral content, lightly sparkling," was sweet and clear. Despite the fact that the springs were located only a few feet from one another, their waters were totally different. It was one of the mysteries of the spa that each spring had its own taste, its own chemical composition, and its own therapeutic effects. The educated palate, the brochure said, could distinguish the waters of one from those of another.

Wary of the highly touted purgative effects of the mineral waters, Charlotte had drunk sparingly from the springs she had visited so far. But at the Elixir Spring, she drank deeply, prompted by the century-old claim that Elixir water gave "strength and courage to the mind." They were virtues that present circumstances put her in need of. Continuing along the route, she came suddenly upon a spring that shot ten feet into the air from the center of a stone well in a picturesque glade. This was the Champion Spouter, another of High Rock's famous spouting springs. At the hiss of the eruption, Charlotte felt a shiver run up her spine. It was easy to see why the ancients had been inspired to build temples at such springs: there was something faintly supernatural about waters that shot out of the ground of their own volition. She was struck by the similarity of the ancient Greek spas to their modern counterparts. The ancient Greeks had also sought to create an environment that was removed from the everyday world. In their cure, the sick took sanctuary in the temple for the night. In their dreams, they were visited by Asclepius, who prescribed drugs, baths, or diets. Miraculous cures were effected. The visitation from the God triggered the body's disease-fighting resources—a concept that wasn't all that different from Anne-Marie's notion of creating an environment in which "our bad habits give us up."

The next spring was the Old Red or Beauty Spring, which was recommended for the skin. It was mineral water from the Old Red Spring that was the chief ingredient in the Body Spa line. In fact, the water was probably pumped to the bottling plant from the cement block structure that stood nearby. The spring was covered by an ornate pavilion, evidence of its historical importance. For a hundred years, spa-goers had been visiting this spring for their rashes and complexions. On impulse, Charlotte splashed some water on her face. As Paulina was fond of saying, "Who knows? It might do some good." Like the waters of High Rock Spring, the waters of the Old Red were high in magnesium. And radium: the Old Red was one of the springs that had been cited in the radium report. On the lintel of the pavilion were painted the now-ironic words: "Clear and transparent are these precious fonts as purest water of the pebbled brook." Beneath the lintel, a sign warning of the radium danger recommended limiting consumption to one glass per week.

The sign brought Charlotte back to the radium controversy. Incited by the Mineral Man and the mayor, the townspeople were up in arms. It seemed to Charlotte that they would be wiser to simply let the issue fade away, but they were deeply offended by the slur against the purity of their waters. Again, she found herself thinking of *An Enemy of the People*. Tom had discovered that it was an investment bank that had been behind the press release. From this, Charlotte had concluded that the radium rumor was connected with the takeover. Perhaps Gary had hired the investment bank to orchestrate the deal. The bank might have planted the rumor in order to depress the price of Langenberg stock. But there was a major flaw with her *An Enemy of the People* theory, which was that by damaging the reputation of High Rock's mineral waters, Gary was also damaging that of his own product. But perhaps he thought he could redeem the reputation of High Rock water, just as the townspeople in Ibsen's play had believed the doctor could redeem the reputation of the baths. Hadn't Gary said as much to the *Society* reporter at the fete?

From the Old Red, Charlotte followed the route down a

ferny ravine to the base of the Vale of Springs. A few minutes
later, she emerged at the Island Spouter. Crossing over the
footbridge, she took a seat on the bench where she had sat with
Art only two days before. She had been avoiding dealing with
the subject of the recent deaths. But it was again pushing its
way to the forefront of her mind. She had gone from feeling
numbed to feeling angry. Adele and Art had both died in the
bathhouse guarded by a beneficent Asclepius whose snake-
entwined scepter was a symbol of man's ability to shed disease
the way a snake sheds its skin. The scepter had now been
raised twice over a scene of death. She wanted to find out who
was responsible, who had violated their sanctuary. The walk
had refreshed her, had given her strength and courage of mind.
Or maybe it was the Elixir water. Bending over, she retied her
shoelaces. At her feet, an arrow-shaped sign pointed uphill:
"High Rock Hotel—.5 Miles." Only five days before she
would have had to take the hill at a slow walk with frequent
pauses. Now she was able to take it at a brisk walk without
stopping. Tomorrow she would graduate to the next grade, an
accomplishment that would earn her a merit pin for her sweat
suit. Such was progress. She straightened up and set off. She
wanted to check in on Paulina before lunch.

The words hit her the minute she entered Paulina's bedroom.
"She was there," said Paulina, pointing at Charlotte with the
sandwich she held in one hand. "She'll tell you what I say is
true."

A much-recovered Paulina was holding court. It was just as
Jack had said; on the third day, she had risen again. She sat
cross-legged (a position remarkable for an eighty-year-old
woman) at the side of her Chinese bed, swaddled in a white
cotton blanket under which she was still wearing the cotton
duster. Her back was to the opening in the latticework railing,
where a young woman in the red smocked uniform of the
Paulina Langenberg salons stood brushing her long, blue-black
hair. A tray holding a plate with the rest of the sandwich and
a bottle of mineral water sat next to her on the bed. She was
conducting business: her black-framed reading glasses hung
from a chain around her neck and her lap was full of papers.
The man to whom she spoke sat in a chair at her back, while

Leon stretched out like an indolent pasha in a chaise longue at the foot of the bed, flipping through the pages of a fashion magazine. Charlotte noticed he was wearing turquoise socks with his conservative gray suit. Were the socks a grudging concession to the flamboyant nature of the beauty industry, or the one expression of exuberance in an otherwise inhibited personality? she wondered.

Jack introduced Charlotte to the stranger, who was a Mr. Bates of Schweppe, Marsden, and Fitt, a New York law firm. Charlotte realized that he must be the estate lawyer, The One with the Blond Wife.

"Come here. Sit," ordered Paulina. She gestured with the sandwich to a chair on the opposite side of the bed.

Charlotte complied. She could smell the sandwich; it was corned beef, and it smelled delicious, as she would expect it to after having had nothing but vegetables, fish, and lean meat to eat for five days.

"Now tell him," ordered Paulina. She nodded over her shoulder at the lawyer, and then proceeded to wolf down the sandwich.

"Tell him what?"

"What Sonny said."

Charlotte hesitated, reluctant to involve herself in the family row.

"Never mind," said Paulina, waving her arm in dismissal. She picked up the rest of the sandwich. "I've got to keep my strength up. I've had a terrible shock." She washed down the sandwich with a swig of mineral water and then reached over for a dill pickle. "I am prostate with grief."

"Pros*trate*, Aunt Paulina," said Leon, looking up from his magazine.

"Prostrate," she repeated.

It was one of Paulina's more endearing traits that despite more than sixty years as an inhabitant of English-speaking countries, she had yet to master the English language. Her speech was riddled with malapropisms.

"So you've come to see me," she said, biting into the pickle. "A poor old woman, betrayed by her own son."

Her voice was weak and tremulous. Despite the fact that she was up, she didn't look well. Even her expertly applied

makeup couldn't camouflage the fact that her usually sharp
eyes were dull and were hung with violet circles. Frannie
would have said that her aura was dim and shriveled. In color,
it would be gray, the color of diminished life force. Or maybe
a dark, dull red, the color of discord and vengefulness. For she
was seething with rancor. According to Jack, she had spent the
morning recounting the tale of Elliot's betrayal to a string of
subordinates who had been summoned to appear before her.

"Yes," replied Charlotte. "I was here yesterday too. It looks
as if you're feeling much better."

"Not much. A little. Not so hard," she chided the girl who
was brushing her hair. "Gently." She returned her attention to
Charlotte. "I was just telling Mr. . . . ."—she directed her
glance over her shoulder to Mr. Bates—"about Sonny. He
called me a despicable old woman." Her eyes misted over.
"Do you believe it?" She continued, her self-pity metamor-
phosing into outrage: "His own mother." Setting down the
sandwich, she reached into her pocket and pulled out a
crumpled ball of paper. "His exact words," she announced,
turning to face the lawyer. She unfolded the ball of paper and
read: " 'You're a despicable old woman, always manipulating
people with your money. That's all you care about—money.'
She returned the piece of paper to her pocket. "You see?" She
turned to Charlotte. "Tell him. Isn't that what Sonny said?"

"That's what he said."

Paulina snorted. " 'All I care about is money.' If I didn't care
about it, who would?" She resumed eating, polishing off the
other half of the sandwich. Then she replaced her glasses on
her nose and picked up the papers in her lap. "Where were we?
I'm disinheriting my son," she said. "I'm glad you're here. We
can use you. We need another witness." She went on to
explain that the document in her hands was the official copy of
her will, which had been stored in her lawyer's vault. Her
black notebook, which lay open on Mr. Bates's pin-striped
knees, was the working copy. She was now making the
changes in the official copy that she had already made in the
working copy.

"We're still on real estate, but after that we're finished,"
replied Mr. Bates, a round-faced man whose jolly countenance
seemed at odds with his choice of profession. He leafed

through the notebook. "Let's see. We've finished with the apartment in Paris, the flat in London, and the villa at St. Jean-Cap Ferrat. I guess we're on American real estate. We've done the Palm Beach mansion. Next would be the Greenwich estate. Page twenty-eight."

Paulina read: "Should my son"—she crossed out the word "son" and inserted the word "nephew"—"Elliot B. Langenberg"—here she crossed out Elliot's name and substituted Leon's—"survive me, I give to him . . ." She went on to describe the Greenwich estate, a Norman-style mansion overlooking Long Island Sound, and then initialed the change in the margin of the document, which was about forty pages thick and bound with a red satin ribbon.

Charlotte was familiar with the procedure as a result of making changes in her own will. For the time being, the changes would be recorded in longhand. If the changes were to be typed in, the new typeface wouldn't match the old, a difference that could provide grounds for the will's legitimacy to be challenged. Although it seemed like an antiquated way of doing things, its purpose was to deter any suspicion that the will had been tampered with.

"What about the Park Avenue triplex?" asked Mr. Bates.

"That too," said Paulina, making the changes. "Everything to Leon." Looking up, she smiled at him indulgently. "Sonny gets zilch."

"Shouldn't we leave him something, Aunt Paulina?" asked Leon. "He *is* your son. What about Palm Beach?"

Paulina dismissed the suggestion with a wave of her hand. "If he wants real estate, he can buy it himself. He's got plenty of money." She reconsidered. "No, you're right. He may have plenty of money now, but if I know him, he won't have it for long. We'll leave him an annuity. Five thousand a year—so he won't starve." She addressed the lawyer: "Make it so he's paid quarterly. Otherwise he'll spend it all at once."

Five thousand a year—it wasn't even enough to keep him from starving; it was only enough to be an insult, Charlotte thought. But she kept her mouth shut and looked out at the golf course. From this height, she could see all eight of the pump houses that supplied the water for the baths. It had started to rain, a cold, steady downpour. The trees lining the fairways swayed in the wind, their light green leaves displaying their pale undersides to the sky.

The hair stylist had finished brushing Paulina's hair and was now plaiting it deftly into a thick, glossy braid. When she had finished, Paulina swung around to face the edge of the bed, disengaged her legs, and lowered her feet onto an antique stepping stool, her legs being too short to reach the ground. From the drawer of the bedside table, she withdrew a tube of lipstick, which she pressed into the girl's hand. Then she dismissed her.

The girl thanked Paulina and headed toward the door.

"Wait," said Paulina. She pushed the tail of the turtle buzzer.

Jack appeared at the door.

"Jack, let me see those." She nodded to a fresh bouquet of red roses that stood next to the bouquet that Charlotte had noticed the day before. The old bouquet was now looking slightly wilted.

Jack brought over the roses and set them on the bedside table.

Reaching over, Paulina pulled out the card, read it, and crumpled it up. "Give them to her," she ordered Jack. "I don't want to be reminded of my traitorous son. Are the others from him too?"

Jack nodded.

"Throw them away."

Jack handed the girl the fresh vase of roses.

"They're Paulina Langenberg roses," said Paulina proudly. "They're named after me. If you're important enough, you get a rose named after you—Queen Elizabeth, Baroness Rothschild." She didn't mention That Woman.

The girl, who didn't quite know what to make of it all, and who seemed somewhat nervous in the royal presence, thanked her and left.

"Can you imagine? No makeup! A pretty girl like that," said Paulina after the girl had gone. "Jack, tell her I insist that all Langenberg employees wear makeup. Set up a lesson for her, and make sure she gets some free samples. If she still insists on not wearing makeup, get rid of her."

Jack pulled out his leather notebook and made a notation.

Paulina then turned to the jolly-faced Mr. Bates and asked if he was still married. When he replied with a mystified "yes," Paulina again reached over to the drawer and withdrew a tube of lipstick. "Blush Pink: it's from our new Body Spa line," she explained. "It will be very nice on your lovely wife."

For as long as Charlotte had known Paulina, she had rewarded subordinates with a lipstick: beauticians, waiters, estate lawyers—it made no difference. The fact that a lipstick didn't carry the same value as it had fifty years before hadn't yet occurred to her. To her way of thinking a Paulina Langenberg lipstick would always be a gift to treasure.

The lawyer thanked Paulina and pocketed the lipstick with a little smirk. Paulina's gratuities were probably the joke of his office.

Paulina then returned her attention to the will, reviewing the pages one by one. When she was finished, she turned to Mr. Bates. "Okay," she said. "I'm ready. I just sign?"

"Aunt Paulina, do you think he'll challenge it?" asked Leon.

"Leon, you're always looking for trouble."

"I know it's not likely, but what if he does?"

"What's to challenge? I have three witnesses right here to declare I'm not a crazy." She turned to Mr. Bates. "Isn't that right?"

"I don't see any grounds on which this will could be challenged," he concurred. "You're under no obligation to leave anything to your son. It's always wise to say that's what you're doing so that it's not considered an oversight, but we've done that." He read from the document: " 'For good and sufficient reasons, I make no provision for my son Elliot, and it is my wish that he not share in my estate in any way, with the exception of the annuity that I have provided for him.' But," Mr. Bates added, "people always try."

"So he can try. He'll just be throwing his money away. As usual." Paulina read aloud from the will: " 'I, Paulina L. Langenberg,' " she said solemnly, " 'the testator, sign my name to this instrument on this sixteenth day of June, et cetera, and do hereby declare that I sign and execute this instrument as my will and that I sign it willingly, that I execute it as my free and voluntary act for the purposes therein expressed, and that

I am eighteen years of age or older, of sound mind, and under no constraint or influence.'" With that, she signed. But although she did so with a great deal of flourish, Charlotte detected a twinge of regret in her expression.

Taking the document from Paulina, Mr. Bates carried it over to a table, where he initialed each of the twenty-odd changes and instructed Charlotte and Jack to do the same. Then they each affixed their signatures to the document, also making a declaration as to their identities and to the fact that Paulina was of sound mind and under no influence. Finally, the lawyer fixed the red ribbon that bound the pages with a drop of sealing wax, into which he pressed the firm's seal. The amended will would not be as good as retyping the entire document, but it would serve as a model for the new document and as a reflection of Paulina's wishes in the unlikely event that she should die before the new document could be prepared.

"I now pronounce you testate," said Mr. Bates. With that, he shook Paulina's hand and put the official copy away in his briefcase.

The deed was done.

Paulina held the black notebook out to Jack. "Jack, please put this back in the cabinet." Reaching into her bosom, she withdrew the key. "One more thing. We need a new spa director. I've decided to make the director of the men's baths—The Italian One with the Muscles—acting spa director."

"Jerry D'Angelo?"

"Yes. The guests like him. I like him. A nice family man. A former policeman—that can come in handy. Tell him it's only temporary, but we'll see how it works out. We'll have to find another medical director too. Start looking around. Did My Mistake get his walking papers yet?"

"Not yet."

"Make sure he gets them on Monday. I want him out," she said as Jack headed toward the glass vitrine. "And while you've got that unlocked, get out a couple of jars of caviar. And then get some crackers and a couple of bottles of champagne from the kitchen. We're going to have a celebration."

Displayed on the lighted glass shelves of the vitrine was an

improbable collection of articles: only in an apartment of
Paulina's would one find a Lalique vase, a horned black
African fetish, and a replica of the Statue of Liberty intermin-
gled with a dozen cans of gourmet food.

"It's safer there," Paulina explained as she noticed Charlotte
eyeing the jars of blanched asparagus and cans of pâté de foie
gras. "If I didn't lock it up these freeloaders would eat me out
of house and home."

Unlocking the cabinet, Jack replaced the notebook on a shelf
next to a jade bowl and withdrew two jars of beluga caviar.

Gravel Gertie would have been envious.

Paulina then turned to Leon: "Now that I've made you my
heir, there's something I want you to do. *Get married!* I want
you to pass the business along to your children. There are lots
of nice girls out there looking for rich husbands. Forty-eight,
and still a bachelor!"

"Yes, Aunt Paulina," said Leon.

"Good." Business concluded, Paulina switched to the subject of movies. Movies were her favorite form of relaxation,
she said. She often went to Times Square to catch the latest
releases. With the blanket draped around her shoulders and her
hair in a braid, she looked like an Indian squaw in a B-grade
western. She was curious about the makeup used in Charlotte's
most recent movie, in which she was made to look as if she'd
aged dramatically.

But before Charlotte could reply, Jack appeared at the door
in the company of a tall, distinguished-looking man in an
immaculately tailored suit. He had a round, balding head and
a dark, handsome face. He was introduced as Dr. Aldo
Castelli, Paulina's personal physician.

"Good morning, Doctor," said Paulina. She waved an arm
at the assembly in her room. "We're having a celebration."

"I see," said Dr. Castelli. Nodding hello to the group, he
crossed the room and took a seat on the edge of the bed. Taking
Paulina's hand in his, he raised it to his lips. "I am very happy
to see that *la bella signora* is feeling better." He spoke with a
smooth Italian accent.

Paulina, whose various personalities ranged from raging
termagant to shrewd businesswoman to benevolent empress,
now revealed still another side of her character: the flirtatious

coquette. "Much better," she replied, batting her heavily mascaraed eyelashes, "Thanks to you, Doctor."

"No, madam," protested Dr. Castelli, "it is the patient who does the work of healing." His expression took on a look of concern. "I'm very pleased that you're feeling up to entertaining. But I want to make certain you're completely well. I'd like you to undergo a complete battery of tests."

Paulina gave him an uncooperative look. It was clear she didn't want to take the time to have a physical exam.

"Besides," he added, "I've come all the way up from New York to take care of you. We want to make the trip worthwhile, do we not?"

Dr. Castelli was a shrewd student of patient psychology. If flattery didn't convince Paulina, getting her money's worth surely would.

He took her hand in his. "Will you do this for me?"

She capitulated. "Whatever you say, Doctor."

"Thank you, madam," he said with a little bow. "I've already taken the liberty of making an appointment for you at High Rock Hospital. Will this afternoon be all right?"

"Yes, yes," she replied, impatient with the specifics. "Now, Doctor," she said, "will you join us for some champagne?"

Charlotte had been hoping for a few minutes alone with Paulina. Now that she was feeling better, Charlotte felt an obligation to fill her in on Art's death and on what she'd discovered about the radium story. But it was obvious that her opportunity wouldn't come today.

Jack had reappeared with the caviar and the champagne, which he was now pouring. As he handed her a glass, Charlotte decided she would leave the task of informing Paulina of Art's death up to him, since he seemed to make a specialty of breaking unpleasant news.

"What are we celebrating?" asked Dr. Castelli.

"I have disinherited my son," Paulina announced.

The doctor frowned. "I am afraid, signora, that I do not consider such a matter a cause for celebration, if only because the rift with your son has caused you such anguish." He smiled. "But I am always happy to drink to the continued good health of one of my most glamorous patients."

Paulina grinned.

"You may not consider it a cause for celebration, Dr. Castelli, but I do," said Leon. He raised his glass in a toast. "Cheers."

"Cheers," said Paulina.

Following her bath that afternoon, Charlotte headed over to the Health Pavilion for an herbal wrap. She remembered Adele's comment that it had made her feel as if she were being buried alive, and wondered what she was in for. But she found it to be, if not a quasi-mystical experience, a delightful one. After being anointed with a sweet-smelling herbal lotion, she was wrapped, mummylike, in warm linen sheets and ordered to rest while the herbs penetrated her skin. And so she had, to the sweet strains of a Mozart concerto. After an hour, the therapist had returned to unwrap her. To her amazement, she had emerged from her linen cocoon with skin as smooth and silky as a newborn's.

She was changing when her ears were assailed by a twangy, high-pitched voice with an unmistakable West Texas drawl: "Charlotte!" it shrieked. It was Mary Jane Jacoby, also known as M.J., the wife of the producer of several of Charlotte's movies. M.J. was not one of Charlotte's favorite people. She was the kind of person who offended by virtue of her sheer stupidity. She simply didn't have brains enough to be tactful. And if not by virtue of her stupidity, by virtue of her insufferable good humor. Never had Charlotte known her to complain, to suffer, to regret: she faced the world with the mindless good cheer of the mental defective.

Turning, Charlotte saw M.J. gliding across the locker room. Or rather, an apparition of M.J.: her chin was locked in place by an elastic chin strap and her round, childlike face was covered by the spa's Black Gold mud pack, the chief ingredient of which was purportedly the same mineral-rich Dead Sea mud that had been prized by Cleopatra (but which Charlotte suspected came from Paulina's Long Island City factory). Only M.J.'s vacant baby-blue eyes and her large, expertly capped teeth showed through the black goo.

"How are ya, honey?" She gripped Charlotte by the shoulders and pecked the air on either side of her face in a Hollywood embrace. In her chin strap and spa-issue white terry-cloth robe and turban, she looked like a swami with a toothache. Or rather, a swami with a toothache who had been playing with matches. On her hands, she wore large, pink, bandagelike mittens.

"Fine," replied Charlotte. "M.J., what are those on your hands?"

"Electric warming mits, honey." She raised her forearms to display the battery packs strapped to her wrists. "They help the moisturizer penetrate the skin. I usually wear 'em just at night, but I figure I might as well wear 'em as much as I can while I'm here."

"I see," said Charlotte, raising an eyebrow.

She suddenly remembered that it was because of people like M.J. that she had always avoided spas. M.J., in fact, could be called a spa groupie: she was one of those rich women with nothing better to do than traipse around from one expensive spa to another in search of eternal youth.

"Now don't you go makin' fun of me, Charlotte Graham," M.J. chided. "When you get to be our age, you need all the help you can get. Speakin' of which, you never told me you were gettin' the treatments. I should have known. No one could look as good as you do and not be gettin' some help."

"What treatments?"

"Cell therapy." M.J. stared at her in disbelief. "You mean, you're not here for the treatments?"

Charlotte shook her head.

"Well, I declare. I thought that's why everybody came here. Of course, this is nice, but why should I travel three thousand miles when I have a whole bunch of spas right at home in California. I'm talkin' about cell therapy, honey. Youth, rejuvenation." She rotated her hips. "Sex-u-al vigor."

Charlotte played dumb. "I thought cell therapy was only available in Switzerland."

"Oh, no. You can get the treatments right here. Dr. Sperry gives 'em." She lowered her voice. "It's cheaper here too. Of course, it's all on the q.t.—the U.S. hasn't approved cell therapy yet. When it comes to anything healthy, you can count on us bein' way behind the rest of the world . . ."

"If it's illegal, how does he get away with it?"

"He only takes patients who've been personally referred.

That way he can be pretty sure they're not goin' to give him trouble. But listen, honey, there's absolutely nothin' wrong with it. They've been using cells for years in Europe. And it works: that's why I look so young." She laughed.

Preserved, was more like it. M.J.'s face had been lifted so many times that it looked as if it would rupture if she assumed any expression other than her perennial ear-to-ear smile.

"If you're interested, I can ask Dr. Sperry to take you on."

"Actually, I was just on my way up to see him for my checkup."

"Why, that's perfect. I'll just call upstairs right this very minute and tell him you're a good friend of mine."

"Thanks."

"Believe me, you won't regret it. I feel a million times better since I started. Irwin does too; it's done wonders for our sex life." She gave Charlotte a dig in the ribs. "Maybe it'll spice yours up a little too."

"I doubt that," said Charlotte dryly.

"Oh, I forgot," said M.J., raising a mittened hand to her lips. "You got rid of Jack Lundstrom, didn't you?"

Unfortunately, the chin strap wasn't enough to stop M.J.'s wagging tongue. "I think it was the other way around," she replied.

M.J. was referring to Charlotte's fourth husband, who had divorced her a few years before. He was a successful business-man who had expanded the family manufacturing company into a multinational conglomerate. She'd always thought she'd find happiness with a man whose achievements matched her, but in a different field. But it hadn't worked out. He hadn't wanted to be Mr. Charlotte Graham. He had wanted someone to decorate his houses and serve as his hostess. But they had parted amicably and remained friends.

M.J. giggled. "That's right. These men—none of 'em can stand livin' in a woman's limelight. I'm sorry, honey, but you go through 'em so fast I can't keep up with you."

In fact, Charlotte had been married for ten years to her second husband, and would probably be married to him still if he hadn't died of a heart attack when she was in her late thirties. Her first marriage, to a hometown boy, had fallen apart when she went to Hollywood. And her third, to one of her leading men, had simply been a mistake. After losing Will, she'd been lonely; he was handsome and charming. He was also a drunkard and a womanizer, but she wasn't going to waste her time explaining that to M.J.

"Anyway, the treatments will get you geared up for the next one. Listen, honey, just because we're almost old enough to collect social security doesn't mean we can't enjoy a little roll in the hay once in a while."

Charlotte had to smile.

· 9 ·

M.J. MIGHT HAVE had her failings, but she could pull the right strings. On her word, Charlotte was sitting in Sperry's office a few minutes later listening to his pitch on cell therapy. It was true she had taken advantage of M.J.'s connections, but she figured the end justified the means. She wasn't sure what she stood to gain from talking with Sperry, but he seemed as good a place to start as any. Frannie's offhand remark that it was Sperry who had been responsible for Adele's death was the only lead she had to go on, and a pretty slim one at that. Yes, Adele could have died of an allergic reaction. In fact, the chances of an adverse reaction were probably greater for someone who was taking drugs. But that didn't explain why Art had died. Nor did it explain the position of the feet. On the other hand, the fact that Sperry was among the first on the scene in both cases raised her suspicions. It reminded her of the popular wisdom that you can always find the arsonist at the scene of the fire. It was also Sperry who had first attributed Adele's death to drowning subsequent to a drug overdose.

As she listened, she wondered how to approach the subject of allergic reaction without tipping him off. At least she didn't dread this meeting the way she might have earlier in the week. Five days of mutually disagreeable spa checkups (Sperry wasn't accustomed to being rebuffed by patients who objected to his constant stream of unctuous flattery) had finally led to a bilateral agreement: she would let down her frosty guard in return for his acting more like the professional he purported to be.

As she expected, he began with "what cell therapy will do for you." According to Sperry, cells were the panacea for all the ills to which the flesh is heir. He reeled off a list of complaints. Sex life slipping? Skin wrinkling? Flesh sagging? Memory failing? Going bald? Feeling blue? Nerves strained? Overweight? Tired out? Suffering from: insomnia, stomach upset, headaches, heart disease, high blood pressure, bowel irregularities, or too small a bosom? Name a condition or disease, and Sperry's patent medicine would cure it. The only major condition he didn't mention was cancer, and that was only because he was smart enough not to invite an investigation by the authorities. His pitch reminded her of that of the European "monkey gland" doctors of the twenties who had implanted thin slices of chimp testicles into the testicles of their male patients. The treatment was supposed to restore youthfulness and renew sexual vigor. In her youth, she'd known several older actors whose putative virility was attributed to doctors who were members of the so-called "erector set."

Actually, Charlotte had no doubt that cell therapy worked. According to Sperry, its efficacy could be attested to by more than fifty thousand satisfied patients. If it didn't work, they wouldn't keep coming back. But so did the charms, prayers, and magic potions that humanity had relied on since the beginning of time. The placebo effect, modern science had dubbed it. The biochemical changes that produce the cure are triggered by simple confidence in the doctor's prescription, even when that prescription is only a sugar tablet or placebo. And what builds confidence more effectively than posh surroundings and a walloping bill? The patient who pays thousands of dollars to be told he isn't feeling up to par because his cells need rejuvenating is ninety percent cured before the injection. For Sperry's patients, there was the added incentive of getting a bargain. Instead of traveling to Switzerland, they could get their treatments right at home. Sperry's fee, which he wasn't bashful about bringing up, was two thousand dollars— cash. As he put it: "No one ever said youth was inexpensive."

Charlotte did some rough mental calculations. Figuring five patients a week, he was making ten thousand a week, or half a million a year. Quite a gold mine. The cells must cost something, but his office overhead was covered by Paulina (at

least until Jack got around to carrying out her orders). With that
rate of return, the risk was well worth taking. And what was
the risk? Injecting sheep embryo cells into the rear ends of a
few hundred wealthy youth seekers would hardly constitute the
kind of threat to the public's health that would merit a full-scale
investigation by the Food and Drug Administration. Unless—
unless someone tipped them off. If that were the case, the
chance that the tipster was a patient was greater than not: a
patient who had had an adverse reaction, a patient who was
unhappy with the results, a patient in tough financial straits—
"give me a cut of the action or I'll turn you in." Frannie's idea
that Adele had died of an adverse reaction was worth looking
into, but this was better. When it came to a motive for murder,
a threat to an income of half a million a year was a strong
motive indeed.

She returned her attention to Sperry, who was now down to
specifics. First she would undergo the preliminary treatment,
in which she would be injected with a small amount of cells,
the purpose being to accustom her immune system to the
foreign protein. She would undergo the treatment itself two
days later, on the last day of her spa visit. The treatment would
consist of an injection of five or six different kinds of cells,
depending on her needs. After the treatment, she would be
required to rest for three days. Bed rest prevented the cells
from being destroyed by muscle contraction. It also allowed
the body to recover from side effects caused by the shock of the
immune system, namely nausea and fatigue. She would also
be asked to avoid alcohol and tobacco, which could damage
the cells.

At this point, Sperry went over to a cabinet and withdrew a
glass ampule containing about half a teaspoonful of white
crystals. "This is what the cells look like," he said, handing it
to her. "This ampule contains brain cells, but it could just as
well be kidney, lung, heart, pituitary, liver, thyroid, testes, and
so on. We use about sixty varieties."

Charlotte examined the ampule. She wondered briefly if
brain cells were what M.J. was getting—if not, she could use
some. She passed it back to Sperry, who asked if she had any
questions.

"Yes. How it works."

"Oh, quite right," he said, wrinkling his nose in a smile. "How it works." He cleared his throat. "As you know, we are all composed of cells."

She could follow that much.

"Each of our cells has a genetically determined life span. When that life span is reached, the cell dies. As more and more of an organ's cells die, the organ becomes less efficient. The heart becomes less strong, the skin becomes less elastic. In other words"—he smiled—"we age."

His words were polished, but they didn't tell her much. "I'm familiar with the aging process," she said dryly.

"Indeed. Aren't we all." He smiled again, displaying his lupine teeth. He continued: "In cell therapy, we use sheep embryo cells to stimulate the regeneration of cells that have been weakened by age or disease. The patient is injected with cells that correspond to the organ whose performance has been compromised. We give kidney cells to patients with kidney trouble, heart cells to patients with heart disease, et cetera."

"Like a transplant," offered Charlotte, playing along.

"Quite right. A highly sophisticated form of transplant, actually. The cells migrate to the affected organ, where they produce a rejuvenating effect. In addition, there's an overall rejuvenating effect. We call it the 'fountain of youth' effect. Senescent body functions are reinvigorated."

At this stage in her life, thought Charlotte, she had no interest in reinvigorating her senescent body functions. The fact that they had become senescent—or at least partially so—was one consolation of her years, whatever M.J. might say about rolls in the hay to the contrary.

But she was curious nonetheless. "I'm afraid I still don't understand how the cells cause regeneration," Charlotte pressed. For all the pseudoscientific mumbo jumbo, she was none the wiser.

"On a biochemical level?"

"Something like that."

"That's a good question." Sperry stared at her blankly for perhaps ten seconds. Hadn't anyone ever asked how it worked before? Then he swiveled around in his chair and gazed thoughtfully out the window. On the wall to the side of the window Charlotte noticed an official-looking medical degree

("Honorable") from the Madras Homeopathic College. After a moment, he swiveled back. "It has to do with DNA—deoxyribonucleic acid, the cell's genetic blueprint."

Yes, she had heard of Watson and Crick.

"I'm afraid it's just too complicated for the layman to understand. Let's just say it's a secret of nature, shall we?"

Charlotte smiled. A secret of nature. Of course.

"Now," he said impatiently, "are we ready or aren't we?"

"Not quite." She wasn't going to let him off the hook yet. "One more question. I'm afraid I'm still a bit of a skeptic."

"Of course," he said solicitously. "That's entirely natural. I wouldn't want you to be anything other than completely comfortable with your decision." He wrinkled his nose. "What else would you like to know?"

"What I'm wondering is this: if cell therapy is the miracle treatment you claim it is, why isn't it accepted by the medical establishment?"

He looked exasperated. "Miss Graham," he said patronizingly, "you are a highly intelligent woman."

"You make that sound unusual," she parried.

Ignoring her, he went on: "I needn't tell you that some of the greatest achievements of science have taken place outside of the scientific establishment." In tones of solemn reverence, he invoked the pantheon of modern science: Galileo, Darwin, Pasteur. It was clear he included himself in this august company. "Nothing's changed," he continued. "The real geniuses still have to buck the establishment. Look at Jonas Salk." He leaned back, warming to his subject. "But when it comes to impeding scientific progress, the government is even worse than the scientific establishment, especially in this country. The U.S. Food and Drug Administration is the most backward drug regulatory agency in the world. Look at cell therapy: it's been approved in six countries." He ticked them off on the tips of his fingers. He leaned forward earnestly. "But not in the U.S. The tragedy is, when the FDA withholds approval of a treatment as valuable as cell therapy, they are compromising the health of the American public."

Charlotte thought he was overstating his case. Cell therapy hardly lent itself to implementation on a mass scale. Each town would need its own flock of sheep and its own private abattoir.

"I know what I'm doing is against the law," Sperry continued more calmly, "but that's the price I pay for being a pioneer. But," he added, "you didn't come here to listen to my sermonizing. Any other questions?"

"Yes. Is there any danger associated with cell therapy? Side effects? Adverse reactions?"

"Good question. I've already mentioned the side effects: nausea, fatigue. As for danger, there's very little. Whenever a foreign substance is injected into the body, there's the risk of an allergic reaction. But that risk is very small. One in a million, if that."

"What if that were to happen?"

"Oh, it usually happens immediately. We'd just give the patient a shot of adrenaline—it would fix them right up."

"That's reassuring," she said. Scratch that idea.

"Well, are you ready to take the plunge?"

"I guess so."

"Good. I can assure you that you won't regret it." He opened his desk drawer and pulled out an appointment book.

Charlotte's eyes casually followed Sperry's tanned hand to the imitation leather cover of the spiral-bound notebook, and then stopped. The appointment book might be a clue. If Adele or Art had threatened to turn Sperry in or had demanded a piece of the action (hadn't Adele said she was hard up?), they must have been his cell therapy patients. And if that were the case, their names would be in his book. She knew she was grasping at straws. But at least there were straws to grasp at. If they had threatened his income, they probably did so in person. Adele had seen Sperry just before she died. But what about Art? If she could see the book, she could see if Art had had an appointment on the day he died. At the least, she could get an idea of how many cell therapy patients Sperry had and therefore how much money he was making.

Sperry opened the appointment book. "How long will you be staying?"

"Until Wednesday."

"Good. Then I'll schedule your preliminary treatment for Monday and your final treatment for Wednesday."

As Sperry recorded her name in a small, neat handwriting, Charlotte wondered whether the book listed appointments for both spa and cell therapy patients or for cell therapy patients alone. If it listed appointments for both, it wouldn't tell her much; there would be no way of distinguishing one from the other. Maybe he had two appointment books, like the double books of white-collar criminals. But a scan of his desktop revealed nothing but a stack of the computer printouts that would tell the new inmates in which column their names were recorded in the giant ledger in the sky.

Having finished writing down her name, Sperry made out two appointment cards and passed them to her. Charlotte had no intention of keeping the appointments. She was only willing to go along with this up to a point.

"We can do the Reinhardt test today if you like," Sperry said. "It's a simple blood test: the Reinhardt Resistance Reaction Ferment Test. It determines which organs are malfunctioning."

"Yes, that would be fine," she replied. The Reinhardt test sounded very useful: organ not functioning fully, test tells all. She wondered why modern medicine had never heard of it.

"The fee is five hundred dollars. If you would like, you can pay me on Monday. I usually require payment in advance, but most of my patients come here with the intention of undergoing cell therapy."

In other words, with money in hand. "That's okay. I have travelers' checks. Will that be all right?"

"Fine."

She withdrew a book of travelers' checks from her handbag and proceeded to sign five one-hundred-dollar checks.

"As you know, cell therapy is illegal," Sperry continued. "For this reason, I must ask you not to discuss your treatments unless you think the person with whom you're speaking is interested in undergoing the treatments."

"I understand."

"Incidentally, if you refer a new patient to me, I'll pay you a referral fee of two hundred dollars."

"I see." That sneaky M.J., she thought. Here she was feeling guilty about taking advantage of her, when all she was after was the two-hundred-dollar kickback. She handed him the checks, which he put away in a drawer.

"Excuse me while I get the Reinhardt test ready." He stood

up. "While you're waiting, you might want to read these." He
handed her a file of clippings on "body servicing" and
disappeared into the adjoining room.

As soon as the door closed, Charlotte started riffling through
the papers on the desk. Under the stack of printouts she found
another appointment book, which meant that the one in which
he had noted her appointment was for cell therapy patients
(which explained why he kept it in his drawer). She picked up
the cell therapy book. Art had died on Thursday. She checked
the entries for that date. There it was, Arthur Dykstra, one
P.M.—one hour before he died. Heart, spleen, kidney, etc.—
he was scheduled for the works. She turned back to Monday,
the day Adele had died. She was there too, scheduled for liver,
among other things. Next to each name, there was a notation
indicating whether the patient was scheduled for the Reinhardt
test, the preliminary treatment, or the cell injection. Turning
back to the beginning of the week, she added up the Reinhardt
tests. Her earlier estimate had been way off. For the week of
June 10, there were seventeen Reinhardt tests, which meant
seventeen new patients. Almost two million a year!

She put the book back and sat down. Leaning back, she
leafed casually through the articles, which were illustrated with
tantalizing picture layouts of the posh clinic on Lake Geneva.

In a moment, Sperry returned with a trayful of test tubes
with colored tops. "I'm just going to draw some blood," he
said, pulling a rubber tourniquet out of his pocket. "It won't
hurt at all."

As Charlotte headed back downstairs a few minutes later,
she asked herself what to do. Should she go to the police on the
vague grounds that Adele and Art had been Sperry's patients?
Or should she see what other evidence she could dig up? She
decided on the latter course. She needed to know more. For
instance, an Interpol check would reveal whether Sperry had
ever been in trouble in England. Jerry could arrange that. At
the desk, a receptionist directed her to Jerry's office in the
basement. At the foot of the stairs, she found herself in a
brightly lit corridor lined with offices. The first office was
occupied by Frannie, who sat with her back to the door,
typing. She was wearing earphones over her monkey's ears.

The second office, she concluded, must be Jerry's; it had a chin-up bar across the door. It was his office, but he wasn't there. A secretary told her that he was repairing a toilet. She expected him back in an hour. Charlotte checked her watch: it was now two-thirty. She would have just enough time for a bath. Her muscles were tense, her nerves taut. Her fishing expedition in Sperry's office had taken more out of her than she had thought.

Emerging from the Health Pavilion, she descended the low steps to the lawn of the quadrangle, startling a turquoise peacock, who folded up his fan and scuttled away, dragging his elegant plumage behind him. The quadrangle was all but deserted. The heat had driven the guests to the boating concession on Geyser Lake or to the pool behind the Health Pavilion, from which she could hear the thump of the diving board followed by the splash of the divers as they hit the water. After the air-conditioned crispness of Sperry's office, the afternoon air seemed heavy, liquid. A couple of kids stood at the south edge of the reflecting pool, feeding gluey pills of white bread to the orange carp. Charlotte paused to watch. She felt a bit like the carp—as if she were swimming aimlessly, on the lookout for the morsel tossed her way by an unseen hand, the morsel that would lend sense to the blackness at the surface, a point of focus from which the recent events would radiate in concentric rings. After a few minutes, she moved on: up another set of low steps to the portico of the Bath Pavilion decorated with the relief of Asclepius.

In the women's lobby she found Hilda reading a gossip magazine. Hilda smiled broadly. Setting aside the magazine, she escorted Charlotte to her cubicle. After nearly a week, Charlotte was familiar with the routine. After changing into a robe and turban, she waited in the wicker chair while Hilda filled the tub, listening to her talk about the spa where she had worked in Budapest, a hotel spa with a marble tub in every room; four mineral water swimming pools; and dozens of treatments, one of which was a carbon dioxide bath similar to the bath at High Rock. But High Rock's water was far superior, she said. It was the best-tasting, the best for baths, and the most healthful, radium or no radium, in the world. But for the spa's menu plans—conversation with Hilda was prone to sudden shifts—she had only criticism. The idea of depriving oneself of food in the name of beauty was alien to the Hungarian soul: apart perhaps from wine, romance, and gypsy music, there was nothing as important to a Hungarian as food. Besides, a woman was intended to be soft and curvaceous. To strive to be anything else was not only denying God's will, it was denying one's womanhood. A wistful look would come over Hilda's Tartar features when she reminisced about the pastry shops of Budapest with their *linzer tortes*, lekvar cakes, and *kugelhopf*.

Another of her favorite topics was the movies. She was an avid fan of Charlotte's and of the Hollywood of the thirties and forties in general. She plied Charlotte with questions: what were the stars' houses like, what were their clothes like, what were their cars like. But there was little Charlotte could tell her that she didn't already know. For modern movies, she shared Charlotte's disdain. She hardly went to the movies at all anymore. She didn't want to see another maniac hacking another unsuspecting baby-sitter to bits or another mobster blasting away another innocent bystander. Charlotte didn't blame her. Unlike the movies of her era, which were uplifting and fun, today's movies were filled with a contempt for human values, a delight in degradation. It seemed to her that Hollywood was filled with vulgar, hateful men who used their position to force their warped vision on the public. It was true that the public went along with it, but she attributed this to the American love affair with the movies. The fact that the public turned out in droves when a good movie did come along was evidence to her of its basic good sense. But it was evidence that was lost on the moguls, most of whom had yet to figure out there was money to be made from quality, decency, and taste.

But it wasn't about the movies that Charlotte wanted to talk. Her thoughts were on Sperry. If he had killed Adele and Art, he would have had to have crossed the quadrangle, just as she had a few minutes ago. And if he had, someone would have seen him. He would have been in full view of anyone looking out a window, of anyone sitting on the terrace of the Hall of Springs. On the afternoon that Art died, dozens of people had been sitting on the terrace, Charlotte and Jerry among them. Even taking into consideration that their attention had been diverted by the Mineral Man, someone would have noticed Sperry. He might have walked under the colonnades instead of crossing the lawn, but there too he would have been readily visible. And certainly he would have been noticed in the women's wing of the Bath Pavilion.

Charlotte asked Hilda if she had noticed anyone unusual on the day of Adele's death.

"I didn't see anybody," she replied as she adjusted the spigot. "I was sitting in the lobby, knitting. When it comes time to check, I find her dead." She rolled back her head and stuck her tongue out of the side of her mouth.

Hilda had missed her calling. She had a vivid way of dramatizing her conversations.

"Is there any other entrance other than the main door? Any way that someone could have entered the building without being seen?"

"No, miss. Only the door to the sun terrace." She pointed down the hall to the door that opened onto the courtyard between the two wings. But there too Sperry would have been noticed. In good weather, the courtyard was filled with sunbathers.

"And the door to the cellar," added Hilda. She stood up.

"Hilda, do you think Mrs. Singer looked drugged?"

Hilda's face clouded over. "I don't know," she replied with uncharacteristic abruptness.

Hilda had probably already been grilled pretty thoroughly on this point. She may have felt guilty. It was probably part of her job to notice if the guests looked drugged or ill. Or maybe she *was* guilty—at the least, of not checking on Adele when she should have.

"Okay, it's ready."

Charlotte removed her robe and lowered herself into the steaming water. Hilda arranged the pillow and floated the towel on top of the water. Then she left to fetch Charlotte a glass of mineral water.

Charlotte leaned back. After nearly a week, the experience was old hat: she was no longer surprised by the depth of the tub, the tingly warmth of the water. No longer surprised, but still delighted.

Hilda returned shortly with the glass of water. Then she

asked Charlotte if the water temperature was all right, which it was. The floating bathometer read ninety-four point three.

"I come back to check you in fifteen minutes," she said. Then she shuffled out, closing the door behind her.

As she sipped the water, Charlotte tried to think back to Monday. She had heard a door closing, and footsteps. She was sure the footsteps hadn't headed toward the lobby. But where? Adele's cubicle was at the end of the corridor. Frustrated, she gave up and surrendered to the bath. Even on as hot a day as this, the water felt wonderful. Her legs floated to the surface, gleaming with a silver sheen. Tucking them into the toe hole, she was reminded of the strange position of the feet. She removed one foot from the toe hole and watched as it slowly rose to the surface. Out of curiosity, she lifted it out over the end of the tub. Then she did the same with the other foot. To accomplish this comfortably, she had to slide herself forward. But it wasn't just Adele's and Art's feet that had been hanging out, it was also their lower legs. Sliding herself farther forward, she gently eased her legs out over the end of the tub. In order to do so, she had to support her upper body with her arms. Otherwise her head would have gone under. *Otherwise her head would have gone under.* Suddenly she realized why the victims' feet had been hanging out over the end of the tub. She slid herself back to an upright position. It was simple! How stupid she had been not to have figured it out before.

Consider the problem of how to drown someone in a bathtub. Granted, such a problem is not one that ordinary people customarily give much thought to, but if they were to consider it, they would no doubt conclude that the most effective way would be to hold the victim's head underwater. If this were their conclusion, they would be wrong. The victim, who would presumably be averse to the idea of drowning, would scream, fight back—kick, scratch, strike out—thereby calling attention to the fact that someone was trying to kill him. Even if the perpetrator were successful, there would be signs of violence on the victim's body or on the murderer's, evidence of a struggle. Circumstantial evidence, to be sure, but evidence enough to raise suspicions. But what if the perpetrator sneaked up on his victim? Sneaked up on him, grabbed his ankles, and jerked his feet into the air. In a tub as deep as this one, the victim's head would be forced under-water. A little thrashing about, then silence. No struggle, no marks, no evidence—except for the fact that the victim's feet would be found hanging out over the end of the tub. It would require some strength, but not enough to exclude anyone other than a total weakling.

It was a theory anyway, a theory worth testing. Reaching over to the chair at the side of the tub, Charlotte checked her watch. It was almost three-thirty. Jerry should be back by now.

Emerging from the tub, she pulled a towel from the heated rack and dried herself off. Then she changed into her white sweat suit. On the way out, she explained to Hilda that she had to cut her bath short because of an appointment. Hilda was disapproving. A bath without the rest period conferred only half the benefit. With Hilda's scolding ringing in her ears, she headed out the big bronze doors. The sun was shining through the clouds. On the terrace, the string quartet was setting up for the afternoon concert. In the women's locker room, she changed into her bathing suit. If she was going to play victim, she wanted to be decent. Then she put her sweat suit back on, stuffed a bathing cap into her pocket, and headed down to Jerry's office, where she found him fiddling with a rusty float valve.

"Toilet fixed?"

Jerry looked up and shook his head in disgust. "For the time being." He laid the part down on his desk. "Someone's got to do it, I guess." He didn't sound convinced. He invited her to sit down and then took a seat himself.

By contrast with Sperry's office, Jerry's was shabby. Paulina only spent her money where it would show. With its chin-up bar and its assortment of other athletic equipment—a push me-pull you, a jump rope, a hand grip—it looked like a high school locker room.

"Andrea told me you'd been here. What's up?"

Charlotte explained that she had a theory about how Adele and Art had died and that she wanted him to help her test it out. She was purposefully unclear. Jerry agreed and they headed back across the quadrangle. It was now close to four. The boys had gone, leaving behind an armada of soggy bread pills that had been rejected by the surfeited carp. The concert had started—the strains of Bellini's "Overture to Norma" floated across the lawn—but the terrace was emptier than usual. The lobby of the Bath Pavilion was also deserted. The only person around was Dana, who was mopping the floor. In the women's wing, they found Mrs. Murray at her station. Jerry asked to use a bath cubicle for an experiment in hydrotherapy. If Mrs. Murray had any questions, she didn't voice them. But, she said, the cubicles that weren't still occupied were being cleaned. She suggested they use the VIP suite, a large cubicle reserved for Paulina and for the wives of foreign dignitaries and the like. Escorting them down the corridor, she unlocked the door with a key from a ring that hung from the belt of her white uniform.

The VIP suite was actually two rooms. In addition to the bath cubicle, there was a well-appointed anteroom. A door opened off the anteroom to a private terrace. The fact didn't escape Charlotte that it was adjacent to the cubicle where Adele had died. Someone with access to the keys could have hidden there awaiting the opportunity to enter Adele's cubicle unobserved.

Instructing Jerry to wait in the anteroom, Charlotte went into the bath cubicle and started drawing the tub. While the tub filled, she stripped down to her bathing suit and pulled her bathing cap over her tightly wound chignon. When the tub was ready, she summoned Jerry.

Upon entering, he let out a low whistle. "Not bad," he said, boldly eyeing Charlotte's figure.

"For an old lady," she said, smiling.

In fact, Charlotte was quite vain about her figure. It was true that her flesh sagged a bit around her knees and that it hung heavy on the backs of her arms (her so-called bat wings), but time hadn't affected her high, firm bust and the long, shapely legs that had literally stopped traffic in a famous scene from one of her movies.

"Okay," said Jerry. "What do you want me to do? Try to kill you?"

"Drown me, to be precise," she said, lowering herself into the tub.

"How do you want me to do it?"

"That's up to you."

Once Charlotte had positioned herself, Jerry stepped up to the side of the tub. "I don't know what I'm getting myself into here."

"That's okay—I'm tough."

Suddenly Jerry was standing over her. She felt his strong arms trying to push her under, one hand on the top of her chest, the other on her head. She flattened her palms against the bottom of the tub and locked her elbows. Pushing her under in this position was impossible. Stymied, Jerry tried again, this time circling his hands loosely around her throat and pushing her backward. She cuffed him gently on the jaw with her loosely clenched fist.

"This is hard work," he said, releasing his grip. Then, trying a third time, he put his hands on her shoulders and pushed her down. Turning her head to the side, she bit his arm gently: she didn't really bite, but rather pressed her teeth into his forearm, which was enough to demonstrate that she could have bitten him hard had she wanted to.

"I give up," he said. "I'm afraid I might get hurt."

"Not so easy, is it?"

He looked at her pointedly.

"That's the purpose of this little experiment. To prove that it's difficult to forcibly drown a healthy, conscious adult woman by holding her head underwater. The same goes for a man. At least, not without some battle scars. Now," she said, repositioning herself. "We'll try it another way."

"Again?" he protested.

She nodded.

"What do you want me to do this time?"

"Stand at the foot of the tub."

Jerry complied.

"Now grab my ankles."

Reaching into the warm water, he took hold of her ankles.

"Now pull."

Jerry pulled her ankles gently. She slid forward.

"No good," she said, returning herself to her former position. "You're being too gentle. Let's try it again—this time for real. Jerk my ankles, hard. And then push them up into the air so that my head is forced underwater. As if you were forcing me to do a backward somersault."

His hands tightened around her ankles. "Okay, here goes."

Charlotte felt her legs being yanked forward. Then she felt her hamstrings stretching as Jerry pushed her legs over her head. The warm, fizzy water rushed into her nose, her mouth. A hand was holding her head under. Try as she might, she was unable to get her head above the surface. Then she felt nothing.

She had blacked out.

· 10 ·

"REFLEX VAGAL INHIBITION," Jerry said. "I should have known," he added, talking as much to himself as to her.

"What?"

He looked over at Charlotte. "In the blood vessels in the neck"—he took his hand off the wheel to point to the side of his neck—"there are sensors that regulate blood flow. When the head is jerked back like that, it sets the sensors off. The sensors send a message along the vagus nerve to the heart—that's the nerve that regulates the heartbeat. That's why you blacked out: reflex vagal inhibition." He shook his head. "Jesus!"

Charlotte glanced at him. The expression on the face that looked out over the wheel was uncharacteristically grave.

Her experiment had been a success. She was unconscious for only a few seconds, but it was enough to prove her point and to give Jerry a scare. He had been ready to start CPR. She felt fine, but Jerry was still shaken. He had suggested a drink and dinner in town. He was batching it, he explained. His wife and children were visiting her sister in Albany. Charlotte had readily accepted. Delicious as it was, she was sick of spa food.

After they left the Bath Pavilion, Charlotte had gone back to her room to change into civvies—her sweat suit was beginning to feel like army issue. Jerry had picked her up in his car a few minutes later. They were now heading down the Avenue of the Pines. A haze of humidity hung over the golf course and the pink of the evening sky was tinged a peculiar shade of yellow. It looked as if they were in for a thunderstorm.

Jerry continued: "I used to see it all the time. Especially

with husbands. They'd put their hands around the wife's neck in an argument—you know?" He took his hands off the wheel briefly to demonstrate. "The next thing they know, she's gonzo. It works the same way as a karate chop to the neck. I used to feel sorry for some of those poor guys. They didn't mean any harm. I remember one guy saying, 'She just went limp, she just went limp.'"

"Didn't mean any harm?" said Charlotte cynically. Unlike Jerry, her sympathies didn't lie with the poor husbands.

"Well, you know. They didn't mean to kill anyone." He looked over at her. "So you're one of those, huh?" Charlotte gave him one of her withering looks, to which he responded with a show of dimples. "Good thing I didn't drown you. I just thought of something else," he went on. "The CO_2 level just above the surface of the water can get pretty high. It can make a person woozy."

"Meaning what? That they wouldn't be as alert?"

"Yeah. That it would be easy for someone to sneak up on them. Occasionally clients actually pass out—that's why the attendants are supposed to check up on them every ten or fifteen minutes."

So she had been right, Charlotte thought. Hilda wasn't being evasive—she just hadn't wanted to admit to not checking up on her client as often as she should have.

Jerry continued: "In the old days, the bath attendants used to hold a chicken headfirst over the tub to demonstrate how much carbon dioxide was in the water. It was a promotion gimmick: the chicken would pass out. Then they'd take it away and it would start flapping and squawking again."

"It doesn't sound like much of an advertisement to me," said Charlotte with a grimace.

"In those days it was. The CO_2 was the big attraction. But it was different then: the clients didn't just come here for a bath—they came for the cure. It was supposed to be good for the heart."

The car pulled out onto the highway. They were following the same route that the jitney bus had taken the day before.

"What was the cure exactly?"

"A series of baths at increasing temperatures and CO_2 levels," replied Jerry. "We don't offer it anymore—it's too

time-consuming and nobody believes in it anymore anyway—
except the boss lady. She takes the complete cure every
June—three baths a day for six weeks."

"No wonder she's so hard-boiled."

Jerry laughed.

In a few minutes they had reached their destination, a
restaurant named Lillian's after Lillian Leonard. Jerry described it as a steak and brew joint and a local favorite. Inside
it was paneled with weathered barn boards and decorated with
old photographs. Many were of Lillian, whose face had been
the most photographed of her day. Among the crowd, Charlotte recognized several of her fellow inmates. She concluded
that Lillian's must rank right up there with Mrs. Canfield's as
a destination for the weak of will.

To avoid being recognized, Charlotte sat with her back to the
dining room. Her face had also been one of the most
photographed of her day and she still looked much as she had
then. Even to young people, her face was familiar from her
recent string of movies. But she would have attracted attention
in any case. Her exquisitely tailored suit and dignified bearing
stamped her with a distinction that was not often to be found
among the blue jean-clad clientele of an upstate tavern.

But although she was the object of a few curious stares, she
was not approached. Taking her seat, she found herself facing
a portrait of Lillian, the amplitude of whose figure was a
testimony to changing styles. Her bosom overflowed her dress,
her upper arms bulged over the tops of her long kid gloves, a
succession of delicate chins festooned her lovely face. It was as
if the flesh that had been displaced by her tightly strung corset
had been forced upward like toothpaste from the bottom of the
tube.

Noticing her glance, Jerry turned around to look at the
portrait. "Those were the days when men liked an armful."

"Times have changed," Charlotte replied. She found it
ironic that so-called liberated women should despise the
womanly curves that distinguished them from the opposite sex.
She was reminded of what Hilda had said, that to starve
yourself to thinness was to deny your womanhood.

"Not for me, they haven't," said Jerry with a wide smile.

"Italian men still like a little extra flesh to keep them warm at night."

"Thank God for Italian men."

He smiled. The dimples were back.

The waitress brought their drink order—a foamy pitcher of cold draught beer accompanied by a bowl of pretzels. It was a sultry night, the kind of night for drinking beer in the air-conditioned, yeasty-smelling interior of a local gin mill. And beer and pretzels certainly beat what was being offered at the spa: a weak white wine punch and a trayful of crudités. Charlotte took a long draught and settled in. She liked the company too.

"I have a toast to propose," she said. She hoisted her mug and smiled. "To the new acting spa director."

Jerry stared at her uncomprehendingly. "Who?"

"You. The One with the Muscles."

"The boss lady is making me acting spa director?"

Charlotte nodded.

He leaned back, silent. "Jesus," he said finally. "That's a surprise. I was wondering who she was going to get to replace Elliot, but I thought she'd move Sperry back up—for the time being anyway."

"Sperry's out too. Now that Anne-Marie's fallen from grace, she's decided there's no reason to keep him around anymore. Jack's supposed to be giving him his pink slip on Monday."

"Aha, the chief executioner," said Jerry. He shifted his attention from Charlotte to the room behind her. "Speak of the devil."

Turning around, Charlotte saw Leon sitting in a booth, engaged in earnest conversation. Sitting opposite him, recognizable only by the back of his head and by the hand-sewn loafer with the worn sole that protruded from the side of the booth, was Jack.

Jerry returned his attention to Charlotte. "I'm impressed by your intelligence," he said. "Now that I'm going to be a big executive, I'll need some spies. If I ever want to find out what's going on in the front office, I'll remember to give you a call."

"Anytime."

"Acting director," he repeated. "Translation: not for long. I'll bet thirty to one that Elliot's reinstated within six months. But at least I'll get a break from the toilet repair routine for a while. What does she call me, 'The One with the Muscles'?"

Charlotte nodded and smiled. "It's better than 'My Mistake,' which is what she calls Sperry."

"I guess," said Jerry.

The menu arrived. Charlotte decided on steak—after all those vegetables, she was raving for red meat—and corn on the cob, which was Lillian's specialty. Lillian Leonard was reputed to have been able to put away a dozen ears at a sitting. Neither was exactly Cuisine Minceur.

The waitress took their order and left.

"Do the police have any leads yet?" asked Charlotte, returning to the subject uppermost in her mind. As she had foreseen, the police had been pressured by the press to upgrade the case to a homicide investigation on the basis of the similarity in the positions of the bodies.

Jerry replied that they had completed all the routine tasks: checked the registers at High Rock Hotel and at the other hotels, combed the buildings and grounds, interviewed the guests and employees who'd been at the scene, checked the license plates of the cars in the parking lot. "*Nada,*" he said.

"I might have a suspect."

"Now that you've told me how it was done, you're going to tell me who did it. Is that it?"

"Not quite."

"Who?"

"Sperry." She went on to tell him about Sperry's illegal cell therapy business, and how a threat to his profits could have provided a motive for murder. She also told him that Adele and Art had been his patients, and that both had had appointments on the days they died.

When she finished, Jerry said, "I knew about the cell therapy business. It's hard to keep secrets around here. But I had no idea he made that much money at it. Good work! You ought to go into the business. I can contribute another damning bit of evidence."

"What's that?"

"That Art Dykstra was an undercover investigator for the FDA."

"He was!" exclaimed Charlotte. "I thought he was a chemist."

"He was, but he was also an FDA investigator. He was here to investigate Sperry. Somebody had anonymously reported Sperry for the illegal practice of cell therapy. I wouldn't be surprised if it was the boss lady herself."

"Jerry, you've been holding out on me."

"Not really. There didn't seem to be any connection to the murders. Until you pointed it out."

"Art didn't have heart disease?"

"He did, but that wasn't why he was here. Or it wasn't the main reason anyway. I guess he figured he could kill two birds with one stone." He grimaced at the unintended pun. "I mean, get some cardiac rehabilitation and find out what Sperry was up to at the same time."

Charlotte sighed. Jerry's news left her more confused than ever. "How did you find this out?"

"From Crowley. He's doing a back history on Sperry now."

"Good. I was going to ask you what you could find out about him."

Dinner arrived—two juicy steaks, french fries, and corn on the cob dripping with butter. In her mind's eye, Charlotte saw an invisible hand making a black mark against her name in the giant ledger in the sky. Whatever gains she had made during her week of abstemious living would probably be wiped out by a single night of self-indulgence.

Over dinner they discussed the case. How would Sperry have gained by killing an FDA investigator? they wondered. Even if he'd gotten away with it, wouldn't the FDA have sent someone else up to investigate? Unless Art had been on the take. Art might have offered to write a clean report in exchange for a kickback. He writes the report and Sperry kills him, not only to save the money, but also to make sure he doesn't talk. But if Art had written a clean report, wouldn't the FDA have said so? Besides, Art didn't seem the type. And then there was the question of opportunity. Sperry had been nowhere near the Bath Pavilion at the time of Art's death. Or if he had, no one had seen him.

In any case, they owed it to Crowley to fill him in. Jerry suggested they drop by the casino after dinner. Crowley was now living there, in a former high stakes gaming room that had been converted into a center for the murder investigation, which now took in both the sheriff's department and the Food and Drug Administration. High Rock hadn't seen so much action since the racketeering hearings in the fifties. According to Jerry, Sperry was now the chief suspect. Or rather, the only suspect. His background would be gone over with a fine-toothed comb; his movements would be scrutinized down to the fraction of a second; his colleagues and patients would be questioned for any information that might be pertinent to the case.

The waitress reappeared to clear away their plates.

"Do you miss police work?" Charlotte asked after the waitress had taken their dessert orders (two crêpes suzette—another of Lillian's specialties and the real Lillian's favorites).

Jerry shrugged. "Sometimes," he replied. "I always wanted to be a cop. I signed up right after high school. It sounds corny, but I got a lot of satisfaction out of it. It's a good feeling—saving the world." Reaching into his pocket, he pulled out his wallet and withdrew a laminated card that identified him as Jerry D'Angelo, detective, third grade. Across the mug shot was punched the word RETIRED. He passed the card across the table to Charlotte. "My souvenir. Fifteen years, nine hundred felony arrests." He added, with a proud smile, "I liked catching crooks."

"I would say so," said Charlotte. She studied the picture. It showed a different Jerry from the one who now sat across from her: a tough, dour-faced man with the kind of pasty complexion that comes from too little sleep and too much fast food. She handed it back to him.

"But I'm glad to be out too. Actually, the greatest danger isn't that you'll get shot. It's that you'll get fat and die of a heart attack or that your nerves will go. The work can drive you nuts. You see only the worst side of life. You start thinking the whole world's like that."

"Was your wife happy when you got out?"

"Ecstatic. She'd been wanting me to quit for a long time. She was always worried." He held up his trigger finger. "I got hurt twice before this. I'll never forget the day I told her. It was on Christmas Eve. I gave her this big package. I told her it was a Christmas present. Inside were my disability papers from the Civil Service Review Board."

Jerry went on to talk about his wife, Rosalie, who'd been his high school sweetheart back in Bensonhurst. They had four children—all girls, all athletes. His oldest was in college. Paulina was footing the bill.

"That's another benefit of leaving police work," he said. "The boss lady might be a bitch to work for sometimes, but so was the city, and the city didn't pay for the kid's college education. If you're loyal to her, she's loyal to you, which is more than you can say of most employers."

"Well said," said Charlotte.

Jerry pulled out a picture: his wife, the plump, dark-eyed beauty whom Charlotte had seen at the fete, and four pretty, dark-eyed girls.

"Jerry, they're lovely," said Charlotte. They all had wide smiles and perfect teeth. The two little ones had Jerry's dimples.

"Thanks," said Jerry, putting the picture away. "What about you?" he asked. "I mean, are you married?"

Either he didn't keep up with Hollywood gossip or he was too polite to admit it. Charlotte replied that she had been—four times. Over her crêpes, which wasn't exactly the dessert for a sweltering June evening, but which tasted wonderful anyway, Charlotte talked about her life. She'd never had any children. In the Hollywood of the forties, having children was considered bad for the box office (it was important for a star to keep her face in front of the public, and taking a year or two out at the peak of a career was thought to be a ticket to has-beenville). By the time she was big enough to stand up to the bosses, it was too late, in the sense that her second husband was soon to die of a heart attack. She had married again, but that marriage had been a disaster. After that, she'd been single for almost twenty years before marrying again. But she wasn't entirely alone. She had half a dozen nieces and nephews and she was close to the children of her fourth husband. Although they had been married for only two years—as M.J. had quite accurately put it, he couldn't live in Charlotte's limelight—

they remained good friends and she'd become a surrogate mother to his two grown daughters, whose own mother had died.

By the time they finished dessert, the adjoining bar was becoming crowded with young singles and it was getting noisy and smoky. A band was setting up in a corner. It was time to leave.

When she returned to her room after their visit to the casino, her head was spinning, and not just from the beer. A haggard Crowley had been glad to hear what Charlotte had to say and had offered a tidbit of his own in return. It seemed that Sperry had abandoned his lucrative Harley Street practice under a cloud of scandal. One of his patients had died as the result of an allergic reaction to an injection of cells. The patient had been sensitized by the first shot and had gone into anaphylactic shock following the second. As a result, Sperry had been ostracized by the British medical establishment. The British, Crowley explained, were less stringent than the Americans when it came to regulating the practice of medicine. A layman such as Sperry (his medical credentials were spurious) could set himself up in practice as long as he didn't perform certain acts, such as operating under anesthesia or prescribing certain drugs. But an Englishman who called himself a doctor, whether or not he was listed on the British medical register, was expected to maintain certain standards of behavior. For those who tarnished the honor of the medical establishment, the punishment was severe: no patient referrals, no club memberships, no chummy backslapping at medical convocations. Sperry's answer had been to emigrate—first to the Bahamas, where he set up a cell therapy clinic that never got off the ground, and then to the United States, where his connections in the carriage trade, along with his good looks and smooth way with women, landed him a job at That Woman's fat farm in Arizona. He had been induced to come to High Rock during one of Paulina's raids on the competition, but in his case Paulina was duped: That Woman had shrewdly taken advantage of Paulina to dump a problem employee.

But although Crowley had learned a lot about Sperry, his efforts had been less successful when it came to actually pinning anything on him. As Jerry had said, none of the dozens of spa guests and employees who had been interviewed had seen him at the time of the murders. He had no alibi—he hadn't actually been seeing patients. Charlotte's interview with him had lasted only twenty minutes—just enough time for Adele to get over to the Bath Pavilion and into the tub. His next appointment wasn't for thirty minutes, during which time he could have committed the murder. It was the same in Art's case: there was an interval of about thirty minutes when he could have committed the murder. But he would have to have been lightning-footed and invisible to boot to make it from the Health Pavilion to the Bath Pavilion and back in that time.

Charlotte restively circled her room, hanging up her clothes, putting away her shoes, straightening the jars and bottles on the bathroom counter, as if by restoring order to her surroundings, she would bring order to the greater chaos. She was by nature a nester. It was a defense against spending so much time in hotels and rented rooms. Her brownstone in Turtle Bay, where she had lived on and off for the last thirty years, was her sanctuary, her retreat. When she wasn't there, she took bits of it with her: a small flower vase of blue and white Canton ware; a picture of her second husband in a Victorian silver frame; an antique rosewood sculpture of the grave and gentle Kwan-yen, the Chinese goddess of mercy and protector of women; a small malachite clock with ormolu mounts; a volume of Edna St. Vincent Millay bound in Moroccan calf. These were the totems of her private life. She paid homage to them now, arranging them on the marble surface of her dresser. Picking up the volume of poetry, she read the poem on the page to which it opened: "The solid sprite who stand alone,/And walks the world with equal stride,/Grieve though he may, is not undone/Because a friend has died." With a pang, she thought of Adele and Art. She was not undone, but nor could she call herself a solid sprite.

Setting the book aside, she walked over to the sliding glass doors, which stood open. She preferred natural ventilation to the artificial chill of air-conditioning. The moon hung low, casting an argent shadow over the lake. To the south, heat lightning shimmered through the clouds. Below her, a broad lawn stretched down to the lake shore. It was dotted with empty Adirondack chairs that seemed to have become animate by virtue of their contact with their former occupants. Some sat alone, staunchly independent of their chair fellows; others were gathered in gregarious clusters of three or four; still others were ranged in a line in mute appreciation of the spectacle before them, the geyser from which the lake took its name. In the moonlight, its fountain shone like a column of quicksilver, creating a host of ripples that slid across the calm, black water. To the west, the lawn was bounded by a path leading down to the gazebo at the water's edge. Behind the path rose a backdrop of trees. The globes of the Victorian lampposts lighting the path made it appear as if the trees were hung with a necklace of giant glowing pearls. As she watched, the globes dimmed to a dull yellow and then went out. She checked the face of her clock with its garland of hand-painted roses: it was midnight.

After changing into her nightgown, she climbed into bed. She had just fallen asleep when she was awakened by the ring of the telephone. It was Tom. He apologized for calling so late, explaining that he'd been trying to reach her all evening. Her brain still muddled by sleep, she had at first wondered why he was calling. In the confusion, she'd forgotten all about the radium. He was calling to tell her that he'd found out the name of the investment banker who'd hired the PR firm to plant the radium story. It was Raymond Innis. Apart from the fact that he was known as an up-and-coming, young M & A man ("mergers and acquisitions"), Tom knew nothing about him. Nor did the name mean anything to Charlotte, although the fact that he was an M & A man would point to a connection with High Rock Waters's takeover of Paulina Langenberg. After hanging up, she lay in bed, the light of consciousness gradually stealing into her brain. Raymond Innis: maybe the name did mean something to her after all. She slid the hotel directory out of the base of the telephone and looked up the number for the front desk. Then she dialed.

Her voice, which was usually husky, was even more so at this hour. "This is Charlotte Graham in room six-fifteen," she heard herself saying. She sounded as if she'd been up all night drinking whiskey. "Is there a guest staying at the hotel by the name of Raymond Innis?"

"Yes, Miss Graham," answered the obsequious voice on the

other end. "Mr. Innis is in room four-twelve. Would you like me to connect you?"

"No thank you," she replied, and hung up.

Raymond Innis was the Role Model. She had been introduced to him one night at dinner—the night he'd spurned yogurt as mucus-forming—but she'd forgotten his name. It was beginning to look as if her *An Enemy of the People* theory was right: Innis, who is hired by Gary, plants the radium rumor in order to depress the price of Langenberg stock, making it cheaper for Gary to acquire Paulina's company. Being a guest at the spa enables Innis to stay on top of the action and fit in a short vacation as well. Like Art, he was probably killing two birds with one stone. In the morning, she would tell Paulina. She would be glad to carry out her promise. Although she liked and admired Paulina, she was becoming concerned about her increasing involvement in the machinations of the Langenberg family empire. She had the feeling that she was becoming the permanent understudy in Anne-Marie's former role as Paulina's confidante. It was a role she wasn't anxious to fill.

Turning onto her side, she invited sleep, whose furtive arrival was ushered in by the syncopated voices of a hundred bullfrogs.

· II ·

A MORNING MIST clouded the surface of the lake like breath on a mirror, but the day promised to be clear and cool. The hot, humid weather that had hung over the High Rock plateau for the last twenty-four hours was gone, banished by the mountain breeze that flowed in through the screen of the sliding glass doors. Charlotte checked her clock: its gilded hands stood at the quarter past nine. She had missed Awake and Aware, breakfast, and Terrain Cure. So much for spa life. Picking up the telephone, she ordered an herb tea and a bran muffin—her penance for her self-indulgence the night before.

After breakfasting on her balcony, she changed into her sweat suit and headed over to Sperry's office for her spa checkup and for the results of her Reinhardt test. The Reinhardt test was as far as she planned to go with cell therapy. She was counting on Sperry's getting fired tomorrow. As she waited in his office a few minutes later, her eye was captured by the cover of the latest edition of a business magazine. The faces of Gary and Elliot peered out from behind a pyramid constructed of Langenberg products and bottles of High Rock water. Picking it up, she turned to the story. Inside was a shot of Leon with the caption "Heir apparent?" News traveled quickly.

She had just started reading when Nicky arrived. As he took a seat in one of the dove-gray chairs, his joints made a startling grinding noise. Looking up, Charlotte saw that he was grimacing in pain.

"My knees," he explained. "The doctors say there's too much weight on them. If I don't lose weight, I'll have to have operations on both of them. That's one of the reasons I'm here."

"Do the baths help the pain?" asked Charlotte with concern. The baths were supposed to be excellent for any kind of joint pain, or so Sperry had said. And Charlotte had noticed an improvement in her bad knee.

Nicky shook his head. "I can't take the baths. I don't fit in the tub."

"Oh. I'm sorry." Sorry that she'd made a faux pas, and also sorry for poor, sweet Nicky.

"That's all right," he said with his sad-eyed smile. "I've lost twenty-one pounds already. Probably a couple of more by now—I'll find out in a few minutes. I want to lose at least ten more while I'm here. That will bring me down to three hundred. My long-term goal is one sixty-five. I know it's going to take a long time, but I'm determined to do it."

"Good for you."

"I have a wish list of things I want to do. I want to run; to ride in a sports car—I mean, to fit in a bucket seat; to wear a gold chain—they don't make them big enough for me; to cross my legs." He demonstrated by trying to raise one leg over the other. "See, I can't do it. Miss Andersen says that if I keep thinking of my wish list, I won't overeat."

"It sounds as if she might be right," said Charlotte. She was happy that Anne-Marie's doctrine of "our bad habits giving us up" was working for someone.

Sperry appeared at the door of his office and summoned Charlotte. After wishing Nicky good luck, Charlotte went in.

The meeting was mercifully brief. Mercifully, because Charlotte was barely able to conceal her contempt for Sperry now that the evidence was piling up against him. But if he knew he was under suspicion, he didn't show it. He was as smooth as ever. After taking the usual weight and blood-pressure readings, he gave her the results of her Reinhardt test.

The test showed that she should get mostly glandular cells, he said. "Glandular cells are especially helpful for post-menopausal women who've experienced a decline in their endocrine secretions." He widened his narrow mouth in a concupiscent leer, revealing his pointed teeth. "We also find that the rejuvenation of the sex glands helps protect against cancer."

Aha, cancer too. She noted he didn't say "cure" but "protect against." "How long will it be before I notice an improvement?" she asked, curious about the time required for her senescent body functions to be reinvigorated.

"Some patients notice an improvement within a few weeks," Sperry replied. "For others, it can take as much as a few months. The results last four to seven years, depending on age and physical condition. For someone your age, the results will probably last only four years."

"Which means that I'll have to come back?"

"Yes. The more often you have treatments, the more effectively the aging process will be retarded. But above eighty we can't do much." He smiled, wrinkling his nose. "Unfortunately, we can't extend the life span. But we can extend the active, productive period of life well into old age."

So there was something cell therapy couldn't cure: death. After a few more minutes of chatting about cell therapy, Charlotte left. Sperry bid her good-bye "until tomorrow," a reference to the preliminary cell therapy treatment that she had no intention of undergoing.

On her way out she crossed paths with Nicky, who headed into Sperry's office in eager expectation of having lost another couple of pounds.

Ten minutes later, Charlotte was riding the glass elevator up to Paulina's penthouse. Jack answered the door. He was dressed in a white tunic of an expensive-looking linen fabric. He looked like a well-kept gigolo, which in a sense was what he was. It was a good thing he worked for Paulina. He had a taste for luxury that would have been satisfied by few other secretarial jobs. In reply to Charlotte's inquiry, he reported that Paulina's nervous crisis was nearly over. She had gotten up the previous afternoon for her tests. Upon her return, she'd gone immediately back to bed, but he predicted that she'd soon be up for good. Then she'd take the cure. It was her habit to take the cure every June. It was also her habit to take it following an emotional crisis. In this instance, the emotional crisis fell in June, which provided a double excuse for being purged in the cathartic mineral waters. Taking the cure, like buying jewelry

and reviewing her balance sheets, was one of Paulina's ways of
dealing with death, disappointment, or, in the case at hand,
betrayal. But if she hadn't yet emerged from the protective
cocoon of her huge Chinese bed, she was, as Jack put it, "full
of her old piss and vinegar." His big blue eyes danced. He was
clearly delighted that his boss was herself again.

Jack escorted Charlotte down the hall to Paulina's bedroom,
where they found her stretched out on her side in a Madame
Récamier pose, a meaty flank thrust less-than-seductively
toward the ceiling. Her cotton duster had been exchanged for
an elaborately embroidered red silk kimono that looked as if it
should be on display at the Costume Institute at the Metropol-
itan Museum. She was conducting business: her heavy black-
framed glasses were balanced on the tip of her nose. *The New
York Times* was clutched in the beringed, ink-stained fingers of
one hand; a buttered bagel in the other. A profusion of papers
was scattered over the pink-quilted bedspread: *Barron's* and
the *Wall Street Journal, Standard and Poor's* and *Moody's*
indexes, corporate prospectuses and annual reports. Paulina
was a woman who kept an eye on her investments. There was
also, Charlotte noted, a copy of the business magazine with
Gary and Elliot on the cover. At her bedside, with his gray
pin-striped back turned to Charlotte, sat a man with whom
Paulina was conferring over a yellow legal pad. At Charlotte's
arrival, he turned around. The man was Raymond Innis!
Charlotte stared. He returned her stare through deep-set,
slightly slanted eyes that were narrowed to slits by his
prominent cheekbones.

"Come in, come in," said Paulina, waving the bagel. "I
want you to meet . . . my banker." She looked at Jack, who
came to the rescue.

"Mr. Innis," he said.

"Mr. Innis, this is Miss . . ."

"Graham," supplied Jack.

"The famous movie star," added Paulina. "You know,
Border Town. And that other movie about the pioneer
woman . . ."

"*Westward Ho*," offered Charlotte. She hadn't realized
Paulina was such a fan. Stepping forward, she shook hands

with Innis. "We've met. We were both interviewed in connection with the murder investigation."

"Oh, that," said Paulina with a dismissive wave of the bagel. Taking a bite, she munched pensively for a moment and then peered suspiciously at Innis over the tops of her glasses. "Why you?"

"I was in the cubicle next to the victim's."

"Did you see anything?" asked the ever-curious Paulina as she polished off the rest of the bagel.

Innis shook his head.

"I hear they suspect My Mistake. Never mind," she added. "We're not talking about it. Bad for business." She turned her attention back to Charlotte. "What brings you to visit a lonely old lady?" she asked, this time without a trace of self-pity.

"Mr. Innis," replied Charlotte bluntly.

"Mr. Innis? You came to see me about Mr. Innis?"

Innis set down the legal pad, leaned back, and folded his arms, calmly awaiting her explanation.

"Yes. I found out who planted the radium rumor. Remember? The reason you asked me up here?"

Paulina stared at her uncomprehendingly for a minute. Then she slapped a palm to her forehead. "I forgot."

"You were right. The radium rumor *was* planted. By Mr. Innis's firm."

At this point Leon entered. Approaching the bed, he kissed his aunt on both cheeks, shook Innis's hand, and nodded hello to Charlotte. Then he took up his usual position in the chaise longue at the rear of the room, the sycophant at the foot of the empress's throne.

"Leon, this is all your fault, this mess," said Paulina, raising a braceleted arm to the heavens with a clank of precious metals. "The sound of a one-man band without the trumpet" is how Charlotte had once heard someone refer to the cacophony created by Paulina's jewelry.

"What's my fault?"

Paulina shot him an aggrieved look. She gestured to Charlotte. "Come here," she ordered.

Charlotte stepped over to the edge of the bed.

Paulina took Charlotte's hand. "I'm sorry. I forgot I'd asked you to look into this for me. I found out myself who was responsible. It was my nephew—he asked Mr. Innis to take care of it. It was a tactic to avert the takeover." She addressed Leon. "What did you call it? Burned ground?"

"Scorched earth," corrected Leon, who was wearing bright yellow socks to accent the thin yellow line in his conservative tie.

"Scorched earth. Sabotage the product so the enemy won't want the company. Leon found out that Sonny was going to betray me and decided to take care of it himself. How sweet." Her voice was caustic. "Don't alarm the senile old lady. My Sonny may be an airhead, but you—you are a buzzard."

"Vulture," said Leon.

"He corrects me yet. A vulture," she hissed. "Leon, listen to me. I am not senile—yet. I am not dead—yet. Until I am, I will handle my own affairs. Understand?"

"Yes, Aunt Paulina," said Leon contritely.

So it was just as Charlotte had suspected—the *An Enemy of the People* theory. Only the party who had planted the rumor to depress the price of the stock wasn't Gary, as she had suspected, but Leon. The theory was right, she had just been on the wrong side of the corporate battle line.

"And you," Paulina continued, turning to Innis. "Until I'm dead you'll do business with me. Not with my son, not with my nephew. With me."

"I'm sorry for the misunderstanding, Mrs. Langenberg. Your nephew led us to believe that you'd approved of the scheme."

"Approved of. Feh." She addressed Leon. "Where'd you get that harebrained scheme anyway? Let me tell you something: if you want to make a company unattractive, you sell off assets, you issue stock, you go into debt. But sabotage the product? That's stupid. Besides, a little rumor wouldn't stop the Seltzer Boy. Not only are you contemptible and deceitful and . . ."

"And a vulture," volunteered Leon.

"And a vulture. You're stupid. Now I'll show you how business is conducted in the real world." She grinned. "If Sonny thinks he can outwit his mother, he's deluded. He doesn't realize who he's up against. The same goes for the Seltzer Boy. Such nerve, taking my company like a rapist. If he'd come to me like a gentleman, maybe we could have talked terms."

Charlotte raised a skeptical eyebrow.

Paulina caught Charlotte's expression and shrugged. "Well, maybe not. But he's not the only one with nerve. Two can play his game as well as one."

"What are you going to do, Aunt Paulina?"

Paulina grinned. "If the mountain won't come to Muhammad," she said cryptically, "Muhammad must buy the mountain."

"That's one way of putting it," observed Charlotte.

"Does that mean you're going to buy High Rock Waters?" asked Leon.

Paulina played her moment with great style. Sliding backward, she propped herself up against the headboard. As suspense mounted, she sat quietly with her eyes half closed. Then, after taking a moment to rearrange the pillows, she announced coyly: "What's sauce for the goose is sauce for Paulina Langenberg."

"But . . ." protested Leon.

Paulina raised a hand to silence him. "I know what you're going to say. That it's impossible, that it would require a two-thirds vote of the stock, of which the Seltzer Boy's company controls thirty-four percent." She looked at Leon over the tops of her glasses. "Tell me. Am I right?"

"Well, yes," he replied.

"Am I right?" Paulina repeated, this time addressing Innis.

Innis played along, although it was clear he was familiar with her plans. "That was Brant's idea, yes. To gain negative control."

She turned back to Leon: "You say it's impossible to fight back. First lesson: you can always fight back. The Seltzer Boy is a little nothing who's attacked a very big, very powerful animal. What he doesn't realize is that the animal is about to bite him back. Correction: swallow him up."

"But how can you?" asked Leon.

"It's not for nothing that I'm one of the world's richest women. I'm going to form a new company to take over the Seltzer Boy. I already own five percent of his stock. I always own stock in the companies I do business with—it's a good business practice. It's not much, but it's a start."

Leon looked stunned.

Paulina picked up the pad and started making notes fast and furiously. "Mr. Banker, tell your team to get up here on the double. Jack, get the company lawyers up here. And call the PR people—we'll need them to get the word out to the financial press. Then get us some food—sausages and so on."

Paulina was one of those people for whom the emotional stress of most crises could be palliated by the administration of food or drink.

"But, Aunt Paulina, a counter-takeover will wipe us out," whined Leon, clearly worried about the security of his new-found inheritance.

She stared at him, steely-eyed. "First, it is *my* money, not *our* money. Second, do you think I'm going to pay cash?"

"Oh, I see," said Leon. He nodded in a businesslike way, obviously a studied effort to appear calm.

"It's called borrowing money, bor-row-ing mon-ey. It's one way that businesses acquire other businesses. That's your second lesson for the day. Isn't that right, Mr. Banker?"

Innis nodded.

Leon was now sitting bolt upright in the chaise longue. "How much are you going to borrow?" he asked. A note of hysteria had crept into his voice.

Paulina consulted the figures on her pad. With a malicious little grin, she announced, "I think we can do it for under twenty-five million."

"Twenty-five million!" Leon jumped up and began pacing the rose-colored carpet at the foot of the bed.

"It would be even more expensive if it weren't for you. Your stupidity is actually going to save us money. Their stock dropped fifteen points after you put that article in the newspaper. Of course it shot back up after Wednesday's takeover announcement. But not to where it had been. Everybody knows the only person who can run Paulina Langenberg is Paulina Langenberg."

Leon leaned against the railing at the foot of the bed.

"You're telling me you're going to spend twenty-five million on a company that's in trouble?" he said, his jaw clenched.

"Bah," said Paulina. "In trouble is when you want to buy a company. We'll be getting a good company cheap. That's your third lesson for the day. For this, I should be charging tuition. If you listen to me, you'll learn more than you ever did at Columbia. Now sit down. You're making me nervous."

Leon continued pacing.

"Sit down," yelled Paulina.

Leon retreated to the chaise, where he sat with his arms folded defiantly across his chest, his lower lip stuck out in a pout.

"Now listen. This is what will happen. Sales will recover. We just need to get the message out that there's nothing wrong with the water. Look at our stock, it bounced right back. Besides, we'll have the Seltzer Boy working for us. He can bring it back. He said so at the fete."

"Who says he's not going to quit?" taunted Leon.

"No one. But I hope he doesn't. He's sharp, the Seltzer Boy. Unlike some people around here." She looked at Leon. She continued: "Now, we must proceed with speed. Let's see," she said, chewing on the end of her pencil, "this is Sunday." She addressed Innis: "Can we get our commitments by Wednesday?"

Innis considered the question briefly. "I think so."

"Okay, we'll announce the tender offer on Wednesday. A sneak attack—if he can do it to us, we can do it to him. If we announce on Wednesday, we should be able to wrap it up pretty quickly. If they're going to tender, they'll want to get it over with by the weekend."

"What have you decided to offer?" asked Innis, who was making notes.

"Fifty," said Paulina. "That's a premium of a hundred percent over the current market price. If we don't reach our goal by the end of the waiting period, we'll raise our bid. But I don't think we'll run into any problems. After the radium rumor, the stockholders will be anxious to sell."

"What's our goal?" asked Leon.

"Controlling interest."

"Aunt Paulina," said Leon. Again he was sitting up.

"What?" she asked impatiently.

He spoke slowly: "High Rock Waters owns thirty-four percent of Paulina Langenberg. You own twenty percent of Paulina Langenberg. That's fifty-four percent. Which means that by acquiring controlling interest in High Rock Waters, you'll be recapturing control of Paulina Langenberg."

Silence. Paulina was at a loss for words. After a moment, she spoke: "He just realized. I don't believe it." She raised an arm. "Leon, that's the whole idea." And then she added, on a sourer note: "If you hadn't been worrying so much about your inheritance, you'd have caught on sooner."

Leon leaned back in the chaise, grinning. His yellow-green eyes gleamed with vengeance. "Brilliant," he muttered. "Brilliant."

"Thank you," said Paulina. Pushing herself up on one elbow, she raised herself to a sitting position. "Now I'm going to get up," she announced. "I have work to do. Jack, get my slippers, the red ones."

Jack opened the door of Paulina's closet, turned on the light, and retrieved the slippers—spike-heeled mules with red angora pompoms—from a disorderly pile of shoes and clothing. Carrying them back into the bedroom, he stooped before Paulina and slipped them onto her tiny feet.

Her business completed, Charlotte rose to leave. But Paulina wouldn't let her go without giving her the roses Elliot had sent. She didn't want to be reminded of her traitorous son, she said. In the same breath, she complained that she hadn't received a bouquet from him yet today.

"Maybe he's on a trip," offered Jack diplomatically, to which Paulina responded, "So he can't send flowers when he's on a trip?"

Paulina dismissed Innis with a lipstick and orders to get to work. Then she marched over to the closet and angrily flipped off the light switch. "How many times do I have to tell you to turn out the lights," she scolded Jack. "Do you think I own the electric company?"

"Who knows?" he replied. "Maybe the electric company will be next."

"Don't be a wiseacre," chided Paulina with a good-natured grin.

"I have the distinct impression you're feeling better, Mrs. Langenberg," said Jack fondly.

Paulina's brown eyes sparkled.

After Charlotte was sworn to secrecy, she was escorted into the living room by Jack, who then disappeared into the kitchen to wrap the flowers. As she awaited his return, Charlotte looked out over the spa. On the esplanade, Anne-Marie was leading the *corps d' aerobics* in alternate toe touches. She stood with arms and legs outstretched like Da Vinci's vitruvian man. The class followed in strict unison as she touched first one toe, then the other. Except for Nicky, who failed to even touch his knees. On the distant terrace of the Hall of Springs, the Mineral Man was wrapping up his act. The audience was smaller now. He was getting to be old hat. After packing up his knapsack, he disappeared into the Pump Room. To either side of the Hall of Springs, guests strolled under the colonnades. Charlotte was fascinated by the spa's architecture. Its balance was restful, but it was also unnerving. She was reminded of the phrase from Blake's poem: there was something fearful about its symmetry. Every column had its mirror image. Looking out, you couldn't distinguish the Bath Pavilion from the Health Pavilion. Unless you looked at the power house, whose brick stack rose from behind the Bath Pavilion like a lighthouse on a foggy sea. Charlotte was reminded of the ancient Persian carpet weavers who believed that a perfect carpet design trapped the evil spirits, bringing bad luck to the owner. To keep out the evil spirits, they deliberately introduced a mistake into each design, a disruption of the pattern, a dissymmetry. The chimney of the power house was like that.

Jack returned with the bouquet of roses and showed Charlotte to the door. In the foyer, she pressed the elevator button and waited. The silence was punctuated by a familiar melody from *Oklahoma*; the string quartet had begun its morning concert. As she gazed out of the long windows overlooking the spa, her thoughts dwelled on Leon: if it had once been Leon who basked in Paulina's favor, the tables were now turned. He was finding out there was a heavy price to pay for being heir apparent to the Langenberg fortune.

The lawn to the east of the quadrangle was dotted with

sunbathers who'd been unable to find a place at the edge of the pool or who simply preferred the grass. As Charlotte watched, a lanky young man in a T-shirt and shorts emerged from the rear of the Health Pavilion and threaded his way among the blankets and chairs to the parking lot. She suddenly realized from his ectomorphic build and loping gait that he was the Mineral Man. Her suspicion was confirmed by the knapsack that he carried over his shoulder. In the parking lot, he got into a little red car and drove away. What puzzled her was how he had gotten from the Hall of Springs to the Health Pavilion. He hadn't walked under the colonnades—she had been looking right at them. Nor had he crossed the quadrangle. He had simply popped up like a jack-in-the box at the rear of the Health Pavilion.

Her thoughts were still toying with this puzzle when the elevator arrived. Riding in a glass elevator was the kind of simple thrill she never tired of. Before her lay a panorama of mountains and of blue sky as hard and clear as porcelain. The clarity of the sky was marred only by a wisp of white condensate floating upward from the stack of the power house, where the mineral water was being heated for the afternoon baths. *Where the mineral water was being heated for the afternoon baths*. It suddenly dawned on her how the Mineral Man had gotten to the Health Pavilion. At the same moment, she realized how Sperry could have gotten to the Bath Pavilion. According to Regie Cobb, the water for the baths was pumped from the springs under the golf course to the power house, where it was heated. From there, it was pumped to the Bath Pavilion. Pumped—through tunnels. There *must* be tunnels. Regie had said the volume of water was sufficient to supply the water for a small town. Large pipes must be required. And Hilda had talked about the pipes getting clogged with the mineral precipitate. They must require constant maintenance. Any sensible architect would have put them in tunnels. Otherwise they would have to be dug up every time they needed to be repaired. And what about the water for the drinking fountains? In the Hall of Springs alone there were fountains for each of three mineral waters. To say nothing of the fountains in the Bath Pavilion and the Health Pavilion. The entire complex, she concluded, must be underlaid by a network of pipe tunnels. She went on to conclude that the tunnels must lie under the colonnades. It made perfect sense: provide a sheltered pathway linking the buildings and a conduit for the pipes in the same structure. So! The symmetry of the architecture was not only the product of a quest for a visual unity, but of a quest for practicality as well.

The elevator settled gently into the shrubbery around the foundation of the hotel. Charlotte emerged into the lobby, and, after dropping off the flowers at the desk with instructions to deliver them to her room, headed out through the revolving doors. On the pillared porch she found Regie Cobb just where she had expected to, sitting on a bench reading a newspaper, his feet propped up against the suitcases of the new arrivals and his eyes shaded by a Panama hat. The minibus stood at the curb awaiting its next load of passengers. Before retiring to the job of minibus driver, the television newscaster had said, Regie had been chief of maintenance. If anyone could tell her about the tunnels, it was he. As she approached, he stood up and, setting aside his newspaper, tipped his hat: a quick touch of his fingers to the brim in an old-fashioned expression of deference to the opposite sex.

"Mr. Cobb?"

"That's me."

"My name is Charlotte Graham." She extended her hand.

"I'm honored, Miss Graham," he replied, pumping her arm. "I'm a fan from way back. I recognized you on the bus the other day."

Charlotte smiled. "I had a question about the spa that I thought you might be able to answer."

"I'll do my best."

"The other day, you said that the water for the baths comes from a grid of springs underlying the golf course."

"That's right."

"And that the water was pumped to the power house."

"Yep."

"Here's my question: how does the water get from the power house to the Bath Pavilion?"

He eyed her speculatively, wondering why she was asking the question. Then, shifting his gaze to the spa, he raised an arm and pointed. "You see those colonnades there. Well, under each of those colonnades is a tunnel. The tunnels house all the pipes."

"How would someone get into the tunnels?"

"There's an entrance in the basement of each building."

Charlotte then remembered something else. When she had asked Hilda if there were any other entrances to the Bath Pavilion, she had mentioned the cellar. She addressed Regie: "So that someone would be able to go from the Health Pavilion to the Bath Pavilion through the tunnels."

"Yep." He nodded. "If you knew your way around."

"Would you be able to show me? It's very important."

He looked directly at her. "This wouldn't have anything to do with the two people who died over at the Bath Pavilion, would it?"

"Maybe."

"I can't. I have to stay here. But Otto could. Otto Klepper, he's the power house custodian. He knows all about the tunnels. He's off today, but he could take you through tomorrow. I'll call him and make arrangements."

"I'd appreciate that," she said. "Thank you."

· 12 ·

THE SIGN ON the power house door said: "Caution: safety shoes and hard hats required beyond this point." Opening it, Charlotte found herself on a catwalk overlooking three large, brick-enclosed boilers. Peering over the railing, she could see an alcove under the stairs where a makeshift office had been set up. A fat man in dark blue work clothes sat at the desk. His arms were folded across his chest and his shiny bald head hung over the back of his chair. On the desk lay the uneaten remains of a bag lunch. He was snoring.

"Hello," she shouted.

Receiving no reply, she descended the stairs. At the bottom, she repeated her greeting. The man didn't wake. Finally she approached the desk. Standing about five feet away, she said "excuse me" in a voice loud enough to be heard above the hum of the machinery.

With a violent snort, Otto Klepper jerked up his head and opened his gray eyes in a vacant stare. He looked just as she would have expected a custodian named Otto to look: round, pink, and with not enough wits to be curious, which under the circumstances was just as well.

"Sorry to disturb you, Mr. Klepper. Mr. Cobb said you might be able to give me a tour of the tunnels."

Blinking, Otto scrambled to a standing position. Despite the fact that Regie was supposed to have notified him that Charlotte was coming, he seemed confused by her presence. "Are you from the state?" he asked.

"The state?" repeated Charlotte.

"Are you here to do an inspection?"

"No. Mr. Cobb sent me. He said you'd give me a tour of the tunnels."

"Oh, you're a friend of Mr. Cobb's," he said, a smile spreading over his sleep-dulled features. "I remember now. I thought you was from the state. I didn't want to get caught napping on the job."

"Oh," said Charlotte. "Of course not." She stated very clearly, "My name is Charlotte Graham. Mr. Cobb sent me. I'd like a tour of the tunnels."

"Well, I guess if Mr. Cobb sent you, it's okay." The smile faded and a look of concentration came over his face. He stared at her intently. "Don't I know you from somewhere? You look familiar."

"I don't think so," replied Charlotte. She didn't want to get into it.

"That's funny. I could swear I've seen you somewhere before." He shook his head in bewilderment. Then he turned to the business at hand: "I'll be glad to take you down. Haven't been down in a while myself."

"Thank you."

"I'll be with you in just a sec," he added, raising a finger. "Jeez, you had me scairt there for a minute," he added with a chuckle. "I thought you was from the state or somethin'."

"So I gathered."

While Charlotte waited, Otto checked the gauges on the boilers and recorded the readings in a logbook. Then, gesturing for her to follow, he set off down a corridor at the side of one of the boilers, flashlight in hand. At the end of the corridor, he descended another set of stairs to a metal fire door. On the door was a sign, now pitted with rust, that bore the fallout shelter logo of black triangles on a yellow ground. It had been years since Charlotte had seen one of these signs. An artifact of the Cold War, it brought back disturbing memories of air raid alerts and brinkmanship and the HUAC hearings. Remembering that the spa had once been a civil defense depot, she wondered if somewhere there was a dusty cache of canned vegetables stockpiled by some provident citizen in anticipation of the apocalypse.

Otto opened the door and flipped on a light switch. A string of light bulbs illuminated a tunnel about six feet high and too narrow for two to walk abreast. Charlotte entered behind Otto, whose bandy-legged. stride put her in mind of a tugboat bobbing at its moorings. By the light of the naked light bulbs, the floor and walls glittered like a crystal cave. What had once been brick and mortar was now encrusted with the precipitate from the mineral water that had leaked from the antiquated pipes. The stale, musty air even smelled of minerals; its acrid odor made her nose itch.

"Watch your step," warned Otto.

The floor beneath her feet was rough and uneven from the mineral deposits.

"This is the oldest tunnel," Otto said, turning to address her. "It was built when the old Lincoln Baths went up. It used to carry mineral water from the old power house to the Lincoln Bathhouse. The Lincoln Bathhouse burned down in the fire. It used to be where the Hall of Springs is now."

Directing the beam of the flashlight overhead, Otto pointed out the various pipes and their functions. The chief pipe was a large, insulated steam pipe that heated the spa in winter. Next to it in size was a new pipe that carried the heated mineral water to the Bath Pavilion.

Otto nodded to the new pipe. "Touch it."

Charlotte obeyed. "It's warm."

"Yep. We heat the water to a hundred degrees. Have to. By the time it gets to the Bath Pavilion, it's cooled down considerable. Of course, this here pipe's insulated. It it wasn't, it'd be as hot as a radiator."

In fact, the tunnel itself was quite warm. Charlotte removed the jacket of her sweat suit and tied it around her waist. Warm—and moist, from the water that leaked from the joints of the old pipes, each drip adding another layer of mineral to the floor that had built up over the decades.

"The new pipe looks as if it must have been expensive."

Otto nodded. "Nickel alloy stainless steel. Costs a fortune," he added solemnly. "But Mrs. Langenberg knows how to spend her money right. This here stainless steel will resist the buildup of the mineral. Yep," he said, patting the pipe as if he were patting a horse. "This baby will last."

He went on to point out the old cast-iron pipes that were now encrusted with mineral scale. Reaching into the leather holster on his belt, he withdrew a screwdriver and pried off a piece of the mineral incrustation, which he handed to Charlotte. "A souvenir," he said.

Charlotte turned it over in her hands. It was thick and heavy, its layers distinguished like the rings of a tree by their different widths and various colorations of reddish brown.

"These pipes are new too," Otto continued, shining the torch overhead at the pipes that carried the Union and Sans Souci waters from their sources in the Vale of Springs to the Pump Room.

The pipes were stenciled with black letters reading "Union" and "Sans Souci." Likewise, a pipe labeled "High Rock" carried the spa's most famous water from its source on the esplanade to the power house, where it was pumped across the street to the new bottling plant.

The pipe lecture over, Otto resumed the tunnel tour. In a few minutes, they had passed through another door into a room that the flashlight revealed to be square, with two doors, one in front of them and one to their right. Otto flipped a light switch on the wall, with no results. "Lights must be out," he said. "Guess I'll have to take care of that one of these days. We're under the new spa now. Overhead is the northwest pergola." Crossing the room, he opened the door in front of them and shined the flashlight into the darkness. "This here tunnel leads to the Hall of Springs."

Charlotte peered in. It was quite different from the tunnel through which they had just passed. High, broad, and clean, with cement block walls, it had the feeling of a high school corridor. The WPA architects had designed the spa for quality. Otto closed the door and shined the flashlight on the other door. "That there tunnel leads to the Bath Pavilion."

"Do these tunnels underlie the entire spa?"

"Yep. You can walk all the way around. On the other side, there's a linkup with the tunnel that leads to the hotel."

With that, he turned back toward the door to the old tunnel, signaling that the tour was at an end.

"Could we go a little farther, please?" asked Charlotte. She still wanted to check out the route Sperry would have taken and to see whether he could have made it to the Bath Pavilion and back in thirty minutes.

Otto checked his watch and shook his head. "I'm sorry, ma'am. I've got to be gettin' back."

"Then could I borrow the flashlight and continue on my own?"

"I wouldn't want you traipsin' through these tunnels alone. You might get hurt or somethin' and I wouldn't want to be held responsible."

Charlotte could see from the stubborn look on his simple face that it was no use arguing with him. "That's okay," she said.

Now that she knew the layout, she could make her own way. Regie had said there was an entrance in the basement of each building.

From the power house, Charlotte headed directly for the Health Pavilion. She decided to start where Sperry would have. If her memory served her right, there was a door at the end of the basement corridor that probably led to a tunnel. From there, she would follow the tunnel around to the Bath Pavilion, timing how long it took her. As she descended the stairs, she found herself feeling smug. She had figured it all out: why Sperry had murdered his victims, how he had murdered his victims, and now, how he had done it without being seen. She was anxious to tell Jerry.

In his office, she found his secretary, Andrea, typing dictation.

Spotting Charlotte, Andrea removed the headphones. "Can I help you?"

"Is Jerry around?"

"He's at lunch," she replied with a smile. "Any message?"

"No. Just tell him I was here." She was disappointed. She would have liked some company.

"Miss Graham, right?"

"Right. By the way, do you have a flashlight that I could borrow for an hour or so?"

"Sure," said Andrea. She located a flashlight in a filing cabinet drawer and handed it to Charlotte.

"Thanks."

Yes, she was smug—sort of, Charlotte thought, as she headed toward the door at the end of the corridor. But she knew that smug was a dangerous way to feel. She didn't trust smug. It was just when you were feeling smug that you flubbed a line or tripped over a prop. If Frannie were to analyze it, she would no doubt say that such mishaps were karmic retribution for the sin of pride. Charlotte's mother had called it cruising for a bruising. Her intellect told her she had the case neatly wrapped up, but her intuition, which she had learned to trust implicitly, told her otherwise.

Like the door at the power house, the door at the end of the basement corridor was posted with the CD logo. She checked her watch. It was now twelve forty-seven. It would have taken Sperry only a couple of minutes to get from his office to here. Having established the time, she opened the door and stepped into the tunnel. After closing the door behind her, she switched off the flashlight and held her palm up to her face. She couldn't see a thing. It was as dark as the pit from pole to pole. And as silent. For some reason, the corny words of "Invicta" always came to her in moments like this. She supposed it was because she had once had to recite them in a movie in which she had played an intrepid Englishwoman marooned in New Guinea. The words of the final stanza now ran through her mind: "I thank whatever gods may be for my unconquerable soul." Switching the flashlight back on, she took a deep breath—the odor was of damp concrete—and set off, following the steam pipe into the darkness as if it were the white line on a night-blackened highway.

She walked at a brisk pace, almost a jog. Sperry wouldn't have lost any time. His goal would have been to get to the Bath Pavilion and back as quickly as possible. Unlike the floor of the old tunnel, which was caked with mineral, the floor here was dirt and gravel. Occasionally there was a damp spot where a pipe had leaked, but on the whole it was easy going. And cool—there was no pipe carrying the heated mineral water to the Bath Pavilion. Shining her flashlight on the ground, she noticed fresh footprints in the damp spots, narrow footprints— proof that she wasn't the first to have entered the tunnels in recent weeks. Judging from the distance between them, they were the prints of a tall man. They could have been a workman's or Sperry's or the Mineral Man's, but she suspected the latter because of their shape, which fit his build, and because of their presence in this section of the tunnels, between the Health Pavilion and the Hall of Springs.

In a few minutes she had reached a door opening into a square room identical to the one Otto had showed her. It was the basement of the pergola at the northeast corner of the spa. From there, she headed west toward the Hall of Springs. At the tunnel's end, she opened another door into the well-lighted basement corridor of the Hall of Springs. To either side were rooms filled with junk: broken chairs and tables, cast-off kitchen equipment, old-fashioned light fixtures. Along one wall stood a dusty stack of High Rock water crates dating from the era of state stewardship. She could see why the state-bottled water hadn't sold. The dark green bottle with its ugly red and black label had about as much appeal as a bottle of laxative. The resemblance may in fact have been deliberate—it was as a laxative that the waters had originally been prized. Overhead, the steam pipe was joined by a pipe carrying Union water to the fountain at the east end of the Pump Room. As she proceeded along the corridor, she picked up first the pipe carrying High Rock water, and then the pipe carrying Sans Souci water to the fountains on the floor of the Pump Room.

At the end of the corridor, another door led back into the tunnels. On this side, there were no footprints, which led her to conclude that the footprints on the other side were the Mineral Man's. If they were Sperry's, they would be here as well. But the fact that there were no footprints didn't exonerate Sperry; he might simply have gone around the other way, to the south. She was beginning to get a feel for the tunnels now: overhead, she could imagine the guests strolling under the colonnades, exchanging biological ages. She soon reached the basement of the northwest pergola, where she had been with Otto. Here she rejoined the pipe carrying the heated mineral water to the Bath Pavilion. She checked her watch: only six minutes had elapsed. Passing quickly through, she turned left into the tunnel leading to the Bath Pavilion. More confident now—she had yet to run into a rat or a bat or a tarantula or any other of the disagreeable creatures she had half imagined to be lurking in the tunnels' dark corners—she picked up her pace.

A few minutes later, she arrived at the door to the basement of the Bath Pavilion. Leaning up against it, she bent over to

catch her breath—the brisk walk had left her winded. She
checked her watch: twelve fifty-four. It had taken her only
seven minutes to get from the basement of the Health Pavilion
to the basement of the Bath Pavilion. Double it, add a few
minutes for going up and down the stairs at either end, and a
few more for doing away with the victim and you had twenty,
twenty-five minutes. And she had been walking—a fast
walk, but a walk nonetheless. Sperry might have cut another
minute or two off his time by jogging, although he didn't seem
the jogging type. In any case, within the space of half an hour
he could have drowned Adele or Art and made it back to his
office in time for his next appointment. He might even have
had a few minutes to spare to run a comb through his
silver-gray hair.

Part one of her mission was complete. Now for part two:
how close were the basement stairs to the cubicles in which
Adele and Art had been killed? In other words, could Sperry
have reached the cubicles without being seen? Opening the
door, Charlotte entered the basement. The part in which she
was standing appeared to have been a laundry: a row of old
washtubs stood on a platform against the front wall and drying
racks hung from the ceiling. Like the structure above it, the
basement was laid out in a U, with the sides formed by the
women's and men's wings. Passing through the laundry area,
Charlotte entered the area under the women's wing. Piled in
the center was a stack of old wicker furniture, most of it
painted an ugly hospital green. At the far end of the stack of
furniture was another staircase. Charlotte climbed it and
opened the door. She emerged directly opposite Adele's
cubicle and face-to-face with Hilda, who was lumbering down
the hall with an armload of laundry.

Hilda stared at her, at first in surprise and then in conster-
nation. "Miss Graham!" she said. Her yellow Tartar eyes
narrowed with suspicion as she took in the flashlight in
Charlotte's hand. "What are you doing here?"

"I was looking for someone," she lied.

"Who?" demanded Hilda.

Charlotte ad-libbed. "Mrs. Jacoby. Mary Jane Jacoby."

"You're not supposed to be here," scolded Hilda. She
pursed her lips in disapproval and waved a gnarled finger in

front of Charlotte's nose. "I'm going to have to report you. You're going to get into trouble."

"I'm sorry," said Charlotte. "I didn't know."

"Come," said Hilda, gesturing for Charlotte to follow. Turning around, she shuffled down the corridor, her corduroy slippers flapping from side to side. Charlotte followed sheepishly in her wake.

"Where are we going?" asked Charlotte. It was clear that Hilda had orders to be on the lookout for unauthorized persons.

"To see Mrs. Murray."

Charlotte felt like a fourth grader being summoned to the principal's office. She put the flashlight away in her pocket.

At the end of the hall, they found Mrs. Murray at her desk.

Hilda presented Charlotte: "I caught her snooping around in the cellar." She added, "She said she was looking for Mrs. Jacoby."

"I'm afraid we don't have bath appointments until after one," Mrs. Murray said curtly. "I thought all our clients were aware of that."

"I'm sorry. I understood from Mrs. Jacoby that she had an appointment at noon," lied Charlotte.

"If you'd checked at the reception desk in the lobby, I'm sure someone would have been able to tell you the time of her appointment."

"No one was there."

"Oh. And when was that?" Mrs. Murray folded her arms across the stiffly starched surface of her bosom and fixed Charlotte with an icy blue stare.

"About—about five minutes ago."

"I've been at the desk for the last ten minutes. Now, if you'd like to follow me to the lobby, I'll check Mrs. Jacoby's appointment for you."

Mrs. Murray led Charlotte out to the lobby, where she looked up M.J.'s appointment, which was for three-thirty that afternoon.

"I hope you'll understand, Miss Graham, that we cannot allow our guests to wander around the Bath Pavilion," Mrs. Murray said. "Our security precautions are necessarily strict, but they have been especially so in recent days for reasons with which I believe you are familiar."

Charlotte nodded agreeably.

"Unfortunately, one of the problems we have to contend with is guests who believe that their fame"—here she paused for effect—"or their connections"—she stared at Charlotte, her eyes narrowing with the full force of authority—"give them special privileges. I hope that you . . ."

But Charlotte didn't allow her a chance to finish. Giving the loathsome Mrs. Murray her most daunting look, a look that had wilted leading men and commanded armies, Charlotte spun regally around on her heel and strode out.

"Bitch," she muttered under her breath.

She emerged from the Bath Pavilion into the light of mid-day feeling like a mole emerging from its burrow. With her jaw firmly set, she shrugged her broad shoulders in an insouciant gesture that was the product of her many years before the cameras. Oh, well, she thought. She was too wise to take offense at the insults of a minor-league martinet like Madeleine Murray. She had accomplished what she had set out to: she knew Sperry could have made it to the Bath Pavilion and back in the thirty minutes between patients. And she knew that the basement staircase in the women's wing would have given him access to Adele's cubicle. She wondered why the police hadn't investigated the tunnels. There were no footprints on the Bath Pavilion side, or any other evidence that they had been down there. Probably sheer laziness. Finding the lights out, they had probably decided to skip it. She had the feeling they were just going through the motions anyway.

Suddenly realizing that she was hungry, she set off across the quadrangle toward the Hall of Springs, her thoughts still on Sperry. How had he known which cubicle was Adele's? she wondered. She supposed he could have checked the appointment book beforehand. He certainly hadn't paraded out to the lobby to check it at the time of the murder. That is, *if* Sperry was the murderer. His guilt was far from a foregone conclusion. Anyone who knew about the tunnels might have come and gone without being seen, including the mysterious Mineral Man. The image of the corridor of offices in the basement of the Health Pavilion popped into her mind. For someone with an office there, for instance, it would have been a cinch to dash over and back. Like Jerry—not that he was a likely suspect. Or Frannie.

By now it was one-fifteen. The terrace was crowded with guests eating lunch. Charlotte threaded her way among the umbrella-capped tables to the bronze doors. She always dreaded crowds for fear of being approached by fans, but so far the guests had gone out of their way to respect her privacy. Such courtesy was one benefit of a place that attracted celebrities. Inside, she headed across the Pump Room to the High Rock fountain.

"The drink's on the house," said the young man who served up a fresh glass of the fizzing water. She drank it down quickly. Her expedition had left her thirsty. As she drank, she imagined the path the water had taken to reach her glass: upward through a fissure in the earth's crust to the spring on the esplanade. From there, through the pipes to the Pump Room, where it was served up to spa guests whose digestive systems had been brought to a standstill by too much rich food. The thought of the pipes brought her back to the problem at hand: after lunch, she would return to the tunnels to see if the staircase on the men's side was a mirror image of that on the women's. She would bet it was, given the spa's symmetry. If so, it would have brought Sperry out next to Art's bath cubicle. She also wanted to check out the tunnels on the southern side on the chance that Sperry had gone around that way.

Having finished her drink, she headed toward a table. She took a seat and studied the menu. She sighed. She wasn't in the mood for zucchini pancakes. She settled on cucumber bisque (sixty-four calories), an *omelette au fromage garni* (two hundred calories), and whipped cauliflower (fifty calories). After giving the waitress her order, she took the flashlight out of her pocket and settled back, glad to be off her feet. In doing so, she felt the piece of mineral Otto had given her press uncomfortably into her side. Taking it out, she held it up to the light. Its reddish brown crystals shone like mica. Running a finger across the surface, she discovered that it was as rough as sandpaper. It would make a good paperweight, a souvenir of the spa.

A voice interrupted her thoughts: "Is that a piece of mineral?"

Charlotte looked up. Her exercise teacher, Claire, was standing at the side of her table. She was wearing a long skirt of an Indian cotton print and a full white peasant blouse over a lavender leotard. With her long, curly, reddish hair, she looked like a young woman from a Botticelli painting.

"Yes. It's from one of the springs," she lied. She didn't want to confess to having explored the tunnels.

"You might get in trouble if they catch you chipping off pieces of the mineral," said Claire with a gentle smile. "You're not supposed to."

Oh, damn, thought Charlotte. In hot water with the authorities again. "I just picked it up," she said. "I didn't know."

"May I join you?" asked Claire. Sensing Charlotte's puzzlement, she added: "I'd like to talk with you. About a private matter."

"By all means," said Charlotte. She gestured to the seat on the other side of the marble-topped table.

Claire sat down. The waitress reappeared and took Claire's order—for an iced herb tea and a bowl of yogurt with fruit topping.

For a few minutes, they chatted about exercise class. With the arrival of their orders, Claire's tone turned more serious. "I have a favor to ask," she announced. "I'm sorry to intrude on you like this, but I didn't know who else to go to." She paused for a moment, picking up her spoon with slim, white fingers sprinkled with freckles the color of the mineral.

As she dipped the spoon into the yogurt, Charlotte noticed a small diamond on her left ring finger, an emerald cut, simple and neat like its wearer. The gold band was still shiny. She suddenly had an intimation of what Claire was about to tell her.

Noticing the direction of Charlotte's glance, Claire held up her left hand to display the ring and smiled. "Yes, I'm engaged to be married," she said. "To Elliot Langenberg."

"Congratulations!" said Charlotte. She didn't know what Elliot's last wife, the fashion model, or the one before her had been like, but she was sure he couldn't go wrong with Claire. And she suspected that Claire would be happy with him as well. She had the feeling he was a kind and gentle man.

Claire continued: "That's what I wanted to talk with you about. Elliot feels terrible about this rift with his mother. I

didn't know anything about it—the scheme to sell his Langenberg stock to High Rock Waters. But even if I had, I don't
think I would have discouraged it. It's been a good experience
for him. He didn't want to go behind his mother's back, but he
had to demonstrate that he's capable of running his own life. I
know that sounds strange to say of a forty-seven-year-old man,
but he's a forty-seven-year-old man who's never stood up to his
mother. Don't misunderstand me, I have great respect for
her—she can be very kind—but she can also be very domineering."

"I would say that's putting it tactfully," said Charlotte.
"Most people make no bones about calling her a tyrant."

"Okay, she's a tyrant," said Claire with a reluctant smile.
"If Elliot had let her, she would have gone on bullying him
forever. Anyway, he doesn't want the rift to go on and I don't
either. It's eating him up. He really loves her very much." She
paused, her slim fingers toying with her spoon. "It's especially
important that relations be patched up now . . ." The next
words came out in a rush: "Now that the baby's coming." She
looked up with the smile of someone who's just completed a
difficult task.

Charlotte felt a thrill of delight rush over her: for Claire, for
Elliot, and most of all for Paulina. Paulina, who at long last
would be a grandmother. Her glance drifted down to Claire's
abdomen, where she could just discern a slight curve beneath
her loose white blouse.

"I'm due in November. I know it's putting the cart before
the horse, but"—she smiled engagingly—"that's the way it
is." She continued: "We were planning to get married anyway.
This just means moving the date up a bit. It was a big surprise
to me too. I'm no spring chicken myself."

Charlotte reached out for Claire's hand. "I'm very happy for
you," she said. "How does Elliot feel about it?"

"He's on cloud nine. We just found out yesterday that it's
going to be a boy—the wonders of modern science and all
that."

"Paulina will be delighted. Someone to carry on the family
name."

"I hope so. That's what I'm concerned about. Elliot's
stubborn—he won't be the first to seek a reconciliation. But I

know it would mean a lot to him if his mother came to the wedding. What I'm asking is this: I wonder if you would do us the favor of telling her—you know, that I'm pregnant—and of trying to patch things up. I'd just hate for this to go on . . ."

"I can't think of anything I'd rather do. I can't make any promises . . ."

"That's okay. It would mean a lot just to know you've tried. I would have asked Anne-Marie, but she's on the outs with Mrs. Langenberg now too. You were the only one I could think of. It's very important, especially now. You see, she might not be around much longer."

"What?"

She sighed. "Elliot found out from her doctor this morning that she had a tumor on her ovary. There's a good chance it's cancerous. Apparently it turned up during the routine physical she had on Saturday."

"I'm very sorry to hear that. Very sorry. Are they going to operate?"

Claire nodded. "Her doctor's making the arrangements now. He said he'd have a better idea of the situation after the operation."

Charlotte nodded.

The waitress reappeared and took Charlotte's dessert order: an apricot mousse at thirty-seven calories and a cup of espresso.

"Have you made any plans for the wedding yet?" Charlotte asked.

"No, but we'd like to keep it small. Immediate family maybe."

"If Paulina has anything to do with it, you won't be keeping it small."

Claire smiled. "Yes, I guess you're right. Well, if she agrees to come, we'll put on any kind of wedding she wants."

"I'll do everything I can," said Charlotte. She squeezed Claire's hand with affection.

Claire smiled and returned her squeeze. "I'd really appreciate it. Well, I'd better be getting back to class."

After signing her bill, Claire stood up and glided out, her long skirt swaying gently. Her erect carriage and athletic grace gave her a sense of quiet dignity that was elegant and womanly. Elliot had made a good choice. Charlotte doubted she would have any difficulty convincing Paulina of that.

But she wondered if by announcing their engagement, Elliot and Claire might be opening themselves up to trouble from another source.

· 13 ·

IT WAS WITH a light heart that Charlotte left. If there was anything she hated, it was a family row. The stubborn pride of people who love one another was the cause of so much unhappiness. And weddings often brought out the worst of it. How many weddings there were in which a pall was cast over the festivities by the absence of a relative who refused to attend. A marriage is hard enough to keep going, let alone one whose beginnings are clouded by disapproval. In many families, the bride's being pregnant would be the cause of just such a furor, but Charlotte suspected it would be just the opposite in this case. What Paulina wanted more than anything was an heir. For despite appearances to the contrary, she was still an Old World peasant at heart. And now she would have an heir—a male heir. No, the trouble wouldn't be with Paulina, but with Leon. Charlotte doubted that he would remain Paulina's heir, and being disinherited was not apt to sit well with someone who'd had time to accustom himself to the idea of becoming one of the world's richest men.

For the moment Charlotte put aside the idea of returning to the tunnels. After dropping off the flashlight at Jerry's office, she headed over to Paulina's. She was met at the elevator by Jack, who looked haggard. The blue eyes under his long, curly lashes were hung with deep, violet shadows and his perennial golden tan had taken on a sallow cast.

"How's she doing?" asked Charlotte, adding, "I heard."

Jack was surprised. "How?"

"From Claire."

He nodded in acknowledgment of the connection with

Elliot. "Pretty well, actually. She's treating this like a business problem: acknowledge it, learn everything you can about it, and find a way to solve it. Only you can't beat cancer the way you can the competition." He paused. "I don't think she fully realizes what she's up against."

Charlotte doubted that. There was little that escaped Paulina. "What *is* she up against? Claire wasn't too specific."

Jack closed the door to the apartment behind him to avoid being overheard. "She has tumors in both ovaries."

"Both ovaries! Claire only mentioned one."

"No, both. Bilateral. That's what makes Dr. Castelli pretty sure it's cancer. She doesn't have any symptoms. Which is why I don't think it's really hit her yet. She'll have to have surgery, of course. If it's cancer, they'll take out both ovaries and the uterus and part of the omentum."

"Omentum?"

"The fat around the intestines. It's standard for this kind of surgery. The operation's scheduled for next week."

"Then what?" asked Charlotte.

Jack shrugged. "Chemotherapy, I would imagine. If it's cancer. My mother went through this: the operations, the chemotherapy."

"For how long?"

"Twelve to eighteen months."

"Oh, God."

"I know. That's one reason why this is really getting to me. My mother died four years ago, just before I came to work for Paulina." He sighed, and then went on: "She suffered terribly. She lived from one pain shot to the next. That was the worst—waiting with her for those shots."

"I'm terribly sorry."

"I was the one who took care of her," he went on. "My father was dead; my sister was living out in California. When she finally died, she weighed fifty-two pounds. She was a living skeleton." He blinked away the tears that had welled up in his bright blue eyes.

Charlotte touched a sympathetic hand to his shoulder.

"I'm sorry. I'm kind of emotional this morning." He smiled ruefully. "Not enough sleep, I guess. This has brought it all back. But I shouldn't jump to conclusions. Maybe it won't be the same for Paulina. If it is, I don't know what I'll do. I don't think I could go through it again."

"I hope you won't have to. Did Dr. Castelli say what her chances are? If it does turn out to be cancer, I mean."

"Yes." He gathered himself together. "Not good. First she has to get through the operation, which is no small feat for someone her age."

"I don't think we have to worry on that score. Paulina's as strong as a horse." She corrected herself: "Three horses."

He smiled. "You've got a point. As for the cancer—because there aren't any symptoms in the early stages, it's usually not detected until it's gone pretty far. According to Castelli, the five-year survival rate ranges from twenty-five percent to seventy-five percent, depending on the type of tumor and how far it's spread. He'll have a better idea next week."

Charlotte nodded. It was really too early to tell.

"It's all been such a surprise, a shock really," continued Jack. "I wasn't prepared for this. In all the time I've worked for her, she's never missed a day on account of illness. Except for her nervous crises. But you can't really count them as being sick." He smiled. "Of course, to listen to her, you'd think she was always on her last legs."

Charlotte laughed. "I know. Her headaches, her indigestion . . . I don't think we have anything to worry about. Hypochondriacs always live forever."

Jack smiled. "I hope you're right. Well, shall we go in?" He ushered Charlotte into the living room. "Miss Graham to see you," he announced.

Paulina was sitting behind her huge Louis XVI desk, her head barely protruding from above a mound of papers. "She was here to see me ten minutes ago." She glared at Jack over the tops of her glasses.

It was the first time since the fete that Charlotte had seen Paulina out of bed. She was wearing a stunning Chanel suit of royal blue silk, accented by costume jewelry of blue and green paste that Charlotte wouldn't have paid fifty cents for at a rummage sale, but that Paulina wore with flair. It was typical of her idiosyncratic style that in addition to the paste, she wore a star sapphire ring the size of a robin's egg. In the walking jewelry store category, Diamond Jim had nothing on Paulina.

"What were you shmoozing about out there? Don't answer—that was a historical question."

"Rhetorical," corrected Leon, who sat in front of the desk.

Paulina shot him a dirty look. "I know. You were talking about me." She pointed an accusing finger. "I can tell from that sad-sack look on your faces. Everybody's walking around here like this was a funeral parlor. Well, I'm not dead yet." She stood up and came around to the front of the desk. Lifting her hem, she danced a little jig. "I'm still kicking. Got that?"

A smile crept across Jack's careworn face.

"Say, 'Yes, Mrs. Langenberg,'" ordered Paulina.

"Yes, Mrs. Langenberg."

She turned to Leon and repeated her jig. "There's still some life in the old girl yet. Got that?"

"Yes, Aunt Paulina," agreed Leon obediently.

"You are forbidden to wear long faces in my presence." Resuming her seat, she addressed Charlotte: "He told you. I might have cancer of my . . ." She pointed in the direction of her lap. "But despite what *some* people may think, I'm not about to croak. The masseuse, The Mousy Girl with the Leg, told me I have a brilliant aura, which means I'm very strong. Besides"—she gripped the ridge of her ear, jiggling the cluster of fake blue and green gems—"I have big ears, like an elephant. Which means I'll live forever."

"You've never looked better, Paulina," said Charlotte. She meant it. Whatever minus value the cancer carried in the giant ledger in the sky, it was more than offset by pluses for will, determination, and vitality.

Paulina beamed. "I've never felt better. Well, maybe a little tired," she added, lest a bid for sympathy slip by. Then she became what was, for her, philosophical. "Anyway"—she shrugged—"if I die, it's no big deal."

The phone rang and Jack answered it in his office, which opened off of the living room behind Paulina's desk. It was Innis, he said.

Paulina picked up her extension. After listening to what Innis had to say, she replied, holding the telephone at arm's length: "I understand what he wants—more money. That's what it boils down to. Tell him Mrs. Langenberg says no, plain and simple. We've made a more-than-generous offer."

While she talked, Jack listened on the other extension and made notes.

Raising her voice, Paulina went on: "A hundred percent above market price isn't exactly peanuts. What does he want, the sky?" Placing a hand over the receiver, she addressed Leon: "That was a rhetorical question." And then to Charlotte: "Sit down. I'm just doing a little business. Leon, will you get us some mineral water, please."

Charlotte took a seat. While Leon fetched the mineral water, she studied the map hanging above Paulina's desk. It was a map of the world with Langenberg factories and salons marked with pins: red for salons, yellow for factories. She looked for countries without any pins—Vietnam, Cambodia, Libya, a few other African countries—that was it.

Paulina was speaking sarcastically: "A wholly inadequate offer? That's what he calls it?" She sighed. "It was down to twenty-five. His stockholders will be making a fortune. Tell him that's it. Not a penny more." She hung up. "The lawyers for the Seltzer Boy," she explained. "Such nerve. We haven't even made our formal offer yet and already he wants us to sweeten our bid."

"Will you?" asked Charlotte.

"We'll see," said Paulina with a twinkle in her eye. "Now, how's my Mrs. Stockholder? Listen," she said, leaning across the desk, "you were smart not to sell out to the Seltzer Boy. You'll make a lot of money sticking with me. The Body Spa line, it's a miracle. The early reorders are in—it's going to be big numbers—very big numbers. It's flying off the counters."

"I'm glad to hear it."

Leon, who had returned carrying a tray holding four glasses and a couple of bottles of High Rock water, gazed proudly at his aunt. "What do you think of my aunt, the eighty-year-old corporate raider?"

"The word's out on the street already," said Paulina. "The market likes it. Our stock's up one and seven-eighths already today. Everybody's happy that Paulina Langenberg is acquiring Paulina Langenberg. Everybody but me. Oh, I'm happy," she added. "But let me tell you—being an eighty-year-old corporate raider is no big deal. An eighty-year-old puppet is more like it."

"What do you mean?" asked Leon as he poured the water.

"That I'm the puppet of the Seltzer Boy. He planned it this way. He knew I'd take over his company. He knows me better than I know myself." She picked up a document and passed it to Leon. "He's sharp. Very, very sharp."

"The proxy statement for High Rock Waters," said Leon.

"Read the paragraph that's circled, 'executive severance agreement,'" said Paulina, pointing with a freshly lacquered fingernail.

Leon set down the bottle and read: "'In the event of a change of control, Mr. Brant will be entitled to three years' base compensation.' Et cetera, et cetera." He passed the document back. "A golden parachute."

"A diamond parachute. We have to pay him whether we like it or not. With stock options, he could end up walking off with millions." She pushed the tail of the turtle buzzer. "Jack, my vitamins."

The telephone rang again. This time it was a different phone, a red one. Paulina answered it herself.

"Paulina Langenberg." Pause. "From Garden City. How nice," she said, her voice sweet as honey. And then: "Much better, thank you. What can I do for you?" For a few seconds, there was silence as the caller voiced her request. "What happens when you use Mineral Lotion Number Three?" asked Paulina. She nodded. "I see. Have you taken the computer test? Good. What is your eye color? Gray. Hair color? I see. What color was it before?" she asked, writing down the reply on the back of an envelope. "Skin color? Do you tan easily? You do, but you burn first. Aha! That's it! That's why you're having trouble."

Jack handed her a saucerful of vitamins. She put them into her mouth one by one, then downed the mouthful with a swig of mineral water.

"That's all right, dear," she continued. "This is what you do: use Mineral Lotion Number Two. Number Three is too strong for you. Take it back and exchange it for Number Two. No, it won't cost you anything. Do you wear pink lipstick?" She listened for the reply. "Well, you shouldn't. Always use lipstick with an orange tone: Copper Rose would be good on you. We'll send you one. That's right, no charge. Just give your name and address to my secretary. My pleasure," she purred. "Good-bye." To Charlotte, she said: "I never refuse to talk to a customer. People don't believe it, but it's true. Isn't it, Leon?"

Leon nodded. "There's a special toll-free number."

"The customer's the real boss." She addressed Leon: "If you think I'm the boss, you're wrong. It's Mrs. What's-Her-Name from Garden City who's the boss. And when I'm dead, don't you forget it. The minute you forget it's Mrs. What's-Her-Name from Garden City who's the boss, you're in trouble."

"Yes, Aunt Paulina."

"*Not* that I'm ready to go yet. Okay, where were we? Oh, the Seltzer Boy. Feh! He can have his money. I'm going to get my company back. If it costs me millions, that's the price I'll have to pay." She looked pained. "Anyway, in the end it will go to my Anne-Marie." She pressed the turtle buzzer again.

Jack stuck his head around the corner of the door.

"Jack, show Mrs. Stockholder Anne-Marie's announcement."

Jack nodded. In a minute, he appeared at Charlotte's side with a recent issue of the *Times*. On the back page of the second part of the Sunday A section was a headline: "Anne-Marie Andersen to wed Gary A. Brant." Above the story was a picture of Anne-Marie looking uncharacteristically demure.

"She's got herself a good one this time," said Paulina. "He's smart, very smart. Even if he did outfox me. Not like that nothing she used to be married to." She turned to Charlotte: "I hear he's the chief suspect in this bath business. Have the police got anything on him yet?"

"Only the cell therapy business." She didn't want to tip her hand.

"Cell therapy—what a fraud. I reported him for it. The food and drug people were supposed to send someone up from Washington to investigate, but they never did. So inefficient, these bureaucrats." She turned around to talk to Jack: "Did you give him his walking papers?"

"This morning," he replied.

"Good riddance to bad rubbish is what I say." She spoke to Charlotte: "Speaking of this bath business, I hear you've been snooping around the Bath Pavilion. Did you find out anything?"

"Oh," said Charlotte, caught by surprise. She should have known Paulina's spies would have reported her. Deciding there was no harm in it, she proceeded to tell Paulina about the tunnels. "Yes, as a matter of fact. I think the murderer might have used the tunnels to get to and from the Bath Pavilion."

"What tunnels?" asked Leon.

"Pipe tunnels. The spa is underlaid by a network of tunnels that house the pipes for the mineral water. They connect all the buildings. Each building has an entrance in the basement. For instance, someone could go from here to the Bath Pavilion without ever going above the ground."

"Is that right?" commented Leon.

"Oh, those pipes," said Paulina, slapping a palm to her forehead. "You wouldn't believe what it cost me for those pipes." She turned to Charlotte. "Thank you for telling me. I like to know what's going on."

"Actually, I came to see you about something else. An engagement."

"I know about it already. I read it in the *Times*."

"Not that engagement. Another engagement. Elliot's."

"Aha! He's going to marry The One with the Freckles?" Charlotte nodded. "Claire Kelly."

Paulina's eyes narrowed in suspicion. "Why are you telling me?"

"She wanted me to. She wants me to pave the way for a reconciliation. Elliot apparently felt badly about going behind your back, but he also felt he had to assert his independence. Claire would like things to be patched up between you. But Elliot won't take the first step."

"So she wants *me* to? Tell her that if she thinks Sonny's stubborn, she hasn't seen anything. That's where he gets it from—his mother. Don't I have my pride? Why should I be the one to make the first move? He was the traitor. He has to come to me." She turned to Leon. "Right?"

"Right," agreed Leon, bobbing his head like a trained seal.

Charlotte had laid the groundwork for her big line. Now she was ready to deliver. After a pause, she continued: "Claire thought you might be interested in making the first overture because . . ."

"I know. Because I'm on my deathbed," interjected Paulina sarcastically. "Well, tell her nobody's going to push me into the grave."

"No, as a matter of fact, that wasn't the reason."

Paulina looked at her as if to say, "Well?"

"Because of the baby."

Charlotte thought at first that Paulina hadn't heard. Had she spoken loudly enough? she wondered. It was as if the gears in Paulina's brain that processed information into compartments labeled marketing strategies, research and development, and accounts receivable had jammed on an undigestible item. With the exception of her nervous crisis, Charlotte had never seen Paulina's face so inanimate. Then a look of innocent delight slowly crept across her ancient, hardened features, like the rise of a warm breeze over the dusky Russian steppes. "Did you say a baby?" she asked in a tremulous little voice.

"Yes," replied Charlotte with a grin. "A boy. She's had amniocentesis. She already knows it's going to be a boy."

"A boy," repeated Paulina softly. And then, more loudly, "A grandson." Standing up, she threw her arms into the air and spun herself around in a spontaneous dance of joy that would have been ridiculous if it hadn't been so touching. "A grandson. I'm going to be a grandmother."

Leon glanced over at Jack, who stood at the door of the office, and then back at his aunt. It was as if he couldn't believe his ears. "That's very nice, Aunt Paulina," he said lamely.

"I can't believe it," said Paulina. "Sonny's going to be a father. God be praised." She slowly lowered herself back into her chair, an exultant expression on her face. After a moment, she spoke: "This girl Claire. I think she'll be good for him. She has a level head on her shoulders."

"I think so too," said Charlotte.

"When's the baby due?"

"November. They're planning on getting married next month."

"Next month. That doesn't give us much time." She rummaged around on her desk for a pencil. Then she retrieved a crumpled ball of paper from the wastebasket. "Such waste," she said, carefully smoothing it out. "How many times do I have to tell you," she chided Jack, "write on both sides!"

But Jack didn't smile. "Excuse me," he mumbled. Turning on his heel, he disappeared into the hallway.

Paulina started scribbling. The gears were in motion again. "Okay, we'll have the wedding in New York. Where is he? I want him to take notes." In irritation, she pressed the turtle buzzer. A dreamy look came over her face. "I wonder what they're going to name him."

"Claire didn't say."

"Maybe they'll name him after Herbert," she said, referring to Elliot's father. She shook her head. "Tsk. Tsk. What are we going to do about her? All those freckles. Thick ankles. No chic. But she has potential. She has nice eyes, warm eyes. What do you think?"

"I think she's very attractive," said Charlotte.

"She just needs some makeup, that's all. There are no plain women, only lazy ones. With a little makeup, she'll be a beauty, my daughter-in-law."

It was difficult for Paulina to understand that not wearing makeup was an expression of liberation. To her generation, it had been just the opposite.

Jack reappeared.

"Where have you been? I want you to take notes."

Jack withdrew a notebook from his breast pocket.

"Okay. One: send her a jar of our freckle cream. Two: schedule her for a make-over at the New York salon. Three: schedule her for a picture at the photographer's—the posh one on Park Avenue. Make-over first, picture second." She paused, chewing thoughtfully on her glasses. "Those hippie skirts, ugh." She screwed up her face in distaste. "We'll have to get her some clothes. Get The Stylish One in the New York office to take her around."

"Judy Dawson?" said Jack.

"Yes. Bonwit's, Bloomingdale's. She can charge everything to me."

Jack nodded.

"Good. That takes care of her. Now where were we? Wedding arrangements. Next month. Check the date with

Sonny. We'll have the reception in Greenwich. A nice jazz band, tasteful, quiet. Celebrity Caterers can do it. They did such a nice job on the fete. What else?" she mused. "The engagement announcement. Call the *Times*. Tell them I want two columns on a Sunday. Like Anne-Marie."

Jack made a notation.

"Only bigger. A double-decker headline at the top of the page. Threaten to cancel our advertising if we don't get what we want."

And so it went—invitations, wedding dress, menu, even the honeymoon, which Paulina decided the newlyweds should spend at her Paris apartment. If Claire had any illusions about her and Elliot leading a quiet life out of the glare of Paulina's spotlight, they wouldn't last long.

"Oh, and get Sonny on the phone," Paulina said finally. "I want to talk to him. And get that girl up here. It's time for bylines to be bylines."

"Bygones, Aunt Paulina," corrected Leon.

"Thank you, Leon," she said cheerfully. "One more thing. Call The Lawyer with the Blond Wife. Tell him to get up here on the double."

"What are you going to do?" asked Leon, a note of panic creeping into his voice.

"I'm going to change my will. I'm going to get my company back and I'm going to have a Langenberg to leave it to."

"But . . ."

Paulina raised a bangled forearm to silence him. "Don't worry, you'll be well taken care of. You always wanted to be financial vice president. I'll make you financial vice president. How's that?"

Leon crossed his arms over his chest for a moment and pouted. Then he rose suddenly from his seat. "If you want to know, it stinks." With that, he stalked out, slamming the door behind him.

Paulina shrugged. "If he doesn't want it, he doesn't have to take it. Jack, get out my will. I might as well start working on it right now. At my age, I might go any minute. I have to have everything in order."

Jack headed in the direction of the bedroom.

"And call the bathhouse. Make an appointment for this

afternoon. If I'm going to keep up with my grandson, I have to be fit." She winked. "As my father used to say, 'Your health comes first, you can always kill yourself later.'"

After a short nap, Charlotte headed over to the Bath Pavilion. Heavy gray clouds had moved in, bringing a steady rain. To avoid getting wet, she had jogged across the esplanade. Anne-Marie would have been proud of her. She took refuge in one of the pergolas that flanked the entrance of the spa while she waited for her breath to subside. It was a pleasant shelter, draped as it was by fragrant lavender clusters of wisteria. It was even lighted: so dreary was the weather that the photosensitive control for the lanterns hanging from the vaulted roof had been triggered. From this cozy niche, Charlotte had a fine view of the esplanade. The archway framed a picture of a wet green lawn bisected by a gravel path. Hurrying along the path was the upright figure of a little woman in a red rain cape. She was carrying a red umbrella of the kind given away as a gift-with-purchase at Langenberg cosmetics counters. She moved with quick little steps, her red bowler hat bouncing up and down.

Charlotte had often come across Paulina walking alone in the city just as she was now. It had always surprised her that someone as rich and famous as Paulina was not accompanied by bodyguards. She supposed the same might be said of herself. But she didn't carry around a fortune in the form of rings, necklaces, brooches, and earrings. Even the ornaments on Paulina's hats were often real jewels. Paulina's attitude toward her jewelry was, "If I can't wear it, what's the point of having it?" Given her nonchalance, she had been very lucky. She had only been mugged once. The value of the jewelry that was stolen was never disclosed, but it was rumored to have been over a million dollars. Luckily, she wasn't hurt. Nor had the incident persuaded her to change her ways: she had shrugged it off with her usual blithe disregard for bad fortune.

"Aha! Mrs. Stockholder," said Paulina, reaching the pergola. She closed the umbrella and tucked it under her arm. "Are you having a bath too?"

Charlotte replied that she was.

"It's a good afternoon for it," said Paulina, looking up at the rain streaming off the roof. "Shall we walk over together?"

Charlotte said yes and rose from her seat.

As they strolled under the colonnades, Paulina chatted about her company's future. She had witnessed what had happened to the competition after the deaths of the company founders. The Eye Shadow Man's company had been taken over by a soap conglomerate that had sold it off piecemeal, while That Woman's company had been convulsed by a power struggle that had led to its ruin; its products had met the ignominious fate of being sold in drugstores and five and dimes. Paulina had prospered from their misfortune. She now had no major competitors for the well-heeled carriage trade, although there were always ambitious upstarts trying to muscle in. But, she confessed, something had gone out of her life with the deaths of her competitors. Much as she had complained about their spying and their thefts of her ideas, she missed them. That's why having a grandson was so important to her. With a Langenberg in the future, she had something to look forward to. And with it, the hope that what had happened to the other companies wouldn't happen to hers.

Charlotte noted the contrast. A few hours earlier it had been, "If I die, it's no big deal." Now it was, "I have a grandson to look forward to."

They had reached the Bath Pavilion. The reception desk was being manned by Frannie's husband, Dana, who was leaning back reading a magazine, his sneakered feet propped up on the marble counter. At the sight of him, a look of outrage crossed Paulina's face. Marching over to the counter, she rapped him over the shins with her umbrella. "Look sharp, young man," she said.

Startled, Dana hastily removed his feet from the counter and scrambled to attention. "Mrs. Langenberg," he said in his soft Carolina accent. "Miss Graham. I'm sorry. I didn't see you. I was just filling in for the receptionist."

"Filling in or not, you should look professional," said Paulina.

"Yes, ma'am," said Dana. "I'm sorry, ma'am. It won't happen again."

"It had better not. You might find yourself out of a job."

With that, she marched off toward the women's wing. In the women's lobby, she draped her cape over the arm of a waiting attendant and then took stock of her surroundings. Spotting a scrap of paper under a chair, she pointed to it with the tip of her umbrella. "Clean that up. We can't have litter on the floor."

Mrs. Murray, who was standing at attention, scurried down the hallway, returning a few seconds later with a dustpan and brush with which she quickly swept up the offending scrap of paper.

Charlotte took great pleasure in seeing her getting her comeuppance.

Paulina marched on down the corridor, on the lookout for the slightest breach of her lofty standards. The staff was lined up on either side like royal subjects for a procession of the queen.

Leaning on the handle of her umbrella, Paulina bent over to study the black-and-white-tiled floor, which shone like a mirror. "How long has it been since the floor was waxed?" she asked.

"Someone comes in every week," replied Mrs. Murray.

"Then get someone else to do it or have it done more often. Do you see these scuff marks?" She pointed out a few barely visible scuff marks on the polished floor with the tip of her umbrella.

"Yes, Mrs. Langenberg."

And so it went: dust balls, unemptied ashtrays, spotted mirrors—all came in for Paulina's criticism. When she finally reached the VIP suite at the end of the hall, the staff seemed to breathe a collective sigh of relief.

It was here that Charlotte and Paulina parted. Charlotte entered her bath cubicle and quickly undressed. She was looking forward to a long soak in the effervescent waters.

Hilda entered a few moments later. "Hello again," she said. She smiled, revealing the wide gap between her large, protuberant front teeth.

Charlotte smiled back. She held no grudge against Hilda. She had only been doing her duty. As had Mrs. Murray for that matter.

Hilda kneeled down to draw the bath. "Do you think you'll

catch the person who killed that poor Mrs. Singer?" she asked coyly.

So she had figured out why Charlotte had been exploring in the basement. "I hope so," replied Charlotte.

"You'd better catch him soon. Some of the guests have stopped signing up for baths. They're afraid." She then left to fetch a glass of water from the fountain. Returning a moment later, she handed Charlotte the glass and then tested the bath, which she pronounced ready.

Charlotte stepped in. The water fizzed like an uncorked bottle of champagne. Hilda adjusted the pillow behind her head and then floated the towel on the surface of the water in front of her face. "The temperature, is okay?" she asked, swirling a forearm in the bubbly waters.

Charlotte nodded.

After wishing Charlotte a pleasant bath, Hilda left to attend to her other clients, diminished in number though they were.

Charlotte settled back, tucking her feet into the toe hole. Her skin was sheathed in iridescent bubbles. She thought again about the Greeks and their sacred springs. It could be argued that the whole of Western religion could be traced back to these sacred springs, to say nothing of medicine, art, and music. By the Golden Age, the early Greek spring temples had grown into huge health resorts, centers for worship and entertainment. Her own craft could trace its origins to these ancient spas, where the first actors sang the praises of the gods. Later, huge outdoor amphitheaters had been built. Charlotte had once visited the amphitheater at Epidaurus, the birthplace of Asclepius. It was a marvel of ancient architecture: tier upon tier of limestone benches coiled into the lap of the mountainside like a giant serpent. Returning in the early morning, she had declaimed the closing lines of *Antigone* to the pale Peloponnesian dawn: "There is no happiness where there is no wisdom;/No wisdom but in submission to the gods./Big words are always punished,/And proud men in old age learn to be wise." It was one of her most memorable moments.

She set the glass down and turned to rest her cheek against the curved edge of the tub, savoring the coolness of the porcelain. Soothed by the carbon dioxide, she drifted off to a Hellenic paradise of sacred olive groves and thyme-carpeted fields. If she were to imagine another life for herself—apart from Lillian Leonard's—it wouldn't be as Frannie's desert hermit, but as an actress in ancient Greece, or rather an actor, since the actors had played both male and female roles.

The scream jerked her back to reality. "Ai-ai-ai!" It came again: a high-pitched wail that reverberated down the corridor like a Klaxon down a silent street. "Ai-ai-ai! Ai-ai-ai!" There was no mistaking the voice.

Charlotte jumped out of the tub and pulled on her robe. She had gotten up too quickly: for a moment, she had to steady herself on the back of the chair as a wave of dizziness overcame her, but it quickly passed.

"Ai-ai-ai!"

She ran out into the corridor. The door to the VIP suite stood open. Entering, she found Paulina sitting bolt upright in the tub, a towel draped over her head. Her knees were pulled up to protect her chest and her white-knuckled hands were gripping the sides of the tub for all she was worth.

Charlotte removed the towel. Paulina's eyes were screwed shut. "Paulina, it's Charlotte. Are you all right?"

Paulina opened her eyes. "Yes," she said. Her head barely protruded from above the rim of the tub. Strands of long black hair had come unraveled from her chignon and mascara smeared her cheeks. "Where is everybody? Somebody tried to kill me."

"Somebody tried to kill you?"

The tops of Paulina's huge breasts, like those of some primitive fertility goddess, bobbed on the surface of the water. Suddenly conscious of her nakedness, she pulled the towel over herself. Charlotte noticed she was still wearing the sapphire ring. The motive wasn't robbery.

"Yes. He went out that way." She nodded toward the door. "Into the hall. He was going to kill me. Drown me. He was trying to hold my head underwater."

"Who?"

"I don't know. I was dozing. A man, a strong man."

"Will you be all right?"

Paulina nodded.

Charlotte ran out of the room. Outside the door, she bumped into Hilda, who had come running in response to the scream.

"Someone's tried to kill Mrs. Langenberg," Charlotte explained.

Hilda's penciled eyebrows flew up in alarm.

"Do you know where there's a flashlight?"

Hilda nodded.

"Good. Go tell Mrs. Murray to call the police. Then get the flashlight and bring it back here to me. And hurry."

Hilda galumphed off down the hallway, her slippers flapping.

Charlotte returned to her cubicle and quickly changed into her clothes. Then she headed back to the VIP suite. As she passed the door to the basement, she could feel the cool draft of the cellar air. It stood wide open.

Paulina had lifted herself out of the tub and was donning a terry-cloth robe. She looked pale, but composed. She was already knotting her chignon back in place. I'm all right," she said, emerging from the inner chamber.

Hilda returned with the flashlight. A small crowd of curious guests was already gathering in the hall.

"Did you tell Mrs. Murray to call the police?"

Hilda nodded.

"Good. I'm going after Mrs. Langenberg's assailant. You stay here with her until Mrs. Murray gets here. When Mrs. Murray gets here, call Mr. D'Angelo at the Health Pavilion and tell him what's happened. Tell him that I've gone into the tunnels after the assailant. Have you got all that?"

Hilda nodded. "Miss Graham?"

"Yes?"

"Be careful."

· 14 ·

AS CHARLOTTE DESCENDED the basement stairs, she wondered if what she was doing was wise. What if the killer was armed? But she had to go after him. She had stood by once while a murderer had fled. Besides, he was probably far away by now. Almost ten minutes had elapsed since the attempt on Paulina's life, enough for him to get halfway around the spa. The most she could hope for was a clue. She quickly reached the foot of the stairs. Which way to go? On instinct, she headed to her right—to the south. She had already explored the tunnels to the north with no results.

Switching on her flashlight, she opened the door. She could hear nothing. As she entered the tunnel, however, her attention was immediately captured by the appearance of the ground underfoot. Unlike the other tunnels, which were tracked if at all only by the long, narrow footprints that she suspected were the Mineral Man's, the ground here bore evidence of recent traffic. She stooped to examine the tracks. None were clear enough to determine the size of the shoe, but she could distinguish two types—the waffle tread of a sneaker and the smooth print of a leather-soled shoe. Standing up, she shined the flashlight overhead. As she expected, the beam revealed two pipes, the steam pipe and the pipe that carried High Rock water from the esplanade to the Pump Room. Although she hadn't explored these tunnels, she felt as if she already knew the layout. She was becoming as familiar with the spa's tunnels as she was with those of the IRT. In a few minutes, she reached the door to the basement of the southwest pergola. Here too there was evidence of recent traffic: the brass knob was polished to a dull sheen by frequent use.

The door was unusually heavy. To her surprise, she discovered that its inside surface was lined with lead. The reason became apparent when she directed the beam of the flashlight toward the room's interior. It was the fallout shelter she had imagined only half seriously to exist, right down to the cache of canned vegetables. But it did make sense, she thought as she entered, the door closing with a dull thud behind her. A basement with a ready supply of fresh water made an ideal fallout shelter location. She shined the flashlight around the room. Sandbags to block the radiation stood against the walls. Some had ruptured, spilling sand over the damp ground. Against the sandbags stood stacks of metal shelving. One was devoted entirely to food. Aluminum canisters labeled flour, sugar, coffee, tea, and so on (there was even one for Ritz crackers) occupied one section. Another section held canned goods now pitted with rust: string beans, tomato soup, cranberry sauce. A second stack of shelving was devoted to household supplies, including a game of Scrabble and a first-aid kit. Still another held survival equipment: a hunting knife in a leather holster, a Geiger counter, several tanks of oxygen. Even a freezer. What had they planned on using for electricity? she wondered. In short, everything for the well-appointed fallout shelter except a rifle to shoot the poachers who hadn't the foresight to build fallout shelters of their own. She felt a little like Carter must have felt on entering King Tut's tomb: here were the remains of a civilization that now seemed almost as remote as that of ancient Egypt, a civilization that believed nuclear war was survivable.

For a few seconds she took it all in: it was both funny and horrifying, like a sick joke. Ritz crackers and Scrabble, my God. Rats she had expected, even a murderer, but not this. It was then she noticed the unusual smell: sweet, like vanilla. She looked down. At her side stood an orange crate that had been turned on its side. On top of it stood several bottles of High Rock water. Protruding from the necks were the burned remains of sticks of incense. She lifted one to her nose: vanilla. Other bottles of High Rock water held candles. Their labels were now obscured by incrustations of multicolored wax. In the center of the room stood a decrepit wicker rocker whose coat of hospital green paint identified its origin as the stack of cast-off furniture in the basement of the Bath Pavilion. The dishes scattered around had clearly been purloined from the spa's dining rooms. It was clear that the former fallout shelter now served a different function, a function revealed by the tiny butts littering the sandy ground at her feet. Adaptive reuse, the planners called it. What had once been a fallout shelter was now a hideout for smoking dope.

She wanted to explore the fallout shelter, but she wanted to make sure first that no one was lurking on the other side. Crossing the room, she opened the door and shined her light into the darkness—nothing. But she did think she could hear the distant thud of footsteps. If they were those of Paulina's assailant, he was already far away—not that she would know what to do if she caught up with him anyway. She turned back to the fallout shelter. A dusty stack of magazines on the ersatz coffee table caught her eye. On top was a pamphlet entitled: "Understanding Your Aura." She wondered if it was the text for Frannie's course. Opening it, she read: "There is a vast world of hidden vibrations beyond those that are measured by scientific instruments . . ." The frontispiece was a crude drawing of a figure framed by a fan of squiggly lines. Underneath the aura pamphlet was a collection of magazines from the fifties. Into her mind popped an absurd picture of fifties' survivalists reading magazines and playing Scrabble until nuclear winter was over. She picked up a 1954 issue of the *Saturday Evening Post*. It was all fifties grimness: "Can Russia Trust Its Slave Armies?" and "Let's Quit Talking Nonsense About the Cold War." Those who romanticized the fifties as a halcyon era of innocence had forgotten the darker side of those quiet years.

As she leaned over to return the magazine to the pile, her attention was jerked back to the present. Sandwiched in among the magazines was a typed manuscript entitled: "LIFE READING ON THE ENTITY BY THE NAME OF ADELE B. SINGER. Born April 11, 1944 in Brooklyn, King's County, N.Y. Date of Reading: June 9. Place of Reading: High Rock Springs, N.Y." Charlotte scanned the first page. It was a brief medical history: height, weight, blood pressure, and so on. It also mentioned a history of alcoholism and drug abuse, repeated hospitalizations for drug overdoses, and two suicide attempts. That it had been culled from the spa's medical records was clear from the fact that it included Adele's biological age (noting that it was ten years older than her chronological age) and her assignment to C-group. Charlotte was puzzled: why was it called a "life reading," why did it refer to Adele as an "entity," and what on earth was it doing down here? She continued reading:

"The Instrument has isolated the vibration of the entity by the name of Adele B. Singer. According to the *akashic* records, the former appearances on the earth plane have been quite varied." It appeared to be some sort of mystical reading of Adele's past lives. She read on: "The entity has experienced previous incarnations in Ireland, Rome, Syria, Peru, and Atlantis." The reading briefly described these earlier incarnations before moving on to the entity's "last appearance on the earth plane," in which it "took part in those journeyings from east to west" known as the Gold Rush. "In 1849," the reading stated, "the entity was involved in selling strong spirits to miners in California. The sale of strong spirits often led to rowdiness and drunken behavior, which sometimes had tragic consequences. The entity's experience of drug and alcohol abuse in its current incarnation is karmic retribution for its past. But although the entity sold strong spirits in its last incarnation, it was also one to whom many came for counsel. From this, it is evident that the entity possesses talent as a counselor. Because of the entity's karmic past, its mission during its present sojourn on the earth plane is to aid people for whom karma has ordained a life of addiction. It was for this that the entity has returned to the earth plane in the present experience."

Setting the document down, Charlotte took a deep breath. According to the Instrument, whoever he or she was (the reading had the smell of Frannie about it), Adele had been a barmaid in her last life. The Instrument had a vivid imagination anyway. Charlotte smiled as she imagined a tarted-up Adele passing mugs of beer across a bar to a row of grizzled prospectors, their necks craned for a glimpse of her cleavage. From what she could gather, Adele was supposed to make up in this life for the sins of her customers in the last. She was reminded of the laws that held the host responsible if a drunken guest killed an innocent person in a car accident on the way home from a party. Except that Adele's fate wasn't a jail sentence, but a new life as an alcoholic in which she was not only supposed to cure herself but to help others as well. When it came to punishment, the law of karma had a vengeful quality to it. If a Roman matron laughs at the cripples, give her a gimpy leg; if a barmaid serves up strong spirits, turn her into a lush. No one could ever say the punishment (or rather the educational opportunity) didn't fit the crime.

She continued reading: "The entity, however, has failed to progress in this life embodiment. Instead of taking advantage of the opportunity for karmic action, the entity has continued to accumulate negative karma. The decay of the physical envelope is a reflection of the entity's spiritual degeneration. The entity has made minor progress in recent months, which is reflected in a slight improvement in the condition of the physical envelope, but there is still much room for improvement. The entity continues to poison the Temple of the Living God; it is a human pillbox." A human pillbox? The Instrument also had a knack for the catchy phrase. She read on, expecting more of the same mystical chitchat, but what came next was far from chitchat. "In order to prevent further degeneration," the reading said, "disincarnation is recommended." Charlotte reread the sentence. *"Disincarnation is recommended."* In other words, it was time to close the book on Adele. She felt the goose bumps rising on her forearms. Was the Instrument predicting Adele's death? Or was the Instrument *responsible* for Adele's death? She read on: "On the other side, the etheric entity will experience a period of rest and reunion with the Supreme Source while it awaits the restoration of the soul in another body.

"The Instrument is losing its energy; it must now revitalize. If we perform right action, we will build good karma. Life is God: that which is constructive grows, that which is destructive deteriorates. We are born alone, we die alone. There is but one Source."

Whew! The Instrument, whoever it was, was off its rocker. She was about to set the document down when the yellow beam of the flashlight caught a few handwritten words at the bottom of the page. She moved it closer. Printed in pencil in a small, neat hand were two phrases: "Disincarnation scheduled Monday, June 11. Mode of disincarnation: water."

A wave of panic rushed over her, the same wave of panic that still occasionally hit her on the stage, that turned her legs to jelly and her voice to a feeble croak. She leaned her head back, gasping for breath. She felt as if a giant block of concrete were pressing down on her chest. Her stomach was revolving like a cement mixer; the vanilla scent was making her nauseous. Closing her eyes, she concentrated on breathing slowly and deeply until she felt the muscles in her chest relax and the wave of panic subside. Then, like a child going over its lessons, she slowly reviewed the significance of the document before her. It was a reading of the *akashic* records, the records that Frannie had described as a chronicle of everything that had happened, was happening, and would happen in the universe. The reading had been conducted by a person who described itself as the Instrument and who believed itself to be capable of tuning in to Adele's vibration in the *akasha* (like tuning into a radio frequency, Frannie had said). The Instrument had received the message that the entity by the name of Adele Singer was recommended for disincarnation. For an early discharge, so to speak. Ergo: the Instrument had taken it upon itself to be the agent of Adele's disincarnation.

Charlotte wasn't sure her reasoning held, but no matter how she looked at it, she kept coming back to the same conclusion. Adele had died on June eleventh. The mode of her death was water. In which case, the Instrument who retreated to this basement hideaway to turn on and tune into the vibrations of the etheric universe was Adele's murderer. Was the Instrument Frannie? Had she been speaking from specific knowledge when she said Adele was "living on borrowed time"? It was also Frannie who had said Adele would be better off starting over in another incarnation. Or was the Instrument one of Frannie's disciples, someone who had taken the Other Lives/ Other Selves course? In any case, it appeared that the Instrument thought it was helping Adele advance on her spiritual journey. A form of karmic mercy killing. Charlotte was reminded of the play *Arsenic and Old Lace*, in which she had once played one of the crazy Brewster sisters. The pious old maids made a practice of helping homeless old men along the path to Jesus with glassfuls of elderberry wine laced with arsenic. "Murdered! Certainly not!" says Abby of a man whose body they have just stuffed into a window seat. Her sister replies: "What we've been doing is a mercy." Only the situation at High Rock wasn't a comedy. Damn, all her theories about Sperry were now shot. That's what she got for being so smug. For it could be said of Sperry with some certainty that he would make an unlikely Instrument. His interests clearly inclined toward the earthly plane.

She shined the flashlight around the room, but there were no other clues: a crumpled candy bar wrapper, an empty can of Coke. She decided to see Jerry. By now, he would be at the Bath Pavilion. She decided to take the reading with her and then changed her mind. The Instrument might get suspicious if it returned and found it missing. In fact, it probably wasn't such a good idea to hang around. She had been down here a little too long for her own good. The Instrument might come back, although it was a better bet that it wanted to get as far away as possible. Again, she fought down a wave of panic. What if the Instrument had come along while she was wandering through the tunnels? She carefully put the reading back in place and then shined the flashlight around the room in a last check for clues. As the beam swung past the door, her heart jumped into her throat. She was sure the door had closed behind her, but it now stood slightly ajar. Mesmerized by fear, she dumbly riveted her flashlight on the opening and watched as it slowly widened. The hunting knife! She grabbed it and quickly removed it from its holster. Then she switched off the flashlight and backed up toward the other door. The room was suddenly bathed in light. The intruder had switched on a flashlight. Then she saw it nudge its way through the opening: the shiny, black muzzle of a gun. She wanted to scream, but nothing would come out. She was gulping for air. Then she screamed.

Screamed, and turned to flee through the other door.

"Charlotte!"

It was Jerry's voice. He was standing there in front of the door, the gun hanging loosely from his hand. The sight of his bull-necked figure was as reassuring as that of the neighborhood cop walking the beat on a deserted street. She breathed a sigh of relief. "Jerry," she said.

"Sorry," he said, putting the gun away in his belt. "Hilda gave me the message. I thought I'd better take this along. Did you see anyone?"

"No. If he came this way, he got away. But, Jerry, I've discovered something else."

"Hey, are you all right?" he said, looking at her more closely. "I didn't mean to scare you."

She must have looked frazzled. "Yes," she said. But even to herself, she sounded not quite sure. "It's not you—I mean"— she looked down at the gun—"that. It's what I've found out."

Jerry nodded at the knife that she still brandished in her hand. "I don't think that would have done you much good." He shined his flashlight around the room. "Hey, what is this? A fallout shelter?"

"Yes," replied Charlotte. She put the knife back in its holster and returned it to the shelf and then pointed to the collection of butts on the sandy ground. "One that's being used as a hippie hideaway."

"So I see," said Jerry. He looked up at her. "Okay, what's up?"

Charlotte proceeded to tell him the whole story, starting with how she'd seen the Mineral Man from the seventh floor of the hotel. From there, she went on to Regie's confirmation of the existence of the tunnels, her meeting with Otto, and her exploration of the tunnels on her own.

Jerry listened intently, interrupting only to say that he'd always known about the tunnel at the end of the basement corridor in the Health Pavilion, but that he'd had no idea the entire spa was underlaid by tunnels.

Charlotte nodded and went on to explain how she'd clocked the time it took her to get from the Health Pavilion to the Bath Pavilion.

"So then it could have been Sperry. He could have made it across and back between appointments."

"Yes, he could have. But he didn't. He isn't the murderer, Jerry." She sighed. "Or at least, I don't think he is."

"Who is?"

"I don't know. Maybe Frannie."

Jerry blinked in surprise.

She handed him the reading.

"'Life Reading on the Entity by the Name of Adele B. Singer,'" read Jerry. "Another Brooklyn kid." He proceeded to scan the health information.

"It's some sort of mystical accounting of Adele's past lives," Charlotte explained as Jerry turned the page. "It was written by someone who calls himself, or herself, the Instrument. At the end, it says, 'In order to prevent further spiritual degeneration, *disincarnation is recommended.*'"

Jerry took his time reading the document. After a minute, he said, "I see it. 'Disincarnation is recommended.' In other words, the Instrument killed Adele at the direction of this Supreme Source."

"It looks that way to me. But there's more." She pointed to the handwritten note at the bottom of the second page.

"'Date of disincarnation: June eleventh. Mode of disincarnation: water,'" read Jerry. "June eleventh. That's the day Adele was killed."

Charlotte nodded.

"So this wacko who calls himself the Instrument kills Adele in the belief that he's doing her a favor." He shook his head. "Some favor. Why Frannie? I know she's a little looney tunes, but that doesn't make her a killer."

"Because she's so involved with reincarnation. She talks about it all the time. And she teaches those courses, Other Lives/Other Selves and You and Your Aura. Look." She showed him the aura pamphlet.

"I see what you mean," said Jerry, studying the pamphlet. "Crowley should be here by now. I think we'd better let him in on this." He grinned. "Looks like you've done it again, kid."

"Only because the Instrument tried to kill Paulina," said Charlotte. "Should we show Crowley the reading?"

"No, we'd better let him come down here and get it. I don't want to tread on his turf any more than necessary."

As they got ready to leave, Jerry ran the beam of his flashlight up and down the stacks of shelving. They spotted it simultaneously: a black object nestled among the cans of string beans and peaches that was an obvious anachronism in a fifties-era fallout shelter.

"A tape recorder," said Charlotte. "Jerry, maybe the Instrument recorded the reading. Didn't you get the feeling that the reading had been dictated while the Instrument was in some kind of trance? Remember, it said at the end that it was losing its energy?"

"Yeah. In which case, the voice on the tape would be the Instrument's." He checked to see if the recorder held a cassette, but it didn't. He then started searching the shelves. Before Charlotte could offer her help, he had discovered two cassettes stashed in a flour canister.

"That was quick work," said Charlotte admiringly.

"Practice. Here," he said, passing her the tapes, which he held with a handkerchief to prevent smudging the fingerprints. "You do the honors."

"Thanks. Don't mind if I do." She slipped the first tape into the tape slot, rewound it, and pushed "Play." The voice on the tape said: "Life reading on the entity by the name of Adele B. Singer. Born April eleventh, 1944 in Brooklyn, King's County, N.Y."

She had expected to hear Frannie's voice. But it was a man's voice—a man with a soft Carolina accent. Not Frannie, but her husband, Dana. She pictured him: a handsome young man with a thick black beard and a graceful brow. Of course. It didn't make sense that a lame Frannie would have traipsed down to the fallout shelter for a joint. Besides, Frannie operated out of the Health Pavilion; it would have been a hike for her. Dana operated out of the Bath Pavilion, which was only a short distance away. One of her first thoughts had been that the killer worked at the Bath Pavilion. If anyone was likely to have figured out the best way of killing someone in a bathtub, it was someone whose job was getting people in and out of one. Maybe it had even happened accidentally once or twice: a slip in the tub—the feet fly into the air, the head is momentarily forced underwater . . . Or maybe, as a karate instructor, he had somehow deduced that forcing the head backward in such a way would have the same effect as a karate chop to the neck.

"LaBeau," said Jerry. "No wonder you didn't run into him—he probably went through the basement and back up the stairs to the men's wing."

"Yes," said Charlotte. But what about the footsteps she had

heard in the tunnel? She wrote them off to her imagination. As Dana's voice droned on, images came to her mind of Dana running to Adele's aid with the resuscitator, of Dana notifying Jerry of Art's death.

"He was one of the first on the scene—in both cases."

"That should have told us something right there."

"Do you know him at all?"

"A little. He's as nutso as she is."

"Why did he do it, do you think?" Frannie had said he was working off the karmic debt he had incurred in a previous incarnation in ancient Rome when he fed the Christians to the lions. Was this the way he was doing it? If so, he hadn't made much progress in close to two thousand years.

Jerry shrugged. "I've given up trying to figure out why people do the things they do." But he did offer the fact that Dana had been a sickly child who'd been spurned by his sports-minded father in favor of his more athletic siblings. As a result, he'd grown up to be a very fitness-minded adult.

Perhaps, theorized Charlotte, his childhood experiences had left him with a pathological hatred of the unfit.

"Then why did he marry a cripple?" asked Jerry.

"Good question." And if he did hate the unfit, why had he suddenly felt the compulsion to start killing unfit guests? Charlotte wondered if Frannie knew. She remembered seeing Frannie typing dictation in the office next to Jerry's. Was it she who had typed the reading?

They returned their attention to the tape. When it came to the part about the human pillbox, Charlotte was reminded of Art, the self-described devotee of the electric pencil sharpener. Maybe he had also been killed because his physical envelope was degenerating.

She pushed the STOP button. She had been struck by a chilling thought. "Jerry, I have a theory. Maybe Dana is killing people who are unfit, using physical fitness as a *gauge* of spiritual achievement."

Jerry looked puzzled.

"The reading gives Adele's medical history, including her biological age, which in her case was considerably higher than her real age. If the condition of the body is a mirror of the condition of the soul, and if the biological age is a measure of the condition of the body—"

Jerry completed the sentence for her. "—then those who don't do well on the Fitness Appraisal are candidates for being hastened along the path to spiritual enlightenment, courtesy of Dana LaBeau."

"Yes."

"Maybe. But that would mean that everybody in C-group would be on his list." He pointed at her. "Including you."

"No. If I've got this guy figured out, he would only be out to disincarnate people who are in C-group because of their self-indulgence. I'm in C-group because of my real age. After all, you can't stick a sixty-two-year-old woman in A-group with all the twenty-year-olds."

"What about smoking dope?" asked Jerry, gazing down at the butts littering the sandy ground. "Isn't that a form of self-indulgence?"

Charlotte shrugged. "Maybe not to him. I'm sure he can find a rationalization for it. Maybe he thinks it doesn't matter as long as he stays in shape. Or maybe he thinks it's all right because it's a means of tuning into the *akashic* records."

"Let me see if I've got this right," said Jerry, his brow furrowed in thought. "According to your theory, you'd be doing pretty well in his book. Your biological age is lower than your real age, which would be a sign of spiritual progress."

"Exactly," replied Charlotte.

"My brains are getting scrambled just thinking about it."

"I know what you mean." In Dana's terms, she thought, the body perfect of someone like the Role Model would be a sign of spiritual achievement. But in her opinion, his obsession with his body bordered on narcissism. And to her, worshipping the body seemed as great a sin as doing violence to it. At least Adele and Art hadn't considered themselves better than everyone else because of the superior condition of their *latissimi dorsi*. They were humble and kind, which should count for something—count for a lot, in fact. But although the gauge theory made no sense to her, it *did* make a crazy sort of sense. This time her intuition was telling her she was on the right track.

"But what about Paulina?" asked Jerry. "How does she fit in?"

"I don't know." Who knew? Maybe Dana didn't like the way she hit him over the shins with her umbrella. She returned her attention to the tape. "Do you want to continue listening to this or do you want to see what else we've got?"

"Let's go on. We might find the reading for Paulina or for someone else. We can always come back to this later."

Charlotte pushed the FAST FORWARD button, stopping to listen occasionally until she came to the end of Adele's reading. After a silent interval came the next reading, for Mary Jane Jacoby.

"Do you know her?" asked Charlotte.

"The blonde babe who fixed you up with Sperry? The one with the inch-long red fingernails and the two-thousand-dollar tank watch?"

Charlotte laughed her low, husky laugh. "I guess you do know her. She's an oil heiress. She's married to a producer I know."

M.J.'s reading also led off with the date and place of her birth, the date and place of the reading, and a brief medical history. It went on to detail M.J.'s past lives as a close friend of the Borgias during the quattrocento and at the opulent court of the Sun King. Leave it to M.J. to be where the action was, Charlotte thought. When the reading came to the description of the entity's attributes, she had to smile. "The entity," Dana's voice said, "lacks mental discipline." The reading went on to say that M.J.'s service to others made up for her failure to discipline her mind. (She was a well-known philanthropist, serving on committees for everything from blind animals to battered wives). By her charitable works, it said, she was building good karma. Her youthful appearance was her reward for correct development.

"A plastic surgeon may have had something to do with it," interjected Jerry.

"Or Sperry's injections," added Charlotte.

The reading concluded with M.J.'s date of disincarnation, which wasn't for twenty-six years. "She's safe," said Charlotte. By then, she would be well into her eighties.

After another silent interval, the voice on the tape resumed.

The next reading was for Nicky, who had high blood pressure, diabetes, and joint problems, and who weighed over three hundred pounds, or had. Nicky, a twenty-four-year-old man with a biological age of fifty-four.

"If anyone's likely to fit your theory, it's this kid," said Jerry.

The date of the reading was June sixteenth—only two days before. "Yes, the Instrument has the records here," said Dana's voice. "The Instrument has isolated the vibration of the entity by the name of Nicholas Makriannias in the skein of time-space. In the composite of the latent or astrological and the material sojourns, we find these influences: the entity has failed to develop the spirit with regard to brotherly love, forgiveness, and understanding. In its other appearances in the earth plane, it has consistently chosen to sit in judgment of its fellow travelers. In the land of its present nativity at the beginning of the present century, the entity worked as a doctor at Ellis Island. In this position, it allowed only the healthiest immigrants to remain in the New Land. As a result, many were deported, and some died on the return journey. In ancient Greece, the entity was responsible for choosing youths to participate in the Olympic Games. As the entity judged others, now it is judged; this is the swing of the karmic pendulum. The entity's current incarnation offers many lessons to be learned in the exercise of the will, which is the greatest faculty of the soul. But because the entity has continued to selfishly indulge its appetites, its condition has not improved. Instead of progressing in this material manifestation, the entity is regressing. The deterioration of the physical envelope is a reflection of the deterioration of the soul. All illness comes from sin; the body is the Temple of the Living God. In order to progress to the next stage in the cycle of rebirth, disincarnation is recommended. In its next incarnation, the entity will have another opportunity to apply the will to spiritual growth that it may emerge from the darkness of disease and anxiety into the light and freedom of unity with the Supreme Source. This is the Universal Law of Evolutionary Progress. The Instrument is losing its energy, it must revitalize. If we perform right action, we will build good karma. Life is God: that which is constructive grows; that which is destructive deteriorates. We are born alone, we die alone. There is but one Source."

This time, the words were on the tape: "Disincarnation scheduled Tuesday, June nineteenth."

"That's tomorrow," said Jerry.

Charlotte nodded.

And then: "Mode of disincarnation: fire."

· 15 ·

CHARLOTTE AND JERRY emerged from the basement of the Bath Pavilion feeling as if they were emerging from some twilight world of the psyche where black was white and vice versa. The women's wing was deserted, but the door to the VIP suite was being guarded by a police officer who stood with his back to the corridor, taking notes. Inside, another police officer was measuring the anteroom and a fingerprint officer was dusting it for fingerprints. At the other end of the hall, a guard had been posted to prevent unauthorized access to the scene. Charlotte and Jerry headed in his direction. When they reached him, Jerry asked to speak to Crowley. If the guard was curious about where they'd come from he didn't show it. He simply asked them to wait with the others in the women's lobby. As in the case of Art's death, those who had been present at the scene were being held for questioning. They sat around in chairs that had been brought in, looking put out, scared, or bored. Paulina was not among them. She had probably been taken to the hospital for a checkup. In front of the building stood three police cars, one with its lights still flashing, and a van displaying the call letters of the local television station. A camera crew was unloading its gear. Paulina wouldn't welcome the publicity. "Bad for business," she would say.

"Here comes the press," Charlotte whispered. She reminded herself to slip out a side door after their interview. When it came to the press, she was as experienced at surveillance and evasion as a guerrilla warrior.

"No talking, please," admonished the guard.

She had forgotten: the police didn't want their sources influencing one another with their accounts of events.

After a few minutes, the door to the room that was being used as an office opened and Dana emerged. As a member of the staff, he would have been among the first to be questioned. Charlotte had to muster all of her self-control to avoid staring at him, this pleasant-looking young man with the nice southern manners and the deranged soul dating back to the Big Bang. He passed through the lobby, taking no notice of them or of anyone else. The thought crossed her mind that he might try to escape before it dawned on her that he was still unaware that they had found him out.

The guard then signaled Charlotte and Jerry to enter. Crowley was seated at Mrs. Murray's desk. Another officer sat next to him, notepad in hand. Charlotte retold her tale, starting with her discovery of the tunnels. Crowley listened impatiently—clearly, he thought there were more pressing matters at hand. But by the time she got to Adele's reading, he was sitting on the edge of his chair. The tapes were the icing on the cake. It was a tribute to his professionalism that he didn't take Charlotte to task for interfering, but acted immediately on her findings. By that evening, two undercover policemen were working at the spa as janitors. Others were assigned to watch the LaBeaus' house and the hotel. Both Dana and Nicky would be watched around the clock. In addition, a policewoman was assigned to watch Frannie on the chance that she was in league with her husband. At the first sign that Dana intended to put his plan into action, he would be arrested and charged with the attempted murder of Nicky and with the murders of Adele and Art.

For the time being, Crowley decided to leave the reading and the tapes alone. He didn't want to risk tipping Dana off. But one thing about their account baffled him: the reference to fire. It baffled Charlotte and Jerry as well. Why wouldn't Dana plan to kill Nicky in the bath as he had the others? It was Charlotte who came up with the answer: Nicky wouldn't fit. Jerry cited the case of a visiting group of Japanese sumo wrestlers, all of whom had been too big for the tubs. Like the sumo wrestlers, Nicky had used the whirlpool bath instead. The fire mode might refer to the whirlpool, Jerry speculated.

Dana could be planning to turn the thermostat up so high that
Nicky would die of a heart attack or heat stroke. Perhaps he
was planning to drug him first. Such "hot tub deaths" were not
uncommon, particularly in California: too much to drink, the
thermostat turned up too high, and the partiers are found
floating like dead fish the next day, an empty pitcher of piña
coladas at their sides. With Nicky, high blood pressure played
into the picture: five of Anne-Marie's jumping jacks were
enough to turn him beet red from exertion, let along the cardiac
workload of coping with a soaring body temperature.

Another baffling fact was that Paulina's assailant had tried to
kill her by holding her head underwater instead of jerking her
ankles. But Charlotte decided to let Crowley worry about that.
The case was in his hands now. She had done what she could
and now felt for the first time since Jerry had confided his
suspicion that Adele's death might be something other than a
simple overdose that she could relax, which was what she'd
come to the spa to do in the first place. After leaving Crowley,
she and Jerry headed directly for Lillian's, where they cele-
brated with a drink—Charlotte indulged herself in a prohibited
manhattan—and dinner. After Jerry dropped her off, she went
to bed and slept for a solid eight hours.

Her alarm went off at the crack of dawn. She had resolved
to devote the entire morning to her spa routine. Although she
would be staying over—she didn't want to miss the outcome of
the drama that was being played out—it was still the last day
of her program and she wanted to make the most of it. Her
follow-up Fitness Appraisal, which would show what im-
provements her stay had brought about in her physical condition, was scheduled for late morning. Then lunch and a bath
and her spa stay would be over. She would be leaving the next
day. She had lost six pounds, but she didn't know what that
translated to in terms of inches. In any case, she couldn't count
her stay as much of a bargain. Per pound, it had cost close to
seven hundred dollars. Besides which, they were pounds that
would creep back on again in a matter of weeks. Experience
had taught her that dieting was futile. She always reverted to
her original weight, which couldn't be called slender, but

which was okay with her. She was of the minority opinion that a little extra flesh never hurt anyone, especially at her age.

But the weather hadn't cooperated with her good intentions. The day had broken cold and rainy. She had begun on the right foot, with a visit to the High Rock Pavilion for two glasses of mineral water followed by Awake and Aware with Anne-Marie, which had been held in the Health Pavilion instead of on the esplanade as usual. But Terrain Cure had been canceled, leaving her with some extra time before her follow-up. She decided to visit Jerry. She wanted to find out what had come of the surveillance of Dana and Frannie. But his office was vacant. A janitor (she wondered if he was an undercover cop) directed her to his new office on the second floor.

"Hey, I like your digs," said Charlotte as she entered. It was Sperry's old office, complete with dove-gray leather chairs and vertical blinds.

"Quite the ritz, huh? Have a seat." Coming around to the front of the big teak desk, he pulled out a swivel chair for her.

Charlotte sat down. "What happened to the previous tenant?"

Jerry shrugged. "All I know is, he's been given the sack and I'm living in luxury. But I suspect it'll be back to the basement for me as soon as the boss lady gets a new medical director."

"Think positively," said Charlotte. "What are you going to do with the casting couch?" she teased.

"Oh, that." Jerry smiled. "Actually it's kind of an embarrassment. If I took the legs off one end, I could use it as a slant board. I hear they're very good for the complexion. What do you think?

"That's an idea. Or you could use it for doing sit-ups." She switched the subject: "I came to check up on what's going on."

"A lot," replied Jerry. "We've got our boy. We were on the right track—it was the sauna. One of our men spotted him doping out the temperature control last night. He's scheduled Nicky for a session on the machines tonight. Presumably he'll suggest that Nicky take a sauna afterward."

"When everyone's gone home."

"Exactly. If I'd been on the ball, I would have figured it out. We reserve time in the machine room at night for the disabled, the obese—people who might be self-conscious about working out with the group. Just getting some of these fat people onto the machine is a major production."

"So the time wouldn't have aroused anyone's suspicions."

Jerry shook his head. "It helps that he's Nicky's exercise advisor. After the workout, he recommends a sauna to soothe Nicky's tired muscles. Then he turns up the heat, locks him in, and waits. For someone with blood pressure as high as Nicky's, it wouldn't take long."

"And it would be written off as an accident."

"Easily. There wouldn't be any clues. He'd just reset the temperature control and unlock the door once Nicky was done for."

"Have you told Nicky?"

"We had to. He's going to play along. He's a spunky kid. By the way, do you remember the tape we didn't play?"

"Something was on it?"

"Crowley went down to the fallout shelter this morning to listen to it. He made sure Dana was busy doing something else first. Nicky wasn't the only one who was scheduled for disincarnation."

"Who else?"

"Someone you know."

Charlotte couldn't think of anyone. "Come on, Jerry. Who?"

"Frannie."

Charlotte stared at him, her large eyes awash with the gray light that streamed through the windows. They were a pale gray, almost white: a dove-gray. "He would have killed his own wife?"

Jerry nodded. "She was scheduled for disincarnation for next week. The mode of disincarnation was air. Suffocation, maybe. A little pillow talk and then the lights go out—for good."

"But she doesn't fit the profile. Her limp was something she was born with. She didn't bring it on herself. In fact, she was supposed to be discharging her bad karma by helping others become more fit."

"Neither did Paulina."

"Was there a reading for her?"

"No. That was one of the things Crowley was looking for.

But actually, Frannie does fit, sort of. According to her reading, she was born with a gimpy leg because she laughed at the cripples in ancient Rome."

"Yes, she told me that. She was a member of Roman royalty. She also told me I was a desert hermit in my last life, very spiritual and pure. I subsisted on nothing but dates and water."

"Dates, huh?"

"Go on," urged Charlotte.

"Well, according to the Instrument, she had already paid her karmic debt by her good works. Therefore, it was cruelty to keep her on the earth plane any longer. She was ready to return as a more advanced being."

Charlotte wondered why he really did it. In marrying Frannie, she speculated, he might have been marrying the sickly self he despised, and by killing her, he might have been killing the cripple in himself. In any case, she was sure the shrinks would have some explanation or other.

"She was supposed to wait for him on the other side," Jerry continued. "Once he was disincarnated, they would be reunited in the etheric plane and then reincarnated together in another life. Soul mates, you know."

"I guess that proves she wasn't in on it. I suppose he didn't say how long she'd have to wait around for him out there."

"As a matter of fact, he did. About forty years or so—you see, he still had a lot of bad karma from his past lives to work off."

"By helping people disincarnate? He's going to have to change his approach. How does making license plates sound?"

"I wouldn't count on it. He'll walk—they all walk. He'll cop an insanity plea—a year in a rubber room and he'll be back on the streets along with all the other maggots who've beat the criminal justice system."

"Maggots, huh?"

"Yeah. You know, those little white worms that feed off garbage. It's a constant tide of maggots out there. They're coming at you all the time. No matter what you do, there're always more of them."

"That's a comforting thought."

Jerry grinned.

* * *

Charlotte knew it would be Frannie who would conduct her
follow-up, but she nevertheless felt a lump rise in her throat as
she saw Frannie waiting for her in the lobby of the Health
Pavilion, her ears sticking out from between strands of lank
blond hair and her game leg tilted out at a peculiar angle.
Seeing Charlotte, she smiled crookedly. She seemed naked,
defenseless, too frail to take the blow. Her marriage, her
future, her beliefs, would all be shattered, maybe even
ridiculed. Again Charlotte thought of the baby mice: blind,
pink, unprepared for exposure to the harsh world outside their
nest. What would she draw on to see her through? But perhaps
she had unexpected reservoirs of strength. People often did. At
least she had the day-to-day routine of a job she loved to
depend on. It was a strange and monstrous feeling, being able
to see Frannie's future being played out like this. Sitting there,
in the heart of the dusky, columned lobby, her slight figure
seemed unreal, a murky image floating deep within a crystal
ball.

Frannie rose to greet her. "Are you ready for the verdict?"

"As ready as I'll ever be."

Again they climbed the staircase to the diagnostic room.
Again they went through the twelve stations. To Charlotte's
surprise, several of her fitness parameters had improved. Her
lung capacity was better, as was her resting pulse—a result,
said Frannie, of the "training effect." She had also lost eight
inches, most of them from her hips.

"See, it pays off," said Frannie, recording the inches lost.

"I guess so," Charlotte concurred, rather weakly.

"You're auric field is brighter than it was too—more
energetic, more shimmery. That means you're more balanced.
The aura reflects the changes in your spirit. When you don't
take care of your body, your spirit suffers, and when you do,
your spirit is more radiant."

"Frannie?" interjected Charlotte. "Remember when you
said that Mrs. Singer would be better off starting over in
another life?"

"Yes." Stepping back, Frannie raised a pensive knuckle to
her chin and gazed intently at Charlotte. Her attention was

elsewhere. "But we still have a problem," she said. "A big problem."

"What?"

Moving around to Charlotte's back, Frannie placed her hands on Charlotte's shoulders. "Your spine is like a steel cable," she said, digging in her fingers. She spun Charlotte around. "Look at your shoulders."

Charlotte looked in the mirror. Her shoulders were hunched up around her neck. The tension was obvious.

"We can't have you going home like that," said Frannie. She instructed Charlotte to sit on the lifecycle and lean over the handlebars.

"There's something I don't understand," continued Charlotte as Frannie worked the back of her head and her neck. "Does that mean that the person who killed Mrs. Singer did her a favor?"

"Oh, no. I probably shouldn't have put it that way. She wasn't making any progress, it's true; but that's not to say she wouldn't have. The only route to enlightenment is through the karmic experience on the earth plane."

"So if you take someone's life, you're robbing them of their opportunity of reaching enlightenment."

"Exactly. If you take someone's life, you're robbing them of the vehicle of experience, the body. A favor—never. To interfere with someone's karmic destiny is the worst kind of cosmic crime."

"I see," said Charlotte. Even within the context of Frannie's strange beliefs, there was no way of justifying what Dana had done.

Frannie finished by raising and lowering Charlotte's arms a few times. "Now look in the mirror."

Charlotte obeyed. It was remarkable: her shoulders now sloped naturally and felt much more relaxed, all as a result of applying pressure to a few small points. "Thanks," she said. "I needed that."

Frannie went on to demonstrate several exercises to relieve shoulder tension. She suggested doing them daily and wrote them down in a fresh copy of the exercise prescription booklet. Then came the second part of the Fitness Appraisal: the computer interview. But this time Frannie instructed Charlotte to answer the questions according to how she'd behaved during her spa stay. If she hadn't drunk any alcohol, she should say she didn't drink. If she hadn't smoked, she should say she didn't smoke. If she had exercised daily, she should say that too. The computer would then calculate her biological age based on the good health habits she'd established at the spa.

Charlotte's health habits during her spa stay hadn't exactly been simon pure, but she played along anyway. To the alcohol question, she answered no (she'd only had two manhattans and a couple of beers), as she did to the smoking question. When she finished, she rejoined Frannie, who had been inputing the results of her physical evaluation.

"I want a pledge," said Frannie as they waited for the printer to spew out the computer's verdict.

"Let me guess. No cigarettes?"

Frannie nodded.

"Cut back on the cocktails?"

Frannie nodded again. "One per day—that's it."

"Okay. What else?"

"Salt. No more potato chips. Your face is already less puffy than it was. Just because your good health and good looks are a positive karmic consequence doesn't mean you should abuse them," she scolded. "Your body is a temple . . ."

"I know, but I treat it like a hotel room."

Frannie grinned.

The printer stopped and Frannie tore off the printout. "On to Anne-Marie," she said, heading toward the exit. Outside of Anne-Marie's office, she paused to rummage through the bag in which she carried her paraphernalia. She withdrew a small package neatly wrapped in red tissue paper. "For you," she said, holding it out shyly. "I've enjoyed working with you."

"Thank you," said Charlotte, touched that Frannie would have gone to the trouble of getting her a farewell present. She opened it up. It was a gift package of plump California dates.

"For inspiration."

"Dates!" Charlotte threw back her head and laughed. "If you think I'm going to come back as a desert hermit, you're crazy. But thank you very much." Charlotte was amused, but she was also sad—sad that Frannie had such a good-natured sense of humor about her off-the-wall ideas.

"Maybe as a Mother Superior in a very posh, very elegant convent," offered Frannie with her crooked smile.

"That sounds all right."

After bidding Frannie a fond good-bye, Charlotte took a seat in Anne-Marie's office to await her follow-up personal consultation. Anne-Marie arrived shortly, striding into the room with the confidence of a champion tennis player walking onto the court.

"I understand congratulations are in order," said Charlotte as Anne-Marie took a seat behind her desk.

"Thank you. Did you see the announcement in the *Times*?"

"Yes. Paulina showed it to me."

"Paulina!"

"She seemed very proud. She thinks you've made a good match."

"Did she? I'm glad to be back in her good graces. But I'm puzzled. She doesn't usually forgive a grudge so readily."

"She may be softening."

"Paulina, never."

"You'd be surprised. Maybe it's because she's going to be a grandmother. Claire's going to have a baby." Charlotte didn't think it was her business to tell Anne-Marie about Paulina's cancer, which might have been another reason for her change of heart.

"Oh, that's wonderful," said Anne-Marie, looking up in pleased surprise. "When's the baby due?"

"November. They're getting married next month. Paulina's already making all the arrangements. Starting with the engagement announcement, which she specified should be 'bigger than yours.'"

Anne-Marie chuckled. "That sounds like Paulina. How is she?"

"I haven't seen her today. But she seemed all right yesterday."

"Good. Such a terrible thing. Do the police have any leads yet?"

"None," lied Charlotte. Anne-Marie was obviously unaware that until yesterday her ex-husband had been the chief suspect. She changed the subject: "Speaking of weddings, when is yours?"

"September fifteenth. We're leaving for our honeymoon on the twentieth. We're going to Nepal."

"Climbing mountains?"

"Yes. It will be Gary's first major expedition, although he's done a lot of climbing in the Tetons. We'll be climbing Annapurna Four. It's one of the easier summits in the Annapurna massif." She pointed to one of the mountain photographs hanging on the wall. "That's Annapurna there."

The photo showed a wall of cloud-hung peaks. It looked immense. Next to it was the photo of the two people on the narrow ledge. She now recognized the sharp-pointed features of Anne-Marie's fellow climber to be those of Gary. It wasn't the way she would have wanted to spend her honeymoon.

"I wish you both luck."

"Thank you," said Anne-Marie. She picked up the printout. "Now, let's see. Are you ready to start climbing mountains yet?"

"Heartbreak Hill is about it for me."

"Heartbreak Hill is as good a place as any to start," she said. She studied the printout. "Well, you're not going to win any prizes."

"I didn't expect to." The spa awarded prizes in the form of a brooch of the Indian maiden to the guests who had lost the most inches and the most pounds during the course of their program. But at least she had earned an achievement pin for graduating to a steeper grade of the Terrain Cure.

Anne-Marie continued: "But you'll be pleased to know that if you maintain the health habits you've established here, you'll cut another three years off your biological age."

At her age, three years was beginning to look like a long time. Though she still didn't believe in all that biological age mumbo jumbo. "The cigarettes and the cocktails?"

"That, and the exercise."

"But I do exercise. I walk. A lot."

"Not enough. You should be taking a brisk forty-minute walk four times a week. That's easy to remember: four and four. At a moderate pace, forty minutes should be about two miles."

"There never seems to be enough time," Charlotte protested.

"That's because you think of exercise as an intrusion on your life. You have to start thinking of it in the same way you think of brushing your teeth—as a part of your day. It will become a pleasure—you'll see."

Anne-Marie wrote down her instructions in Charlotte's booklet. "You'll notice that we're not giving you a lot to do. Only the shoulder exercises and the walking. We don't want to overwhelm you."

"That's good."

"But that doesn't mean we're not encouraging you to do more. What I'm writing down is the bare minimum. By the time you come back next year, you should be ready to run up Heartbreak Hill."

"I doubt that."

Charlotte spent the next half hour being bombarded with self-improvement advice. She left with her booklet full of instructions and her head full of resolutions and promises, including one to return next year.

She always felt uplifted by a resolution to turn over a new leaf, no matter how ephemeral she knew it to be. She therefore found herself feeling the sting of irritation less acutely than usual when she ran into M.J. in the lobby of the Health Pavilion.

M.J. explained that she was in-between treatments. She had already had a manicure and a pedicure and would be returning to the salon in a few minutes for a facial, a haircut, and a perm. "A complete make-over from the neck up," was how she described the rest of her treatment.

Charlotte repressed the urge to comment that a complete make-over from the neck up was just what M.J. needed.

M.J. wriggled her fingertips to display the polish on her inch-long nails. It was a revolting shade of purple. "I know it's vulgar, but I couldn't resist," she giggled. "Blackberry Brandy—it sounded so good. My toenails are Chocolate Mousse. After a few days at this place, you start pickin' colors because they sound good to eat. That reminds me, have you been to Mrs. Canfield's yet?"

Charlotte replied that she hadn't.

"Oh, so noble. I must confess that I have. But I only had a

cup of coffee and a chocolate truffle. It couldn't have done me much harm. Look," she said. Thrusting out her right breast (whose dimensions Charlotte knew to have been augmented by an implant of silicone), she proudly displayed the brooch that was pinned to the jacket of her light gray B-group sweat suit.

"You won the prize!" said Charlotte. "Congratulations."

M.J. nodded proudly. "For losin' the most pounds in the Four-Day Rejuvenation Program," she said. She stood on her tiptoes to whisper in Charlotte's ear: "Strictly on the q.t.—it was the laxatives that did it."

Charlotte raised an eyebrow.

"I know it's not real weight, but it gives you a psychological lift to lose four pounds in a day, you know?" She slid her hands down her hips and rotated them in an imitation of Mae West. "Irwin's going to l-o-v-e the new me. Listen, Charlotte, did you ever get your cell injections?"

"No. Just the Reinhardt test."

"I'll bet you were goin' to get glands. All the older ladies get glands. But don't worry. You can still get 'em. Dr. Sperry's goin' to open a new clinic in Mexico. A friend of mine's goin' to back him. When it opens, I'll give you a call. It'll still be a lot cheaper than goin' to Switzerland."

London, the Bahamas, High Rock, Mexico. Sperry was like the street vendors in New York who fold up shop when they see the cops coming, only to resume selling gold chains and wristwatches on another corner fifteen minutes later. He was probably getting out of the country one step ahead of the FDA.

"Thanks," said Charlotte. She wondered if M.J. would still be able to collect her two-hundred-dollar referral fee.

"It works, I guarantee it," M.J. went on. "Look at me: my biological age is only thirty-seven. Do you believe it? I owe it all to Gil, I mean Dr. Sperry. Isn't it terrible that they fired him? I know cell therapy's against the law and all that, but it isn't like he's a murderer or anything."

"Not it isn't," agreed Charlotte emphatically.

"Anyway, I'm goin' to be even younger by the time I check out of here. I have my follow-up later on. I wouldn't be surprised if I got down to thirty-five. Which would mean I've still go a lot of years left."

Another twenty-six, according to the Instrument, Charlotte thought.

M.J. continued: "By the way, you never told me your biological age."

"That's right," said Charlotte. "I never did."

It was the next morning—Charlotte's last at High Rock. She was sitting in Crowley's cubicle at the casino with Jerry and Jack. Crowley was filling them in on what had happened. Jack had been dispatched to the meeting by Paulina, who claimed to be too busy to take the time to hear what the police had to say. In truth, she probably didn't want to. If Charlotte knew Paulina, she was already well on her way to forgetting that an attempt had ever been made on her life. She had an amazing ability to block out the negative events in her life. If it was bad, it hadn't happened—it was that simple.

Crowley sat behind a desk piled high with papers, among them the gruesome souvenirs of two murders and one murder attempt. Among the papers, Charlotte could see a copy of Adele's reading, a photo of Art's nude corpse lying on the tiled floor, and a police sketch of the VIP suite.

He was explaining that Dana had been picked up last night after locking Nicky in the sauna.

"Did he confess?" asked Jack.

"Sort of," Crowley replied. "He really had no choice. We had the reading and we had the tapes"—he nodded to Charlotte—"thanks to Miss Graham—and we'd caught him more or less red-handed. His excuse was that he was acting as the Instrument of this Supreme Source."

"The devil-made-me-do-it defense," said Jerry.

Crowley looked disgusted. He also looked pale and worried, despite the fact that he finally had a murderer behind bars.

"How's his wife?" asked Charlotte.

"Okay," replied Crowley. He explained that a policewoman had been sent out to the LaBeaus' house after the arrest to stay with her until her sister arrived. At first, she'd been stunned. She hadn't said anything. But she was now talking, which was a good sign.

Jerry took over: "She thinks he might have come under the influence of an evil spirit guide. She said that you have to be careful when you're dealing with out-of-the-body experiences, that all of the spirits you encounter in the etheric plane aren't necessarily good ones."

Charlotte remembered what she had said about opening yourself up to an entity: you never knew what might come jumping in.

Crowley addressed Jack: "Back to your question. He admits to killing Mrs. Singer and Mr. Dykstra—that is, he admits to being the Instrument—but he swears up and down that he had nothing to do with the attempt on Mrs. Langenberg's life."

"Did he have an alibi?" asked Jack.

Crowley nodded. "Ironclad. He was minding the reception counter in the Bath Pavilion while the receptionist took a break. At least half a dozen people saw him there. Including Miss Graham and Mrs. Langenberg."

"Which means what?" asked Charlotte. "That there's another murderer?"

Crowley looked grim. "It looks that way."

Another murderer! Another murderer would explain a lot. Why there was no reading for Paulina. Why Paulina didn't fit the profile of the other victims (the murderer couldn't have known about the cancer and it wasn't something she had brought upon herself anyway). Why a different technique was used. Crowley was right: there had to be someone else. Her mind was racing. Knowing that the police had a suspect—that much had been in the newspapers—Paulina's assailant had probably counted on her murder being blamed on the suspect. But what he couldn't have known was *how* Adele and Art had been killed. In trying to kill Paulina by holding her head under, he'd given himself away. She was reminded of Diamond Jim's quote: "Never play another man's game." It was advice he could have benefited from. But who would have wanted to kill Paulina? A business rival? With Paulina out of the way, Gary would retain control of his company and hers. But he had planned on Paulina's taking over his company, or so she had said. A relative? By killing Paulina before she could change her will back, Leon would remain her heir. A vindictive employee? Paulina's habit of firing people (or rather, having them fired) was bound to have provoked resentment. Maybe this time the killer *had* been Sperry.

"What about Sperry?" she asked. "Is he still around? I heard from one of the guests that he's going to open a clinic in Mexico."

"He's in L.A.," said Crowley. "He flew out yesterday. He's staying with one of his clients. The L.A.P.D. is keeping an eye on him."

"Jack, when did you fire him?"

"Monday morning."

"Jack fires him on Monday morning, and someone tries to kill Paulina on Monday afternoon."

"It's a possibility," said Jerry.

"Did the fingerprints show anything?" asked Charlotte.

"No," said Crowley. He and Jerry exchanged looks.

"What is it?" asked Charlotte.

"It's just that they rarely do." It was a procedure, Jerry said, that was usually performed more for its public relations benefit than in expectation of any results. "The public expects a detective to scatter a lot of black carbon around and go over it inch by inch with a magnifying glass," he said. But there were lots of reasons why fingerprinting was rarely helpful. First, any criminal with half a brain either wore gloves or wiped his prints. Second, getting unsmudged prints was difficult, and when you did, they usually belonged either to the victim or to the others at the scene. Third, even unknown fingerprints were no use unless you had some idea who they belonged to. The idea of a central file through which fingerprints could be identified was a myth. Not only did fingerprints submitted to a central file have to be accompanied by a list of names of the people whose prints they were to be compared with, the people whose names were on the list had to have been arrested on a federal charge; otherwise, their prints wouldn't be on file. "Footprints," he went on. "Now footprints are another story."

Footprints! As Jerry said the word, a bell went off in Charlotte's head. Something about the idea of footprints was important in this case. She imagined herself back in the tunnel. The long, narrow footprints between the Health Pavilion and the Hall of Springs, the Mineral Man's footprints. No, that wasn't it. The footprints between the Bath Pavilion and the fallout shelter—that was it! Part of it. The other part was the soles of the running shoes on the marble counter in the reception lobby.

She addressed Crowley: "Was Dana wearing sneakers when you arrested him?"

"Yes. Running shoes, I think."

"The kind with waffle treads?"

"I think so. Why?"

"There were two sets of footprints in the tunnel. One was a sneaker, a running shoe, with waffle treads. The other was a regular shoe. But the second set was pretty unclear."

"And you think the other set might belong to the second killer?"

Charlotte nodded.

"We'll look into it." He nodded to his assistant, who made a note. "Well, I guess that's it," said Crowley. He rose from his seat, signaling that their meeting was at an end. He turned to Jack. "We'll keep you informed of any new developments. Please give my regards to Mrs. Langenberg."

"I will," said Jack. Jerry stayed behind to compare notes with Crowley. But she didn't go directly back to the spa. After declining Jack's offer of a ride, she struck off toward town in search of a hardware store.

Fifteen minutes later, she was headed back to the spa on the minibus, a newly purchased flashlight in her bag. She would be driving back to New York after lunch, but there was something she wanted to check before she left.

Back at the spa, she headed directly for the Bath Pavilion. The baths weren't open in the forenoon, but she was able to get in through the unlocked door to the sun terrace and enter the basement unobserved. She quickly made her way past the stack of wicker furniture and through the laundry area to the tunnel. Inside the tunnel, she switched on the flashlight and shone it on the earthen floor. She had wanted another look at the footprints. What she saw looked like the mud at the edge of a desert watering hole. The ground had been so tracked up by Crowley and his men that it was impossible to distinguish one print from another. No matter—if the killer was Sperry, he'd have left some prints on the other side. Passing through the fallout shelter, she turned left into the unexplored tunnel. The ground here was muddy from seepage. And in the mud there

were footprints. Their imprint was as clear as that of a signet
ring in a drop of sealing wax. Kneeling, she shined the light on
the one closest to her. And then on another. Just to make sure.
She now knew who had tried to kill Paulina. It was someone
who knew about the tunnels. Someone who stood to lose if
Paulina changed her will. He had been running. She could see
where his feet had slid in the mud. Walking to, and running
back. So she hadn't imagined the pounding footsteps. Step by
step she followed them—through the tunnel to the basement of
the pergola where she'd taken shelter from the rain, and from
there into another tunnel, where a dark opening midway along
the south side marked the junction with the tunnel leading to
the hotel. Like the tunnel between the power house and the
spa, the tunnel leading to the hotel appeared to be low and
narrow and encrusted with mineral.

It was here that the footprints stopped. He had come from
and returned to this tunnel. She stooped to get a closer look:
there was even a fan-shaped mark where he had pivoted to
turn. She was about to stand up when something in her brain
registered a flash of white just inside the entrance to the tunnel.
She had just figured out that it was a white coat when she felt
a heavy object come down over the back of her head. Her last
image was of something like stars floating in a void of black at
the fringes of her consciousness. Not stars exactly, but rings,
concentric rings, like the rings of a tree.

· 16 ·

"ARE YOU ALL right?"

The fuzzy blur in front of Charlotte's face congealed into the solid, reassuring face of Jerry. "What are you doing here?" she asked.

"I tracked you. I'm pretty good at footprints myself. I figured you'd be too impatient to wait for Crowley."

"What happened?"

"You tell me."

Charlotte raised a hand to the back of her head; it felt bruised but there was no lump. "Somebody hit me over the head."

"I figured that much out. With the butt of a flashlight, I'll bet. If it weren't for that thing on the back of your head, you'd be a lot sorer."

"You mean my chignon?" teased Charlotte.

"Hey, it's called a bun where I come from." In one hand, he held a flashlight; in the other, an object wrapped in a handkerchief. His gun was tucked into his belt.

"What's that?"

Jerry unwrapped the object. "A hunting knife. The one from the fallout shelter, the same one you almost used on me."

"He was going to use it on me?"

Jerry nodded.

"What would he have done with me?" She knew it was a stupid question, but she was still dazed. She couldn't think.

"I don't know. Stuff you into the freezer in the fallout shelter until he got a chance to bury you somewhere." He grinned, displaying his dimples. "Put you in cement shoes and dump you into Geyser Lake."

"Very funny. Any other ideas?"

Jerry shook his head. "Did you see him?"

"Only a glimpse. White—a white coat."

"That could have been anyone."

Anyone: Sperry, but he was in California; Dana, but he was in jail. Suddenly it all came back to her. The rings, like the rings of a tree. The hand-sewn loafer protruding from the edge of a booth. He had returned to the tunnel to erase his footprints. She was the only one who knew what his footprints looked like. That's why he'd tried to kill her.

Raising herself up on one elbow, she gripped the rock-hard muscles of Jerry's upper arm: "It's coming back now, Jerry. I know who it was."

It was the next morning. Charlotte hadn't gone back to New York as she had planned. She'd spent the afternoon at High Rock Community Hospital, waiting around for her skull to be X-rayed. As it turned out, she was fine. Not even a minor concussion. But she hadn't been ready to leave yet either, at least not until Paulina's assailant had been caught.

Paulina sat on the chartreuse velvet couch at the far end of her living room. She was dressed for business in a black-and-gold-checked suit and a black silk blouse. Down her bosom cascaded a half-dozen strands of Russian amber beads, which were matched by the yellow stones on her ears and on her finger. She was chewing on a hunk of Hungarian sausage.

Charlotte and Jerry sat facing her. They had been drafted by Crowley to explain what had happened. They'd just finished telling her that her assailant had been picked up on the Thruway near Buffalo at about eight the night before. He'd been heading west in her Mercedes, who knew where to.

Jerry had already explained about Dana: how he'd had an alibi and how that had led him to the conclusion that there was a second killer. He had then explained why the realization that there was a second killer had prompted Charlotte to return to the tunnels for another look.

"How did she know they were his?" asked Paulina about the footprints.

"By the imprint of the holes in his soles. Charlotte had noticed the holes on an earlier occasion. In fact, he'd pointed them out to her. He was making the point that he wasn't in the job for the money, I think."

Paulina snorted. "Wasn't in it for the money."

"Charlotte had suggested to the police in his presence that the other set of footprints might belong to the second killer. He'd gone back to the tunnel to erase them when he ran into Charlotte. He knew she would already have recognized them, which is why he tried to kill her."

Paulina didn't seem unduly upset at the revelation that the man who had tried to kill her was her secretary. She sat calmly munching on her sausage. In fact, she loved drama; if she was part of it, all the better. "What about the shoes?" she asked, eager for every scrap of detail.

"They were in the car," replied Jerry. "By the way, your car will be returned to you within the next couple of days."

"Tell them to return it to New York. I'm leaving today," said Paulina. But she was more interested in the shoes. "He was going to throw them away?"

"I would imagine so. The police made comparison casts at the scene this morning. They matched the casts of his shoes, as did the fingerprints on the hunting knife he was going to use on Charlotte. We have him cold."

"He always seemed like such a nice boy."

"But what was the motive?" asked Anne-Marie, who had arrived a few minutes after Charlotte and Jerry with Gary, who had flown in for merger talks with Paulina. Also present was Claire, who had been drafted to fill the vacant spot at Paulina's side after Jack's mysterious disappearance.

Jerry answered in one word: "Mercy."

Anne-Marie looked puzzled.

"It was to have been a mercy killing," he explained. "In part, anyway. He thought he would be sparing Mrs. Langenberg the pain and suffering of a long, slow death from cancer."

"You have cancer?" asked Anne-Marie, shocked.

Paulina nodded. "Maybe. I found out a couple of days ago. I have tumors on both ovaries. I didn't get a chance to tell you. But don't worry," she added, stabbing another hunk of sausage. "I'm not going to die—yet, anyway."

Anne-Marie decided to take Paulina's word for it, for the moment at any rate. She turned her attention back to Jerry.

"His mother died of cancer," Jerry continued. "He told Charlotte about it. Apparently, she suffered terribly. He was afraid Mrs. Langenberg would suffer too. I suppose she was a mother figure to him. Maybe he felt guilty that he hadn't done something to relieve his own mother's suffering. Who knows?"

"He wanted to spare you," said Charlotte.

"Spare me! Spare himself is more like it. If I want to be dead I can kill myself already." She washed down the sausage with a swig of mineral water. "By the way," she asked Claire, who sat on the sofa beside her, "did you call the young man I told you about? The one who works in the men's store on Madison?"

Claire responded that she had.

"Was he interested?" asked Paulina. Claire replied that he was.

It was typical of Paulina that she viewed the whole affair as an inconvenience. Never mind that Jack had tried to kill her—who was going to take care of things now that he was in jail? It was also typical that she already had a replacement in mind.

"That was part of the motive anyway," Jerry continued.

"What was the other part?" asked Anne-Marie.

Charlotte picked up the thread of the narrative: "He may have been thinking about putting Paulina out of her misery, but he probably wouldn't have done anything about it—for the time being anyway—if Claire hadn't gotten pregnant. Once he knew Claire was pregnant, he had to act fast."

"What did that have to do with it?"

"When Paulina found out about the baby, she decided to change her will back. She had cut Elliot out after he sold his stock to High Rock Waters, but she'd decided to reinstate him. If Elliot were to become her heir, it would mean that he would eventually take over the company."

"I don't get it," said Anne-Marie. "Why would that make a difference?"

"If Elliot were to become boss, Jack would lose his job. Jack's the one who's been reporting on Elliot all these years. He wasn't Elliot's favorite person. He always knew his days would be numbered if Elliot took over, but he never gave it much thought until Paulina cut Elliot out of her will. It was then that he began to realize he might be able to stay on."

"But why would he want to? I mean, if he wasn't making that much money."

"It wasn't the money, it was the life," Charlotte continued. "He was hooked on it: the travel, the four-star hotels, the champagne and caviar. He was the first to admit it. In what other secretarial job would he have a Matisse hanging in his bedroom? You see," she explained, "he was Leon's . . ." She paused, trying to decide how to phrase it.

"*Innamorato,*" interjected Paulina. As usual, she was way ahead of everyone else.

"Is he gay?" asked Anne-Marie.

"I don't know," replied Charlotte. "I don't know that Leon is either. But it doesn't really matter. The point is that Leon had a sort of crush on him. It's understandable. He's very handsome and he can be very charming. If Jack had killed Paulina, Leon would have remained her heir."

"I see," said Anne-Marie. "Which would mean that Jack could have kept on living in high style."

"Exactly," said Charlotte. She was struck by the similarities between Dana and Jack. Dana too had believed he was helping his victims. But in both cases it was really their own self-interest that was the motive.

The police had questioned Leon, Charlotte added, and concluded that he wasn't involved. He'd gone back to New York to nurse his wounds. The arrest had probably been more of a shock to him than it was to Paulina.

Jerry continued: "If you consider the fact that Jack thought he could get away with it, you have a very strong motive. He thought Mrs. Langenberg's death would be blamed on the bodies-in-the-bath murderer. He didn't know the bodies-in-the-bath murderer would be caught and that he'd have an alibi."

"He did know about the tunnels, though, thanks to me," said Charlotte.

"What tunnels?" asked Anne-Marie.

"The spa is underlaid by a network of tunnels," said Charlotte. She went on to describe how she'd theorized in Jack's presence that the killer might have used the tunnels to get from one building to another. "At that point," she said, "he realized he could kill Paulina and get away with it."

"Except that he didn't know how," interjected Jerry. "He didn't know the victims' ankles had been jerked into the air." He explained briefly how Adele and Art had been killed. "He thought their heads had been held underwater. Which Charlotte discovered wouldn't work."

"Least of all on Paulina." She looked over at Paulina. "I seem to remember your saying something like, 'Nobody's going to push me into the grave.' "

Paulina chuckled like a merry elf. "I was right, wasn't I?"

"Well, unless anyone has any other questions, I'll get back to work," said Jerry. "I haven't accomplished much in the last three or four days." He extended his hand to Charlotte. "I hope you'll be back to see us."

"I will," she replied. She invited him and his family to visit her in New York and then bade him good-bye with a big hug. "Thanks for everything," she said. "The New York P.D. lost a good cop when they lost you."

Jerry grinned, all dimples.

Once he was gone, Charlotte rose to leave as well. She still had some packing to do. She would be leaving soon with Paulina, who had invited her to share a rented limo, being temporarily without her car and driver. Paulina had decided to cut her cure short. She had, she said, "business to attend to." But Charlotte suspected that beneath her calm exterior, she may have felt nervous about continuing with the cure. And who could have blamed her?"

But once again Paulina wouldn't let Charlotte go. "I need someone to take notes," she insisted. "Claire's still getting used to me. Aren't you, dear? It will just take a few minutes." She turned to Gary. "I don't think this is going to take very long, do you, Mr. . . ."

"Brant," supplied Charlotte. The role of Paulina's secretary was one she'd had plenty of opportunity to bone up on.

Gary smiled. "It depends," he said.

Paulina had a twinkle in her eye. "Claire, dear, will you please get Mrs. Stockholder a pad of paper. Thank you, dear," she added as Claire got up. She then turned to Charlotte.

"Besides, as a stockholder in Paulina Langenberg, Inc., this concerns you. Okay, let's get down to business."

With that, Paulina dismissed the subject of the attempt on her life, probably for good. Settling back, she removed her shoes and raised her feet onto a footstool. "Claire, dear, will you please get us some more salami and some crackers. The crackers are in the cupboard above the stove."

The turtle buzzer was conspicuously silent. It was one thing to treat the hired help like slave labor, but another when the hired help was about to become a member of the family.

"Yes, Mrs. Langenberg," said Claire. She handed Charlotte a pen and a legal pad and glided off toward the kitchen.

"Thank you, dear," said Paulina. "Make sure you write on both sides," she ordered. Then she picked up a document from the coffee table. It was the proxy statement for High Rock Waters. "It says here that in the event you leave your position as a result of a change of control, I have to pay you three years' salary, plus stock options, et cetera."

"That's right," said Gary.

"Such nerve," said Paulina, shaking her head. "You know what I think? I think you planned on this, on my taking over your company. Am I right?"

"Let's say I didn't expect you to roll over and die."

Paulina smiled. "Why not? Everybody else around here seems to. Never mind. What are you going to do if you decide to leave? Thank you, dear," she added as Claire set the crackers and salami on the table. "Very nice—you didn't just bring the box; you put the crackers on a plate."

Claire rolled her eyes at Charlotte. It was clear that being Paulina's lady-in-waiting wasn't a job she relished.

"What am I going to do?" repeated Gary. He looked over at Anne-Marie. "Well, first we're getting married. Then we're going to climb some mountains. After that?" He shrugged. "I might start another business. I'm thinking about something in the home video line."

"Jeans, running shoes, mineral water. Very profitable. Now this home video. Very clever, this home video—watching movies at home. You have a good nose for trends. What home video stocks do you recommend?"

Gary reeled off a short list.

"Get this down," she ordered. "And make a note to call my broker." She turned back to Gary. "What about going to work for a bigger company?"

"I don't think so," he replied. "Once you get chief executive in your blood, it's hard to go back to working for someone else." It was clear that Gary had no intention of staying on, whatever enticements Paulina might offer. He was going to pull the rip cord of his golden parachute.

"So," said Paulina, eyeing him appraisingly, "you like being the boss." She offered him some crackers. "Eat," she ordered. "If you're going to be climbing mountains, you'll need your strength. Good," she added as Gary helped himself. "What if you went to work for a bigger company as the boss?"

"What are you driving at?"

Paulina smiled beneficently. "I'm an old lady. I'm not going to be around forever. For a while—fifteen, maybe twenty years—but not forever. I've devoted my life to building this company. I built it product by product, promotion by promotion, country by country. You know what that's like."

Gary nodded.

"Do you know what happened to The Eye Shadow Man's company? It was sold to a *soap conglomerate*. They didn't know how to run a beauty company. Two years later it's pfft—nothing. I don't want that to happen to my company. I don't want the company I've worked and slaved for all my life to be sold off to strangers. I want it to be around for my grandson. A beauty company needs a heart and soul. The decisions have to be made by one person: a creative person, but a person who's shrewd with money. A person who's capable of commanding respect, a person with authority. A person with nerve."

Gary's heavy black eyebrows were knitted in concentration.

Paulina continued: "I'm old. I'm tired. Now they tell me I might have cancer. I'm ready to retire. But who am I going to turn my company over to? Not my nephew. He has no imagination. He's good with numbers, but he's not creative. My son?" She gazed lovingly at the photo of Elliot that had been restored to a position of prominence on the end table. "My son, he's very creative. But he doesn't have the business sense to run a big company." She extended her arms. "But you're creative, *and* you're a good businessman."

It was the perfect solution to Paulina's succession problem. Gary would be, in effect, prince regent, guardian and preserver of Paulina's empire, intermediary in a dynasty of Langenbergs.

Her speech over, Paulina folded her arms across her bosom and awaited Gary's response. As an afterthought, she added: "Besides, if I have to pay you, I might as well get my money's worth."

Charlotte could see the wheels spinning in Gary's head.

Before he could reply, Paulina went on: "You want trends? We've got trends. Our spa line, it's a miracle. I'll tell you why: it's scientific. Today's young women don't have the time to fool around with a lot of makeup. But they want to take care of their skin and they want to do it simply, quickly, and effectively—one, two, three. That's the theme of the spa line: twice a day—one, two, three. That's what we say in our ads."

Gary interrupted Paulina's spiel: "I'm very interested. In fact, I have a couple of ideas of my own about areas for expansion."

"Yes?" said Paulina, all ears.

"Frozen foods, for one. A line of low-calorie, all natural frozen dinners called Spa Cuisine. I think it would do very well. The young, upscale, health-minded professional who doesn't have time to cook doesn't want a frozen dinner that's loaded with salt and additives."

"I like it, I like it," said Paulina. Her eyes were shining.

"Also video tapes. A line of exercise instruction tapes based on the classes at High Rock: aerobics, yoga, body work."

"Anne-Marie could do them."

"That's what I was thinking," said Gary, looking over at Anne-Marie, who glowed with happiness. "About the job. We'd have to talk terms."

"Of course. Your lawyer, my lawyer. They'll talk. You rooked me once, you're not going to rook me again. I have terms too. One is that you make my nephew financial vice president; I promised him the job. The other is that you find a place for my son. Creative vice-president or something. Maybe I'm getting wiser in my old age. I can see now that I've used my son badly. I've tried to force him to be a businessman when he's not. But he's very creative. He could be useful to the company: packaging, design, advertising. He has artistic talent. That painting there"—she pointed proudly to the abstract that hung next to the Picasso drawing—"is one of his."

Gary turned politely to look at the painting. "Very nice," he said. "What about your son?" he asked. "Is he going to resent my position?"

"I've already talked with him about it." She took Claire's hand. "Oh, I'll provide for him. I intend to reinstate him in my will. He'll control a large block of stock. He'll be rich, he'll be doing the creative things he likes to do. But he won't have the day-to-day responsibility of running the company, which he didn't want anyway. Isn't that right, dear?"

Claire nodded. "I think he's always thought of it as a burden, the idea that he was expected to take over someday."

"He'll be very happy. He's going to be married to this lovely young woman and he's going to have a son, who *will* be interested in running the company." She pinched Claire's cheek. "Did you get the freckle cream I sent?"

Claire nodded.

"Use it twice a day. You have to be very careful with your skin."

"Yes, Mrs. Langenberg."

"Paulina, call me Paulina," she said. She fingered Claire's white peasant blouse. "You shouldn't wear white. You're too pale for white. It makes you look washed-out. You should always wear clear colors; clear colors will enhance your beautiful coloring. She has beautiful coloring, my daughter-in-law."

Claire laughed. She had a laugh like a clear brook.

The phone rang.

"Can you please answer it, dear?"

Claire did. "There are two reporters downstairs," she said, placing a hand over the receiver. "They want to interview you about the merger of Paulina Langenberg and High Rock Waters."

"Good, tell them I'll be right down." She addressed Gary: "I had the PR people in New York send them up. I thought we might have something to announce. You talk to them too—

you're good at that. The press always makes me nervous."
Reaching into her bosom, she withdrew a key, which she
handed to Anne-Marie. "Anne-Marie, could you please get me
some vodka? In the bedroom."

Anne-Marie left to fetch the bottle.

"Mrs. Stockholder! Thank you for filling in as my secretary.
And thank you for everything else. I have a lot to thank you
for, don't I?" Turning, she opened a drawer in the end table.
"Here," she said. She pressed a lipstick into Charlotte's hand.
"From the Body Spa line," she said proudly.

"Thank you," said Charlotte.

Anne-Marie returned with the bottle.

Grabbing it by the neck, Paulina tilted it skyward and
swallowed a belt that would have made a Russian gasp. "For
courage," she said. Then she put on her shoes, checked her
makeup in a hand mirror, and stood up. "Okay," she said as
she rose to her full height of four feet ten. "Let's go."

Charlotte returned to her room to finish packing. Into her
suitcase went her collection of souvenirs from High Rock Spa:
the chunk of mineral, the prescription booklet with her
shoulder exercises and walking regimen, the farewell package
of California dates, the sample bag of Body Spa products,
and . . . the lipstick. At ten of one, she called a bellman and
headed downstairs. In a corner of the lobby, she spotted Gary
and Paulina talking with the reporters. Or rather, Gary was
talking. Charlotte could hear him mixing his metaphors: he
was saying something about the many rows that needed to be
hoed before the final details could be nailed down. Paulina was
leaving all the talking up to him; she was passing on the
scepter. At the desk, Charlotte picked up the low-calorie box
lunch that the spa provided for departing guests. Then she
headed outside to wait for the limo. Under the columned
portico, she came across Regie Cobb sitting next to a tall,
gangly young man.

"Are you leaving?" he asked.

"In a few minutes."

"I'd like you to meet my son, Doug. He wants to be an
actor. He's studying acting at High Rock State. He's also a
fan—he's seen all your movies."

"Well, almost all," corrected Doug.

"There are some I hope you were lucky enough to miss," she said. The young man looked familiar, she thought as she shook his hand. She glanced down at his feet. They were very long and very narrow.

"You're the Mineral Man!" she said.

"Yes. It was Dad's idea. Something to do during summer vacation, to keep me in front of the public. I work nights at the hospital too. You know, you were the first to guess. How did you know?"

"By your height." Her glance flew to the red knapsack on the bench behind him. "And by your knapsack. Besides, you were very important to me in solving a difficult puzzle, one that involved the tunnels."

"What?" he said.

The limousine had arrived. "Your father will explain. I have to get going. It was very nice meeting you. Good luck in your acting career." She said good-bye and then headed over toward the group that was emerging from the hotel.

In the lead was Paulina, wearing a black gaucho hat decorated with a star-shaped pin of glittering pavé diamonds. Behind her came Claire, who carried the train case in which Paulina stored her jewelry. She held it out in front of her ceremoniously, as if it contained the relics of a saint.

Gary and Anne-Marie and a couple of photographers brought up the rear.

"I want you to take a picture of us in front of the hotel," Paulina ordered the photographers. Grabbing Gary's arm, she struck a pose.

But their attention had been captured by a bigger fish. "There's Charlotte Graham!" said the one.

Deserting Paulina, they came over to Charlotte, circling her with their cameras like a boxer circling his opponent. "Look this way, Miss Graham." "A big smile, Miss Graham." "Chin up, Miss Graham—let's see that beautiful jawline." All the while, the shutters were clicking, clicking, clicking.

Out of the corner of her eye, Charlotte had registered the look of annoyance that crossed Paulina's face as she was upstaged. Now she watched as Paulina relaxed her expression and threw up her hands as if to say, "Life's too short for such worries."

As the photographers continued to click away, Paulina marched over to the limo, whose liveried driver stood at attention at a rear door.

"The front door, please," she said.

"Yes, madam," he replied. Moving up to the front of the long black car, he ceremoniously opened the door on the passenger side.

"I always sit in front," she explained. She slid onto the seat, her hat barely visible above the dashboard, and settled back against the cushion.

"I always like to see where I'm going."